"Refreshing. Gruenfeld's la... ...onstrates that this up-and-coming author is as adept at legal twists and turns as he is at police drama and psycho-thriller chills. Gruenfeld handles the legal elements, including the trial, with aplomb."

—*Publishers Weekly*

"Intricate plotting and intrigue, dripping in courtroom maneuverings and politics, by an engaging writer."

—*Los Angeles Daily Journal*

"Gruenfeld is a fine writer who marries a well-crafted plot with finely wrought characters. A legal thriller with both a heart and a mean left hook."

—*West Coast Review of Books*

"Gruenfeld returns in top form, this time delivering a first-rate courtroom thriller with a twisty two-track plot that will keep most readers guessing right up through the denouements. A worldly-wise legal shocker."

—*Kirkus Reviews*

"Gruenfeld packs this lengthy thriller with intriguing characters and a colorful narrative."

—*Booklist*

"A truly ingenious tale with one plot reversal after another, and surprise is part of the fun. It is the serpentine plot that is the novel's strength and the reason lovers of crime and trial drama should find this yarn to be one of the best to come along in a while."

—*Baton Rouge Sunday Advocate*

THE HALLS OF
JUSTICE

LEE GRUENFELD

AN ONYX BOOK

ONYX
Published by the Penguin Group
Penguin Books USA Inc., 375 Hudson Street,
New York, New York 10014, U.S.A.
Penguin Books Ltd, 27 Wrights Lane,
London W8 5TZ, England
Penguin Books Australia Ltd, Ringwood,
Victoria, Australia
Penguin Books Canada Ltd, 10 Alcorn Avenue,
Toronto, Ontario, Canada M4V 3B2
Penguin Books (N.Z.) Ltd, 182–190 Wairau Road,
Auckland 10, New Zealand

Penguin Books Ltd, Registered Offices:
Harmondsworth, Middlesex, England

Published by Onyx, an imprint of Dutton Signet,
a division of Penguin Books USA Inc.
Previously published in a Dutton edition.

First Onyx Printing, July, 1997
10 9 8 7 6 5 4 3 2 1

PUBLISHER'S NOTE
This is a work of fiction. Names, characters, places, and incidents either are the prod-
ucts of the author's imagination or are used fictitiously, and any resemblance to
actual persons, living or dead, events, or locales is entirely coincidental.

For Helen, Michele and Cherie
—women who love me with no questions

Revenge is a kind of wild justice, which the more man's nature runs to, the more ought law to weed it out.

—FRANCIS BACON (1625)

In the halls of justice,
the only justice is in the halls.

—ANONYMOUS

Prologue

Vinny Rosamund banged the sides of both fore-fingers against the wooden bar, keeping time to the tune blaring out of the jukebox. To any listener of even moderate sophistication, the music was unforgivable tripe—simplistic rhythm, sophomoric instrumentation and enough overwhelming bass and percussion to hide the whole gooey mess behind a mask of sonic overload. To Vinny, lost in his Mitty-esque heavy metal fantasy, it was tonal genius of the first order. The mindless chords and visceral beat felt by the stomach before the ears were just what he needed right now. He felt his spinal cord being plucked, all his muscles and organs vibrating in sympathy, and he swayed back and forth with his eyes half closed, never missing a beat with his fingers, banging harder now, unmindful of the pain. The music was sheer bliss, the commotion around the bar pure heaven, the cold Scotch still dripping down his esophagus a stream of icy and delicious fire. Great stuff, cocaine: never lets you down.

A man in the seat to Vinny's right turned and nodded toward the beating hands. "If you wouldn't mind . . ." the man said politely.

Vinny quieted his fingers and sized him up: mid-thirties, below-average height, bit of a paunch, soft hands, his posture not poised and ready but indifferent and amateurishly vulnerable as his eyes flicked between Vinny's face and hands. Threat assessment: minimal.

"Wouldn't mind what, dickwad?" Just loud enough to turn a few heads, including that of an exceptionally well-dressed brunette a few tables away from the bar.

Fear, as Vinny had intended, flitted across the man's eyes. "Never mind."

Vinny paused and stayed perfectly still, watching the fear grow as the guy tried to figure out how big of a mistake he'd made. "Never mind, uh-huh." He gave it another second and resumed the drumbeat, a little louder than before. "Fuckin' A, never mind." He waited for relief to wash over the asshole's face, but was unable to read what everyone else in the immediate vicinity saw only as disdain as the guy turned away to resume an earlier conversation.

Vinny looked like a man lost in his own world, but that was another thing a line of good blow will do for you—make you aware, heighten your senses and sensibilities, put you on predator alert without it looking that way to the civilians outside who thought you were just stoned and couldn't see how ready for anything you truly were. That's how he knew the pretty brunette was watching him from that table near the other end of the bar. Hey, no big deal. The babes watched him all the time. What was not to like? He was a classical good-looker. Shade under five-ten, dark brown hair that could fall casually wherever he directed it to, a medium frame that reflected both the hours in the gym and the anabolic steroids he subjected it to, enough of the latter to inflate some muscles but not enough to bring up telltale acne on his back. He had the kind of narrow, menacing features the babes were crazy about, surely the result of some inner qualities of wariness and strength rather than an accident of genetics unrelated to his persona.

The babe was watching, no doubt about that. He'd seen her several times since he'd walked into The Alley, one of the more upscale of a series of upscale saloons on Montana Avenue in Santa Monica. She had to be watching him, because he'd nearly bumped into her three times, and it was like she was everywhere at once, and he sure as hell hadn't done enough nose candy to cause *that*. He'd have liked a closer look, but it would never do to acknowledge his awareness of her, and he remembered enough anyway. Mid-twenties, he figured, judging from the flawless skin. An athletic type who moved easily within her clothes, the fabric of her pleated skirt hurrying to catch up as she walked, the soft folds of the material seeming to caress her legs rather than cling to them. An excellent chest, too, from what he could see. Not the sort of pendulous novelties that would hit her knees by the time she was thirty-five but the soft, roundish kind that beckoned like satin pillows. Wide eyes, a soft nose, full lips—a great-looking broad. No wonder she was looking at him. They'd make a terrific couple, is what she must be thinking.

He waited until he was sure her face was turned in his direction, then looked at her full on and saw that she wasn't looking at him but at that asshole on his right, who was looking back. Vinny looked from the asshole to the babe and back again, and smiled crookedly. "Little out of your league, geek." The geek dropped his head quickly, obviously embarrassed to have been caught in the middle of some kind of impossible fantasy.

Vinny would show him how it was done. He looked at the babe, parted his lips and wiggled the tip of his tongue back and forth at her. The chick seemed startled and drew back reflexively, a little of the drink she was holding sloshing around in her glass. No problem. Standard reaction. Uptight rich types always pretended to be shocked at the direct approach; then they got over it and you could get down to business. Saved a lot of time.

He'd already turned back to the bar and closed his eyes to let her know he had correctly anticipated her response and had no reason to wait around for verification. He drummed a little more, supremely confident of her continued attention, then opened one

eye and looked in the mirror to where she should
have been, but saw only an empty chair. Must be
the wrong angle. He waited for a particularly strong
fwhoomp! from the digitized bass drum and angled
his body slightly as he crashed his fingers down on
the bar, sneaking a direct peek at the table, but the
chair was still unoccupied.

Diane moved to the happy hour hors d'oeuvres
table, where Lisa was picking through the salad
platter trying to find a tomato that didn't look like it
had been artificially ripened by ammonia chloride
gas as it rode up in a truck from Florida, knowing
full well they all had. "You believe this guy?" Diane
said, bending to Lisa's ear to be heard over the din.

Lisa turned to get a view of the bar. The weird-
looking guy with the expensive leather half coat
was rocking and banging away, seemingly oblivious
to the rest of the patrons but opening an eye every
three or four seconds to look surreptitiously around
the room or at himself in the mirror. His cuffs were
pulled back enough to reveal a Rolex watch, and he
kept his unused fingers splayed out rather than
curled back into a fist, the better to display the
tigereye sapphire ring on his left hand, the high-
carat diamond pinky ring on the other.

"A regular Mr. Wonderful." Lisa bit into the
tomato slice and out of habit bent her neck forward
to keep the ensuing stream of juice and seeds from
spilling onto her blouse, but no such effluvia issued
forth from the desiccated ex-vegetable.

"He keeps looking at me."

"Everybody looks at you. Everybody looks at me.
What about it?"

Diane shrugged a shoulder. "He made a lewd and
obscene gesture at me."

"Spoken like a true lawyer; can't you just say he
flipped you the bird or something?"

"Well, he's creepy."

Lisa had to admit that was true. "Very full of himself, too. Like he's waiting to be noticed by some
panting chick."

"Yeah." Diane smiled. "Don't you just love the type?"

"Oh yeah." Lisa held up the stringy remnants of the tomato and managed to gracefully rid herself of the mess by wrapping it in her unraveling napkin. "Why're you looking so glum, anyway? You won the case today, didn't you?"

Diane's lips tightened and her eyes narrowed as she looked away. "Yes, but I shouldn't have. Not that quickly."

"Oh, stop. This rate, you'll make partner in a year." Why would her sister be downcast over a major victory in court?

Vinny had by now decided that it was way uncool to be looking around as much as he had been. He was already way past cool, his gray silk suit perfectly offset by the white shirt worn with no tie and the top three buttons undone. The leather coat was a great touch, too. A bit warm for it, really, but it was such a beauty, and a helluva contrast to the pinstripes and worsteds all around him. Sure does make a guy stand out, especially from the half dozen geeks wearing LA Stars hats. The NFL's latest expansion team was undefeated so far this season, but hell, all it's good for is laying down bets; you don't have to get sappy about it.

"He's gotta be roasting in that thing," Diane observed, pulling her mind away from the scene in court earlier in the day. "Who the hell wears leather in southern California this time of year?"

"Why's he bother you?" Lisa asked. "There's a million guys like that within three miles of this place."

"'Cuz he's looking at me."

Lisa glanced at the bar. "No, he's not."

"Well, he was."

"Okay, tell you what." Lisa wiped her hands with the remains of her shredded cocktail napkin and looked around for a place to toss it. There was never anywhere to put garbage or an empty drink glass in these places. "I'll go over there and kill him."

Diane turned her head away from the bar to face Lisa. "Oh, would you really?"

"Sure. Shoot him between the eyes. That be okay?"

"Ahh, you're just kidding me."

The music, preprogrammed by The Alley's owner according to his matchless insight into the musical tastes of his patrons, which equated well to their perception of his cheap Scotch poured into expensive bottles, changed rhythm, slowing in tempo but sacrificing nothing in intensity. An undoubtedly sloe-eyed nymphet of dubious ethnic origin purred unintelligible words to an equally undifferentiated Euro-punk melody augmented by soaring, synthesized strings. Nearly swooning in quick recognition of one of his all-time favorites, Vinny Rosamund dipped his shoulders, shot his cuffs, and prepared to pound out the new, more profoundly complex rhythm with four—count 'em, a full four—fingers, an inarguable demonstration of super clicked-into-it-ness that could not help but be noticed by that bimbette, wherever the hell she was but no doubt still looking at him.

Diane rolled her eyes upward and stamped a foot. "I mean, God, lookit this guy!"

Lisa paused, her drink raised halfway to her mouth. "All right, already! Wanna go mess with him?"

Vinny turned to leer momentarily at the blond a few places to his left. She didn't even honor him with the courtesy of a disdainful sneer but simply turned away, as though he had never been there in the first place. Vinny was having a difficult time with the fact that The Alley was filled with doctors, lawyers (including deputy DAs, defense attorneys, corporate counsel and tax specialists), stock and bond brokers, financial consultants and entrepreneurs of varying stripe, most of whom spilled out of the massive, high-rent Colorado Lakes professional complex several blocks away each evening starting at around seven. The fancy cars in the lot didn't bother him, as none was much fancier than his own black Cadillac. It was more an attitude kind of thing. And if he wasn't wearing a tie, so what? His suit was certainly as expensive as most of those around him.

As he prepared to ignore the ignoring from the blond, his eye caught a glimpse in the mirror of the babe from the table returning to her seat. She glanced briefly at his reflection, curled the sides of her mouth up ever so slightly in what might have been a smile, and then bent toward the table before he could respond or even stop his hands from their incessant drumming. She unhurriedly picked up her glass from the table, turned casually and headed back toward the far wall of the bar, disappearing behind a sea of dark suits. It broke his rhythm, and he had to force himself to concentrate on the music to get his hands back in synch.

No mistaking that smile. Happened to him all the time, no surprise there. Cagey bitch, though. Where'd she go?

" 'Scuse me." Female voice, from over his right shoulder where an arm protruded toward the bar. By instinct he leaned to the right to block her way, make her brush against him. Her hand dropped to the bar impatiently, where it seemed to prepare to wait until he got whatever childish irritation he was planning over and done with. He pursed one side of his mouth and tried to close his eyes and raise his eyebrows at the same time, very James Dean-ish, and turned toward the voice. His eyes snapped open and his mouth lost its curling sneer.

Same chick.

"You mind?" she said, reaching toward the stack of napkins on the inside edge of the bar.

"No. Huh-uh." Now where the hell had she come from? Vinny turned back toward the wall to his left, a dumb move considering she was standing right here next to him and, as expected, couldn't spot her there. A speck of white fluttered in his peripheral vision as the babe's arm brought the retrieved napkin across the bar, and he turned back to his right in time to watch her head off in that direction. He stared at his hands, resting on the bar where he'd left them, the music forgotten for a moment. He sensed rather than saw the geek to his right looking at him.

"You got some kinda fucking problem, pal?" Vinny said without looking at the guy, stressing the *g* at the end of "fucking" so the asswipe wouldn't think he was a lowlife.

The guy kept looking at him, without turning away, eyes calm and steady. Vinny fixed him with his most steely and terrifying gaze. "I said, you got—"

" 'Scuse me, sorry," came from his left, and he whipped his head around in time to see the same goddamned broad reach across the bar for a swizzle stick, then flash him a brilliant smile before turning to walk away.

"Hey, wait a minute!" he yelled, quickly surveying the room in the opposite direction where he was sure she'd headed not half a minute before. By the time he turned back to her, she was gone once again. And the geek was still looking at him.

Vinny turned to face him. "I'm askin' you again, shithead, what the fuck are you—"

"Hey." Big guy, sitting to the geek's right. Maybe six-two, well into middle age but dangerous look- ing, dressed in an ill-fitting, inexpensive suit that only heightened the appearance of some serious musculature beneath. He stood full up and took a half step toward Vinny, no trace of fear in his eyes. At the same time, the broad reappeared from off to the right.

So there was Vinny, the bitch looking right at him, Paul Bunyan stepping into his face. He felt his neck grow hot, and a familiar trembling begin in his arms. No matter what happened now, all he could do was fuck up. Even the nine-millimeter Beretta pressed against his chest gave him no com- fort. What was he gonna do, pull out a piece in a bar full of yuppie scum, kind of people probably got up at four to hit the gym before work and would like nothing better than to be heroes? And to top it all off, he was seeing double. Oh, for Chrissakes, there were two babes watching him now, but they were both the same babe.

No, wait. He should have noticed before. Different outfits. Twins? Jesus H, a pair of goddamned *twins* was fucking with his head. And now the giant was moving forward, one arm upraised. *Oh, shit . . .*

"Buy you a drink, pal?"

What? Vinny blinked his eyes. "What?"

"C'mon." The giant draped an arm casually over Vinny's shoulders. "Settle down, lemme buy ya a beer."

The geek sniffled once and picked up his drink. The giant was turning Vinny forcibly toward the bar. The twin broads were leaning in toward each other, giggling into their hands. The geek chuckled and took a sip from his glass, shaking his head slightly in unmistakable derision.

The big guy wasn't even going to beat him up, man to man. Wasn't going to let him salvage his manhood at the cost of a bloody nose. Instead, he'd expertly defused the situation, broadcasting his assurance that he could squash Vinny like a bug if he had to, so there was no need to. The babes were still giggling. Vinny wasn't even worth the effort it would take the guy to blacken his eye: just another piece of street trash eight fathoms out of his depth. The blond three stools down was ineffectively hiding a smirk behind a plastic straw clamped between her lips. And the big guy was still trying to turn him toward the bar.

Vinny slapped the arm from across his shoulders. The giant stepped back in feigned fear, put both hands up in the air. "Whoa, easy there, big guy."

Vinny wasn't a big guy. Everybody could see that. It was like calling him "little dick." Everybody in the entire bar was staring at him now; he could feel it, could feel his ridiculous sharkskin suit shining like a thousand-watt klieg light from beneath the folds of the equally ridiculous leather coat. Here he was again, as he had been so many times before, and all he could do was fuck up, as he had done so many times before. He estimated that it was at least four miles to the front door, a daylong swim against the current of sneering and disdainful bar patrons and those two giggling, brainless bitches. All he was doing was having a simple drink and listening to some music, not bothering anybody, and those two had to go and make trouble.

Best thing would be to turn back to the bar and have a drink with the giant who anybody in his right mind and not whacked out on coke and booze could see was a cop. Best thing would be to smile at him, offer a hand in reconciliation and manly humility, knock back a few and get the hell out of there even though you'd come there to do business but you could forget about that because this guy was not only a cop but a regular.

That was the smartest, most savvy and streetwise thing to do so Vinny spat at the man's shoes, eyed him defiantly for a second and then turned and walked deliberately toward the door, swaying his hips so the leather coat swished back and forth behind him, letting the citizens know they'd met their match, trying to ignore the mounting laughter behind him, some of it coming from the giant whose shoes Vinny had had enough brains left to miss but most of it coming from those cock-teasing, stuck-up bitch twins.

"I don't know why things like that bother you so much, Lisa," Diane said to her sister as they walked arm in arm out the front door of The Alley an hour later, well before the rest of the crowd would begin drifting out.

"Because I'm a professional, that's why. Would I cater a party and not give the guests a place to put a dirty napkin or an empty glass?"

"But this wasn't a party and those aren't guests."

"Same difference." They walked toward the far end of the lot. "And besides, it's stupid for business: the quicker you get people to realize they don't have a drink, the quicker they'll buy another one."

"You're not a professional, you're an anal compulsive."

"Goddammit!" Lisa shouted.

Diane stopped awkwardly as Lisa came to a

sudden halt. "Now what? You gonna bitch about the tomato again?"

Lisa pointed toward her car, a two-door Lexus in dark green, listing unnaturally to the rear. "I got a flat."

"Oh, for heaven's sake." Diane disengaged herself from her sister's arm and walked toward the car. "Why's it leaning backwards like that?"

Without waiting for an answer, she stepped around to the other side and looked back at the car. "Uh-oh."

"Uh-oh, what?" Lisa walked to the other side of the car and followed Diane's gaze toward the ground. "Hey, wait a minute."

Both stared at the second flat tire without speaking. They were far from the front entrance of The Alley in a poorly lit corner of the parking lot.

Lisa grabbed Diane's arm and started to push her forward. "Let's go back and—"

"Trouble, ladies?"

Diane felt her sister's grip tighten. They both knew, without turning around, whose voice it was.

"Oh, shit," Lisa whispered.

"Easy," said Diane quietly. Then, in a louder voice, "No. No trouble." She started to walk forward but the sound of his footsteps coming up from behind and to the right stopped her. He seemed to materialize out of the dimness as he came to a stop in front of the car.

"Two flats. Can you imagine that? Hm hm hm." He had one arm across his chest supporting his other elbow, chin in his hand in an attitude of surprised contemplation. "Some coincidence."

Diane took a breath and tried to steady herself. "Yeah." She held on to Lisa's arm and started to push them both forward again.

"Hey, where you goin'?"

Diane tried to force their pace as she said, "To get some help," but Vinny had already stepped in to block their path and they had to stop.

"Help?" He opened his arms and held up his

hands in a gesture of confusion. "You don' need no help. You got me."

"If you don't mind . . ." said Lisa.

"But I do mind."

"Listen," said Diane, raising her voice in a thinly veiled warning to him that she was about to scream, "we're going to—"

Almost quicker than they could see his hands, Vinny reached into his jacket and yanked out the Beretta, slamming it forcefully onto the hood of the car, the explosive sound shocking in the quiet night. Any thoughts that this might be some minor retribution for the incident earlier in the evening ended with the realization that he had not only slashed two tires but now also put a deep dent in the gleaming hood of the car.

"You're going to what?" He waited for an answer he knew wasn't coming. "I said, you got me. You think you need anything more than me?"

Diane tried her best to objectively appraise the situation but didn't need to go any farther than the creep's face. Even in the poor light she could see his flared nostrils and the watery glaze of his eyes, and it wasn't hard to detect the raspy voice and sniffly breaths. His whole evening's supply was probably already up his nose, and it was barely nine o'clock.

"I'm askin' you, you think you need more than me?" No mistaking the menace now. It wasn't the false-front bravado that was laughably evident inside the bar but the voice of rage and unrequited humiliation. Hell hath no fury like an emasculated street punk.

"No," said Diane, unable to keep the fear from her voice.

"No, what?"

"No, I don't need more than you."

"Right." He nodded, then stood up straight. "Right."

"So," said Lisa, equally terrified, "you're gonna, you know—you're gonna change the tires?"

Vinny froze. "Am I gonna what?"

"Are you—I mean, you said we don't need . . ." Her

voice trailed off, hope of approaching the situation rationally quickly dissipating in the dank night air.

"You're asking me am I gonna change your tires?" Vinny looked down and shook his head, then idly scratched the back of his neck. "You fucking cunt," he said casually.

Bile rose with sickening suddenness in Diane's throat at the abrupt cessation of even the semblance of civility. As long as some thin veneer of polite social discourse remained, however slight and affected, there was the hope that he might settle for scaring them and then let it go. But this last utterance carried with it the unmistakable intimation that the game had taken on a new and harrowing twist, and with it, no further need to pretend that it was anything else.

"What do you want?" Diane asked in her most commanding tone, as though she were cross-examining a hostile witness.

Vinny looked at her. "When I'm good and fucking ready, I'll tell you." He picked up the gun and pointed it directly at Lisa, waited for her to catch her breath and for Diane to step protectively closer to her, then waved it to their right. "Get in."

Diane forced herself to look where he was pointing and saw a late-model black Cadillac four-door parked in the shadows off the pavement of the lot.

"Please . . ." Lisa began.

"Now," Vinny said, placing his free hand around the one holding the gun, pointing it steadily and professionally.

As the two women neared the car, Vinny stepped in behind Diane and nudged her shoulder. "You drive. You"—he tapped Lisa on top of the head with the tip of the gun—"in the back."

The two sisters stopped with their hands on the door handles, both knowing that the act of getting into the car carried with it an unmistakable inevitability of unspoken dimension, the lights going down and the curtain drawing back on a play with an indeterminate plot; the dread that filled their hearts was boundless.

Vinny snapped his fingers. The sisters opened the doors and got in. Vinny hesitated for a moment and then opened a third door and slid in beside Diane. He gestured and they closed their doors. He reached into a pocket and withdrew a set of keys, inserting them into the ignition.

"Start it," he said to Diane, but when she reached forward to take hold of the key, he leaned over the backseat suddenly and held the Beretta an inch from Lisa's face, causing her to gurgle a choked scream. He looked from Lisa to Diane and back.

"Either one of you tries anything stupid," he said quietly but with conviction, looking back to Diane, "I shoot the other one in the eye."

The black Cadillac cruised carefully north on the San Diego Freeway. As per instructions, Diane kept it as close to sixty miles per hour as possible. The speed limit was fifty-five, but Vinny Rosamund knew that, on a California freeway, anybody sticking to the limit was automatically suspect of being drunk or on the lam. Getting ticketed for doing sixty in Los Angeles would be like getting busted for dropping a candy wrapper on the street in New York: contrary to the laws of nature.

Near the off-ramp to the Getty Center, Diane spotted a black-and-white LAPD car with two uniformed officers coming up two lanes to their left but had little time to contemplate any plans.

Vinny inclined his head toward the cops. "Do it," he said calmly, without even looking backward or at Diane, "and I'll kill them both." He curled the fingers of his left hand and idly flicked at a cuticle. "Done it before"—he blew on a fingertip—"and I'll do it again."

"Where are we going?" Lisa ventured weakly in a small voice.

Vinny didn't respond, as though he hadn't heard, then turned halfway around and scratched the side of his neck with the gun barrel. "Special place. You're gonna like it. Might even love it." He gestured toward the windshield. "Get off at the Ventura. That way." He jerked a thumb to the left, westward.

Diane took a last, wistful glance at the police car and began easing into the next lane.

"Use the blinker. Nobody teach you howda drive?"

They stayed on the Ventura Freeway for about twenty minutes, until Vinny directed them off at Kanan Dume Road. Heading south toward the Santa Monica Mountains, Diane stared hopefully ahead but saw only dark, empty hills. She knew the area. There was nothing through the pass until you hit Malibu, and she knew they weren't going that far because this was too roundabout a way to have come. Unless the creep had purposely taken a freeway route because he felt it safer than navigating around on surface streets. Maybe that was it. . . .

"Pull over."

Startled, Diane jerked the wheel slightly and was answered by the rumble of tires running over the gravel breakdown lane. "Pull over?" she repeated.

"Take it easy, dammit!" Vinny reached for the wheel and turned it back to the left as Diane eased off the gas.

The unlit road was inky black, the surface immediately ahead illuminated by their headlights, but nothing else was visible outside the two thin cones of light. Diane slowed the car and pulled it off to the side. Vinny reached for the key and turned off the ignition, then threw the gearshift lever into park so he could pull the key out.

Diane chanced a peek at her sister in the rearview mirror. What the hell was this? Was he going to drop them off here and let them make their own way out? Surely he wasn't stupid enough to pull anything right here. The road was not heavily traveled at night, but it was the main link between northern Malibu and the west valley, and cars were sure to pass by at least every few minutes. Marching them off into the thickets made no sense: how long would an abandoned Cadillac have to sit before it attracted attention?

Vinny opened the door and got out, took a few steps and stopped, keeping his back to the car. Diane heard the sound of a zipper and turned her head to see Lisa looking at her quizzically. The noise of a heavy stream of urine hitting soft sand followed.

Vinny never bothered to look back to see what they were doing. He had the keys so they weren't driving anywhere, and he would be able to hear any attempt to get out of the car and sneak up on him. Besides, these weren't cops or wiseguys, just two scared chicks who probably never did anything braver than drink red wine with fish.

He finished, raised up on his toes and jiggled once or twice, then zipped back up. The Beretta was tucked under an armpit, and he pulled it out as he turned back to the car. He reached for the open door and slammed it shut without getting in, then opened the rear door. He leaned down and smiled broadly.

"Can't deprive you of my company, huh? Don' seem fair."

He took off his leather coat and suit jacket, got in and closed the door, tossing the keys up front to Diane and putting the jackets on the front seat. "Get moving." He turned to Lisa and ran both hands through the hair on either side of his head, the point of the gun tracing an arc through the air.

Diane hesitated and Vinny reached for her hair without looking at her, grabbing a fistful and shaking it back and forth. "I'm not gonna tell you again."

She scrambled to locate the ignition key, holding the key ring up so she could see it while Vinny still had her head pulled back. She reached forward to try to put it in the ignition, and Vinny let go as soon as he felt the tug. Lisa drew back and tried to wedge herself against the door.

When they were moving again, Vinny moved his head as if he were relieving a cramp in his neck and said to Lisa, "Sit on your hands."

Lisa said nothing but tried to find her sister's eyes in the rearview mirror.

"Hey, I'm talkin' to you! Now do it!"

Slowly, Lisa put her hands to either side and slid them under herself, leaning left and right to do so. She hadn't realized until now that she'd had her arms wrapped protectively around herself since they'd left The Alley parking lot, and the sudden physical vulnerability she felt made her breathing speed up. Diane heard it and it frightened her.

"Don't move," Vinny said as he shifted the gun to his left hand and reached for her with his right. Lisa gasped and Diane started to turn around. "Keep your eyes on the road," he said, "and don't make me tell you again."

Vinny stopped his hand short of Lisa's face, then moved it down until it came to rest below her throat. Slowly, he undid the top button of her blouse. Lisa let out a small sound.

"Whatsa matter? Nobody ever touch you before?"

Lisa closed her eyes, desperate to free her hands but too afraid to do it.

"Now shuddup. Don't make me tear nothin'."

Diane fought to keep from crying. "Please. Don't do anything to her. Don't hurt—"

"Shut the fuck up!" Vinny yelled loudly, filling the enclosed space with the anger in his raspy voice. Diane winced and tried to bury her head between her shoulders to escape the sound that seemed to carom around the car. Vinny moved his head so he could see Diane in the mirror, and waited until the venom in his voice had the desired effect and it was clear Diane wasn't going to cause trouble.

After an unnaturally long time, he turned back to Lisa, glared at her and then finished undoing all the buttons on the front of her blouse. He spread it apart and sat back, then hooked the tip of the gun barrel underneath the fabric of her bra. "Take this thing off."

Lisa was crying full bore now, no longer worrying about whether giving visible vent to her fears would worsen the situation by openly acknowledging it. "Please," she choked out between sobs, "I'm begging you, don't make me do anything anymore. . . ."

Vinny didn't answer but pushed the tip of the gun against one of her nostrils, pointing it upward as though to drive it inside. Lisa closed her eyes and emitted a gurgled squeal, the terrible feeling of a gun against her face almost more than her mind was able to absorb. One idle twitch, a quarter-inch movement of his finger, some slight neuronal miscue and a lead slug would explosively pulverize everything inside her skull.

Diane heard the sound and felt that her own mind might not be capable of dealing with the horror of someone hurting her twin sister mere inches from where she sat. "Don't!" she screamed. "Don't do it; leave her alone!"

Vinny pushed the gun upward and Lisa shrieked.

"Y' hear that?" Vinny leaned forward and put his mouth near Diane's ear. He pushed the gun once more and Lisa tried to scream again, but the sound barely made it past the choking in her throat. "I asked you did you hear that."

Diane tried to see through her own tears and not drive off the dark road. She hit the steering wheel hard with her hand, wiped her eyes and hit it again. "I heard," she managed to get out.

"Good." Vinny sat back and turned once more to Lisa. "Now take it off!"

Lisa edged her hands out from under her. In order to get at the clasp at the rear of the bra she had to pull the blouse out of her skirt. When the hook was disengaged she stopped, letting the bra hang loosely. Vinny made a downward motion with the gun and she pushed the straps down over her shoulders and into her sleeves, letting the cups fall to her waist.

Vinny stared at her exposed breasts. "Excellent," he said, with more breathlessness and less nonchalance than he would have liked. "Whadda you got to be ashamed of?" He stared a moment longer, then tapped Diane on the back of the head with the Beretta. "Hey, you, you got the same ones?"

"What?" Diane had been keeping her eyes on the

road and wasn't sure what he was talking about. "The same what?"

"The same tits. I mean you're twins an' all, right? That means you got the same everything. So, what: you got the same tits?"

When she didn't answer, Vinny slapped the back of her head with his hand. "Answer me!"

"Yes! We have the same everything, okay?"

"Don't crack wise to me, bitch." He reached over the seat and rummaged in the pocket of the leather coat, pulling out a small glass vial and sitting back. "Same everything, huh? Like a two-for-one sale, I got me here." He cackled at his own wit and put the cap of the vial in his mouth, twisting the bottle and spitting out the cap when he was done. Without taking his eyes off Lisa's exposed chest, he tapped some white powder onto the back of the hand holding the gun, then seemed to think better of it and upended the bottle so it emptied completely. He raised it to his nose and snorted the powder in loudly, sniffling heavily several times and baring his teeth with the effort to retain it all. He tossed the empty vial on the floor and exhaled with pleasure.

He glanced casually out the window and sat up quickly. "Whoa, hold it: turn here. Right here, dammit!"

Diane slowed the car and turned into a side road, but it happened too fast for her to be able to catch the name on the street sign. A small, rational part of her had been trying to memorize details of their route.

"Real slow," Vinny said, relaxing back into the seat. "Slower." When the car was down to about ten miles per hour, he said, "That's good right there." He reached across the seat and poked at the rearview mirror until it was angled uselessly upward.

Diane couldn't see anything in the backseat. Vinny—she didn't know his name—had stopped speaking. She tried to drive steadily so she wouldn't anger him, but new sounds coming from the rear swirled around her and crazed her until she was completely disoriented and couldn't seem to tell the road from the sky.

Her sister's desperate sobbing was more than she could bear. She could make out fabric rubbing against fabric, the sound of something being torn open, a rhythmic slapping, an occasional grunt or moan from the bastard with the gun, a foot hitting the floorboards. Sometimes the back of the front seat would get hit and she could feel it banging at her back. Through it all was the misery of Lisa's pitiable crying, and even that began to recede as preternatural defense mechanisms in Diane's brain began to systematically shut down her mind against the onslaught of unendurable emotional pain from the atrocity being committed against her sister.

But near the moment where she knew for certain that her world as she remembered it was forever gone, a gleeful cry of "Hey, you! Lookit this!" arose from the backseat, and a hand came over and headed for the rearview mirror and yanked at it, adjusting it to somewhere near its former angle, and as she looked up the whole scene came blasting over into the mirror and reflected directly back through her eyes, searing deep into the center of her brain. Diane screamed and slammed her foot onto the brake.

She felt their bodies hit the back of her seat, but the car had been going so slowly that there were no cries of pain, just an angry grunt from Vinny. She heard him scrambling desperately to right himself.

"Get out!" he was yelling. To whom? Diane heard the back door fly open forcefully and looked in the outside mirror to see Lisa leaning out the door, trying to pull her disheveled clothes around her. Then she was outside, tumbling in the soft grass as the result of a shove from Vinny's foot.

He followed a moment later, anger crazing his eyes. He grabbed the front door and tore it open, shoving the Beretta forward until it was inches from Diane's forehead. "You, too! Now! Goddammit, don' you fuck with me!"

She was an automaton now, obeying blindly, her

mind somewhere on another world. The only
instinct remaining to her was that of survival, but
that included Lisa as well. It always had, throughout
their entire lives.

"Don't you move!" Vinny said to Lisa. "Don't you
fucking move! You just watch!"

Vinny held the gun in one hand, and now Diane
saw that he was groping himself with the other. He
still had an erection. She started to take some small
comfort in the fact that he had been interrupted
before completing the act, but now she noticed
something peculiar: it was unnaturally bright,
almost white, reflecting what little light bounced off
the surrounding vegetation from the headlights of
the car.

It was a condom. *The bastard's wearing a rubber!*
Diane tried to integrate this information even as he
moved toward her. Was this sick sonofabitch worried about catching something? What in the holy
hell kind of—

"Move!" he was yelling at her. Diane followed
where he was pointing and found herself in front of
the car, caught in the headlights.

Vinny turned to make sure Lisa was still in sight,
which was difficult because of the light now in his
eyes, but his words were directed at Diane. "Take off
your clothes, bitch, and don't you fucking make me
say it twice."

His voice was a mixture of cocaine, alcohol, years
of Christ only knew what kind of twisted street
morality and a fresh dose of unencumbered rage.
That he was serious was no longer just a guess—she
had seen him desecrating Lisa in the mirror. She
hurried to comply before he got any madder and
promised herself only to stay sane.

Vinny turned to see her, to verify her nakedness,
then craned around to talk to Lisa one last time. "You
watch this, you sorry bitch." He turned back to
Diane and began walking toward her. "You watch
real good. . . ."

PART
ONE

1

This story does not have a happy ending. I am telling you that up front so there are no hard feelings later.

My name is Salvatore Milano and I am a deputy district attorney in the county of Los Angeles. Modesty aside, I am head deputy in the Santa Monica branch, responsible for all of the other deputy DAs in the office. I assign the more complex or high-profile cases that come in, and I supervise prosecution of some of the more difficult ones. Occasionally, I try a case myself. But no matter who in my office handles a situation, ultimately it's my responsibility. The elected district attorney does not call junior-birdmen deputies when something goes wrong; he calls me.

My office on Main Street (honestly, that's its real name) is one long block east of the famous Santa Monica pier, newly rebuilt following a devastating series of storms in the mid-'80s. It's a Tuesday morning in November, the day after powerful Santa Ana winds finished blowing superheated desert air across the basin and out to sea, washing the skies clean of stagnant pollution. This condition occurs a half dozen times each winter, or what passes for winter in southern California. When that happens, we are treated to achingly beautiful vistas seen through air so clear the visibility is virtually unlimited. From the roof of this building you can actually make out drilling rigs in the Santa Barbara channel thirty miles away, but what is really capturing my attention is a slight south swell combined with an easterly breeze that I know instinctively is shaping the waves a few hundred yards away into dead perfect curls. I am sorry that I didn't get up a little earlier to hit the surf for a few gentle rides before coming to work.

Instead, I'm doing my best to listen to Marsha Jones, an intensely brilliant Harvard Law graduate who sorely disappointed her professors by opting for a prosecutor's job rather than a position with any of the hundreds of corporate law firms who trampled each other to get to her. Improbably, Jones is not only black and female but also one-quarter Native American, which means those firms would have gotten not only a hell of a lawyer but three separate check marks on their affirmative action scorecards as well. She has confided to me that the only bad part of being a black female Harvard Law graduate is that everybody thinks she got in because of some veiled quota the school was trying to meet, when in fact her law school admission test scores were among the highest recorded that year.

I'm only half-concentrating but something she says gets my attention. How to get her to rewind without looking like I was sleeping? "I'm sorry, wait a minute. In a museum?"

She drops her papers onto her lap and *harumphs* noisily. "Holy shit, Milano, I'm sorry I was talking so loud. Did I wake you?"

"Matter of fact, you did. But as long as I'm up . . ."

"Lemme start over. Trust me, you're gonna love this, okay?"

She puts the papers on the floor and rises, grabbing my cup of cold coffee and walking over to the hot plate just outside my office door as she speaks. "There's this exhibit over at the Bohemian Loft—on Colorado?" She leans in to look at me and I nod. I know the place, a showcase for artists that usually favors the skilled and talented over the merely fashionable. The latter need no special showcase, as they are more than adequately represented throughout the area, where ability at one's craft is not a prerequisite to obtaining a grant.

Marsha leans back over the coffeepot. "A guy named Hanson. He makes the most incredibly realistic human figures you've ever seen."

"I've seen his stuff," I call out.

"People will walk right up to these things and stare at them from inches away; they can't believe they're not real people."

She hasn't heard me. "I said I've seen it," I yell. She's right; they are amazing. One figure is a museum guard, leaning idly against a wall. You can stand and observe a few feet away as people walk up to it to ask directions, grow indignant when it doesn't answer, get wide-eyed in astonishment as they realize that they've been talking to a wax model.

Marsha walks back in carrying two fresh cups of coffee: regular for her, decaf for me, both black. "Anyway, seems a guy was visiting the exhibit and he decides to have a little fun. He leans back against a wall, puts one foot up against it, and stands perfectly still."

I take a sip of the hot coffee. I have no idea where this is going.

"Sure enough," Marsha continues, "after a few minutes people are looking at him and trying to figure out if he's one of the statues. There are these two elderly women, and one of them walks up to him, puts her face right in his, and just stares. The guy waits a few seconds, then he yells 'Boo!' real loud, right at her." Marsha takes a sip of her own coffee and makes a face. The regular is not used very much and goes inky real fast if no one makes a fresh pot.

"And . . . ?" I prompt, intrigued now.

"And, she falls flat on her ass." Marsha sets the cup down and picks her papers up off the floor. "Breaking her hip in the process."

I shrug. "So she sues the guy, the museum, the artist, the people who made the floor—what's that got to do with us?" The old woman will probably go into litigation turbo-mode, but those are all civil actions. We are concerned only with criminal cases.

"Well," Marsha says, drawing this out for her own amusement, "seems this particular lady is rather well-off, a high-society type, and she's not interested in the money. What she's interested in is justice."

"Jeez, I hate when that happens." I really do. The search for justice is usually really a quest for revenge. Not that there is necessarily anything wrong with retribution, mind you—a little more old-fashioned, up-front anger in our legal system might go a long way in curing some of our societal ills—it just gets a little uglier in the hands of the self-righteous who dress it up as though they were doing society a giant favor by avidly pursuing their private grievances.

"She believes that this guy was malicious in his intent to harm her—"

"She thinks the guy wanted to break her hip?" I interrupt.

"No, not necessarily, but she does believe he wanted to cause her some distress. I almost think she's happy she got hurt physically because a case for just mental anguish might have been tougher to prove, especially in a criminal proceeding."

"I'd say that was a pretty damned good bet. So what's she swearing out, assault?"

"Battery. With intent to inflict great bodily harm."

"You can't be serious. The guy didn't touch her!"

"I know." She sighs. Marsha has a heavy caseload and doesn't need this right now, but the politics of the times demand that we treat every legal hangnail as a major coronary. "I explained that to her. She says it wasn't a threat or verbal abuse, something that allowed her to contemplate the words and grow fearful as a result; it was the physical nature of the loud yell that made her jerk involuntarily and fall."

I tilt my head back and moan. "Lord, why me?"

"What do you mean, you? I'm the one's gotta deal with this."

Yes, but you're not the one who is going to catch holy hell if this gets out of control and goes public. "What's your recommendation?"

Marsha clears her throat. "I'm going to take it to the grand jury."

I look at her like she's gone temporarily insane, but I can see she doesn't need me to straighten her out on this one so I stay quiet and listen.

"The lady is still in the hospital, for at least two more days. I'll go and see her and tell her this is of the utmost urgency, it has to be done right away, this afternoon if possible."

"Why?"

"So she can't be there, dummy."

"Aahhh . . ."

Marsha smiles. "She doesn't get to see my enthusiastic and passionate presentation of the facts of the case as I request the indictment."

"Which the grand jury tells you to go stick in your ear."

"*Precisemente*. At which point the distraught perpetrator of said heinous crime pays a visit to the victim and cries out his remorse in an impassioned plea for mercy."

I love this woman. "What's the guy do?"

"He's an unemployed musician. Volunteers his accordion at children's shelters."

Awesome smells are starting to arise from the chi-chi oceanfront restaurants preparing for the lunch crowd. I remember I haven't eaten anything yet today. "Christ, she'll probably adopt the poor bastard. Well done."

She says nothing but enjoys the compliment and reaches for her next case. I know she has three she wants to discuss, the last an important matter. I hear some muffled voices through the doorway and look past Marsha to see Marty McConagle in the doorway.

"Sal, you got a minute?" He's telling me, not asking.

"Hey, Marty. Can it wait?"

Marsha twists around in her seat, and McConagle says, "Hiya, Jones. Mind excusing us a few minutes?"

Marsha looks back at me for marching orders, and I look at McConagle. His normally gregarious face is different now, a little blank and restrained. He knows the ropes and would not presume to break up a meeting unless there was a good reason. Marsha looks back again and apparently sees the same thing I do. She starts to gather her papers and stand up.

"Oh, sure, the old boy network plotting how to perpetuate the power elite," she says, slipping the case files into her attaché. She looks to Marty for an appropriately sarcastic return shot but gets only a weak attempt at a smile, and then she hurries up, knowing now that something is definitely wrong. As she passes him in the doorway, she slaps the side of his arm lightly.

"Later, Jones," Marty says. Then he steps into my office and closes the door behind him, without even a backward glance at Marsha's receding form. Now I know there is trouble.

Marty is a top investigator in my office, sort of a cop's cop, a six-foot-two, 210-pound second generation Irishman with large features and expansive gestures who likes to actively flaunt his political incorrectness. He knows he can get away with most anything because he is personally responsible for more convictions in this office than any three of my attorneys combined. He quit the LAPD's SWAT team after being wounded during a hostage situation in a Beverly Hills jewelry shop. The perpetrator who shot him copped a plea and went free; Marty decided that maybe the greatest good in the war on crime was to be found not in apprehension but prosecution. He does not faze easily: his failure to leer suggestively at Marsha Jones is not a good sign.

I point to the chair previously occupied by Marsha, and he drops himself down onto it heavily. It's difficult to assess how recent his shave is, owing to his florid complexion and light beard, but I believe he has not shaved yet today.

"Bad news," he starts.

"No shit. What, Delaney's out of pumpernickel raisin again?"

Not even a smile. "Got a call at home this morning from Patty Salerno, about four A.M." Patricia is an officer on the Santa Monica police force, a decorated cop and a good friend to this office. "Was a rape out near Mulholland."

"Mulholland? Why'd Santa Monica get the call?" Mulholland is up in the Malibu area, a different jurisdiction.

Marty clears his throat and sniffles. "Victim called in directly. They're from here."

"They?"

He nods. "There's two of them. Sisters." I frown in disbelief. "Twins," he finishes, and waits.

I know Marty. What he has seen has built up layers of psychic scar tissue not easily penetrated. The only thing that would warrant this level of concern would be something that hits home. "Diane and Lisa," I venture tentatively, afraid of the very sound of those words, as though their mere utterance might make manifest what, for now, they only abstractly describe. Marty nods.

I need a moment, and by silent assent, Marty lets me have it. My first thoughts go to Diane, and if Marty suspects that there is something personal here, he hides it well. Maybe he doesn't know. For sure Diane Pierman has no idea, such courage as I might possess never having screwed itself to the sticking post. I usually tell myself that a relationship between a management-level prosecutor and a rising defense attorney is unwise and doomed from the start, but this transparent pretense wore thin months ago. Diane, like her sister—what am I talking about: *exactly* like her sister—is about five-ten, which puts her an inch taller than I. She is also graceful and athletic, while I am clumsy and prone to periods of paunchiness that only ill-considered diets and manic exercise can counter, and then only temporarily. This is not to demean myself or incur the wrath of California's self-esteem storm troopers. I have my good points. But they don't include the gumption to ask Diane Pierman out, though such a scenario has fueled many an interesting fantasy.

Raped. Boiling up in the back of my mind are images I can't control and feelings I don't like. "Tell me," I say.

Marty settles back now, having given me the bottom line first so I can concentrate. I must make sure I'm mindful of Marty's own personal feelings, since he also knows the Pierman twins well. The four of us are always running into each other at various civic functions that are part of the general networking of aspiring professionals on the west side. I remember that Marty and I had seen both sisters just last night, and this thought suddenly chills me: only several hours later, somebody had . . . what, exactly? I need to let Marty tell me.

"I don't have all the details, just the outline. Counselors took over right away." Standard procedure. The conviction rate on forcible rape is so low that the prevailing philosophy is to give first priority to the well-being of the victims, including their mental stability, rather than traumatize them further with relentless and ineptly handled interrogations. But the collection of physical evidence is vital, as is drawing out any information that might aid in a quick apprehension of the perpetrator. Rape crisis therapists are trained in how to walk the fine line.

"Collection of physical evidence" is a polite euphemism for an unavoidably frightful and humiliating invasion of the victim's person, almost a slow-motion replay of the rape itself as the affected orifices and their surroundings are poked, scraped and examined under the brutal glare of bright lights, usually by a male physician. Again images creep unbidden into my head: the two women lying back on sterile, narrow hospital tables, their faces contorted with crying and streaked with tears, eyes tightly shut as they pray for this part to just please, God, end so they can go home and stand under a shower for hours until it's all washed away. I don't have any firsthand case experience on crimes like these, but I've read the brochures.

"You with me, tiger?"

"Yes," I answer reflexively, though it takes me another second to snap myself back.

"They were south of Thousand Oaks, pretty far down the way on Kanan Dume Road toward Malibu."

"In a house?"

Marty shakes his head. "In the woods. Diane had a cellular phone in her handbag. She called Pat Salerno. Not sure how they know each other, but I think there was this case, some creep client of Diane's swore he was innocent, he was framed, whatever. I forget his name. Diane believed him and asked the chief if he'd check it out." That would be Darryl Christianson, chief of police in Santa Monica, hired last year as a progressive and enlightened reflection of community values. Fourteen months on the job disabused him of a great deal of that romanticism.

I just realized what case Marty is talking about. "Peter Friehling."

He snaps his head up. "Friehling, that was it! Howdja know that?"

I feel my jaw setting itself tight, against my will. "I prosecuted that case. Or would have if it'd *been* a case."

"You lost me."

"Got dismissed at the prelim."

"At the prelim?" Marty asks in great surprise. "That's not like you, me boy-o."

Damned straight it's not. "Salerno's part was months ago, which is why I didn't put it together while you were talking. I never even got to interview the sonofabitch defendant."

"When'd all this happen? The dismissal, I mean."

I put my hands over my face and rub my eyes, hard. "Yesterday."

Marty's face betrays his surprise, an unusual occurrence. "Whu' happened?"

I take a deep breath. We're getting sidetracked. "What the hell ever. Anyway . . ."

"Anyway, they musta appreciated each other or something, Diane and Pat. So Diane thought of her first when she, you know, when she got into trouble." He pauses, uncomfortable. "Heard you had a date lined up."

"It wasn't a date!" I exclaim too loudly, and quickly get hold of myself. "Just needed somebody for this stupid barbecue thing. Business obligation." It wasn't a date, not at all, just something to do when we both had nothing to do and I didn't want to show up alone. That was it. Diane agreed with me all the way.

I look away toward the window. "And I was going to call it off today anyway."

"Why? On account'a she beat you up in court on this Friehling thing?"

I need to get off this topic. "Were they hurt? Where are they now?"

Marty jerks a thumb toward the door and makes a jiggling motion with his hand. I reach forward, hitting the speaker button on my phone and punching a digit.

"Lemme guess," says a female voice before I have a chance to say anything. "One real, one unleaded, both black."

"How'd you know?" I say.

"McConagle looked like shit," my secretary answers, then clicks off.

"You do, you know," I say to Marty.

He waves it off. "They're okay, physically. Doesn't look like they were hurt at all. Least not what I could see, but then . . ."

There's no need for him to finish. The door opens and

Marion Muriyaki walks in holding two styrofoam cups. "You should drink tea," she tells Marty sternly.

"Was up to me, I'd wear a freakin' kimono, too," he says, accepting the steaming coffee gratefully.

"Officer Salerno is going to call in about twenty minutes," Marion says to me as she puts the second cup on my desk and removes the old one. "She's at the hospital."

"Should I call her?"

She shakes her head. "No need. Should I put her through?"

"Yeah," says Marty before I can answer.

Marion grunts at him. "Maybe I should ask you for a raise."

"Not 'til you learn to make coffee like an American," he answers as she leaves the office, pulling the door closed behind her.

Marty takes a long sip, and he appears to welcome the burning from the hot coffee. "Head-wise, they're not so good. Lisa especially, but Patty got them to go to the hospital."

"St. Matthew's?"

"Yeah. Then she called me. Time I got there two counselors were already on them, and so was Eberfield."

"That's good." Steven Eberfield is one of the best rape trauma physicians in the county, on retainer to the Santa Monica police and a half dozen others in the area. "We get anything on the guy?"

Marty doesn't answer right away but sets the cup down on my desk and reaches into his jacket pocket for the standard police-issue black notebook. He doesn't flip it open. "I can give you the details, but you've already seen the guy."

"What are you talking about?"

"In the bar last night? Remember that greaseball tried to pick a fight, the slick one with the shiny suit?"

Of course I remember. I start to feel weak. "He waited for them after you blew him off?"

Marty shrugs. "Must've."

Now I know why Marty looks like his dog just died. It's quite possible that whatever this guy did to the twins resulted from the humiliation dealt him by Marty in front of an entire room full of well-dressed yuppies. All as a result of his perceived rejection by Diane and Lisa, hardly subtle in its own right. No way was the guy going to take it out on Marty himself, so . . . ?

"You got this from them? Directly?"

"Yeah. From Diane, anyway. Lisa wasn't talking."

I can't let Marty stew about this. "Shouldn't we get to the hospital? What's this call from Salerno about?"

He seems to perk up slightly now that action steps need to be planned. "She's gonna call us soon's we can see the girls. Or we can go over there and wait."

"What about the guy?"

"Police have a good make on the car. My guess, we'll get him before the day is out. I think he was in the bar dealing blow so if we have any trouble, I'll squeeze one of the solid citizens in there tonight, get a name."

Marty shares my contempt for the real cocaine-buying public, the ordinary people who refuse to consider that their harmless, victimless little crimes subsidize a scourge of almost biblical proportions. Subconsciously, they believe their supply comes from the same place as sun-dried tomatoes and free-range chickens rather than the clockers that feed the stuff free to schoolchildren until they are ready to steal from their parents to buy the next vial.

"I think you oughta handle this one yourself," Marty is saying. "The case, I mean. Not give it to anybody else."

I'm tempted to ask him how he came by that opinion. I suspect that he's just making things easier for me, knowing that I want to do just that, but if it comes from him, I don't have to justify it or squirm my way around my personal interest.

"This is gonna be visible," he goes on. "Top dog should show the flag, roll up his sleeves."

The problem is, I'd really like to know which of several possible competing motivations are at work here. Does he think I want the case because of my feelings for Diane or because he thinks I want to run against my boss in the next election? I appreciate his silence on the subject because, truth is, I don't know myself, and after yesterday's courtroom fiasco, any political ambitions I might have harbored have probably hoisted sail and left port.

"Good point. I'll consider it when we see what we

have." It is, of course, as good as done, and Marty graciously lets it go.

"What was Friehling about?" Marty asks.

"Huh?"

"That case, the one with Diane Pierman and Salerno."

There is little more we can do until we hear from Officer Salerno, and it's obvious neither of us is going to do anything else productive until that happens. "Friehling," I say absently. I can't help but shake my head at the too fresh memory.

"This guy, Peter Friehling, he's picked up on a tip just as he's leaving a dock in the Marina, the one with all the fancy charters?" Marty nods. It's a section of the Fisherman's Village tourist trap in Marina del Rey where expensively outfitted boats tie up, a favorite spot for dropping off smuggled drugs owing to all the crowds and boat traffic.

"The feds and a bunch of local jurisdictions are in the middle of this enormous raid, everybody stepping all over each other and complicating things. In the middle of all this they pinch Friehling walking away on the other side of the parking lot. He's not holding, but they got some scared mule swearing Friehling was on the boat and there's about six kilos in the hold, and the mule says Friehling spent the last hour haggling over distribution."

"Possession with intent, conspiracy . . ." Marty starts ticking down the possible charges.

"Minimum. I take the case because I was legal adviser to the team setting up the bust. And who walks into the prelim representing Friehling?"

"Diane Pierman. How come?"

"How come? She's a young associate with Marchetti, Parnell & Kozinski. They're under retainer with some very bad guys. Friehling isn't that high up in the organization, but they have to protect him to show the rest of the mob that everybody gets taken care of. The firm kicks it down to Diane; what's she gonna do, tell them she doesn't like the case?"

Marty doesn't need to be lectured on the pressures facing a budding associate with her eye on a partnership who has hitched her wagon to the prestigious firm's star. "So what happened?"

"Friehling swears to her that he was an innocent party, which is why the feds got a phone tip on him: it was a diversion from the real players."

"Did he have money?" Marty means when he was picked up.

"Nothing. But there was over three hundred grand on board and no other buyers in sight."

Marty sees the basic idea right away. Friehling came on board with the money to make a buy. An amateur, he came alone and unarmed. Somehow he was ripped off and hustled off the boat, the hard guys knowing it was safe: what was he going to do, go to the police and complain about being robbed? By some extraordinary good luck, he stepped off the boat probably within seconds of its being raided by the authorities, but someone on board, a "mule," or carrier, started pleading that the main guy was making an escape across the parking lot. In light of the mule's detailed description and willingness to testify, the authorities had no choice but to pick Friehling up. They charge him with about fifteen federal and state counts, all of them felonies.

"What's Friehling's story?" Marty asks.

"He said he was there to buy a kite for his kid." I hold up my hands. "I mean it. The guy's got no priors. Diane gets her boss to plead with Chief Christianson to investigate his story, and Christianson gives the case to Pat Salerno."

My throat is getting dry, whether from the talking or the strain of the morning's events, I can't tell. I take a sip of coffee as Marty waits patiently. It's something cops, ex- or otherwise, do very well.

"Salerno decides to squeeze the mule, take him through every single detail of what went on during the exchange, see if she can poke enough holes to show Friehling was never really on the ship." The boat was not the primary incoming vessel, just a tender that met the big ship somewhere off shore in international waters. It was part of the complex distribution network for narcotics. An ocean-worthy ship or multiengine plane carries the goods in from South America and is met along the way by smaller, faster runabouts that either tie up and accept parcels or pick up parachuted air drops. These smaller boats then head for any of hundreds of shoreline pickup points ranging the entire length of the west coast.

"I saw the videotapes of her interrogation," I continue. "An amazing job. She caught him in about a thousand inconsistencies, and he was almost pleading to be taken outside and shot, which would probably have been a good thing for him considering that he ended up fingering the boat captain."

"I'm gonna guess," Marty says. "One of Pontanegro's boys."

"Who else?" The very mention of that name makes the muscles in my back start to tighten. Sylvester Pontanegro is a particularly notorious and elusive drug kingpin operating somewhere in southern California, one of a new breed of impossibly vicious wiseguys totally devoid of any sense of proportion. "But Salerno is no dummy. She pulls Friehling back in and says to the guy, if the tip to the feds was bullshit, if you had nothing to do with the delivery, how'd the mule describe you so good? How come he even knew you were out there? How'd he even know who the hell you were if you were just buying a kite for your kid!"

Marty laughs. "And that's when he tells her about how they ripped him off, offers to turn state's . . ."

"What's he got to lose, giving up the operation to try to save his own ass? He's not about to stand up for Pontanegro's people, who not only took all his money but fingered him as well, and the mule's already blown the captain anyway. Except Salerno figured, who the hell needed his cooperation when the boat guys had already been pinched with the cash and the goods? So we re-arrested him based on his confession, and it was a good bust because it was practically at the request of the guy's own attorney, who asked the police to look into it in the first place!"

Marty is still smiling. "You gotta love this fucking business."

"Yeah, well," I say, sobering now. "We arraigned him all over again, piled on a few more charges. Yesterday we're in front of Arigga, Diane and I, doing the new prelim." That I had a slight infatuation with her didn't trouble me, from an ethical point of view. It didn't make me want to ease up on her client. To the contrary, I knew that nothing impressed a lawyer more than a good job by another lawyer. "I really put the pedal to the metal on this one, all the ducks in line, every inch airtight." I don't tell Marty that I even marched in some of the younger lawyers in my charge, just to show them how the old master handles things.

"I have a feeling this doesn't end well," Marty says.

I hold up a hand: *just wait a minute.* "Diane gets up to make the obligatory bullshit motions—hearsay violations, illegally obtained evidence, coercion—"

"No probable cause, improper jurisdiction—" Marty continues for me. It's standard defense procedure, so your client thinks you're really pulling out all the heavy ordnance on his behalf even though there isn't a chance in hell of getting enough of them seriously considered to warrant not being bound over for trial.

"So I'm listening to this with half a brain, the other half rehearsing for the bail motions and all the other usual stuff, and all of a sudden"—I sit up and square my shoulders—"I think I hear Arigga say, 'granted,' like from somewhere out in left field."

"Which ones?" Marty asks.

"All of them."

He looks at me with a confused frown. "Whaddya mean, all of them?"

"I mean, all of them. He grants all her motions and before I even know what's going on, he dismisses the case and Friehling runs from the courtroom like an Olympic hurdler."

It is a day I will never forget. I looked at Diane, expecting a shit-eating grin of triumph, but she was back down on her chair, looking as confused as I was. Pat Salerno was not even in the courtroom to witness it, probably having assumed, as I did, that it was a mere formality preparatory to trial or a plea bargain. Some people I didn't recognize but who were dressed a good deal better than I came to the defense table and shook Diane's hand amid hearty congratulations, but there were still no signs of satisfaction on her face as she mechanically accepted the accolades.

I didn't see her afterward until The Alley, where I made up my mind to call off our non-date. How would it look if a suspect I'm supposed to prosecute and she is supposed to defend is mysteriously released a few days before we show up together at some function? Somehow, I didn't get around to speaking to her.

My anger at Judge Constantin Arigga dissipated somewhat as I recalled the numerous times I'd come before him on other matters and he'd behaved as his usual self: tough, quick-tempered, generally fair and very knowledgeable about the law. I also saw that he was aging quickly, and I tried to chalk off the humiliating Friehling episode to the unpredictable vagaries engendered by too many years under too much pressure. It was too easy for judges to dismiss charges: while they might suffer a little in the press, there was no possibility of reversal on appeal, which judges fear more than most anything else.

"Tough break," Marty says when I've finished the story about Peter Friehling.

"I still get mad thinking about it. It was like Arigga lost his mind for a few minutes at the wrong time."

I thought of saying something to a reporter present at the prelim but forced myself to stay silent. It has gotten me into trouble before, like the time I spoke to the press about the trial of a woman in northern California who shot the alleged molester of her son. The suspect had not even had his trial yet, one in which he might have been convicted and sent to jail, and I ventured the observation that the mother could have saved herself a lot of trouble by waiting to see if the law would do for her what she decided prematurely to do for herself. When pressed, I also mentioned that allowing private citizens to exercise rights reserved for the state is an invitation to the decline of Western civilization. The DA, using language I thought him incapable of, dressed me down severely, not for the sentiments expressed but for a lack of sensitivity for the feelings of the victimized citizenry. My retort that, in this particular case, the victimized citizen was the one lying dead of a shotgun blast to the head prior to his statutory day in court, brought no concession from the DA, who went on to say that I had no business opening my mouth in the first place about a case not even in our jurisdiction. I had to give him that one. At thirty-four, it's not easy being one of the youngest head deputy DA's in the state, and my boss's support is important to me. "Pick your battles carefully," he told me when I got the job, and it turned out to be a useful platitude, especially when dealing with him. If I do decide to run against him in the next election, at the moment a doubtful proposition, I wonder if that would constitute the careful picking of a battle.

We managed to kill a few minutes of waiting time, but now Marty stands up abruptly and opens the door. "I don't like sitting around. Let's go to the hospital and wait there. Coffee's better anyway," he says, making sure that Marion hears it. She curls a lip and sneers at him.

"Salerno calls, tell her we're on our way," I tell Marion.

"How long you gonna be?" she asks.

"No telling."

2

I hate hospitals. They're supposed to be temples of healing, the scientific equivalent of Lourdes, but I can never get past the fact that you have to be sick and in pain before these modern-day wonders do you any good. And then the whole concept is one of simple rescission, restoring you to normalcy, or as close as they can get. It isn't like you come out smarter or more physically fit or with skills you never had before. As soon as you're just well enough, you're out.

I know that this detestation of hospitals is traceable to my New York upbringing, which began somewhere south of the middle-class economic threshold. My visits to the hospital generally consisted of forced marches to Coney Island General to watch relatives slowly die in the wards, doing their best to constrain their moans in my presence, their pain coming instead through their eyes. I watched my adored grandmother as a lifetime of learned behaviors were suppressed under the weight of new ones, such as those required to ensure that the bored and irritable nurses arrived on time with the blessed painkillers. Get one of these ladies angry, say, by asking for a glass of water, and you could doom yourself to recurring episodes of progressive agony as the minute hand on the industrial-size clock over the nurses' station ticked past your appointed medication time with excruciating slowness.

It is said that the most powerful trigger for the recollection of early memories is smell; the intermingled odors of disinfectants and a half dozen exotic and unidentifiable substances as I walk through the doors of St. Matthew's in Santa Monica transport me instantly, and I have to struggle to maintain my equilibrium. St. Matthew's is a considerable improvement over Coney Island, substituting well-maintained and cheerfully colored tile for peeling green paint. But the presence of the standard gaily colored children's pictures and museum prints only underscores for me the basic premise of the hospital. At least in Coney Island the depressing physicality of the place was honest with respect to what was going on within the walls; here in St. Matthew's, all these tasteful decorations are like hanging pictures of Tahiti in a jail cell: they only increase the perception of the contrast between how the patients/prisoners are feeling and how much better off they wished they were.

However, this visit is not about me, not about my problems or eccentricities. I am here for Diane and Lisa Pierman, not to minister to their medical needs but to see that justice is done, a phrase that rings hollow in my ears right now. The only justice I can offer is apprehension and prosecution of their attacker, and I already know that this attempt at balancing the scales is a feeble one. For these two women there will be no rescission, no restoration of their former selves, like they might have expected had they the flu or appendicitis.

Officer Patricia Salerno meets us at the entrance to the emergency room, as though she knew we were coming. Marion's doing, probably. Pat is another transplanted New York Italian who did not endear herself to her family by opting for a career in law enforcement. In that we have something in common. My father was a baker, as was his father, and a basically honest man. But when Michelangelo "Mikey" Prestigiacomo, a midlevel functionary in the Sabbatini crime family, found out that my grandmother was living her last days in Coney Island General, he immediately arranged for her transfer to a semiprivate room in Columbia Presbyterian, for which he earned my father's undying gratitude. I didn't know at that time exactly why Prestigiacomo did that, what he could possibly want from a baker—it became somewhat clearer later—but when I came out of NYU law school and joined the Brooklyn DA's office, word on the street was that Mikey was not amused.

Patricia's story is somewhat similar, as I discovered during a joint commiseration session yesterday following Judge Arigga's dismissal of charges against Peter Friehling, just before I left for The Alley. Her brother was a troubled and searching soul but nevertheless dear to her, despite his part-time job as a numbers runner in East New York. His "organization," as he liked to refer to it, was a rattle-trap agglomeration of high school dropouts with laugh-able mob aspirations, and when they pressured Pat's brother to take the fall for a botched factory robbery, promising him an elevated position in the organization when he got out of prison, Pat, herself only nineteen at the time, decided to step in and put things right. She colluded with the prosecutor to refute her own brother's testimony and implicate his "superiors" at the same time. It worked, but the mean streets were no longer safe for her and she headed west. She has, heretofore unbeknownst to me, become a good friend to our investigations department.

"Hey, Sal," she says to me, forcing a smile. "Brought your bodyguard, did you?"

"Protect him from you," Marty responds for me, but his return bon mot is purely reflexive banter: his heart is not in it.

I look past her shoulder but don't see any activity in the emergency room reception area. "What's going on?"

"They're upstairs," she answers, flicking her eyes toward the ceiling. "Seems they have a more comfortable room for cases like this." Neither she as a cop nor I as a prosecutor is very familiar with "cases like this." We have a sex crimes unit to handle them, and Pat specializes in narcotics.

"Like what?" I ask.

"Where, uh, I guess the problem is more mental than physical?"

A strange way to put it, but I see what she means. Forcible rape is among the most psychically devastating of crimes but need not necessarily result in any serious physical harm. Modern physicians with the appropriate training are aware of the need to take immediate steps to lessen the psychological damage.

"How they doing?" Marty asks.

"Not so good," Pat answers. "Especially Lisa. Diane's holding her own, which isn't to say she isn't pretty busted up, but Lisa hasn't been able to stop crying."

"But he didn't hurt them?" I ask. She knows I mean physically.

She shakes her head. "Not as far as I could tell. Doc'll know better. But, uh . . ." She hesitates, and we let her find her own time. Pat is not normally at a loss for words, so I know there is something more. She clears her throat. "Seems the guy made them watch. I mean, each other. While he was doing it."

"Christ Almighty," Marty says with a rasp.

I want to keep myself calm and under control, but I don't want to appear callous either. I feel as if there is a menu of behaviors for me to choose from but I cannot effect the appropriate mix, so I'm silent for a moment. Maybe I should just be myself, but I'm not sure what that is. In the absence of any external cues, I decide that the only mode I am safe in is that of my profession.

"Can we see them?" I ask.

"I don't know for sure. Diane, probably."

She turns and we follow. I let Marty take the lead, in some sort of subconscious hope that whatever there is to be seen hits him first. Pat bypasses the elevator, and we climb two flights of stairs and emerge from the stairwell onto the third floor. Doctors and nurses give us a longer look than normal as we pass on our way down the hall, like they all know who we are and why we are here. Pat is not in uniform, having been summoned out of bed by Diane's call, but these people have seen her before and they know who she is.

I find that we are in a corridor with a series of small examining rooms. ER is usually at ground level so it surprises me that we are on the third floor. Then I see a set of stirrups as we pass an open door and realize that these are ob-gyn rooms. We come to a room even smaller than the rest. It has an engraved plaque mounted beside the door that informs the visitor that it has been furnished by the Westside Rape Treatment Project. Inside there is carpeting, a couch, three chairs, a table with magazines and two boxes of tissues, some fresh flowers, a poster with lilies announcing a Monet exhibition in Paris fifteen years ago and a yellowing, hospital-issue electric clock on the wall. There are ashtrays as well, a concession in deference to victims who smoke and don't need the added stress of enforced abstinence on top of everything else.

There is another door on the opposite wall. As we enter the room, it opens and a smallish woman emerges. She is carrying a bag in one hand, a notebook and tape recorder in the other. Pat waves us over and introduces her.

"Sal, Marty, this is Priscilla Fields, from the Rape Treatment Project."

She holds out a hand and I take it. As expected, her grip is firm and strong. Professional. "I know who you are," she says as she shakes with both Marty and me. "Pat told me you were coming."

"Can you talk to us for a few minutes?" I ask.

"Of course." She turns to sit and motions to us to do the same. I'm surprised to see that she doesn't have the jaded look of most crisis intervention or emergency services workers, the kind of attitude that is not really uncaring or unsympathetic but calloused in self-defense. She looks haggard and troubled, whether because she has been up all night or because of what she has heard, I cannot tell. Maybe it's a front for we two males who have no way to sympathize with the victims and can never hope to understand and so forth and so on. Nevertheless, it's a law enforcement matter now and we are in charge and that's all there is to it, as she had better understand.

"I apologize for being so out of it," Priscilla says. "I never get used to this. . . ." She wipes away a tear that has formed in the corner of her left eye. "Sorry."

"We're gonna need to see them," Marty begins, as I am too busy silently chastising myself for having jumped to an obviously erroneous set of conclusions about Priscilla Fields. "But we don't need to ask 'em stuff you already got, except maybe to fill in some blanks."

"I understand." Priscilla seems to be pulling herself together within the comforting confines of prescribed procedure and recognizable authority. She seems appreciative of Marty's solicitousness toward the victims.

Marty pulls a tissue out of one of the boxes on the table

and hands it to her. "Officer Salerno tells me there's two of you here, that right?"

She nods. "Uh-huh. I was with Diane, and Renata Cito is with Lisa."

"How come they're separate?" I ask. It would seem to me that they would want to be together, to help each other.

"Diane insisted on it," Priscilla answers. "To preserve the case, she said. Renata and I both taped everything. Diane said get two separate statements so nobody can say they got together and made things up."

This is a relief, on two counts. First, Diane has her wits about her. Second, as she correctly reasoned, the separate statements so soon after the event will be invaluable in gaining a conviction, assuming we catch the perpetrator. I'm also hopeful that she made it a point to remember as many details as possible while her ordeal was underway. That she was able to direct Pat Salerno to their location is a good sign. It's my guess that her training in criminal law and her awareness of what needs to be done is part of what is holding her together. It might also explain why Lisa is faring less well.

Priscilla fills us in on some details, although she will not give us the tape without Diane's permission. Marty takes notes, in bullet-point form, highlighting the salient details: committed at gunpoint, repeated threats of death and bodily harm, rapist appeared to be under the influence of narcotics. My emotions jump tracks among shock, rage and pity so many times I have to consciously will them to one side in order to concentrate.

The rear door opens again, and I recognize Dr. Steven Eberfield as he emerges. He is shorter even than I, by about two inches, slightly overweight and more jowly than his forty-five years might warrant. All in all, it is a pleasant appearance, almost teddy-bearish, which might in part explain his success in his chosen field. There is a school of thought that holds that the examining physician should be a male because it helps the victim get past the notion that all men are monsters, but from what I've read, the gender matters less than the attitude. Eberfield is carrying a brown paper bag about the size a grocery store would use to pack two quarts of milk.

He looks distracted, but his expression brightens as he walks forward and extends his hand. "Sal, every time I see you it's trouble." In addition to this particular specialty, Eberfield is a highly regarded trauma physician in general. We've used him as an expert many times.

"Funny, I feel the same way about you." I reach to shake his hand. "This is Marty McConagle, investigator in my office."

"I know the name," Eberfield says, nodding at Marty. Then he looks back at me. "So, you gonna run for DA or what?"

I can't hide being startled. "Cripes, is nothing sacred anymore?"

"In politics? Get serious."

"Got a minute?" Marty asks him, reaching for another chair. He and I are side by side on the couch.

"Sure, sure. Hell else am I gonna do?"

When we are all seated, I say to Eberfield, "You looked a little concerned. Is Diane all right? I mean, considering."

Eberfield knits his brow. "She's fine. Better than Lisa. But physically, they're both okay."

I nod, relieved. "So what can you give us?" He knows what I mean. What has his examination revealed that impacts the case we want to make against the suspect?

Eberfield scratches an ear and makes a face. "Hate to tell you this, Sal, but you're not gonna have much here."

"How so?" Marty asks.

Eberfield stretches his neck a little and doesn't bother to consult his notes. "No obvious semen traces, even under ultraviolet, but we'll send the scrapings to the lab for an acid phosphatase test. If it's positive, we'll go to DNA."

The absence of semen is not good news. Sophisticated DNA tests can conclusively link traces to a suspect, even if the semen has intermingled with the natural secretions of the victim.

"Same for both women," Eberfield continues. "No bruises, no vaginal or vulval tearing, no abrasions, just a little residual dilation and some labial redness and inflammation . . ." Eberfield lets his voice trail off, and I look at him with lifted eyebrows. He shrugs.

"Wait a minute," Marty says. "You're telling me there's no evidence of rape? Is that it?"

Eberfield looks uncomfortable. "Nothing obvious. It looks like intercourse took place—did Pris tell you the guy used a condom?"

I whip my head around to look at Priscilla.

"Not all that uncommon," she says, "on account of AIDS."

I know that is true. Use of a condom has even been offered as a defense, most notoriously in a case where the victim begged the rapist to use one, and he then claimed the sex was therefore consensual.

"So why test for semen?" Marty asks.

"Because they leak," Eberfield says. "A lot more than anyone would like to believe."

"About how much time passed between the two rapes?" I ask Priscilla.

She looks up into the air and thinks for a moment. "Way I understand it, couldn't have been more than five, maybe ten minutes. Why?"

"Because," I answer, "I bet he didn't ejaculate twice in that time. Who was second?"

"Diane," she answers, and Eberfield nods.

"Her clothes are dirty," he says. "It happened on the ground. Lisa's was in the car."

"Can you ask them?" I say to Priscilla. "Can they tell if he climaxed?"

She looks at Eberfield, who says, "Not sure it's gonna buy you all that much, Sal. Pre-ejaculatory secretions can also be traced. Best thing, we just check them both."

"I'm gonna visit the site," Marty says. "See if I can find the thing." He will also look for any items that might have been inadvertently dropped and see if he can find the spot where Diane was on the ground. Anything to corroborate the details. "Doc, could this look like consensual sex?"

Eberfield starts to shake his head, then seems to change his mind. "On paper, from the physical evidence, yeah, maybe. Just some rough intercourse. But I've been through this a thousand times and I'm telling you, it was forcible rape. No question." He looks at Priscilla, who nods her agreement.

Marty pushes the point. We have to be sure. "Not a revenge thing, change of mind, maybe?"

"What do you mean?" Priscilla asks, stiffening.

Time to rescue Marty: he's only doing his job. I speak for him. "He means—and he's asking because we have to—any chance that they went with the guy willingly, then got cold feet and decided to set him up?"

I expect Priscilla to get huffy but she stays in control. "You haven't done many rape cases, am I right?"

I admit that this is true.

"Fraudulent reporting is rare. It does happen once in a while. But when it does, it's usually well after the fact, not immediately following. In this case, there's not a chance."

"Why're you so sure?"

Priscilla leans forward, but Eberfield puts a restraining hand on her arm. "Sal, you know what goes on in there?" He jerks a thumb over his shoulder. I shake my head. How can I tell him I'd rather not? For the last few minutes I've managed some kind of clinical coldness, and now he's going to tell me what's been happening to Diane?

Eberfield leans back on his chair. "Woman comes in, she's scared, confused, sometimes in clinical shock. I make her stand on a sheet of paper and take off all her clothes. When she's naked and putting on one of those hospital gowns, I fold up the paper and stick it in a plastic bag with a label, in case something useful fell down while she was getting undressed. Then we bag up all the clothes, each item in a separate paper bag, being sure not to fold the underwear across any potentially incriminating stains. If anything's wet, we air dry it before packing it away.

"Next thing I do is lay her down on the table, turn down the lights and examine every inch of her with a Wood's lamp. It's ultraviolet. If I see anything fluoresce in blue-white or orange, it's probably dried semen. Other colors is other stuff. I do this while the victim is barely breathing because she's terrified all over again, some strange galook staring at her in a darkened room with a weird blue light.

"Of course when that's all over we've hardly begun. Now I start collecting all the stuff I found under the lamp, scraping if it's dry, swabbing if it's still wet. 'Moist secretions,' we call them. Could be semen, blood stains, saliva, what the hell ever. Oh, wait a minute, I forgot something: before I start with the lamp I make her pull up the gown and sit on a sheet of paper with her legs spread. Then I take a comb and run it through her pubic hair a few times so any debris will fall onto the paper. Where the hair is matted, I cut it off and bag that, too, and then I take reference samples for comparison, various lengths and from different parts of the pubic region. Those have to be plucked, by the way, not cut. Hurts like hell."

I feel myself growing pale. Marty is as still as death. Eberfield isn't finished.

"We also take pictures. Bite marks, bruises, particulate debris. Close-ups, stick the camera right where it's needed, wherever that might be. Then we spread her legs again, wide this time, and open her up with a speculum and start sticking things in her vagina, taking multiple swabs, doing the same thing in her anus and then her mouth, if circumstances warrant. We check these not only for semen but to see if any diseases got transmitted. Then a little more close-up work with a magnifying lens. All the while I'm dictating what I found to the nurse. The victim gets a full-scale, detailed rundown of her anatomy, and—" he holds up the brown paper bag and gives it a shake—"she gets to see little samples from her most intimate parts bottled, wrapped and neatly labeled with enough paperwork to assure a proper chain of custody. And then . . ." He sets the bag on the table in front of me and leans back, folding his arms across his chest. ". . . and then, she gets to put on some strange clothes because we've taken all of hers away, and sit in this room so a couple of uniformed cops can ask her four thousand questions before she can go home and take a bath."

After a moment, Marty shakes himself and scratches at his ear. I am still staring at Eberfield.

"Point is," Priscilla says quietly, "who's going to voluntarily put herself through that to lay a false claim of rape?"

"It happens," Eberfield says. "Once in a while. Someone looking for revenge, for some money. Someone maybe cheated on her husband and woke up sober and scared and made up a story to cover it. Rare, but it happens, but only when they don't know what they're in for when they get here." He folds his hands on his lap. "Not these two. No way."

After several moments of strained silence, I clear my throat and ask if I can see them.

"Wish you wouldn't," Priscilla says, but not in a pushy way. "There's not a lot more you're gonna learn that isn't on this tape"—she pats the recorder—"and I bet she'll let you have it. You have to understand," she continues, her voice lapsing into a more tutorial and practiced tone, "their shame is acute. It's hard to understand in this day and age, but the ancient bugaboo about being defiled, being made dirty, even if it isn't their fault?" She shakes her head. "It's there in every case. What they really need is to get the hell out of here, go home and get cleaned up."

I already knew that part, but it's good to be reminded.

"I suggest they go home together," Eberfield says to Priscilla. "To one of their homes."

"How come?" Marty asks.

"Their humiliation with respect to each other is a factor here. They each watched while this sonofabitch raped the other. These two were not into anything kinky—it's easy to see that—and probably never even saw other people having sex, certainly not each other." He stands up and arches his back. "I think they should spend time together and talk the whole thing through, and the sooner the better."

Priscilla nods vigorously. "Nobody can help them like they can help each other. But I'll tell you this." She stands as well, the better to make her point. "You need to catch this guy."

"Of course we do," I say.

"No, you don't understand." Marty and I get up and she pokes a finger in his chest. "I can tell you what's gonna happen. They're gonna pull together and get on with things, but it's all gonna revolve around nailing this bastard and putting him away. It's the only justice they're gonna get short of castrating him themselves, and nothing rests until it's done. You see what I'm saying?"

Marty nods. We both know this is true in nearly every

case of violent crime. He turns to me. "We'll get him. Somebody at the bar has to know who he is, we'll get a good fix on the car, positive ID from the girls should be easy." He turns back to Priscilla and squeezes her shoulder, willing palpable reassurance into her. I think maybe he's trying to suck some of her own strength into himself. My own efforts to suppress disturbing images are failing badly.

"We'll get him."

3

I've read magazine articles about it, of course. About how men feel toward women who have been raped. I thought myself above such Victorian irrationalities, and still do, and even as Diane Pierman and I talk quietly over drinks in the outdoor section of a restaurant at the end of the Santa Monica pier, a part of me is wandering through my mind looking for clues as to whether that is still the case. Or ever really was.

The twins are the daughters of Ilosha and Galina Pirosmanishvili, their names before they became Jack and Anne Pierman. Ilosha was a distant relative of the great Russian naive artist of the same last name and shared some of his creative spirit. Where his cousin, prior to the revolution, painted vivid representations of farmyard animals, Ilosha wrote dissident essays and poetry during the early years of the cold war, earning the enmity of Soviet hard-liners. They did everything they could to make his life miserable without actually accusing him of anything, engineering an extra level of hardship into the already unforgiving daily lives of a Muscovite family.

"The chief vice of capitalism is the unequal distribution of wealth," he wrote. "The chief virtue of communism is the equal distribution of misery." Galina shared his political passion and did her best to keep the two little girls fed, each government-sanctioned setback only increasing her anger toward the state. When local merchants were warned that selling food to the family would not be looked upon kindly by the authorities, they had little choice but to plan an escape.

Ilosha volunteered to write a libretto for the Kirov Ballet's production of *The Nutcracker*, and his three-year-old daughters were accepted into the company essentially as set decoration for a dream sequence. Galina, an accomplished seamstress, took a low-paying job sewing costumes for the dancers. Lulled into inattention by the dissidents' apparent assimilation into the centrally directed artistic mainstream, the authorities were caught unaware when the family failed to make the return trip from a cultural exchange performance in Vienna. The timing of the plan was fortuitous, coming as it did during a period when any Soviet rebel who railed loudly against the evil empire, and who could write more than ten words in a row without a spelling error, was hailed in the west as a hero of democracy. It was a time when America took great pride in the highly visible assimilation of defecting Soviet cultural figures, and Ilosha Pirosmanishvili might have achieved greater notoriety were he not overshadowed by the likes of Nureyev, Baryshnikov, Solzhenitsyn and Yevtushenko. The family was welcomed at the American embassy in Rome, feted and housed in New York, and eventually moved to California.

In the style of many of the children of immigrants, the two girls excelled in school, easily surpassing their more jaded and less appreciative American friends. Diane eventually chose law school, graduating from UCLA with honors. Despite a torrent of fervent offers from the top corporate law firms, in a photographic negative of Deputy DA Marsha Jones's career she opted for Marchetti, Parnell & Kozinski and the much different life of the criminal defense attorney, her small bid to carry on her parents' fight for justice.

Lisa, on the other hand, finished her undergraduate degree and decided to go into business straightaway, combining her love for cooking with a keen mind for commerce. Starting with working small parties and supplying specialty items to restaurants, she eventually focused on the demanding but lucrative specialization of catering for location shoots in the film industry. It was perhaps the most hard-to-please customer base imaginable but one also capable of almost fanatical loyalty to any service business that could cheerfully accommodate its needs and keep the exacting and eccentric creative types happy. The referral network was deep and powerful as well, and Lisa's thriving company was in constant demand for the private parties of the rich and famous who rarely argued price.

It was the great American dream of politically sophisticated immigrants, a wondrous irony in which their children, in a glorious transmutation of their own struggles, dispensed food and justice in the promised land. I wonder if Jack and Anne know yet what has happened to their daughters, but I don't ask Diane, who I notice is drinking Glenlivet on ice with no water, in contrast to her more usual daiquiris and other fruity drinks.

I can tell the sisters apart, but not easily. Lisa, despite the ever-present temptations of her occupation, is a bit leaner, giving a more angular quality to the delicate features they both share. She also tends to wear her hair a little shorter and pulled back, to facilitate keeping it out of the way when food is being prepared or served. Diane's face is slightly fuller, softer, and set off with a good deal more of the dark brown hair she often wears loose around her shoulders. Her clothes are usually more formal, as befits a courtroom litigator. Both of them smile easily, and neither seems to have been hardened by a lifetime of fighting off unwanted advances from battalions of men. They are both single, both uninvolved as far as I can tell, both deeply committed to their respective professions. In our circle of westside professionals, they are highly thought of, on many levels. Diane's face is somber now, and she is still wearing dark glasses despite the sun having dipped into the Pacific more than twenty minutes ago.

It took us less than a day to get a good fix on Vincent Rosamund but another three to actually apprehend him, although we cannot assess any criminal liability against him in that regard: we have no evidence that he knew he was being sought, and he will almost certainly profess his innocence when he is arraigned. As far as the law is concerned, he had no duty to turn himself in. Marty McConagle worked through Thanksgiving, forgoing dinner with his family, which gave me a twinge of guilt, so I canceled a dinner date with a lawyer from Orange County and hung around the office awaiting word and trying uselessly to be useful. Marty was characteristically grateful. ("The hell good're you gonna do me? Go, go and eat; what is it, a lawyer again? What is it with you and lawyers all the time: can'tcha talk about anything with a broad except shop?" I pointed out that he himself married an FBI agent, but that was different, he said, and when he was through fuming I told him I would coordinate things by phone from my office. "We got radios now, Sally," he informed me. "They give one to everybody, they're really neat as hell; wanna try mine?") But when it was all over I knew he appreciated my largely symbolic gesture of support, knew that I did not take him for granted. Besides, I really didn't relish a date with another lawyer talking shop, nor did the thought of Thanksgiving dinner in a restaurant particularly appeal to me. Sitting here with Diane makes me glad I didn't go through the motions just so I wouldn't be alone on a holiday.

So Vincent Rosamund is now in custody, and I would have expected Diane to have drawn some small comfort from this. On the contrary, her anxiety seems to have increased, and I slowly come to understand that, prior to his apprehension, Rosamund represented to her some distant abstraction she didn't have to confront. Now that he's in jail, his is a palpable presence, as was made clear earlier this afternoon during the identification lineup.

Diane and Lisa both viewed the lineup separately, but their reactions were similar. Lisa went first. Marty brought her into the darkened viewing room that was separated from the brightly lit enclosure on the other side of the one-way glass. He started giving her instructions ("Take your time and look at each one in turn, then—") but she interrupted, pointing with a badly trembling finger to the man third from the right.

"That's him," she said through gritted teeth, unconsciously taking a step backward toward Marty.

"Are you sure, ma'am?" asked a detective assigned to the case.

"I said that's him." She turned to the detective, arms

wrapped around herself, hands balled into fists. "No mistakes. I'm positive."

Marty clapped her gently on the shoulder. "Well done," he said, then led her out a different door than the one she had come in while they brought her sister in. Diane had no sooner entered the room than she shot an arm out toward the glass and also identified Vincent Rosamund. As with Lisa, the detective made certain she looked at all the other faces so she could say in court she did, but the ID was a lock. Several minutes earlier, Marty himself had picked Rosamund out of the lineup as the man who had hassled both of us at The Alley.

"So what'd you file so far?" she asks me now.

"A single rape charge."

Her surprise is expected. "But there were two! And kidnapping, assault, brandishing a weapon, uh"—she hunts around, feeling that the list ought somehow to be a lot longer—"carjacking . . . ?"

I can't help but smile at Diane's lawyerly and technical assessment of criminal culpability. "I know all that. The initial charge was just to get him inside while we complete the bill of particulars. We want to have a full set of charges without amendments, ones that'll stick, so we're playing this very carefully."

Diane nods and leans back. "What about flight to avoid prosecution?" She has not asked me on whose behalf the rape charge was filed—hers or Lisa's—and I don't bring it up. In fact, Lisa was listed as the complainant. I'm not sure why I did it that way. Just flipped a mental coin, I imagine. I shake my head in answer to her question and explain that Rosamund can maintain he didn't know he was being sought. That Diane even asked such a naive question is not a good sign.

"But he committed a crime and fled the scene!" she protests, whipping off the dark glasses. There is some residual puffiness around her eyes.

"We have no grounds to believe he knows he committed a crime." I hold up a hand before Diane can react to that point, and I don't remind her that there is no flight unless the suspect was actually physically pursued at the scene. "Without knowing what he's going to plead, there's no way to know if he believes a crime has taken place."

Anger is beginning to creep into Diane's face and voice. "You're not seriously telling me this bastard is denying what happened!"

"He isn't denying it. He isn't doing anything except being exceptionally cool and exercising his fifth amendment rights." Nailing a clever criminal is a good deal like making a Hollywood motion picture: given all the rules and constraints, it's a miracle it ever happens at all.

"We may have more luck tomorrow," I go on, "when his attorney hits the scene. We're going to try to get him to talk to us, with his lawyer present, and then we'll arraign him in the afternoon." We have forty-eight hours to either arraign him or release him. Over a long weekend like this one, we can wait until Monday. The defense attorney always harbors the hope that an early appearance of cooperation on the part of the suspect, coupled with a lot of reasonable doubt as to his guilt, will lead toward his release before arraignment with the profuse apologies of the police. This isn't going to happen, although we might cultivate the illusion that it's a possibility. What we really want is as much information as we can get out of Rosamund and his lawyer, if not about the crime itself, then at least about the strategy the defense is going to employ. Unfortunately, I already know who Rosamund's attorney is, and I already know the usual tricks will not work.

I've been doing my best all evening to play it straight with Diane, answering all her questions honestly, no matter how painful. I'm going to need her to trust me later, and setting the groundwork for that trust is important. I have not even come yet to the crucial part of the conversation, but now is the time. I signal the waiter for two more drinks, even though neither of ours is quite finished yet.

"Go ahead if you want to," Diane says, smiling for the first time this evening.

"Scuse me?"

She points to my chest. "Tell me you don't have some stinky stogie parked in your jacket somewhere, and that we're sitting outside because the air smells so good."

"It's awful to be so transparent," I say, reaching into

my pocket and pulling out a No. 2 Upmann. Cigars are my less-than-secret passion, due in no small part to the warm feelings that surround me whenever I smell the delicious aroma of a truly fine specimen. We didn't get to see much of Pop during the day because he worked from before sunup each morning straight through until early evening, but after dinner he was all ours. We were certainly not rich, but my mother never begrudged him the luxury of one fine cigar a day, and accompanying him to the tobacco shop to select the assorted Romeo y Julietas, Partagas, Montecristos and other exotically named imports was a special treat. To this day it is difficult for me to distinguish between the inherent deliciousness of the curling smoke and the memories of those cocooned moments of perfect security and warmth. It was a sad day in the Milano household when the government imposed an embargo on trade with Cuba.

"Sure you don't mind?" I ask, even as I begin to remove the top of the special leather carrier that holds a single cigar.

"Not a bit. I like the smell."

I chose this table because it faces out onto the north side of the pier, and a light breeze is blowing from the south, so I won't have to waft smoke past the unappreciative. I clip the end with my portable guillotine snipper and sniff the middle of the cigar in anticipation.

"You gonna fiddle with that thing all night or tell me why we're here already?"

No sense even making a pretense of not knowing what she is talking about. I light a match and hold it to the tip without drawing in yet, slowly cooking it before pulling in the flame and getting a good glow going. The blue cloud moves lazily back past my head and out to sea.

"I have to make sure you're both going to testify," I tell her. I'm assuming she speaks for Lisa on this decision as well. I know the question is just a formality, but I need to make certain she understands all that is implied, and I'm quite stunned when she hesitates. I had expected some indignation from her that I would even wonder about it: she's been calling Marty's office three times a day to check on progress in finding and arresting Rosamund. Clearly, the strongest case for the prosecution is the twins themselves, acting as witnesses for each other, exploiting their personal credibility that is sure to emerge in their testimony. I start to explain all this and she stops me.

"Sal . . ." She takes a sip of her drink. "You have any idea what it takes for a woman, especially a professional woman with visibility in the community, to stand up in public, admit she was raped and give the sordid details?"

"I think I do," I mumble halfheartedly, reluctant to initiate that piece of the conversation. "But we're going to win this one. People will know that you didn't—"

"People will know shit," she says angrily. "So what if you win? This pig is going to say and do anything to get himself off the hook, make up insane stories about Lisa and me, paint us like twenty-dollar-a-trick hookers or nymphomaniacs. And when the jury deliberates and finds him officially guilty, what are we left with?"

I feel it best to keep silent: it's a rhetorical question.

"Right now," she goes on, "you've done a pretty good job of keeping it quiet." I've pulled in some favors from the usual courthouse journalists in exchange for special treatment once it all comes out. If it does. In particular, I have preyed upon the sensibilities of Eleanor Torjan, crime reporter for the *Los Angeles Times,* with whom I have struck up some sort of symbiotic relationship over the years. I know this one will cost me dearly, because she put up much more of a struggle than usual.

"But if there's a trial," Diane is saying, "journalistic courtesy is out the window, and we're left with a lifetime of men looking at us cross-eyed, wondering, believing there must be at least some truth to what Rosamund says in court, on the public record." She wraps both hands around her drink, seems to get some solid point of reference from the stinging cold. "We're damaged goods, don't you see? Even if he's convicted, people will wonder—" She is crying now, looking past the local issue of convicting Vincent Rosamund and considering the rest of her life. But I cannot give up, even though I'm having difficulty forming a counterargument.

"I'm not sure that's all true, Diane." It sounds lame even as I mouth the words.

"Doesn't matter," she says. "Of course we're going to testify." She leans forward, reading the look of surprise I cannot hide. "I just wanted to make absolutely sure you know what's involved. What it means for us."

"But I was the one who started to tell you how—"

"You started to make a speech," she says without rancor. "It's the standard speech to get victims to testify, with the standard disclaimer about how difficult it will be. I didn't need to hear it, but you needed to hear me. Now you've heard it." She takes her hands off the glass and folds them on the table. "We'll testify."

I lay the cigar down in the ashtray. Hitting it only every minute or so will keep it from getting harsh. "Even if what you say is true?"

"Yes." She lifts her chin ever so slightly, a defiant gesture more to reassure herself than me. "Is there going to be a trial?"

"I don't know. Depends on how much pressure we can put on Rosamund and his attorney to plea bargain, but I gotta tell you: we're going to want a hell of a lot more than they're probably willing to give." I believe we have a solid case against Rosamund, and while we might be able to offer some small concession to avoid the cost and bother of a trial, as well as the exposure for Diane and Lisa, it will not be much. We have a strong case, so how would we justify a compromise?

"You're about to tell me Lisa and I have some say in that, aren't you." It's a statement, not a question.

I nod. "What you're telling me, you two could do without a full-bore trial and the publicity." I know there won't be any feminist rebuttal from Diane following her speech to me. What she says is true: even though the voices of enlightenment decry any attachment of shame or guilt to the injured parties in a rape, on the individual level things are a good deal tougher and more difficult to sort out. People are the way they are, not the way we want them to be. Diane, being a criminal defense attorney, knows this better than I. For my part, I am terrified of the confusing change in the direction of my feelings toward Diane, a direction to which I, with my enlightened social sensibility, always felt immune. I feel a burning need to sort them out, but I have to save it for later: there's work to be done here.

"On the other hand," I force myself to continue, "you have the right to some righteous retribution."

Diane looks past me to the Santa Monica Mountains rising from the shore at Malibu, their peaks burning in the last orange touches of the sun that is already well below the horizon. "What are we looking at? There's a problem, right?"

I shrug. "Maybe. I don't know." I take a deep drag on the cigar and let the smoke out slowly, then set it down and look at her. "Dr. Eberfield found no evidence of violence or forcible sex on you or Lisa. Rosamund wore a condom, you told us. Both of you were seen drinking in a bar earlier in the evening, a known high-class pickup joint." I wait for her to protest and am impressed when she does not. She understands perfectly: while it doesn't look good on paper, she knows that I know it is misleading and irrelevant. I'm just playing devil's advocate by making the defense's case as they are likely to do later. "Both of you were seen to smile at Rosamund following a sexually suggestive but not necessarily obscene gesture by him, a gesture that could be termed an advance."

I may be doing this too well. "You know we were teasing him," she tests me, just to make sure. "His 'gesture,' as you put it, was lewd and we were paying him back."

"I know that. I was there, and so was Marty McConagle, who effectively threw him out, perhaps before you and Lisa could follow through and get something going with Rosamund. Maybe you had to wait until later because of that."

She nods and gives this some thought, perhaps to demonstrate to me that she is being cool and rational under fire, perhaps because she really is. Maybe the two are not distinguishable. "Legally, it doesn't make a bit of difference even if I held up a sign asking him to expose himself."

She is quite correct. "But it could play on the sympathies of the jury," I tell her.

She shakes her head hard. "According to the law—"

"According to the law, Peter Friehling should be in jail, too, but he isn't, is he?" I say this with force, to drive home the point that judges and juries are unpredictable even where the law is clear, but she misinterprets this as a low blow, as though I am still seething over her victory in Judge Arigga's courtroom.

"Oh, so you're going to bring *that* up again, are you?" she says lightly.

"You know what I'm trying to say."

Her shoulders slump. "Net result is that it all hinges on our testimony, and you want to know if we can take it."

"That's it."

Diane leans forward to make her point. "What happened to us is the worst thing, by far, that's ever happened to either of us. Our lives will never be the same; you understand that?"

I do not want to believe in the inevitability of this. "I don't know. With time . . ."

"Sal, tell me something." Her eyes bore into my own. "Why did you ask me to that barbecue?"

"That was just business!" I blurt out.

"Since when is a law school reunion business?" She puts her hand on my wrist, preventing me from picking up the comforting cigar. "You were attracted to me, weren't you? Before, I mean, at least just a little. I know I was to you."

I have been hitting her over the head with the hard realities of the situation, asking her to face them squarely. Oughtn't I to do the same? "I'd be lying if I said otherwise. What's not to like?" I raise an eyebrow in comic suggestiveness.

She ignores my weak attempt to hide my discomfort and doesn't take her eyes off me. "How do you feel now?"

This catches me off guard, and the immediacy of it makes me hesitate. "So much for *that* budding romance," she says, and takes her hand off my arm. The cessation of that tenuous connection makes me feel suddenly isolated. "And thus endeth the lesson," she adds, unnecessarily, sitting back on her chair and looking once more out to sea.

"That's not fair. You ask a question like that, you gotta give a guy a second or two."

She studies my face for a second. "You're telling me it makes no difference?"

I sense that, somehow, with that exquisite sensitivity

available only to the deeply suffering, Diane is reading my very soul. To be dishonest now would not only be transparent but destructive of the confidence I need to build with her. "I don't know."

It's the right answer. I can see it on her face. It is also a lie. "No. I do know. It doesn't make any difference."

It is the first time in this conversation she appears to lose her composure, but I am afraid the sweetness of the moment is about to be lost, stolen by the man with a scowl on his face who is heading in my direction, eyeing the cigar burning in the ashtray. I don't need this right now.

"Excuse me," he says with unexpected deference, pointing to the stogie. "What's that you're smoking there?"

"Upmann?" I say warily.

"Ahh." He reaches into his pocket and withdraws his own cigar, a large double corona. "Prefer Punch, m'self."

Diane giggles, pushes back and stands up, sniffling. "Be right back. You two studs go ahead and bond."

The stranger has saved me from an awkward situation, and we debate the relative merits of Honduran versus Nicaraguan wrappers until Diane returns and he retreats to his own table, wishing us well. By silent assent, Diane and I agree to drop the matter, as nothing could be more destructive at this point. I cannot believe the lightness in my heart, and it's hard to get back on track.

I tell her that Rosamund is being represented by Gustave Terhovian, and any lingering tenderness evaporates instantly.

"Terhovian?" she repeats, blanching at this casually dropped bombshell. Terhovian is one of the heaviest-hitting defense lawyers in the county.

"Uh-huh."

"But he's been out of action for months!"

"What can I tell you?"

Diane knits her brows, trying to remember something. "I heard his kid was into drugs, was in one of those counseling deals where the whole family has to get involved. That's what people've been saying, anyway. All he's done the last couple months are little things, some plead-ings, parole hearings, like that."

Terhovian has a reputation for taking on cases only if he believes the defendant is truly innocent, a career-long strategy that plays heavily in his favor for those occasions in which he knows the defendant is really guilty. This ongoing scheme is well-known to prosecutors throughout the county but the general public sees it otherwise, according to the image Terhovian has carefully and patiently cultivated over the years.

"So who the hell is Vincent Rosamund to rate a lawyer like that?" Diane is saying.

"Not sure, but Marty tells me he thinks he might be some kind of player in the drug business. He's going to check it out." Marty also thinks Rosamund was at The Alley trying to sell cocaine he trimmed from some large buys, a street-level, punk move that would not seem to square well with any kind of status in an organization but that Rosamund maybe felt would buy him entrance into social circles that would normally reject him. And in the case of his addicted customers, that turns out to be true.

As to why Terhovian would take the case, I have no idea. The publicity would certainly not be favorable—quite the opposite, in fact. It is possible that, if Rosamund is really in drugs, his people are offering an irresistible amount of money, but I doubt that would sway Terhovian either. I have never had cause to doubt his basic integrity, even if some of his methods are questionable.

"What's possible," I tell Diane, "is that Terhovian feels the odds are stacked so high against Rosamund that he deserves a fair shake."

"That might fit. Gus probably figures he's the only one good enough to see that he gets one." She looks at me lev-elly. "Are the odds stacked against him?"

I can say with confidence they are, and give Diane some of the comfort she has been seeking from me. "There's nothing in your backgrounds to suggest that either of you would engage in the kind of casual, consen-sual sex that he might wind up alleging." I look into her eyes—apprehensively, I should add—for any kind of sign that this might be an overstatement, but all I get back is calm assent. "A tidal wave of witnesses will attest to that.

There are witnesses to Rosamund's obscene gesture, including McConagle."

"And you."

"Forget me. You want me on the stand under Terhovian's cross-examination?"

She waves it away. "Stupid. Sorry." My voluntary testimony might constitute an automatic waiver of the right to keep my private conversations with the Piermans to myself and open the door for defense counsel to ask me anything he wanted.

"There is the fact of the two slashed tires on Lisa's car," I continue, "your disheveled condition on being picked up by Officer Salerno, and your agitated state of mind in front of several professional witnesses."

"You can forget the therapists."

"Why?"

"Not credible. They make great expert witnesses on general matters, but in an individual case, they're biased toward the woman's side and jurors won't believe they're objective."

It is a good point.

"The doctor's good," she observes. "But the absence of physical evidence is going to hurt." She is thinking like a lawyer again. A faraway look comes into her eyes. "You gotta ask yourself, why was he that careful?" She snaps back into focus. "You suppose he's done it before? Been in trouble for it?"

That thought, an obvious one now, never occurred to me. "You mean, like he's a practiced rapist?"

Diane spreads her hands apart. "Might explain a couple of things. Can't McConagle check?"

"Maybe, when we're sure we have a proper ID." We cannot yet assume that Vincent Rosamund is his real name. It might even have been somebody else's at one time. It's not too hard to check, but it takes some digging. "He can also argue that you staged your acute agitation in the aftermath of an experience you regretted only in retrospect, although that's where the therapists and Eberfield might come in handy." Eberfield's little lecture on examining room protocol comes back to me and I suppress a shudder. "You should also know that no weapon was found on him, and he doesn't appear to have a permit for carrying one, at least not in any California county."

"If that's his name," Diane reminds me.

"True."

"And he's a scumbag. Not clear that applying for permits is one of the things people like that worry about on a daily basis."

"Au contraire." I have to disagree on that one. "They worry a lot. No sense getting pinched on some minor piece of avoidable bullshit. Remember, Capone was busted only for tax evasion."

Diane nods her head, leaves it hanging slightly. The strain of trying to maintain an outward posture of dispassionate legal objectivity is beginning to take its toll. I don't really need her ideas on how to pursue the case, but I felt that involving her, treating her like a colleague, might help restore some of her crumbling self-respect and resolve one or two lingering doubts about resuming her career. But it is enough now. She's tired and losing her concentration, stirring her drink with the tip of her forefinger without being conscious of what she is doing.

"Tell me about Lisa," I say, sitting back and tapping ash from the end of the cigar.

She lifts her head and looks out the window. The deep orange glow cast by the dying sun on low, distant clouds suffuses her face with a soft radiance. Gazing disconsolately toward the horizon, she looks frail and vulnerable, and it seems to me as though this is not a condition imposed upon her by outside circumstance but rather something that came up from within, that had been lurking there all the time, kept effectively hidden until the torment of recent events won out over her resistance and it finally just bobbed up. My guess is that the effects of her trauma go beyond the obvious feelings of outrage and desecration, that what is troubling her most is the shock of her until-now successfully repressed fears swirling upward and making themselves known to her consciousness. Like many high achievers—and I count myself among them—she has carefully constructed a persona of concrete walls, iron safes and secret compartments, all crafted to hide essential truths from herself, as though the garnering of accolades and professional successes were not only a denial of those truths but an actual eradication of them as well. It would be a shock to discover that they had really been right there all along.

"I think Lisa's going to be fine," she says after a very long time. I don't know if she is really referring to Lisa or herself as she speaks, but it occurs to me as I listen that it makes very little difference.

Diane turns back to me and notices her finger in her drink, smiles in mild embarrassment and licks it off. It might have been an erotic gesture under other circumstances, but not now. "We've talked about it for hours, endlessly, forcing ourselves to relive each minute over and over."

I nod in approval.

"We've gotten to some kind of perspective that makes it a little easier," she goes on. "If I pull myself back, explain it to myself intellectually, I can make myself grateful for some things: we're both alive, we weren't hurt physically, not any more than in a rough game of touch football"—she looks at me slyly and I wince: it's a backhanded reference to my tripping her during the annual district attorney/defense lawyers charity game— "we're not pregnant or infected with anything, and the sonofabitch is in custody."

I'm not buying it, although I don't say so. That might work for a few minutes at a time, on a sunny afternoon occupied with taking depositions or filing briefs or meeting with clients. But what about when she crawls into bed at night, when she is truly alone, just herself and the darkness and the demons? If I were with her, would I hold her comfortingly in my arms and rock her to sleep, or would my own demons intrude between us, insinuating rude images into my brain, of a car, a dark night, a gun, the woods . . . ? Phrases like *residual dilation* and *labial redness* keep flashing on my consciousness, and that strangely familiar confusion—*what's the right thing for me to be feeling right now?*—is clawing at me from somewhere deep inside.

I try to concentrate as Diane speaks. She is rambling, free-associating, saying whatever comes into her mind. It flatters me that she's comfortable enough in my presence to open herself up like that, and I listen, supplying only the occasional grunt or encouraging facial expression to keep her going. As she continues, I try to find a pattern in her words, to understand what is lurking beneath them. It isn't difficult.

"What I keep coming back to," she says, "what I can't get out of my mind's eye, is that prick's face, that smug, shit-eating grin and those eyes with no conscience." The venom in her voice is startling, especially when contrasted with her relative equanimity the rest of the evening. "He doesn't even realize, he has no goddamned idea"—there are tears in her eyes again, tears of frustration and raw anger, not of self-pity—"not the slightest notion of what he did to us, what it means!"

Her hands are balled up tightly as they rest on the table. I have no doubt that if she could put one of them through Vincent Rosamund's face and out the back of his head, she wouldn't hesitate to do so. But strong as her words are, I can see that they are failing to express the full extent of her fury, and she is not up to the effort of trying. She looks out at the ocean again and her voice becomes quiet, more reflective.

"For me, I seem to dwell less on the actual, you know, the sexual part, than on feeling so absolutely helpless at the hands of somebody so twisted they find joy in your suffering. I didn't know him, couldn't predict anything. I didn't know if he planned to kill us, or if he hadn't made up his mind, or what. So I felt myself trying to manipulate the outcome. But I didn't know him. It was like"—she waves one hand around, searching for the right metaphor—"like playing chess without knowing the rules. You make a move, see how the guy reacts, make another move. I'm pandering to every sick whim, hoping it will save our lives, not knowing if maybe I'm really killing us, and all the time I hate him more and more because he's forcing me to become someone else to satisfy him, and satisfying him became my whole universe, and who the hell was this bastard to come along and make things so the only point of my entire life was not to get him mad?"

She has banged a fist into the tabletop, turning a few heads in our vicinity, which we ignore. "You know that bumper sticker?" she asks me. " 'Guns don't kill people: people kill people'? It used to make some sort of sense, but . . ." She shakes her head, opens the fingers of one hand and looks at her palm. "He has this chunk of metal in his hand. One nervous twitch of his finger and one of us is dead, forever. Just"—she snaps her fingers—"like that. Without that gun, I could have rammed the police cruiser on the freeway. We might have run for it when we stopped the car or even overpowered him, kicked him in the groin, whatever. But not while he had the gun. Not while he could kill us, even at a distance, like remote control. That gun made the difference." She sits back and something seems to occur to her, and she taps the tips of two fingers on the table. "That gun made him God."

"Then again," I say, "if you'd had your hand wrapped around your own gun, none of this might have happened."

She doesn't miss a beat. "Or I might be dead instead of just . . ." A hand wave. ". . . whatever."

She goes on, and I keep listening, but I already got what I came for, assurances of their full cooperation in the prosecution. And the subterfuge in inviting Diane for a drink doesn't trouble me. As much as I want to put vicious and dangerous criminals away, I know that, as a rule, there is little recompense for the victim of a violent crime. If you are cheated at business or unfairly fired from your job or your roof caves in because the builder cut corners, you can seek financial redress in the civil court and have the wrongs righted. But if you are a victim of a violent crime, the visceral satisfaction of seeing the perpetrator go to prison is a fleeting and surprisingly ungratifying experience. What he took, you don't get back.

"I want you to know something," I tell her after a decent interval. My cigar has gone cold and I pause to relight it, cooking the tip again before drawing in air to get a good burn. Diane's eyes have cleared, and she is focused again as I continue.

"We're going to pursue this with everything we've got, no holds barred. The DA is backing us fully, not even making his usual budget noises."

"That's gotta be a first," she says, smiling.

"It is." It isn't. There is always plenty of money for the

big, visible cases, the career makers. Or for certain less publicized cases when a certain head deputy threatens to quit on the spot if there is even a hint of interference or fiscally motivated constraint.

"I thought that would make you happy," I say to Diane, who again looks distant and distracted.

"Oh, it does," she hurries to assure me. "I was just thinking . . ." She shrugs a shoulder and leans forward again. "What about a fast-food waitress, or a welfare mother in a similar situation, without the kind of resources I'm getting? What happens to women like that? What do they get?"

"Justice is blind," I say mindlessly.

"If you believe that, then *you're* blind. I'll tell you what they get: they get long lectures about the risks, not to mention the expense, of going to trial, the public exposure they'll suffer, and the likelihood they're gonna lose anyway after they've spilled their guts all over the courtroom and the newspapers."

"I'm taking it on myself because of you. Because we're friends." Maybe we could be more. Maybe we will be more; I don't know.

Her features soften and she reaches for my hand, taking it in both her own. "Don't misunderstand. I love it that you're doing this. It's one of the things that keeps me going, and Lisa, too. I wouldn't change it for the world."

I nod, slightly ill at ease. I don't know what to do with my hand. Squeeze a little, put my other hand over hers, pull back? I let it lie there, a dead fish.

"I just don't want to forget that I'm privileged, that I have it better than others might. You understand, don't you?"

I nod again. She is aware now of my discomfort, doesn't know what to make of it. It occurs to me that she may be thinking again that she is soiled goods, that this is the source of my uneasiness, and I want to disabuse her of that notion definitively. But with studied grace she takes the initiative and relieves me of that burden.

"Hey, counselor," she says lightly, uncurling her fingers from around my hand and patting my wrist. "Wouldn't do to let the citizenry see us holding hands in public, would it?"

I smile at her. "What the hell, we're on the same side."

"Sure. Now. But what about when I'm defending some low-rent creep against one of your storm-trooper deputies, huh? What then?"

So she plans to resume her career once this is all over. The thought gladdens me.

She laughs, for the first time since all of this started. Then she looks at me slyly. "Mind if I ask you a personal question?"

"I wish you would. Been a little one-sided so far."

"Not that personal. You really going to run for DA?"

I've been sloughing off that question with wisecracks for weeks now, maybe because I don't have a clear answer myself. The first time one of the politicos I play golf with said I ought to consider it, a small thrill ran through my spine. It is, of course, a career pinnacle for a prosecutor, short of anything on the federal level. And I have little doubt that I could do the job a damned sight better than one Gerard Beckman. But the thought of waging a campaign, running around telling everybody how great I am, fighting my own boss while still working for him, promising political favors . . . ? Then there is the question of possibly losing the election and where that might leave me.

"I'm thinking about it."

"Seriously?"

"You don't think about something like that any way but seriously."

"I think you'd make a terrific DA."

"Why?"

"You're a great lawyer, you're good at supervising people, even defense attorneys respect you—"

I shoot her a skeptical look.

"It's true. Believe me. And Beckman's a hack, so wrapped up in politics and glad-handing he's not really doing his job."

"I'm not sure I have the connections."

"So you don't owe favors either, right?"

I've already thought of all those things. I also know that Beckman is despised by most of the deputy DAs in the system. The question is, would they side with me openly in a campaign against their well-connected boss or lie back and play it safe? That's the thing about being a deputy DA: in any county there's only one place to get a job if you want to be a felony-level prosecutor without working for the federal government. Blow it and you either go into defense work or move.

"The thing is," I tell Diane, "all of those things are good but they're a weak basis for a campaign. You need something, I don't know, something *big* on your ticket, something to get you on the map. Otherwise you're just another good lawyer."

"Like Beckman had Stilwell." That would be Keith Stilwell, a rock megastar from Manchester whose albums went to number one before they were even in the stores a day. He had a little side business of bringing in kilo bricks of pure heroin hidden in his equipment boxes whenever he came to the States on tour. Beckman prosecuted the case brilliantly. I know it was brilliant because I knew the three deputies who worked on it eighteen hours a day for three months only to watch him take all the credit.

"Yeah. Like that. I don't have anything like that."

"Well," Diane says enthusiastically, "maybe the Rosamund case'll put you on the map." She smiles again. "Then maybe I won't feel so bad about all that exposure if it gets you the job."

I smile back. It's a wonderful sentiment. "I don't think so, but thanks for the thought. This one's too easy, too straightforward. Hardly the stuff elections are won on."

"Ah." She grows thoughtful. "Still: I bet something'll come along. You should do it, Sal."

I'm getting uncomfortable with this. It's no secret that most professionals are ambitious and desirous of advancement, but this usually occurs without any outward displays of covetousness, hidden beneath a standard set of appropriately modest behaviors. You do your job and the right things generally happen, albeit slowly. But when you run for election, it's all spilled out on the table, and your heretofore discreet mannerisms are transformed into outlandish and shameful self-aggrandizement. I want the job but I'm not sure I have that in me. I've always hated it in others, like Beckman. It occurs to me: if I run against him, and have to become like him to win, what's the point in the first place?

* * *

I shake my head, attempting to clear it. One last procedural question for Diane and the business of the evening is concluded. "Listen, would you be more comfortable going through the detailed testimony prep with someone else on my staff?"

She knows I'm dropping the other subject and lets it go. "Like who?"

"Like Marsha Jones. I want her to assist me in trial." And she is a female.

"That'd be great. I appreciate it." Any transitory mirth that might have lingered leaves her features. "Not exactly the sort of thing I feel like discussing with the likes of you."

"Understood. But it will come out in court."

"I know that. I'll be okay, especially if we rehearse it until I'm numb. What's the schedule?"

I signal for the check. Diane protests, insists on paying, but this is an official witness meeting, I tell her: the county will pick it up. They won't really. "We're going to arraign him tomorrow afternoon, and I have a case meeting scheduled with Marsha and Marty midmorning. So if you could meet with her crack of dawn-ish, it would be helpful."

"That's fine. Not exactly getting great sleep these days anyway." She asks me if she and Lisa can be kept out of the prelim and out of the pretrial hearings when the case gets to superior court. I tell her I think that may be possible.

The waiter arrives. I wave off looking at the check and hand him my credit card. Diane picks up her purse from the floor near her feet and slumps back on her seat. "So what do you think, Sal? Is it going to be okay?"

I have no idea on what level she is asking the question. Does she mean the case, her testimony, her life? Then I realize it doesn't matter what she meant.

"It's going to be okay," I tell her with all the confidence and assurance I can force into my voice. "Trust me."

4

One of the hard facts about the law is that it is not enough to have the staff of righteousness with you, to be on the side of truth and justice, to be passionate and eloquent about a cause you know with certainty is right. No matter how airtight your case, the legal system is rife with peril when it comes to achieving your goal, be it an acquittal or a conviction. It has always seemed to me that the system is a fraternity hell-night gauntlet of statute, procedure and intricacy, a single-elimination contest in which one wrong move on any step of the way knocks you out of the tournament. Winning is not so much about being right as it is about surviving the obstacle course, prevailing over the endless pitfalls.

The trick is to convince yourself early on that your cause is just and then forget about it, put all the indignation aside and get down to the hard work of winning. Stay as detached as possible, favoring the methodical and painstaking over the fervently righteous. You will resurrect the passion at trial, letting it build during cross-examinations and come to a furious head in your closing argument, but the case is often won before trial, in the preparation.

Marty McConagle, Marsha Jones and I are meeting late morning of the day we are going to arraign Vincent Rosamund. We have been here before, the three of us, many times. I consider myself an enlightened manager, and I make it a point to spread the work around, give everybody a chance to round out their experience and earn their wings in trials by fire. But when it is really important, when something special is at stake, either because I ardently believe in it or my boss, Gerard Beckman, tells me in no uncertain terms to do a good job ("Don't let anybody else fuck this up, Sal," is how he typically tries to motivate me regarding the importance of a particular case), it is Marty, Marsha and I.

Thankfully, neither of them asks me what makes this case so important. I'm not sure I could give an acceptable answer if they did, to them or to myself. It's just something we all sense, maybe just friends helping each other out. Is it so terrible to exploit one's position and abilities on behalf of friends, if it doesn't compromise anybody else along the way? This is what I decide, and let it go at that.

Diane and Lisa met with Marsha just before dawn; this time of year, early December, that's around six-thirty. It is now nearly four hours later and they have just finished. Marsha looks more subdued than usual. While there is no denying her dedication, Marsha is generally able to keep her emotions in check, a necessary talent for anyone who daily swims in the streams of human despair. The investigating prosecutor's job is not to provide a comforting shoulder; it is to preserve a legal case so the perpetrator who caused the trouble gets convicted and punished.

But now, in our case meeting, Marsha doesn't look cool and detached; she seems distracted and troubled. It's probably because in this case, quite possibly for the first time in her career, she personally knows the victims, knows they are friends of Marty's and mine. It may have made her mind race back to other victims, most of whom were just faces and stories and evidence, made her realize that they, too, were loved by others for whom the crime was not just another case but a profoundly wrenching nexus in their lives.

Marsha is tenacious and skilled and is still in the ranks of the "individual contributors," as we euphemistically refer to nonmanagers, because she reserves some of her zeal for fighting against supervisorial assignments, and I have learned to leave her as unencumbered by administrative details as I can. Her conviction rate is one of the highest in the office, despite routinely receiving the toughest cases, the dogs that others are afraid to take on because of the low probability of conviction. Her *winter* pleas are also some of the best around.

In our office, we unofficially rate plea bargains according to which side we think got the better deal, given the facts of the case and the likely outcome in court. If our case is shaky, the evidence tainted, the witnesses recalcitrant, and we settle for a lesser sentence when we know the suspect is guilty as hell, we say *we gave away the courthouse*. If we can get someone to cop to a heavy sentence with only some small concessions to avoid the risk and expense of a trial, we call it a "winter" plea. There are many creative and apocryphal explanations for this term, but its origin is quite prosaic: a reporter from the old *Herald Examiner* stood nearby as one of our deputies referred to a *winner* plea, and she misheard it as *winter*. She wrote it up this way in her article, convinced she was giving her readers an inside glimpse into the private lexicon of our little fraternity. When the laughter in the office died down, the term stuck, and even expanded: a moderately good plea became a "flurry," one close to what we could have achieved at trial is a "blizzard," and there are enough variations in between to challenge an Eskimo's much-vaunted thirty-six different words for snow.

Marsha never lets a suspect cop a plea below a Buffalo snowstorm unless her case is so bad it would probably get thrown out in pretrial. One of the reasons she gets away with it is the fear on the part of many defense attorneys of seeing her at work during trial. She is relentless and has an unparalleled work ethic, treating every case as if it were the Nuremberg trials. I know that in the present situation she's been getting some help from a friend of hers in the sex crimes unit in our downtown office owing to her own lack of experience in that field. Being black doesn't hurt her, either: not only does her color preclude charges of prosecutorial racism against minority defendants, it also makes some defense attorneys just a wee bit cautious about casting aspersions on her character or motivations in court for fear of being labeled racists themselves.

Vincent Rosamund has agreed to talk with us prior to

his arraignment, a remarkable occurrence given his experienced silence thus far. We have little time to get ready.

"It looks very tight, very clean," Marsha tells me, sitting on the chair opposite my desk, perched on the edge rather than in her more typical half slouch. Marty is in his usual spot by my west window, one buttock resting on the sill, one leg dangling and idly swinging back and forth. Marsha doesn't use words like *airtight* or *open and shut* or any of the other phrases of certitude so beloved by television lawyers and cinematic police captains. There is no such thing as an airtight case, no such thing as certainty of conviction, and to presume that there is invites carelessness and defeat.

Which is not to say that one cannot be confident. "I interviewed both of them this morning," Marsha goes on. "Separately. Their accounts of the incident match to the smallest detail." I decide to forgo sharing with her the part of my conversation with Diane in which she described how she and Lisa spent countless hours going over those same details, albeit for reasons other than those of case preparation.

"They been talking to each other," Marty offers. "Couple of weeks gone by, you gotta figure they're gonna get it straight."

"True," Marsha replies. "But what's important, everything they say now is consistent with the notes the therapists took in the hospital and what they told the doc."

Marty nods, satisfied. "Their heads screwed on okay?"

Marsha shrugs and looks down at her notepad, which is blank. "Depends what you mean. Case-wise, we're all right. They'll get up there and say their piece; they'll handle cross okay, especially Diane. She knows all the tricks."

"Whuddya expect?" says Marty, smiling. "Used 'em all herself, one time or another."

"Wonder what she's going to feel like on the other side of that fence," I muse out loud. There is surprisingly little rancor between prosecutors and defense attorneys. We all know the other guys are just doing their jobs as best they can, searching for technicalities, obscure precedents, flaws in the other side's case, anything that will allow them to fulfill their official mandate to put on the best case possible and their personal mandate to wallop the crap out of the other side and emerge victorious, toasted to and hailed at the same watering holes frequented by their opposite numbers, many of whom will probably be there to witness the celebration. My question is one of curiosity rather than ill will.

"I wouldn't worry about it," Marsha assures me. "I get the impression they'll put up with most anything to put this slimeball away. It's almost like . . ."

She trails off, hunting for the right phrase, and this gets Marty's attention. I already know what she is trying to say.

"Like what?" Marty asks.

"Like a mission," I answer for her.

"Yeah," she says. "A mission."

"How'd you know that?" Marty asks me, puzzled.

"Had a long talk with Diane," I answer. "Last night. I wanted to make sure she and Lisa were ready to take this on. Without them, there's no case."

"And?" Marsha prompts me.

"It's become a holy crusade. Like nothing else in the world matters until it's over."

"Yeah," she says, nodding. "That's what I got from them, too. Only not in so many words."

It's not really a new story. One of the single biggest obstacles impeding the victim of a violent crime from putting his or her life back together is the uncertainty of how and when the criminal case against the perpetrator will be resolved. What we are talking about in this meeting is only a slight variation on what Priscilla Fields told me in the hospital: get Vincent Rosamund behind bars as quickly as possible without getting too hung up on maximizing the duration of the sentence. If we could get fifteen years and do it quickly and avoid a trial, don't push for twenty and prolong the agony for Diane and Lisa.

We stay silent for a second or two, until Marty slaps his thighs and says, "So let's get to work, unless you think we should talk more about how winning is better than losing."

I hold up my coffee cup and shake it at Marty, who picks the pot up off the burner near the window, reaches over and pours me some. "We're weak on physical evidence," I say, mopping some drops off the side of the cup with my finger.

"Worse than that," Marty says, pouring some coffee into his half-empty cup. "Bugger was downright gentle, you look at it closely."

"Best I can figure," Marsha replies, "he wasn't trying to be Don Juan; he was covering his tracks."

"He did it damned well, too," Marty observes. "Not like a rapist to leave nothin' behind."

"Hang on a second," I caution. "He was still rough before the penetration."

Marsha shakes her head. "Not so's you can prove. He pressed the gun into Lisa in several places, and there are some slight bruises, but nothing that would stand up as battery, not direct evidence, anyway."

"Just so we understand, among us," I begin, making sure the two of them are paying attention before I continue. "We don't have any doubts about the twins' stories, do we?"

Both are emphatic in their assertions of the sisters' credibility. "But it's going to make our case a whole lot more difficult," Marsha adds, not intending it to impeach their story but as a matter of case-planning strategy.

"What I'm thinking—" I begin, but Marty cuts me off.

"—the bugger's done it before, eh? Like he's had practice or somethin'."

Just what Diane thought. "Maybe. You have any luck on his background?"

"Some." He reaches into his back pocket and pulls out the standard police notepad, not much bigger than a deck of cards, flipping over the cover and thumbing through his notes. "Bakersfield seems to be home territory." He stops on a page and folds the rest of the pad behind it. "Remember I was bettin' he was dealin' snow in the restaurant?" He purses his lips and nods his head without waiting for us to answer. "Sure'n he's into the big boys somehow, organization in Kern County." That's north of Los Angeles County; Bakersfield is the seat.

"How high up is he?" Marsha asks.

"That's the strange part," Marty answers. "Not very, but he's hobnobbin' with the mucky-mucks. I called some old friends up there, DEA types, so this is all on the QT, right?" He looks from me to Marsha meaningfully.

"Doesn't do us much good if we can't use it," I protest.

He waves it away. "You couldn't use this anyway. Not relevant. Only interestin'. Seems our lad is a hot-tempered young buck, shoulda risen much higher, takin' into account all the time he's got in the ranks." Marty enjoys lapsing into his feeble rendition of Irish brogue whenever he has the floor or a good idea or is telling us how he cleverly saw what others missed.

He goes on to explain that Vincent Rosamund is one of those scary freaks so prized by crime syndicates. He is ambitious and willing to undertake any assignment, no matter the risk. This makes him a valuable commodity in the kinds of daring excursions these people frequently undertake to expand their power base, an eager front man anxious to prove his manhood and his value.

At the same time, their quick tempers and uncontrolled egos make them unpredictable and unreliable. As a rule, these types are short-timers, either because they die young or burn out. Often, when their usefulness is eclipsed by their danger to their superiors, they are given a series of assignments of rapidly escalating risk until their demise is no longer a matter of *if* but of *when*. Other times, when they begin to catch on to the fact that there is no hope of advancement, that they have been played for suckers by the very people whose good graces they covet, their only reward is quiet elimination, usually at the hands of the next generation of up-and-comers who have not yet realized that their ultimate fate will be the same.

Marty believes that Rosamund has survived this long because the organization wants him alive as long as possible. He is also a more visible player than most, and his early retirement would not send the right message to the troops. As Marty speaks, I also realize that Rosamund is a sociopath, and there is no creature on earth, of any species, that frightens me more than a human being without a conscience.

"And here's somethin' you're not going to like, me boy-o," he says to me.

"What's that?"

He clears his throat. "Seems one of our lad's little

escapades a while back involved runnin' a boatload of recreational pharmaceuticals up the coast from Baja." He stops there.

"Yeah . . . ?" I ask him.

"Plastic bottles dropped from airplanes? Picked up and run to the Marina in fishin' boats . . . ?"

I let out my breath, loudly, without realizing it. "Friehling."

He holds up a hand. "Maybe. Maybe not."

"What do you mean, maybe? What the hell else?"

He shrugs. "Cheeky bastard, isn't he?"

That's one word for it. There are nine ways the runner on that job could have gotten caught or even killed. "Anything you can prove?" I ask as a formality.

"You kiddin'?"

"So he's a hothead and a punk," Marsha says. "We knew that already. What do we do with it?" She's thinking about the case: not justice, not revenge for my humiliation in Arigga's court in front of Diane, not nailing Rosamund for crimes other than the ones before us. Just the case.

"I don't know," I answer. "Maybe we can use it against him if we have to plea bargain."

"Now you mention it," Marty says, in that offhand, casual style that always presages something of significance, "I have a bit of an idea."

"I bet you do," Marsha says.

Marty dumps his coffee in the plastic-lined wastepaper basket—he does it to annoy my secretary, Marion—and picks up the pot, gesturing with it as he speaks. "The man's a visible player. Too visible to be disappeared"— he pours himself a fresh cup—"maybe too visible to be abandoned in his hour of need."

"You mean by his organization." Marsha has uncapped her pen and is tapping it on her notebook.

"Just so. I'm figurin', maybe his handlers can't let him down in public, on account of their reputations. It might compromise their ability to recruit fresh blood." The bosses' attractiveness to people wanting to get in on the life is largely a function of how well they treat their own, not just in terms of payment but in the degree to which they come to their defense if they get into trouble. I'm not endorsing this line of reasoning just yet, but it would explain why they got Gustave Terhovian as Rosamund's attorney, so I want to see where it's going.

"Let's say you're right. What then?"

"Ah." Marty resumes his perch on the windowsill, gesturing with his cup so that the coffee sloshes precariously toward the rim. "I know you're wantin' to get bail denied, but let's say you can't, on account of it isn't a capital crime and there bein' no great bodily harm and all. Still, let's say bail is high. And he posts it. Now what I'm figurin', he hasn't got that kind of scratch, so somebody else—"

I see now. According to California law, if a suspect posts bail, we have the right to inquire as to the source of the funds, to make sure it's not an illegal source. In this case, even if the money is not provably unlawful, we will know who put it up and therefore we will know something about Vincent Rosamund.

"What's that gonna tell us?" Marsha wants to know.

Marty turns up one palm. "That, I have no idea just yet. A fishing expedition, to be sure, but I'm bettin' we get something useful out of it."

I may not want to know what "useful" is. It might be something Marty can use to apply pressure on Rosamund but is not appropriate from a strictly legal perspective. Regardless, I doubt if it will work.

"We're talking rape here, Marty. It's not like he got popped doing a deal or making a run. Who're they going to show off to, protecting a rapist?"

He waggles an admonishing finger at me. "Makes no difference. It's them against the law, all the time. Their guys are always fuckin' up, even if it isn't business, and if they don't get protection, it makes everybody look bad. And lookit—" He stands and begins pacing. "It's only rape. Not like he did something against the organization. These guys don't get excited about hurting women; they don't give a shit." I glance at Marsha to see if she is taking offense, but she is nodding in agreement. "These bastards feed crack to nine-year-olds," Marty is saying. "One of their people rapes a couple'a civilian chicks, who cares? You think that's worth losing some gonzo wild-ass runner who nets 'em zillions every time he cokes up and goes on a job?"

It makes sense. "But why waste time on a head case who's only going to wind up in prison for the long haul one day anyway? What's the point?"

"The point, me boy-o, is that if they put up a wad of dough, spring him, and he never shows up back in court, he'd shoot the president if they asked him to."

"Nuh-uh." Marsha is shaking her head. "First of all, a guy on the run isn't worth much to them, especially if every uniform in the country's got his picture in his back pocket. And second of all, they wouldn't lose just the bond; they'd lose whatever they backed it with, like maybe somebody's house. Suppose we get bail set at a million? You figure he's worth that to them?"

Marty sees the point but doesn't give up. "Couple other things I found out. Like he's got a rap sheet up there with a handful of arrests but only minor convictions, like for possession without intent. Nobody ever made the big stuff stick, and the guy's never done time."

"Does sound like he's being protected," I venture.

"An understatement, laddie. Some of those arrests don't show charges."

Marsha and I both look up. "No charges?" she says first.

"*Nada.* Like somebody made them go away. Just the code 'CA' next to the entry."

"Mis-entries on ACD's?" Marsha guesses but I shake my head. An ACD—adjournment in contemplation of dismissal—is a temporary suspension of proceedings granted by the judge. If the defendant stays clean for some period of time, usually six months, all record of the arrest is deleted and he gets a clean slate with which to start his life over. A mis-entry in the computer system may happen occasionally, but not the same one to the same person more than once. The odds are too great, although the code 'CA' could be a two-character shorthand designation for ACD.

"I don't like that," I tell Marty. "You got any more sources?"

"All over Kern. I got phone calls in everywhere."

"You know," Marsha says, "what we've basically got is Diane and Lisa's personal reputations, their integrity and the credibility we hope they show on the stand. All of that's going to be crucial."

"So you're wondering," Marty says, picking up the thread, "is there a way we can get Rosamund's dope connections in, make him out for the sleazebag he is."

"Not going to be easy," I caution them. "Judge thinks we're trying to sneak in anything irrelevant or prejudicial, he's going to drop a house on our heads."

"Let's worry later about how we get it in, Sal. First let's find out if there is anything." She turns to Marty. "Can you check to see if he's got any official employment anywhere? Social security number, W-2s, that kind of thing?"

"Sure, that's easy. But we're probably gonna find out he's on the payroll of the Corleone Olive Oil Company or something."

Marsha laughs and leans back on her seat for the first time since we started the meeting. Then she says seriously, "I'm still not sure I understand how someone like that could be so valuable to the organization." She looks at me. "You said the feds were in on this Friehling business, right? So, they've gotta know more. They just never tell us anything."

Marty breathes deeply and exhales toward the ceiling. "You want me to talk to my friends in the Bureau?"

It's not a casual question. We know Marty can only go to that well so many times. Marsha looks to me for support, and I give it to her. "I think that'd be good, Marty."

He nods his agreement. "But here's what I don't get: the guy hasn't said a word since he asked for a lawyer. . . ." The smartest move Rosamund can make, and something hardly anybody in similar circumstances has the presence of mind to do, especially the truly guilty who should know better. "All of a sudden he agrees to this interview, couple hours before he gets arraigned. Now why is that?"

Marsha shrugs but I take a guess. "It can only be because his lawyer told him to."

"I hear that's Gus Terhovian," Marty says.

I nod in affirmation. "It is. Only thing it can be, Gus figures he can derail this whole thing prior to arraignment, but I find it hard to believe he really thinks that's a possibility."

"I'd love to be a fly on the wall for this one," Marsha says, almost wistfully.

Marty and I will be there, but Rosamund and Terhovian were specific: no women or the interview is off.

We talk some more but are basically finished. The three of us agree to reconvene in my office at the end of the day.

5

It would be hard to design a more nondescript entrance to the police station of a city as well-known as Santa Monica. It faces out onto a back parking lot, with squad cars parked just a few steps away. A protective wall shielding the glass doors contains bronze plaques memorializing five police officers slain in the line of duty. The last is from 1969.

The lobby is smaller than my living room. The first thing you see on the left is an automated teller machine placed there by the credit union. Two reception windows sit at the far end, with a corridor going off in either direction from there.

There is a man standing just past the chairs on the right with his hands in his pockets, briefcase on the floor between his feet, looking at a display case containing pictures of the city council, the chief of police and his top officers. He looks familiar but I can't place him right away. His face is gaunt, haggard, the ears sticking out unnaturally, and his eyes have the hooded look of the chronically anxious or paranoid, not normally the kind of personality with which I tend to associate. He is also much older than I. His posture is slightly stooped, and his clothes seem a bit too large for his frame. He has a prominent nose, high cheekbones and full lips, and there is already a bit of five o'clock shadow, albeit not as dark as it probably was in his younger days. It is a Slavic face, but less proud than it might once have been. I think that this is a man who has recently lost a good deal of weight, without his having needed to in the first place.

"Jesus," Marty says, nudging me in the ribs. "Is that Terhovian?"

It is, and the realization makes me falter in my walk toward the interior of the lobby. Marty slows down as well. "The hell's a matter with him?" he whispers.

"Can't imagine." My first thought is that he must have been ill, which would explain his absence from the court scene these past few months. That no one I know seemed to be aware of this or of what the nature of the illness might be, tells me it's not something as simple as pneumonia but may be more along the lines of a heart problem or prostate trouble, not uncommon among men of Terhovian's age, which I would guess to be well over sixty. Whatever it was, it has taken its toll: he does not look like the vital and robust courtroom fighter with whom I have done lusty battle on a number of occasions.

By the time we get to him I have recovered enough to be genial. "Gus—" His head jerks around at the sound of my voice, eyes searching out the source of the disturbance, a surprised and strangely apprehensive look considering his easy familiarity with this venue and the high likelihood of his being recognized and hailed here. "How the hell are you?"

He takes his hands out of his pockets as I step forward, a smile beginning on his lips but not his eyes as he realizes it's me. I offer my hand and he takes it, his own hand bony and thin but still capable of a strong grip. I have noticed that older men on the fade always give a hard, firm shake, as if they were trying to funnel their waning vitality down their arms and demonstrate that they still have the old stuff.

"Still kicking, Milano. You?"

"The same. You remember—"

"Sure. McConagle, right?"

"Nice to see you again," Marty says, offering his own hand. "Haven't seen much of you lately."

"Yeah, well . . ." Terhovian takes his hand back, makes a small flipping gesture with it, as though shaking off an errant speck of dirt. "Can't hang around these depressing places your whole life, can you?"

Marty looks around the lobby. "I hope not."

"So, Gus," I start right in. We don't have that much time prior to the scheduled arraignment, and much as I would like to chat with him and find out what's been going on, I want to maximize the available time with Rosamund. "What say we go visit with this poor, wayward youth you're representing."

A cloud seems to pass momentarily behind his eyes, and he hesitates, almost like he was going to say something and then thought better of it. I'm not sure what the big deal is: prosecutors and defense attorneys are always ribbing each other about their respective chosen sides of the bar. Most realize that the majority of attorneys practicing criminal law didn't pick their philosophy and then build a career out of it but chose a course of action opportunistically, based largely on happenstance, and then tailored their rationalizing social orientations to fit. Thus, many of my old deputies, who ranted on about the burning need to enforce the law and punish evildoers, now fill the ranks of high-paying criminal defense firms where they rant with equal vigor about the cultural injustices that turned their criminal clients, through no fault of their own, into the real victims.

"Certainly," Terhovian says calmly. One-on-one, he is always friendly and quite civil, saving his oratorical pyrotechnics for where they count, in front of the judge or the jury. He has never felt the need to score ego points, never bothers with the petty one-upmanship in off-the-record or trivial conversations, but saves his shots for where they will have an impact on his case. Terhovian evaluates his effectiveness in the system the same way a professional sports coach looks at his season, not at the box scores but the final result: it doesn't matter if it is pretty or clever or groundbreaking, all anybody ever really remembers later on was whether you won or lost, what your winning percentage was. Terhovian worried his opposition because he truly didn't seem to care if, during the various procedures attendant to his defense of a client, he looked weak or ineffectual or sloppy or distracted or displayed any of the thousand other potential image flaws that so seem to concern everybody else, just so long as he won. You could insult him or cast aspersions on his competence or do damned near anything else that would infuriate less-experienced lawyers and cause them to lose concentration, but none of those things ever worked on Terhovian, and you quickly learned that the only deleterious effects of these sophomoric jabs and barbs were on yourself. And when you got back to the office, nobody asked if you bettered defense counsel in the trading of insults; they only asked if you won.

We make our way down the corridor to the right of the reception windows, a short left and a right placing us in front of the heavy steel door with a red sign reading NO GUNS PAST THIS POINT. No weapons are ever carried into any facility where multiple prisoners are kept. Just outside the door are a dozen small lockers, each no larger than a half-gallon milk container, with keys on straps sticking out of the locks on those that are open. Marty removes his service pistol and puts it in one of the empty lockers, closes the door and removes the key.

A window cut into the door opens, steel wire mesh protecting the opening. A solidly built black woman of about forty-five peers out at us. Doreen Sumara has been with the city for twenty-two years, the last seventeen as manager of the jail. Her eyes are knowing and cautious, but there is humor there as well.

"McConagle, you packin' heat under that jacket?"

"No way."

"I'll pat your ass down, you sneak somethin' in here."

"Lookin' forward to it, Doreen."

The heavy door swings open and the three of us enter. McConagle tries to kiss Sumara but she squirms away and makes a sound of disgust.

The jail was built in 1933 as part of the WPA program and, like other projects of that era, is substantially overengineered. It is all concrete blocks and steel, structurally impregnable but also ponderous and imposing. The multiple layers of paint on every metal surface give the place the feel of the interior of a naval vessel, and even though we are on street level, the sensation of having descended to get here is overpowering. The jail can hold eighty-eight prisoners on its three levels and on hot summer days routinely fills to overflowing.

Ten thousand suspects are processed through each year, and rules of conduct to govern their behavior are posted everywhere on ancient pieces of oak tag with faded lettering made by the kind of cut-out stencil kits I used in grade school a lifetime ago. The basics have not changed much: you are allowed two visits a day by two people, not including children, unlimited visits by your attorney, three phone calls, including to a bail bondsman, and a call to the bail commissioner who can change the standard bail if you give him a good story. Every prisoner booked into the jail has bail immediately and automatically set according to a printed schedule. It is called presumptive bail, and it is a gruesome formula. Rape? $50,000. But of a spouse, only $40,000. Lynching? $25,000. Train-wrecking? $200,000. Add $10,000 if you used a gun, $15,000 if you have a prior felony on your record, and so forth. As soon as my office got wind of Rosamund's arrest, we had a bail deviation form on file with the commissioner that ensured this suspect was not going anywhere prior to arraignment.

Detective Dan Pappas meets us at the booking window just inside the door. He has arranged for Rosamund to be held in this jail as a favor to Marty, since the DA's office doesn't have a holding tank of its own. It's only for a short while: if we don't arraign him within forty-eight hours, we have to let him go. Normally, Rosamund would have come under the sheriff's jurisdiction, since the sheriff has custody of all prisoners in the county. He would have been taken to the inmate reception center downtown and transported by bus to all his required court appearances, a tedious process prone to screwups and requiring a good deal of advanced planning. But Marty has a good relationship with the Santa Monica PD—not all of my investigators do—and they have agreed to hold Rosamund for us, the pretext being that at least part of the alleged crime was committed in Santa Monica and the victims did call the SMPD for help, even if it was from a different city. From here, it's less than a two-minute walk through the parking lot to the courthouse.

Pappas grudgingly concedes a perfunctory handshake with Terhovian, and it's clear there is enmity between the two. I have no doubt that the canny attorney has gotten many of Dan's collars back on the street in record time, and I am equally sure that Dan has come down hard on many of Terhovian's clients and gone out of his way to press the cases to conviction, even where a plea bargain might have made some sense.

"We got him alone," Sumara tells us, pointing to a door just a few feet away. "He's in a holding cell just over there."

She makes a hand motion and a jailer brings Rosamund out. He's still wearing the street clothes he was arrested in, although his belt, shoelaces, tie, watch, wallet and all of his jewelry have been taken, inventoried and placed in an envelope that is kept in a locker behind the booking window. He is left without anything to either barter or kill himself with.

It's not easy to maintain your dignity in this environment, especially when your wrists are cuffed, but Rosamund does manage to retain some of the arrogance and swagger I remember from The Alley. He notices me first and gives me that crooked wiseguy smile, then he looks to Marty and back to me, and the smile widens. I know what he's thinking, that without this burly investigator to protect me he could have taken me out at the bar without half trying, that the only reason I'm in control of this situation now is that I'm protected, that I am a coward at heart. He tries to bore into my eyes with his own and I let him for a second, so that he thinks his Manson-like glare will disturb my equilibrium.

"He looks a little smaller without the sharkskin suit," I say to Marty when I've let it go on long enough.

"Nah. Was the elevator shoes did it."

The smile drops a bit at the corners of Rosamund's mouth. Terhovian sets down his briefcase and holds up both hands. "Let's forget the clever byplay, shall we? There is serious business to transact here."

"I got us a room in the detective bureau," Pappas says, motioning to the jailer to escort Rosamund up to the second floor. As they move off, Terhovian close behind, Sumara holds me back.

"We got him K-ten," she says. "You want it that way?" While integration has been a watchword of the civil rights movement for many decades, in custody the entire housing philosophy is based on strict rules of segregation. Each prisoner is asked to voluntarily fill out a questionnaire on arrival and it is bluntly probing: What is your sexual preference? Have you ever been a police informant? Have you ever belonged to a street gang? A prison gang? Ever been charged with a sex crime, an assault, have you ever escaped from custody, do you have enemies in jail . . . ? It contains virtually all of the questions any one of which would make you the target of a civil suit if you tried to ask it during a job interview. Here, they are used to assign various keep-away categories. Standard procedure in a high-profile case is to designate the suspect K-10: no mixing with any other prisoners.

"Hell no," Marty answers for me, looking back to where I'm standing with Sumara. "Let him mix it up with the people, see how he likes it."

"You tellin' me this guy's never been in before?" Sumara asks him.

"Got a feeling he's had favors."

This doesn't sit well with Sumara, as Marty knew it wouldn't. Somehow, and I have never been able to figure this out, she harbors no ill will toward anyone in her custody, never seems to display the slightest contempt, not even for the repeat offenders. This jail being a Type I facility, virtually all of the people in her care are pre-arraignment, which means they have not yet been formally charged with anything, and while she knows with a certainty that nearly all of them are guilty, she treats them as the law prescribes, innocent until proven otherwise. Which is not to say she is careless or unmindful, just fair and humane, but she doesn't hold with special treatment for anybody.

She looks to me for confirmation of Marty's instructions to mainline Rosamund when we return him, and I nod.

The interrogation rooms in the detective bureau are too small to hold us all, so Pappas has arranged for an administrative conference room.

Marty and I are the last two in the room. "Enjoying your stay so far, sir?" he asks Rosamund as we enter.

"Mr. McConagle, do you mind?" Terhovian says. He

looks at the police reporter to make sure he isn't taking anything down yet, but Errol Northers, seated off to the side of the table, has his hands in his lap.

"No problem, Gus," Marty says amiably. "Just trying to lighten things up." His jabbing at Rosamund is not childish play but part of an attempt to annoy and disorient him as much as he can before the questioning starts.

Pappas motions to the jailer to remove Rosamund's cuffs, and I notice something interesting: as soon as the metal bands are off his wrists, Rosamund lays his hands down on the table top and leaves them there. It is the only time I can ever remember when somebody in custody did not immediately start rubbing their wrists, trying to work out the feel of the cold steel restraints. It is one of those expected reflexive responses that is just another in a series of minor humiliations that remind the prisoner who is in control. For certain, Rosamund has been through it before, is tuned in to the kinds of mind games that take place in these situations. His quiet hands on the table are meant to convey to us a high degree of self-possession, and they would if I were not reasonably certain that he was doing it on purpose rather than naturally. He also makes a point of not turning to see the police sergeant standing behind him.

"Yes, well," Gus replies, "my client wants to cooperate in every way possible and do everything he can to help move things along and get this matter cleared up."

"Why?" Marty asks him.

Terhovian is flustered for a moment, fiddles with the buttons on the front of his jacket with his birdlike fingers. He was not expecting a response to his standard offering of cooperation. "What, uh, what do you mean, why?"

"I mean why?" Marty says, taking off his jacket and draping it over the back of a seat. "Man's in custody, charged with rape and kidnapping . . . why's he wanna be so helpful?"

Terhovian doesn't quite know what to make of this. Marty turns to Rosamund. "That true? You wanna coop-erate with us? Get this moving?" Marty has pulled out the seat but pauses before sitting in it.

Rosamund looks to his attorney, not expecting him to

be thrown by this overweight, ill-mannered Irish street cop. "Absolutely," he says.

"Why's that?"

"Because he's innocent," Terhovian finally manages to say. "He's innocent of these ridiculous and spurious charges, that's why."

"Oh. He wants to cooperate so he gets off, is that it? Is that what you're telling me?"

"He wants to be absolved of these charges, certainly." Terhovian hoists his briefcase onto the table, trying to look casual and unconcerned.

"Ah." Marty finishes pulling out the seat and steps around in front of it. "Okay. Y'see, I thought you were trying to tell us he wants to cooperate 'cuz, like, he's a model citizen or something, wants to do his civic duty. That's what I thought you meant." He sits down heavily and pulls the seat forward, resting his forearms on the tabletop. "But he's cooperating because he wants to get the hell out of here, right?" He looks at Rosamund. "Izzat right?"

Pappas and the sergeant try to stifle their smiles. They've seen this before, Marty disabusing the suspect and his lawyer of any notion that they are the ones controlling the action, making it clear from the outset who holds the cards and that stock platitudes and posturing will be of little use in this setting.

Terhovian tries to pointedly ignore Marty and looks at me instead. "Mr. Milano, why the mention of kidnapping? I was given to understand that there was only the charge of rape."

"I changed my mind." Marsha changed it for me. She was afraid that we might have difficulty arguing against bail if there were only the single sex crime charge, especially if there was no great bodily injury—GBI, as it is referred to. Adding in kidnapping with intent to commit a rape increases the seriousness and will bolster our bail argument.

"Why was I not informed?"

"Just made the decision a little while ago."

"Hmm. Well. I would have thought, given our gesture of cooperation, you might have been a bit more forthcoming with us."

"You'da been less cooperative?" Marty asks sarcastically. "His civic duty extend only to rape or what?"

Terhovian cannot hide his annoyance with Marty as he addresses Pappas. "Detective, may we start now?"

"Sure." Pappas nods toward Errol, who places his hands on the keyboard of his machine. One of Terhovian's other conditions of this meeting is that no video or audio taping take place. It's a wise move: Rosamund's smart mouth and arrogant manner will come off badly on tape but if he watches his words carefully, he will do better on the written record where facial expressions and bodily gestures don't appear.

We start by giving our names to the reporter. After Rosamund gives his, Marty says, "That your real name? Rosamund, Vincent J.?"

"Yeah, it's my real name."

"Swear him in, Dan," Marty says to Pappas without taking his eyes off Rosamund.

"Raise your right hand," Pappas says. "Do you, Vincent J. Rosamund, swear to tell the truth, the whole truth, and nothing but the truth?" He leaves out *so help you God,* another in the City of Santa Monica's eager capitulations to modern enlightenment.

"Yeah." Rosamund says it with a sneer; Terhovian shoots him a withering look, and he corrects himself. "Yes, I do."

"Good," Marty says. "Now, is your name Vincent J. Rosamund?"

"He just said it was," Terhovian jumps in.

"I want it under oath," Marty tells him again without taking his eyes off Rosamund.

Terhovian points to Pappas. "When he said, 'Do you, Vincent J. Rosamund . . . ,' it *was* under oath."

Rosamund appears unfazed by the exchange. "Can I have one'a those?" he asks, pointing to the pack of cigarettes Marty is pulling out of his shirt pocket.

"Sure." Marty shakes a few up from the pack, grabs one with his mouth, and slides the pack over to Rosamund, who makes a show of taking one as far from the one Marty took as possible. Then he slides the pack back across the table. There is no smoking allowed in any city facility, but try telling that to a bunch of cops and detectives in an interrogation situation. Or try denying a prisoner who has voluntarily agreed to cooperate.

Marty lights up with a disposable butane, then sets the lighter down in front of him. Rosamund rolls his eyes upward at this juvenile move and says, with exaggerated exasperation, "Fine, can I get a light, too?"

"Oh, gee, I'm sorry," Marty says with feigned apology. "Here you go." He picks the lighter up and tosses it, wide of the mark, trying to make Rosamund scramble for it. Rosamund, not moving, watches it fly by and hit the floor, then motions to it with his eyes, knowing he isn't supposed to leave his chair. Pappas waves and the sergeant steps over, picks it up and slaps it heavily to the table in front of Rosamund. More petty games, more useless points. I nudge Pappas in the elbow to begin and give Marty a *that's enough* look. The corners of his mouth turn down slightly in the effort to suppress an impish grin.

"So, Mr. Rosamund—mind if I call you Vinny?"

"Mind if I call you Dan?"

"Vincent—" Terhovian admonishes gently.

"Sorry. Sure, Vinny's fine."

"Okay then, Vincent. Let's see if we can't make this easy on everybody, whaddya say? Why don't you start by telling us about the events of November twenty-first."

Rosamund shrugs. "What events?"

"Great!" Marty picks up his hands and drops them back onto the table with a loud slap, then turns to Terhovian. "Thought you said your guy was ready to cooperate. What the hell is this now?"

Terhovian turns to Rosamund. "Vincent?"

"I'm askin', what events is he talkin' about?"

"Okay, Vinny," Pappas says, rising to take off his jacket, as if in preparation for a long session. "We'll play it your way. Me, I got all day."

"His arraignment is scheduled for three," Terhovian says.

"We can do it at five," I tell him. "That'll give him more time to be cooperative."

Pappas has his jacket off and is hanging it on the back of his chair. "Vinny, you're charged with kidnapping and raping one—"

"Charged?" Terhovian interrupts.

"Okay, you wanna get technical . . . gonna be charged. You've been arrested on suspicion of kidnapping and raping one Lisa Pierman."

I watch Rosamund carefully and see his brows knit together in confusion. He is wondering why Diane has not been mentioned. From the corner of my eye I see Terhovian tapping his lip with one finger, wondering the same thing: is this some kind of trick? Neither of them says a word. The reporter has his fingers on the keys but is not pressing any of them. In the record, there will be no mention of a long pause. All the conversation will appear to be seamless and continuous. Terhovian knows this, knows he can take all the time he wants to think, and regardless of what that might communicate to the rest of us, on the written record it will vanish. He has undoubtedly briefed his client as well.

But I know this game, too. "Is there some reason why you're taking so long to answer?" I ask. "Did you not understand the question?" Errol's hands dutifully go to work, typing in my comment.

"What are you talking about?" Terhovian says immediately. "Detective Pappas has barely even finished the question." Errol puts that in, too. Sides are even.

After a few seconds Rosamund sits back, apparently having processed the information about a single rape charge and decided he can do nothing with it. He looks at Pappas. "I know I'm charged with that. What I'm asking is, where and when was this supposed to've happened? 'Cuz I have no idea what you're talkin' about."

Pappas, hands folded in front of him, purses his lips and taps his thumbs together, and Marty takes over for him. "Yo, Vinny, November twenty-first, evening of, The Alley on Montana—any of this coming back to you yet?"

Rosamund scrunches his face up in a frown of deep concentration, thinks about it for a second. "You mean those two twins?"

"Yeah, I mean those two twins."

"How come only one of them filed a complaint?" he asks.

Pappas stops tapping his thumbs. "You mean you raped 'em both?"

"I din't rape nobody."

"You didn't," Pappas echoes without inflection.

"Nope." Rosamund thinks for a moment, then turns his hands up on the table and idly lets them flop back over. "I mean I fucked 'em, sure, but I din't rape nobody." The soft, smooth tapping of Errol's fingers on the keys falters momentarily, then resumes.

"You admit you had sex with them?" Pappas asks. "Both of them?"

Rosamund grins his lopsided grin. "Hell, yeah, who wouldn't, you know what I'm sayin'? But I sure as hell din't rape nobody." He looks around, pleased with the reaction he has caused and which none of us can hide. Except Terhovian: his expression has not changed one bit. Either he is even cooler than I had thought or this is well rehearsed.

"So that's why I'm a little confused here, detective," Rosamund is saying. "I mean, if one of 'em is sayin' I raped her, how come the other one isn't? Kinda makes you wonder, don't it?"

He thinks he has us, so Pappas lets it hang in the air for a moment before answering. "Doesn't make me wonder, Vinny. I think you did 'em both, and we're gonna get you for both. Just maybe one at a time."

Terhovian picks up his yellow legal pad and leans back so he can write on it without anyone else seeing. I know what he's writing, a note to himself to make sure that if we are going to press two sets of charges, they are combined into a single action for purposes of trial. His motion will be granted as a matter of course, but that doesn't bother me. The only reason we're holding off on the additional charges is to make sure we have as perfect a complaint as we can. We can add them later, or if Rosamund is allowed to make bail against our objection, we can heap them on right away and argue against bail.

"Detective, I told you, I din't rape nobody. I din't do no kidnapping, I din't have no gun—"

"Who said anything about a gun?" Marty asks.

"Ah, f'Chrissakes, you gonna play games with me now?"

Terhovian clears his throat and leans forward, holding the yellow pad to his chest. "I believe the wording in the complaint says that my client used a gun to effect the kidnapping, is that not correct?"

It is. We just have not yet brought a separate charge involving his actually *having* the gun. "That's true," I admit.

"Okay, look," Pappas says, holding his hands out above the table, quieting everybody down. "Vinny, why don't you just tell us in your own words what happened that night."

"What happened when?" he asks, all wounded innocence. "You mean in the bar?"

"In the bar, afterwards, with Diane and Lisa Pierman."

Rosamund shrugs, a gesture that says, *sure, no problem; can't imagine why, though.*

"I'm in this bar on Montana, The Alley? You guys know the place, you were both there, am I right?" He looks from Marty to me and back again, but we don't respond.

"Keep goin', Vinny," Pappas tells him. "This is your statement."

"Sure, sure. So I'm in this place, it's like the best pickup joint in town, see, great-lookin' broads; they're only there for one reason an' everybody knows it. It's in the air, like."

It is a gross exaggeration, but thinking ahead to how this might sound at trial, he could make it plausible, could get a half dozen of the local stud puppies to testify to it. I'm starting to get an uneasy feeling about where this is going.

"Anyway. I'm standin' at the bar, not botherin' anybody, and I'm lookin' in the mirror and I see this great-lookin' chick, she's starin' at me. I mean, right at me, no doubt about it. I know the look, you know what I'm sayin'? So I turn around to see her, I smile at her, right? And she smiles back."

"You do anything else except smile?" Marty asks.

"What am I gonna do, twenty feet away?"

"What I'm asking, did you just smile, or what?"

"Ahhh, well, y'know, maybe I like, I don't know, made a face or somethin.' "

"A face?" Pappas says.

"Yeah, a face."

"What exactly?"

"Exactly, I don' know. What, you remember every time you made a face what you did, exactly?"

"All right, then what?"

"Then, if I remember, she gets up and walks away, and I'm thinkin', Jeez, where's she goin'? I thought we were, like, startin' somethin' there. And then—I can't believe this, I just can't believe it—there's two of 'em! Two of these incredible-lookin' broads! And I'm thinkin', this can't be happenin', and they're both lookin' right at me. So I gotta be real cool, sure as shit don' wanna blow this, and I turn back to the bar, see if they come on to me, make sure they really want it, you know? Don' wanna force myself on nobody."

"Sure," Pappas says. "You're a gentleman, right?"

"Absolutely. And that's when this guy"—he points to me—"starts botherin' me. I got this terrific thing going, and this guy's got a problem; he doesn't like me bangin' on the bar or somethin.' "

Pappas points a finger at Errol's keyboard and then at me. "You're indicating deputy DA Milano?"

"Yeah, Milano," Rosamund answers, and Errol keys it in.

"That face you made," I ask. "The woman said it was a lewd gesture."

"A *lewd* gesture?" Rosamund parrots back, stretching out *lewd* like a hooting owl might, mocking my formal terminology.

"Yes, lewd. Like she didn't like it."

"Izzat so?"

"Yeah, that's so."

"Well"—Rosamund hitches up his shoulders and leans forward onto the table, resting on his forearms and gesturing with his hands—"then maybe you can tell me why this broad who didn't like it, couple minutes later, she walks right up to me, steps tothe bar to grab a napkin, she rubs her arm on my back and smiles at me."

I feel my stomach begin a slow rumble. What Rosamund has just described is precisely what happened. But that is not really what happened. Not *really*. Pappas looks at me, but I keep my eyes on Rosamund as he continues.

"Sounds to *me* like she liked it." He turns away from

me and back to Pappas, showing him that my feeble interpretation of events is not worth talking about anymore.
"This is so cool, but then she walks away and a couple
seconds later the other one comes at me from the other
side. I can't believe it! Both of them! Jesus, I mean have
you ever . . . ?" He eyes Pappas, appraising him. "Nah,
pro'ly you never did."

I feel Marty tense up beside me. His thought patterns
must mirror my own. Diane and Lisa were toying with
Rosamund, doing their twins trick, playing with his head.
Now here is Rosamund telling us he knew all along there
were two of them, which I know is an outright lie, and
believed that they were coming on to him in a sexually
suggestive manner. But there is not one single fact in his
recounting of these events that I could dispute. He has
even admitted that his banging on the bar was disturbing
me. It's like the blind men describing the elephant, each
exactly right but each completely wrong, too.

"Never mind," Pappas says. "Then what?"

"They were playing with you, not coming on to you,"
Marty says.

"Huh?"

"They weren't trying to get you in the sack; they were
goofing on your sorry ass."

"How you know that?"

"They told me. And I saw it."

"Bullshit. That's what you're sayin' now, now they got
a plum up their ass about the whole thing."

"I saw it, too," I say, falling into it with Marty, even
though it can do us little good. None of this is going to
rattle Rosamund.

"Yeah? Well, even if that's so, how the hell am I supposed to figure that out, huh? Two gorgeous chicks,
smilin' at me, hangin' around, rubbin' up against me,
what am I, fuckin' psychic?"

Pappas glares at Marty and me both. We're not here to
win arguments but to create a record, one which will hang
Rosamund, not give him a stage on which to spin his
fables. "Then what?" Pappas prompts him.

"Then what? I'll tell you what: this gorilla over here"—
he points to Marty—"picks a fight with me. I'm doin' shit
and he puts himself in my face, like he's protectin' this

guy"—again, he points to me—"and before I know it, I'm out on the goddamned street! Made me look like an asshole in front of the whole joint." He slumps back on his seat, a petulant scowl on his face.

"So I understand this," Pappas says, "and for the record: Mr. McConagle steps in between you and Mr. Milano and picks a fight with you?"

"You got it."

"Uh-huh. Then what?"

"Then, I walk around. I'm thinkin', if he hadn't stuck his nose in, I'd be off with those two chicks already. So I hang around."

"Hang around where?"

"Around the bar, up and down the block."

"Why?"

" 'Cuz I was waiting for them, that's why."

This gets my attention. "You were waiting for Diane and Lisa Pierman?"

"Course I was. Shit, wouldn't you?"

"You were waiting for them why?" Pappas asks.

"What the hell do you mean, why!" Rosamund asks in a loud voice. "I just got finished tellin' you, these two broads came on to me big time, the hell you want me to do, go away just on accountta this goombah hasslin' me?" He makes a dismissive gesture with his elbow toward Marty, who remains motionless, his face devoid of any expression Rosamund can read. I can read it, though, and I hope he stays motionless.

"So you were waiting because you wanted to have sex with them," Pappas asks calmly.

"Yes," Rosamund answers with exaggerated enunciation, as though explaining something simple to a retarded child. "I was waiting because I wanted to have sex with them. Because *they* wanted to have sex with *me*."

"I see. Keep going."

Rosamund waits for a second, then cracks a few knuckles first on one hand, then the other. "Like I said, I was walkin' around, up and down the block, out back sometimes. I'm in the parking lot, the far end, and I see them come out together—"

"About what time?" Pappas asks.

"I dunno, maybe nine?"

Pappas nods his head a few times. "So this was, what, maybe an hour later?"

"Later than what?"

"Than when you left the bar?"

"Yeah, so?"

"Nothing." Pappas waves one hand as though shaking off a piece of lint. "Just, I was wondering, if these women wanted you so bad, how come they hung around all that time, 'stead of coming right out after you left?"

For the first time, there is a visible crack in Rosamund's armor of self-confidence. He thinks for a long time before answering, which he does with a leer. "Hey, detective, you know how women are, right? Doesn't look good they should go zoomin' out the door right away. All their friends, all those doctors and lawyers, maybe they don't want 'em talkin', they shouldn't know what the little *poons* do in their spare time."

He waits for a response from Pappas but gets none. "So they come out, and I see they're lookin' around."

"Looking around how?" Marty asks.

"Lookin' for me." He inhales deeply on his cigarette, almost forgotten as he was speaking.

"How do you know that?"

Rosamund exhales loudly. "Ain't you been listenin'?" he says through a cloud of smoke. "We practically had a date; what the hell else are they gonna be lookin' for?"

They were watching out for anybody who might be prowling around in the lot. It won't help to point this out, so I keep still.

"Go on," Pappas says.

"I don't know what car they're drivin' "—so much for getting him to admit he slashed Lisa's tires—"but I see they're headin' for this green number at the other end of the lot, so I head that way, and when I get there, they're lookin' down and shakin' their heads, all upset. So I look and they got two flat tires."

"How'd you know two were flat?" Pappas asks.

"Whaddya mean? I looked."

"Which side of the car were you on?"

"Um, lessee, the left, I think."

"And there was a flat?"

"Yeah, like I tol' you."

"Rear tire?"

"Yeah, rear."

"So how'd you know the other one was flat, too?"

Rosamund pauses for a moment, then says, "I'm walkin' up from one side; I see the tire is flat. One'a these broads is lookin' at the other side so I walk around that side to see, and it's flat there, too."

"They haven't seen you yet?"

"Uh, no."

"So you walk up to one side, look at the tire, then walk around to the other side, look at that tire, and they still don't know you're there?"

"It wasn't like that."

"What was it like?"

"I tol' you: as I'm comin' up to one side, I'm still pretty far away, I see the flat, I head for the other side, by the time I get there I see the other tire, then they see me."

"They didn't see you as you were walking up?"

"Not's far as I know."

"How's that possible, Vinny?"

"Hey, how the fuck should I know!" he nearly shouts. "Why don't you ask them!"

"I did. They say you sneaked up from behind."

"Horseshit!"

"Did you slash the tires, Vinny?"

"Whaddya, nuts? I'm gonna nail these two broads, you think I'm gonna start the night by cuttin' their tires?"

"Yes or no?"

"No." He angrily crushes out his cigarette in one of the cheap aluminum ashtrays scattered along the table.

"Whaddya gettin' all excited for, Vinny?" Pappas asks in a quiet voice, unfazed by Rosamund's display of indignation. In fact, the more Rosamund loses his composure, the calmer Pappas seems to get. He is used to preening, posturing and outbursts of emotionalism from suspects. He reads the histrionics like they were Rosetta stones to the unspoken, windows onto the truth. It is only when the suspects are unruffled and controlled, like Rosamund was when we started, that Pappas gets nervous because then not only does he learn nothing, he loses the upper hand. Now that he has rattled Rosamund, he's starting to settle down.

"You're trying to trick me, that's why." Rosamund folds his hands again, but this time it's to suppress the anxiety they betray. Now without a cigarette to fondle, he eyes Marty's breast pocket covetously.

"Not true," Pappas replies, in a hurt tone. "I'm just trying to understand, is all, trying to help you get it all sorted out. You say something, it doesn't make sense, hey: I know you're a little spooked, it's easy to make mistakes, am I right?"

"I ain't spooked and I ain't makin' mistakes so don' do me no favors, okay?"

"Valet guy says you came out and asked which car was the twins' over an hour before they came out. So you knew which car was theirs. That a mistake?"

"Fuck the valet guy; how'm I s'posed to remember shit like that? I was lookin' to get laid, not gettin' ready for no goddamned interrogation! You wanna know what color socks he was wearin'?"

Pappas throws up his hands in surrender. "No offense here, Vinny. Go ahead and tell it your way. I see a problem, I'll just keep it to myself."

A good deal of the arrogance has left Rosamund's face, replaced by consternation and confusion. While Pappas's probing may have shaken him up, it also let him, and his attorney, know where there were problems in the story, problems they might be able to fix before trial. At least that's what Rosamund was thinking. Terhovian's thoughts are elsewhere: if Pappas is willing to point up some logical flaws, that must mean that there are larger ones he is not highlighting but which we will leap on at trial. The message is that we aren't worried about our case, that we're willing to toss him a few evidentiary bones in this session only to demonstrate that there is much, much more to come, and maybe this suspect would be better off trying to cop a plea. Terhovian, as usual, maintains a perfect poker face. If he does want to deal, there is no reason to do so now. Better to wait and see if he can get more of our cards on the table.

But now Rosamund thinks he may have blown it. Pappas has told him he is going to keep quiet. It is pure nonsense, of course: Pappas had not been pointing out problems to be a nice guy but because it served his purpose. If he has more to say along those lines, he will say it, but now he has Rosamund thinking his wise mouth cut off his pipeline of information. My guess is that Pappas is covering for himself, because the fact is that when you look at it closely, so far there are precious few holes in Rosamund's story. Rosamund doesn't know this, but Terhovian might, and I myself am starting to get a little spooked by this lawyer's taciturn uncommunicativeness. *What the hell can he be thinking!*

Rosamund takes a moment to gather himself. "I asked them do they want a ride someplace, they say sure."

"They both say it?" I ask, inviting a thousand-watt glare from Pappas. He is trying to create a particular kind of gestalt and I am in danger of ruining it.

"No, they both don't say it, one says it, okay?" Rosamund seems relieved that someone besides Pappas is in on the conversation, and I realize that I may have broken some of the tension the accomplished detective is trying to stir up. *Which one?* I would like to ask Rosamund, but I don't.

Pappas looks back at Rosamund and waits. We all stay silent until he picks it up on his own.

"So we get into my car and head out." He stops. Pappas stares. The rest of us do nothing. "One of 'em, I don't know which, she's in the back with me doin' the nasty and the other one drives. Then we get to these woods somewhere and I do the other one, the one was driving, on the ground. Bing, that's it." He folds his arms across his chest and stops.

Pappas continues to stare at him, and Rosamund gives it right back. Errol's hands are poised above the silent keys.

Pappas starts to nod, very slightly at first and then more pronounced. He leans back and hooks his thumbs under his belt. "You want another cigarette, Vinny?"

"Yeah."

Pappas nods at Marty, who takes his pack out and slides it across the table, with the lighter this time. Vinny reaches for it, a little too hurriedly.

"Hey, Milano." Pappas looks over at me, no trace of his earlier irritation with me apparent in his voice. "You got one'a those stink sticks you're always hitting on?"

"I do." I reach for my briefcase, open the cover and pull

out a leather holder, taking out two cigars and holding them up. One is a double corona, the other a huge Churchill-size, both Arturo Fuentes, rich, powerful and slow-burning. Pappas points to the Churchill and raises his eyebrows; I hand it over, then take out a clipper and a box of sulfurless matches as well.

"Must you?" Terhovian asks.

"Your client started it," Marty says, jerking a thumb toward Rosamund.

"You can always go outside, counselor," Pappas tells him, and Terhovian makes a waving motion. I can't tell if he is dismissing the invitation to leave or whisking away smoke that has not even started yet. Pappas takes the clipper and lops off the end, holding up the cigar and letting Rosamund know in no uncertain terms that he plans to be here for a while, certainly for as long as it takes to smoke this giant log.

"You through, Vinny?" Pappas says as he licks the clipped end of the cigar. He does this to make sure the dry wrapper doesn't peel off when he holds the match to the other end and turns the whole cigar to get an even light. This is not his first such smoke, I am pleased to see.

"Yeah, I'm through."

Pappas starts drawing in the flame and speaks around the smoke as he lights up. "So (puff) you don't mind (puff) I ask you (puff) a couple questions, right?"

Rosamund shrugs and says nothing. Pappas hands back the matches, and I proceed to light my own. "You see any problems, Milano?"

"One or two." As I strike a match, Terhovian makes a show of scraping his chair away a few inches farther from mine. "You say Diane was driving?"

"No, I said one of 'em was driving; I don' know which one."

"She just got in and started it up?"

"Yeah."

"With you in the back with the other one?"

He hesitates. Maybe we have a witness. Maybe somebody saw them take off. Maybe somebody saw them when they stopped to switch drivers. He doesn't know, but he sees that I know the details. My only source is the twins themselves, and I have never doubted their story, which is why I feel safe hitting him with discrepancies, knowing my version will stand up. I am not disappointed.

"Uh, no, I did. I started in the front. Yeah, I forgot."

"No problem. Like Detective Pappas said, a little mistake is understandable now and again." I wait to see if he chastises us again about assuming he makes mistakes. No such reaction this time. He sees that it may be better to allow himself a little slack. I wonder why Terhovian doesn't jump in to protect him. "So you were in the front; where were they?"

"One in the front, one in the back."

"Then what?"

"Then, we switched."

"Where?"

"I dunno, someplace."

"How long after you started?"

"Couple minutes, who knows?"

"Why?"

"Why what? Why'd we switch?"

I nod. He grins again. "Can't do much with the one's drivin'."

"So, you got out, and . . . ?"

"I got in the back. Yeah."

"Where was the gun?"

"Very funny."

"What's funny?"

"What'd I need a gun for? They were all over me, man."

"What was Diane—the other one—what was the other one doing while you were in the back with her sister?"

"Cheerin' me on, man. Watchin' in the mirror and waitin' her turn."

"Why'd you leave them in the woods, Vinny?" Pappas decides it's time to jump out of sequence, a good way to trip up a spin artist. "You had such a great time, them giving it up so easy . . . why leave them out there?"

"Yeah, well . . . that." Rosamund takes a long, thoughtful drag on his cigarette. The room is getting uncomfortably smoky, even for me. "One of 'em, I don' know which—"

"Was it the one you fucked first or second?" Pappas asks casually, and it throws Rosamund. In Pappas's mouth, the word sounds as bad as *rape*, but since Rosamund used it first himself, there is no protest available to his lawyer.

"First. I think. Yeah, the first one. Had all these damned snaps on her dress." He looks directly at me as he says this. I have no idea why, but somehow he seems to know it is going to hurt me terribly to hear this. He is right, but only partially; it would have been much worse if it were Diane he was talking about. The thought shames me. "She says she's got some coke, we could do it in the car. I ask her, is she kidding? Carrying dope around in my car? I don' go for shit like that."

Marty lets a half-snort go, and Pappas hangs his head down and shakes it, smiling broadly. "You don't go for shit like that."

Rosamund is embarrassed and starts to say something, but Terhovian cuts him off. "My client is appalled at the thought of illicit substances being carried or used in his vehicle."

Pappas looks up in amused amazement. "Jesus, Gus, give us a break, will ya'? Whaddya think you got for a client here, the surgeon general?"

Terhovian extends his arm and points at Errol. "Let me emphasize in the record that Mr. Rosamund objected to the commission of a felony in his personal vehicle!"

Pappas laughs and points to Errol as well. "Let me emphasize in the record that I'm the fucking Easter Bunny!" Errol starts to enter it in, and Pappas lays his hand over the recording keys. "Just kidding, son." Still laughing, he turns back to Rosamund. "Okay, so one of the sisters tries to do some blow in your car and you get all huffy about it. Then what?"

"I told her to get rid of it and when she didn't, I wouldn't let her get back in."

"She was out?"

"Yeah. I mean, well yeah, she was outside."

"When'd she get out?"

"Right after we got there."

"Why?"

"So she could watch."

"Ah. So she watched you fuck her sister?"

Rosamund shrugs. "Yeah."

"You got a phone in your car?"

"Yeah."

"Why didn't you call somebody to come get them?"

"We, uh, we had an argument—"

"You mean like, what, like a lover's spat, that kind of thing?"

"About the dope. So I was mad, they were mad, they din't give me anybody's name to call—"

"You asked them?"

"Uh, I don'—I can't remember. They din't seem to care. But I felt bad about it anyway. So how'd they get home?"

"One of 'em had a portable cellular phone," I tell him.

"Oh, well whaddya know about that? See, no wonder they din't give a shit!" He says it with a self-deprecating grin, as though we duped him into feeling bad when all the while Diane and Lisa were perfectly able to fend for themselves. I'm certain he already knew Diane had used a cellular phone without my telling him.

"She used it to call a cop," I continue, "to tell her that the two of them had been kidnapped and raped."

"Boy, I din't realize they were that mad."

"What do you mean?" Pappas asks.

"Well, shit, it's obvious, in'it? They get pissed off and make up this bullshit story about how I grab 'em and rape 'em, dont'cha get it?"

"I don't think it's a story, Vinny," Pappas tells him.

"Well I don' give a shit what you think! You got any evidence? They get beat up any? You take some samples—?"

"You used a condom," I say.

"Course I did; whaddya think, I'm one'a these assholes does strange snatch without a rubber? What the hell, don't you read the papers? And hey"—he turns back to Pappas "—what kinda guy rapes somebody and stops to pull on a rubber, I'm askin' you?"

We continue along similar lines, but we can't shake him. He has covered his tracks too well, and there is little to confront him with other than a string of inconsequential discrepancies. If this goes to trial, and Terhovian elects not to put Rosamund on the stand, even those will not come out. Instead, Terhovian will try to evoke his client's version by asking Diane and Lisa leading questions on cross-examination, which he can do if he first asks the judge to let him treat them as hostile witnesses. *Isn't it a fact, Ms. Pierman, that you suffered no bruises because there was no force involved? Isn't it a fact that my client had enough concern for everybody's health that he even employed a condom, insisted on its use? Is it not true that you passed within twenty feet of two police officers and did nothing to attract their attention? Sorry, what did you say? Because of the gun? What gun? There was no gun!*

There is a knock at the door. The sergeant opens it slightly, looks outside and motions to me. I get up and see that it's Marsha outside. She's pointing to her watch and whispering loudly to me.

"It's four o'clock, Sal! Goldman's getting ticked off. You get anywhere?"

I shake my head. "He's hanging tough, but at least we know what their case is."

"That everything was consensual, right?"

"Yep. And I think they can do it without putting Rosamund on the stand, although I gotta tell you"—I turn my head slightly to look at Rosamund, who has calmed himself considerably—"even if he goes on, he's got a hel-luva story."

"Gus'll never put him on," Marsha says with convic-tion. " 'Cuz if it's him against the twins, he's toast."

It's a valid observation. Diane and Lisa are our only evidence, and if it comes down to a matter of personal credibility, Terhovian is better off getting his client a nice haircut, dressing him in a conservative suit and letting him sit quietly for the whole trial.

"You better wrap this up, Sal, or he walks in an hour."

"I know. Tell Goldman we'll be up in twenty minutes. Thirty, tops."

Marsha gives me a look but eventually leaves, and I go back to my seat. Pappas asks me if I have anything else.

"No. Get him out of here." Pappas nods at the sergeant, who nudges Rosamund's elbow and unclips the handcuffs from the back of his belt.

As he holds out his hands, Rosamund starts to talk to me. "Hey, Milano, you know what I—"

"Vincent!" It is the loudest I have heard Terhovian speak today. Rosamund tears his eyes away from me and glowers at his lawyer, but he holds his tongue. The sergeant tells him to put his hands behind his back, cuffs him, and a moment later he is gone.

Terhovian relaxes. "Well." He looks around the room and turns a palm up at Errol, raises a questioning eyebrow to Pappas.

The detective turns to the reporter and waggles his finger at the machine. "That's it, Errol. We're done."

The reporter nods and starts to pack up. We all remain silent until he leaves; then Terhovian takes the floor.

"In light of the foregoing, Mr. Milano, I trust you will cancel the arraignment and drop the complaint."

"Sure, Gus. Maybe I'll give him cab fare home, too. You think we bought all of that crap?"

"You have no evidence, Sal. On what do you plan to argue for a conviction?"

"For starters, we have two victims and two eye-witnesses."

"Who are the witnesses?"

"The victims. They each saw the other get brutalized by that sweetheart you represent. Now, who do you think a jury is going to believe, the Piermans or your client?"

"Mmm, mmm," Terhovian murmurs to himself, looking for all the world like a senile old man gone off into space for a few seconds. "So, am I to understand that you wish to carry on with this case?"

"You bet your ass," Marty answers for both of us.

"An apt phrase, Mr. McConagle, but one perhaps more suited to your own anatomy, and the deputy district attorney's." Terhovian drops his writing tablet into his briefcase, clicks it shut and lifts it off the table. "I'll expect a transcript of this meeting by morning, Mr. Pappas."

"You'll have it."

Terhovian gives me one more long look and turns to leave. "See you in court, gentlemen."

When he is gone, Pappas looks up in surprise. "That's it? He's not even gonna try to cop a plea?"

I'm still looking at the door, glad Pappas posed the question I was about to ask, in those exact words.

"He looks terrible," Marty says. "Wonder if the old guy still has his marbles."

"Yeah. I hope he doesn't make a fool out of himself in court. He was a helluva lawyer for a long time." I turn to Pappas. There is business to be handled. "You gonna walk Rosamund over right away?"

"Probably already there. Shall we?"

Municipal court, Department Three, is on the second floor of the county building. It's a much larger room than most of the others. There are two audience sections of about thirty seats each, separated by a double-wide aisle. The jury box is on the left, and the judge's podium is quite far from the bar demarcating the audience. In the wide expanse between the audience and the judge are two attorneys' tables—one for the prosecutors and one for the defense lawyers—two glassed-in clerks, a court reporter's desk and two bailiff stations.

There is a constant flow of activity in the room. Each of the two attorneys' tables has three or four lawyers working at any one time, other attorneys are moving in and out of the area or queuing up at the clerks' windows, a Spanish-language translator is flitting from suspect to suspect and at least seven marshals are milling about, most with specific functions and others on standby, just in case. The deputy district attorneys and public defenders are conservatively dressed and neatly coiffed, and you can easily spot the private defense attorneys by their ponytails, wildly patterned ties, earrings, boots and European-cut clothes in the case of the males, permed hair and flamboyant handbags for the females. Usually, there are at most only one or two private defense attorneys present at any one time, if any. Nearly every prisoner uses the public defenders.

Arraignments are done en masse, and a group of prisoners is being moved out as I come into court. I'm more than a little surprised to see Eleanor Torjan sitting in the second row of seats, scribbling notes on a steno pad. She notices me and waves. I hold up a finger to Marsha, who is anxiously waiting for me up front, and make my way toward Eleanor.

"We had a deal, right?"

She holds up her hands in a defensive gesture. "Just

taking notes. For that story you promised me for the future, remember?"

"I remember, and you remember you get it only if there *is* a story."

"Understood. So where's your guy?"

I point with my chin toward the bailiff's door on the other side of the bar. "Just coming over from lockup."

"You talk to him?"

I nod. "Says the twins went with him voluntarily."

Eleanor shakes her head in amusement. "What a crock. I know Diane; she wouldn't even get into an elevator with a fuckup like that."

Eleanor always looks like she has been rode hard and put away wet and speaks like it, too, fancying herself part of the old breed of hard-boiled, big-city reporters. It is only partially an affectation, though. Like police officers or paramedics, it's easy to become inured to the pathos and the suffering, and Eleanor tends to see everything as a story, not as something that actually happens to real people in their real lives. For her, this case will have a well-defined beginning, a meaty middle and a neat end, and somewhere in her subconscious she doesn't believe that any of the participants truly exist on either side of that time line. But at least the persona she has manufactured for herself ensures a high level of journalistic integrity: if we have a deal, I know it is solid. I suspect that Eleanor has a secret wish to be summoned by the court someday to reveal a confidential source, which she will refuse to do, and be jailed for contempt—for a reporter the next best thing to winning a Pulitzer.

"So what've you got? Usual physical evidence?"

"Nope. Not even semen."

She frowns. "You're kidding me. You sure he did it?"

I explain about the condom and the lack of apparent force. She sees right away that it's irrelevant. "If he's not denying there was nooky, semen doesn't matter one way or the other, right? Basically, it's his word against theirs."

"Sound familiar?"

Eleanor's laugh is sardonic. "Nobody rounds up witnesses to a rape."

"He did for this one."

She becomes still. "What're you talking about? Who?"

"Diane and Lisa."

It takes her a moment to catch on. "They watched each other?"

"He made them."

"Christ," she breathes. Eleanor is not easy to shock, but this makes her stop for a moment. "They coming here? The twins, I mean?"

I shake my head. "We don't need them. I'm trying to keep them away as much as possible."

"Can't keep them away from the trial."

"I know. I'm hoping it doesn't come to that."

"You gonna let him cop?"

"Maybe. He's going to have to take some serious time, though."

Any thought I might have had that Eleanor finds these events personally disturbing vanishes as she taps her steno pad. "This goes to trial, all bets are off, you know that. This is above-the-fold stuff."

"I know." I sigh. Eleanor's eyes dart to the front, and I turn to see Marsha waving at me frantically. I wonder how long she has been doing that and how long ago Eleanor noticed without telling me. "Look, I gotta go."

"Give 'em hell, Ace. Good luck."

Good luck? An interesting take on journalistic objectivity, but I suppose that if reporters in Washington can play tennis with cabinet secretaries, congressmen and press aides, Eleanor Torjan of the *Times* can wish me good luck.

Municipal court is the window of entry for every criminal case, no matter the severity. At the initial arraignment, charges are read, bail motions are heard and a date is set for the preliminary hearing if the case is a felony, which this one is. In the hearings, a judge will listen to arguments from both sides and determine whether the case should be "bound over" to superior court, where all felony cases are tried.

I wave to Brad Kamen, a marshal I know well. The marshal's department handles most of the enforcement duties in municipal court, like the sheriff's department does in superior. "Where are we at?" I ask him.

He holds up a hand and pulls the two-way radio from

his belt. Every marshal has one, and at times it seems they are all talking at once. I could never figure out how all the communications get coordinated.

"Kamen to base," he says, and there is an answering squawk I can't decipher but seems clear as a summer's day to Kamen, who holds the radio close to his mouth and says, "What's on the way?"

"Twenty-six bodies on the way up," I can make out as the answer. "Just gettin' 'em hooked up." In this day of enforced enlightenment, it is a wonder that "bodies" is the standard phraseology applied to prisoners being moved throughout the county building and that none of the assembled judicial personnel objects.

"You get that?" Kamen says to another marshal, who nods and begins rearranging spare chairs to accommodate them all. He turns back to me, and I slap the side of his arm in thanks before stepping back into the audience section. Three of my deputies, including Marsha, will be handling the bulk of the arraignments. I'm only interested in one case today.

The door to the right of one of the bailiff's stations opens and a marshal walks in, making sure the way is clear before he turns and motions to one of his colleagues. Both wear disposable rubber gloves, as does anyone handling congregations of prisoners. A procession of the newly arrested, all in street clothes, shuffles in amid the clattering of chains and handcuffs. As they are seated, several are forced to raise the chains over their heads and twist so that they don't become entangled with their fellows. The restraints are not removed until everyone is seated.

Again, strict rules of segregation apply. Three of the twenty-six are female, and they are seated in the first row of the audience, which is set off from the aisle by a small swinging door. A marshal is seated with them as baby-sitter. Five Spanish-speaking subjects are placed in the front row of the jury box to facilitate access to the translator. Nine others occupy the back row of the box, and the rest overflow onto seats lined up along the bar. These last are nonviolent offenders with short records who pose little threat to court personnel. Altogether, it is a full house, and this is already the third batch of arraignees today.

Vincent Rosamund is the only one charged with a violent crime. He's placed at one end of the jury box, and a marshal stands less than three feet away. Rosamund's clothes probably cost more than all the other prisoners' combined.

Once they are all seated, the activity that ceased for their arrival starts up again in earnest. Several of the public defenders approach the prisoners and have individual discussions about their cases. Each conversation takes less than thirty seconds, even though this is the first time the attorneys have had a chance to interview some of their prospective clients. The marshals in the room, in that manner of those in positions of authority in the midst of people in trouble, engage in self-conscious, forced jocularity and kidding around, swaggering their free-ness as if to underscore the contrast between their situations and those of the prisoners about to be arraigned, enjoying their control, or maybe just hiding their discomfort. They seem to be in a constant state of delight that it is not they being judged in the dock; the deputy baby-sitting the females in the front row of the audience even banters with the prisoners. It's Monday, and most of the bits of conversation I can catch are about tonight's football game. The L.A. Stars are, miraculously, still undefeated, and people are daring to hope for a shot at the Super Bowl. This astonishing possibility is of much greater immediate concern to courtroom personnel than anything else that might be going on in here, all of which is, to them if not to the prisoners, routine.

After the room is called to order and judge Ephraim Goldman manages to quiet things down, he turns to address the prisoners as a group. He is required to do this, even though nearly all of them look either bored, contemptuous or asleep, except perhaps the one or two who have never been here before and are trying to look uninterested so the others will not ridicule them later for being frightened. Goldman takes his job seriously and tries not to let the grind make him forget who he is and what he represents.

"Ladies and gentlemen, you have certain rights in this

court which are granted to you by the Constitution of the United States and the laws of the State of California. You have the right to a speedy and public trial. If you have been charged with a misdemeanor or an infraction, you have the right to be brought to trial within thirty days unless you agree to waive that time. If you have been charged with a felony, you have the right to a preliminary hearing within ten days."

As he speaks, the only other sound besides the shuffling of papers is the quiet drone of the translator whispering to the front row of the jury box. She looks earnest, as if the Hispanic prisoners are paying rapt attention. Most of them know the rules better than she by now.

"You have the right to be represented by a lawyer or by yourself. If you want a lawyer and cannot afford one, the court will appoint one for you at no expense. You have the right to confront and cross-examine all witnesses against you, and you may subpoena witnesses to appear. You also have the right to remain silent and not say anything at all. And, you have the right to reasonable bail."

That concluded, he starts calling cases one by one, and what follows is a rhythmic litany, almost religious in its strictly mandated, ritualized repetition, the judge-priest leading the way and the suspects-congregation chanting responsively.

Shaneel Williamson, you are charged under section eleven-three-fifty-two of the Health and Safety Code with one count of the sale of rock cocaine. Do you understand the charge against you?
Yes.
Do you have a lawyer?
No.
Would you like a lawyer?
Yes.
Do you have money for a lawyer?
No.
Would you like the court to provide a lawyer for you?
Yes.
Court appoints the public defender. How do you plead to the charge?

The PD takes over now. Defendant pleads not guilty, your honor.

Okay. Preliminary hearing is set for December eight. Motions on bail?

Your honor, says the deputy DA, the defendant has seven priors on similar charges, including two counts of grand larceny. He has also spent sixteen months in state prison and is currently out on parole. People request bail be set at thirty thousand dollars.

Defense?

Your honor, defense requests an OR report.

Bail is set at twenty thousand pending OR report. Next case.

And so it goes, over and over, with little variation. Today, aside from possible court appointees, Rosamund is the only defendant with his own private lawyer. It doesn't surprise the other prisoners. Rosamund is, after all, the only white face in their midst.

There is some conversation between the attorney tables, and then a PD walks over to one of the females in the front row and says, "They're offering time served for no contest." I know the suspect; she is completely illiterate and never made it past the seventh grade but she knows exactly what the PD means: if she accepts the charge, they will consider the time she has spent in lockup awaiting arraignment to be her sentence, and she can go free as soon as the arraignments end. She takes the deal—with her record, the addition of a no-contest plea to petty larceny means little. The woman next to her, who is homeless and a hard-core alcoholic, is fined fifty dollars for urinating in public, and the fine is suspended because of time she has already served in custody awaiting arraignment. She is free to go as soon as the proceedings end.

As Rosamund's case number approaches, Terhovian heads for the defense table. I walk through the swinging door and take my place next to Marsha as the bailiff calls out the case number. Judge Goldman ruffles through some papers and then looks over at the jury box. "Mr. Rosamund." The prisoner raises his hand, and the marshal escorts him to the defense table to stand with his attorney.

This is not usual, but of the twenty-six cases being called, twenty-three are for sale of cocaine as a result of a midnight sweep of the park, and this one is clearly different.

"Mr. Rosamund, you are being charged with violation of section two-sixty-one of the California Penal Code." He doesn't add, *an act of sexual intercourse accomplished against a person's will by means of force, violence, duress, menace, or fear of immediate and unlawful bodily injury on the person or another.* Descriptions of sex-related crimes are never read out loud in open court for fear that the accused will be mistreated by his fellow prisoners when he is returned to lockup. Murderers, thieves and pushers seem to have an interesting way of summoning up self-righteous indignation in the presence of a sex offender. "Do you understand this charge?"

Rosamund looks to Terhovian, who nods and inclines his head toward the bench. "Yes, your honor," Rosamund says.

"Further, you are charged under six-sixty-seven-point-eight." *Kidnapping with intent to commit felony sexual offenses.* "You understand that charge?"

"Yes, sir."

"How do you plead on these charges?"

"Not guilty on both counts, your honor," Terhovian answers.

Goldman nods. "Okay, motions on bail?"

Marsha stands up. "Your honor, prosecution requests denial of bail."

"On what grounds?" Terhovian demands. Goldman lets this minor usurpation of his authority go.

"Your honor," Marsha says, referring to notes she has made on her yellow legal pad, "the defendant has a prior record in another jurisdiction. Further, we have reason to believe that he is engaged in the commerce of controlled substances—"

Hearing this, Rosamund jerks his head around to Terhovian and starts yammering something at him. The attorney puts a restraining hand on his arm but not before Goldman takes notice and makes his annoyance known.

"Mr. Rosamund, you will have a chance to respond."

"But wait a minute—!"

"Mr. Terhovian! Please instruct your client to keep silent or we'll do this without him here!"

Terhovian whispers in Rosamund's ear and order is quickly restored.

"As I was saying," Marsha continues, unruffled. She is pleased that Rosamund has demonstrated a lack of decorum in front of the judge. "We have reason to believe he deals drugs, and might do so again if released. Further, this was a particularly vicious crime that he could easily commit again. He has no ties to the community, and we believe that he is a very high flight risk. I would like to point out that he was captured in another county, and then only after three days of searching."

Goldman mulls it over. "Pretty stiff request there, Ms. Jones. There's no GBI; you think it's fair to let him sit that long before trial?" I'm impressed that the judge has read enough of the paperwork to know there was no great bodily injury.

"I think it's fair, your honor, and it shouldn't be that long. The people will be ready for trial shortly after the preliminary hearing is concluded."

"Mr. Terhovian?"

The attorney rises creakily to his feet. "This is absurd, your honor. My client's priors all involve minor offenses. And he may not have ties to this community but he most certainly does in Bakersfield, in the county just north of our own." He turns to look at Marsha. "And may I respectfully point out to my colleague that the failure of local police to take my client into custody for three days is their problem, not ours. My client had no idea he was being sought and was therefore under no obligation to make himself available to the authorities."

"Is that true, Ms. Jones?" Goldman asks.

"In a manner of speaking, your honor," she says sarcastically, rising. "If he kidnapped and raped a woman and didn't know somebody would come after him for it, if he didn't even believe he'd committed a crime, I'd say we were dealing with a pretty dangerous character. Second, if he's got such great ties to Bakersfield, how come we couldn't find him? And as for his minor offenses, I don't consider possession of narcotics a minor offense, and those were just the ones he was convicted of." She pauses for a breath. "The people are convinced he's gonna fly, your honor, and we strongly urge the denial of bail."

It's an unusual request and one Goldman does not take lightly. He wants to make sure, at least for the record, that he has afforded the other side as much opportunity as possible to rebut our request. "Defense counsel?"

"We renew our objections, your honor. The court's own guidelines for bail recommend certain dollar amounts for these charges, and we see no reason why anything in excess of these ought to be imposed."

"Whaddya know," Marsha bends to whisper to me. "He isn't arguing for OR." Own recognizance: letting the defendant out on his own without bail. I have a feeling Terhovian was going to try for it before Marsha got up and masterfully rendered that expectation moot. Most of what she argued was speculation and supposition, but that's the nice thing about bail motions: the normal rules of evidence don't always apply.

"Those are guidelines, counselor," Goldman is saying. "My job is first to protect the public, and second, to make sure he comes back. I'm required to take into account the seriousness of the offenses charged, the fact that use of a firearm is also charged, that there is an allegation of the use of a controlled substance . . ." He lets his voice trail off and rubs his chin for a few seconds, probably realizing that he has just made Marsha's argument better than she did. I've been in Goldman's chambers. There is a little plaque on the wall that reads, SALUS POPULI SUPREMA LEX: the people's safety is the highest law. "Nope, I'm gonna grant prosecution motion. Bail is denied."

"But your honor—!" Terhovian begins.

"You can renew your motion for bail after the preliminary hearing, counselor. And Ms. Jones"—Goldman points his gavel at Marsha—"I expect you to make good on your promise to get quickly to trial if and when you're in superior. Today is the twenty-eighth, Monday, so ten days is the eighth, okay?"

There are no grounds for anybody to object. Goldman is only being polite, and so Marsha and I nod.

Terhovian does not. "My client will be sitting in jail, your honor. Under the circumstances, ten days seems excessive."

"It's a strain just to get it in then, Mr. Terhovian. And it is within the statutory limit. I would have thought you'd appreciate the extra preparation time, but ... Mr. Milano?"

"We'd prefer to stick with the date you specified." I am diplomatically reminding him that there is no obligation for us to be ready sooner than that.

"Swell," Goldman answers, then addresses his clerk. "Preliminary hearing in this matter is set for Thursday, December eighth." He turns back to us. "I'll hear this one myself."

I'm not certain why Goldman wants to do the prelims, but I suspect he senses that the defense is going to be standing on a lot of technicalities, playing fast and loose with obscure rules. Goldman's knowledge of statute and regulation is vast and legendary, not just the written word but the all-important case law that circumscribes actual application, and the lawyer has not been born that can take advantage of him on that score.

For our part, we couldn't hope for a better judge. It isn't that Goldman is biased in favor of the prosecution: contrary to popular belief, attorneys do not necessarily want a judge who is reputed to incline to their side. In many instances, judges who know they have such reputations purposely overcompensate in the other direction.

Goldman's chief virtue is his utter consistency and predictability. His application of the law is evenhanded and by the book. You know with certainty that he is not going to come winging in with radical reinterpretations or get lulled into honoring speciously argued motions just because some highly regarded, ex–law school professor turned private practitioner applies a patina of academic elegance to them.

Rosamund's arraignment lasts less than ten minutes, and we are finished.

"Is this gonna be a problem?" Marty asks me, referring to the preliminary hearing only a few days away. The purpose of the hearing is to determine if there is sufficient evidence to hold Rosamund to answer in superior court, where felony cases are tried.

"No," Marsha tells him before I can answer. "The preliminary's just going to be a formality. Hell, I could do it tomorrow if I had to."

We are up in Marsha's apartment in Marina del Rey, the top floor of a fourteen-story building two blocks from the ocean. Facing north, it has one of the most stunning views in the area, starting from the Venice pier to the west, encompassing the northern half of Santa Monica Bay and the Malibu coastline, the Santa Monica and San Bernardino Mountains, a good deal of the LA basin, and a piece of the marina itself, the largest small-boat harbor in the world. On this crisp November evening, looking down on many square miles of quietly glowing lights stretching off to the east and the dark, placid ocean to the west, it is easy to forget for a few moments the madness below.

"We don't really need any more time for the prelims," I explain to Marty. "We'll even use some of that time to start preparing for the trial itself, get a head start in case Terhovian forces a close-in trial date. Like she said, the prelims are a formality."

Marty is leaning against the balcony railing, watching the line of airplanes descending over Point Dume in preparation for their landings at LAX. They will march in orderly procession eastward over the basin until reaching the Coliseum, site of the 1984 Olympics, then turn around and come screaming in over South Central, site of the 1992 riots. On a night like this it isn't unusual to see the lights of as many as thirty planes at one time, most in several clearly defined formations, some in seemingly random orientations overhead. "You worried about that interview today?"

I am. The more I examine it, the more apparent to me the internal consistency of Vincent Rosamund's story. I know he is lying, the jury may even suspect he is lying, but in a criminal proceeding the entire burden of proof is on the prosecution. It isn't enough to arouse suspicion in the minds of the jurors; we must convince them beyond a reasonable doubt of the defendant's guilt. If Rosamund's story *could* be true, and if that possibility can be assumed without too great a leap of faith, the jury must find him innocent.

I'm famous for this kind of morbid pessimism, this extraordinary talent for launching myself into fits of depressive melancholia set off by the flimsiest of triggers.

Marsha is prone to no such self-indulgent lapses. "I

don't think it's a big deal. I think what we have here is a practiced rapist who's learned how to cover his tracks."

"We're not going to be able to show that without more evidence than we've got," I remind her.

"We're going to imply it." She is sitting on a beach chair half-in, half-out of the opened sliding door to the living room. We're out here despite the chill in the air so Marty and I can smoke. "And we don't need it anyway. What you seem to keep forgetting is that we have two of the most innocent victims I've ever seen, who happen also to be the most credible witnesses I've ever seen."

"I was hoping it wouldn't come to that." I sip some of the Strega liqueur Marsha keeps on hand for me. She thinks I'm the only person on the planet who drinks the stuff. Marty thinks I'm the only one who has ever even heard of it. "I'd really like to plead this one out. Spare the woman the publicity."

"Speaking of that," Marsha says, "what was Eleanor Torjan doing there today? I thought you had some deals with the press."

"I do. She's taking notes, just in case. Once the Piermans appear, or we go to trial, it's going to be hard to keep the lid on. That's why I want them kept away."

"Hold it a second." Marsha pauses partway through a sip of her single malt on ice. "You telling me they're not going to be at the prelim?"

Marty takes notice as I nod. "That's the plan."

"Then I think we got a problem." She sets her drink down.

Marty turns full around toward us. "I know they don't need to be there, Sal, but you think it's such a hot idea?"

"I'm trying to protect them, Marty."

"That's real gallant, Milano, but you're undercutting your own strategy." Marsha sets her drink down on the Astro Turf–like matting covering the concrete balcony floor. "If you want Rosamund to cop a plea, we need to overwhelm him right away. The twins are our strongest suit. I mean, one listen and everybody's going to know they're on the level. Terhovian's going to have to roll over."

Marty sees where she's heading and takes up the cause. "If they don't speak up at the prelim, somebody's gonna wonder why. That fancy-ass lawyer's maybe gonna think they're not such great witnesses. So where's your pressure then?"

Marsha nods her agreement with this analysis. "Then for sure there's going to be a trial and for sure they're going to be splashed with ink."

"We're going to have to take that chance." I don't like being authoritarian, but the fact is I have already had this conversation with Diane and promised her she wouldn't have to appear. I take responsibility for the decision, or at least I appear to in front of Marsha and Marty, not because of any modern management theory of motivation but because I don't want them thinking the complainants are shaping our case strategy.

"I don't think their presence will make that much difference," I explain. "Terhovian knows they're going to be unbeatable on the stand; he doesn't need to see it in the prelim."

"Then why isn't he trying to cop now?" Marty asks.

"Because there's no need. He wants to take a look at our hand before the trial, see how strong we are: do we have any other corroborating witnesses, any physical evidence"—I shudder slightly, and see Marsha do the same, at the mention of this weakest part of our case—"and then he can make a decision."

"Yeah, but meanwhile his client's stewing in jail, and he doesn't look like he stews easily."

Marty makes a good point, and I have already had the same thought. "I know. That part I don't get, either. Maybe they figure ten days isn't too high a price to see where we're at."

Marsha thinks this over, then leans back on her chair. "Okay, I'll go along. I'm not nuts about keeping the twins out of the prelim—"

"Me neither," Marty throws in.

"—but that's Diane and Lisa's problem. Me, personally? I don't give a damn if he cops or not; I think we'll whip his ass at trial. But I think you should tell Diane and Lisa we've got a whole lot better chance at a plea if they do the prelim themselves. Otherwise, this lady thinks they're going to be testifying at trial, and that's going to be a good deal messier."

It doesn't escape my notice how easily Marsha figured out that the Piermans, or at least Diane, were calling the shots on their appearance, or how smoothly she let me worm out of it.

"Let's forget the preliminary," I say. "We're in and out; I'm not worried about it. What I'd like to know, what's my old friend Arigga going to do with it once we get to him?"

Constantin Arigga, the judge who runs the master calendar court. The same man who embarrassed me in front of Diane Pierman by letting her defendant client walk on a string of dubious technicalities.

Marsha laughs at the mention of his name, taking fiendish delight in my painful memory. "This time, you don't need to worry. Arigga's got a daughter in college, an only child, and he thinks she's a gift from the angels."

"Where'd you hear this?"

"Ah, just stuff you hear. The old fart hates rapists, probably thinks half the world is stalking his kid. Basically he's a decent guy, you know."

That is true. For the most part, barring the occasional inexplicable lapse, Arigga is a respected and knowledgeable jurist. He arrived from Kern County less than three years ago and is already running the master calendar court. I have always suspected that he achieved this position because Supervising Judge Douglas Nyqvist, who runs the whole show in this branch, might have thought he made one too many judicially questionable decisions. Removing an elected judge outright is a rare and drastic move, but putting him in charge of the master calendar was a creative solution. The consequences of errors are less dire there and more easily—and less visibly—correctable.

That is my opinion, but it isn't universally shared. Many think highly of Arigga, and they chalk off my negativity to lingering resentment over what they refer to behind smirks as "the Friehling frolic." It seems that, of the several others who also on occasion have suffered from his incomprehensible rulings, all are fellow prosecutors, which only adds to the prevailing sentiment that this is nothing more than sour grapes against a defendant-biased judge. Regardless, I am forced to admit that, generally, I have received fair treatment at his hand.

"Besides," Marsha says, "he's just going to do the pre-trial stuff, and that's all bullshit anyway. It's not like he's going to hear the case at trial."

She's right, and I need to shake this off. "You get any more leads on this guy?" I ask Marty.

"Still digging. I got calls in to Bakersfield, some guys I know up there; maybe I can get underneath those missing charges on his sheet. I think Marsha's right, that he's pulled this stuff before. Maybe that's what was on the sheet and he got it yanked somehow." None of us has yet gotten over how well Rosamund managed to cover his trail on what appears to have been an impulsive act of revenge.

Marsha rubs a finger along the side of the glass to scoop up some of the condensate that is dribbling onto her jeans. "You need to read their statements, you know."

"I will. Tomorrow." I turn to the right, toward the east, to see the lights twinkling at the Mt. Wilson Observatory. They are a good indication of the general visibility, as I learned when I lived here. On nights when you could count eleven separate yellowish lights up there, visibility was essentially unlimited. Tonight there are six, maybe seven.

"We need to be prepared to go to trial quickly," I say. "I think that's Terhovian's strategy, to rush this in front of a jury. I don't know why, but that's what he wants. And if we want Rosamund to cop, we better slam into this thing like a pile driver."

"I don't have a problem with that," Marsha says confidently. "The faster the better, far as I'm concerned. We got every duck in line, and one way or the other, this bastard's going away."

Marty looks at his watch and walks over to Marsha's big-screen television, the main reason we're meeting here. It's almost game time. "Let's hope these clowns keep it up," he says, referring to his newly beloved L.A. Stars, taking down the remote control and pressing the power button. They're only beloved because they're having a winning season. Otherwise he curses them mercilessly. "The week shouldn't be a total loss."

"When are you gonna announce, Sal?" Marsha asks me out of nowhere.

"Announce what?"

She rolls her eyes and gives me an exasperated look. "I don't want to work for that schmuck forever, you know."

I look down at my drink. "You don't work for him; you work for me."

Marty grunts without turning in our direction. I thought he was intent on getting the set tuned.

"Shit rolls downhill," Marsha says. "Right through you, sometimes, right to me."

I fiddle with my shoelaces. "Don't know that I'm going to. Don't know that I've got enough juice, enough arrows in my quiver."

"You're good at what you do," Marty says, still toying with the controls.

"May not be good enough."

"Hell, Beckman got in; he doesn't even have *that* going for him."

Marsha and I both laugh. "The office's buzzing with it," she says. "You let it go on much longer and people're going to start to wonder, maybe you don't have the *cojones*."

"That supposed to be a challenge? Like to my manhood?"

"Hey, whatever it takes. Practically every deputy in the county will back you, you know that."

"Yeah, all the junior birdmen." Beckman's term. "Lotta clout, there."

"They're gonna kick off. You through with this enthusiastic campaigning now?" Marty backs up without taking his eyes off the screen and dumps himself into the easy chair directly in front of the set. They're right: I'm going to have to decide this one way or the other before too long. I wish I didn't have to do it while the Rosamund case is pending.

I step back out onto the balcony to take in the view. This used to be my apartment, when I first got to LA, having heard that the Marina was the hottest place on the globe for singles to live. I didn't know at the time how many of those singles were in fact new divorcées, desperately lonely and ready to hook up with the next pretty face that could make the pain go away.

I've never been good about meeting women. I've found, though, that, once they got to know me a little and

were able to get past the less-than-Tarzanish physiognomy, their attraction for me deepened. Unfortunately,
the feeling was rarely mutual, and I pretty much resigned
myself to the low probability of ever finding someone I
could rationally anticipate spending the rest of my life
with. Observing the goings-on in the Marina tended to
continually confirm my determination not to end up as
one of the walking wounded desultorily dragging their
equally miserable progeny to the movies every Sunday
afternoon; visitation day in the Marina rivals that of Sing
Sing in terms of numbers and depression.

It's almost Christmas. I hope that for Diane and Lisa
future holiday seasons will not bring back memories of
how terrible this one was. That, too, I take as part of my
responsibility in this matter.

6

As expected, Vincent Rosamund has been held to answer
in superior court not only for the original felony charges
but also for new ones we added during the preliminary
hearing in front of Judge Goldman. These include various
kinds of assaults as well as use of a firearm during the
commission of a felony. Once we prove to the jury's satisfaction that the basic crimes took place, these add-ons
are mere formalities and will add years to Rosamund's
sentence.

The additional charges still don't include those involving
Diane. Marsha and one of our paralegals researched the
case law exhaustively and are convinced the charges are
correct, trying to assuage my paranoia about getting all of
this down perfectly. But I stick to my guns and decline to
file charges on Diane's behalf. I want to see how Terhovian
is going to approach things and then lodge those additional
charges.

Rosamund has already been remanded to the custody of
the county sheriff and has been taken downtown to the
inmate reception center of men's central jail. From there
he was shipped off to the county jail in Sylmar, then
brought back this morning for his new arraignment in
superior court. As with the preliminary hearing, we
expect this to be a cakewalk, an orchestrated recitation of
the standard speeches followed by a date for the pretrial
hearings. We promised Goldman a speedy trial if he

denied bail, and Marsha and I believe we can be ready in well under six months.

We are in Judge Constantin Arigga's master calendar court. A deputy sheriff working lockup brings Rosamund in from the cage, just a short distance down the corridor behind the bailiff's door. All of the prisoners in lockup on the first floor have been brought in from various county facilities, having already been arraigned in municipal court. They are here for various kinds of hearings or trials or, in Rosamund's case, superior court arraignments. They are all dressed in prison coveralls of various colors. The meaning of these colors depends on which facility they are housed in. Orange might mean the prisoner is homosexual or from one of the honor ranches up north or is handling his case *pro per,* acting as his own attorney, and needs to be identified so he can be allowed access to the law library. Other colors indicate a keep-away status. Rosamund is dressed in blue, mainline status, to be mixed in with the general population.

Arigga doesn't like to waste time. "Defense counsel: waive formal reading of the information?" The documentation against Rosamund was originally called a complaint; here in superior, it becomes "the information."

"We do," Terhovian says as he stands up.

"Milano. You doing this one or what?"

"Yes, your honor. Marsha Jones as co-counsel."

"Great. So what are we looking at here?"

"People can be ready in six months," I tell him. Proposition 115, the Crime Victims Justice Reform Act, has made it much harder for defense attorneys to drag out their usual arsenal of endless continuances and other delaying tactics that gradually erode the prosecution's case and needlessly torture the victims. If Terhovian needs more time to get ready, he must be prepared to explain exactly why, and if his excuses come up lame, he had better start canceling his vacation plans. I'm hoping that my little display of confidence and preparedness shakes him up a bit.

Judge Arigga merely grunts and says to Terhovian, "I assume defense waives time?" He picks up a pen and starts to make the appropriate notation on the information file.

"We do not, your honor."

Arigga stops writing, bends his head forward and looks at Terhovian above the tops of his glasses, holding a hand to his ear. "Come again?"

"We do not waive time, your honor. We would like this trial to begin in sixty days."

Marsha looks at me. "Is he serious?" she whispers.

"He looks serious," I say, but I can't believe he would do this. By law, Rosamund has the right to have a trial within sixty days of the arraignment, which is California's official definition of "speedy," but the defense always waives this right as a matter of routine so they can have more time to prepare their case. The operation of the court depends on this standard defense concession. Otherwise, it would be like air traffic controllers enforcing aircraft separation standards to the letter: instant gridlock. Even the framers of Proposition 115 didn't expect every trial to happen *that* fast.

"Are you serious?" Arigga asks.

"Quite serious, your honor. We would like a pretrial date within ten days."

Arigga rests his chin on his fist and drums the fingers of his other hand on the disheveled pile of papers in front of him, papers representing a depressingly crowded court calendar intolerant of further strain. "Mr. Terhovian," he says after many seconds, "the prosecution has requested a hundred eighty days to prepare—down from the nine months they probably really need, I should add—which strikes me as quite reasonable. And as you know, we are backed up the proverbial wazoo with pretrials in this court."

He pauses, waiting for a reaction from Terhovian, who stands perfectly still and says nothing. He is technically not obligated to speak, as he has not been asked a question, but the informal nature of these proceedings would normally demand some kind of response.

In the absence of same, the judge continues. "Counselor, are you telling me you can be ready for trial that quickly and still do a credible job for your client?"

"I am ready now."

"And I cannot persuade you otherwise?"

"We wish to exercise our statutory right in this regard."

"I see." It is apparent to me that Arigga is irritated, but

it would be unseemly for him to display it when someone before him is merely demanding what is rightfully his, even if it does violate the unwritten protocol of the court. Arigga looks at our table and gives me a small shrug, then turns to his desk-blotter calendar. "Today is Monday the twelfth, ten days is Thursday, the twenty-second. Anybody got a problem with that?"

Marsha and I are nearly speechless but she is outwardly calm, thinks for a second and says, "I believe I may have some sentencing hearings scheduled for that day."

"Then let's do it earlier," Terhovian says, and I see some muscles in Marsha's jaw line tighten. There doesn't seem to either of us to be any conceivable way Terhovian can be ready to go to trial that quickly, and for us it will be a nightmare of frantic preparation.

I stand up next to Marsha. "The twenty-second will not be a problem, your honor," I say as nonchalantly as I can. "The sentencing hearings are in another part—sorry, I mean department—and I'll get them rescheduled." All courtrooms in Santa Monica were renamed as "departments" last year but I still can't break the habit of calling them "parts," especially when I'm under stress.

Arigga looks relieved at our acquiescence, even appreciative. "Anything else?"

This is where Terhovian gets to make a new motion for bail. Marsha is staring at the pile of papers before her, and it appears that she's still fretting over the impossibly early trial date. I nudge her to shift her focus to arguing against any new bail motions. She reaches for her notes just as we hear Terhovian say, "Through here, your honor."

Marsha snaps her head to look at him in disbelief, and I quickly jump up and say, "Same here." If Terhovian declines to ask for bail for some reason, I want us out of here as soon as possible in case he changes his mind.

"Defendant is remanded to sheriff's custody," Arigga says to the bailiff, who jots it down on a list with all the lockup prisoners' names on it, so he knows where to distribute them all when their hearings are concluded. Rosamund has not moved or said a word since he was brought in. I hustle Marsha outside and down to our offices.

* * *

"Jesus, what the hell was that all about?" she asks.

"Which part?"

"Start with him not making a new bail motion."

"The only thing I can guess is that he didn't get good news, or maybe got no news, from the OR investigator." This is someone appointed by the court to do background checks and make recommendations as to "own recognizance" releases. One of the things she will do is get an opinion from the arresting officer and factor that into her report. Maybe she spoke with Marty McConagle and is still reeling from that particular opinion. "I'm a lot more worried about going to trial in sixty days."

"What the hell," Marsha shrugs. "We can be a damned sight better prepared than Terhovian can. If we don't show him our hand for another thirty or forty days, no way Arigga can fault us for that. Then what's he gonna do, still insist on a quick trial?"

It's a good argument. We're required to share our evidence with the defense to allow them to get ready to refute it, but there is nothing that says we have to do it before we're ready, so long as the judge doesn't feel we are delaying on purpose. With a trial in only sixty days, nothing we do is likely to be construed as purposeful delay.

"Besides," I observe, "he'll probably cut his own throat in pretrials, making tons of motions." We've got to be allowed time to prepare responses to them, and Terhovian can't object to the time stretching out as long as his own motions are the cause. I shake my head. "No way this trial starts in sixty days."

"What if it does?"

"Then we walk around smiling and bristling with confidence, raring to go, no problems at all, and work twenty hours a day to get there."

"I had a feeling you were going to say that. And speaking of bristling with confidence, I wish I hadn't asked for six months in there. Makes us look weak against Terhovian's two months."

That is true. We shouldn't be doing anything to indicate apprehension on our part, which would hurt our negotiating position in the event of a plea bargain. But Marsha couldn't have known what Terhovian was up to in advance. She thought we were being speedy.

"So what about the pretrials?" she asks. "You'll handle them, right?"

"Right. Not much to prepare. Mostly I just want to see what's on his mind, get an idea of what his defense is likely to be."

Marsha takes a deep breath and lets it out slowly. "I hope we can get him to cop to something. I hate the thought of Diane and Lisa exposed like that."

That makes two of us.

Judge Arigga will be handling the pretrial hearings and motions.

By mutual agreement, owing to the potentially high-profile nature of the case and the willingness of everyone to keep it quiet, this first meeting is to be informal, held in Arigga's chambers. I was surprised by Terhovian's acquiescence in this regard, since the threat of publicity is a standard defense ploy to bully the victims in a sexual assault case, but I elected not to indulge my curiosity and ask him about it for fear of provoking him into a change of heart.

I walk into Room 108 on the first floor of the county building, and am surprised to find it empty except for bailiff Drew Stengel. I'm on time but I know that Terhovian is always several minutes early. Stengel looks up and smiles. "Salvatore, *come sta'*?"

"Bene, grazie; e le?"

Stengel watches a lot of gangster movies, thinks all Italians are mafiosi, which is all right with me because he likes mafiosi, a forgivable lapse of judgment for anyone who has never lived outside of southern California. He's a big man, almost as wide as he is tall, about six-foot-two. For all his physical presence, he is remarkably soft-spoken, one of those rare people in law enforcement so confident of their abilities they see no need to flaunt them. He is affable and menacing, glib and wary, all at the same time, and is one of three bailiffs in this building assigned to courtrooms where the worst, most violent offenders regularly appear. Any notions a suspect might have about starting trouble or escaping are quickly dispelled after a cursory examination of this imposing LA County deputy sheriff.

"Am I the first?" I ask him, walking up the center aisle toward the bar separating the front half of the room from the audience gallery.

"Nope." He jerks his head toward the rear door of the courtroom, the one that leads to a corridor along which all the judges' private offices lie. "Other guy's already here, in chambers."

"Good. When's the boss coming?"

"You mean Judge Arigga? He's already in there."

I come to a stop with my hand on the little gate that allows access to the front. "What do you mean?"

Stengel looks to the right, then back at me, his head cocked at a comical angle. "Uh, how else can I put it?"

"They're in there together?"

This is highly improper. Terhovian and the judge together without me constitutes an *ex parte* conversation, a situation that is presumptively unfair to my side. I see now that, behind his blithe joshing, Stengel looks uncomfortable. He's an experienced hand in the courtroom, probably knows as much about law, or at least procedure, as most of the attorneys who troop through here.

He shrugs, taps the side of his leg. "I started to say something . . . you know . . ." He shrugs again, a gesture of helplessness. What influence does he have with a high-ranking judge, one that also happens to be his boss?

How should I handle this once I get inside? I'd be much better off just forgetting about it. Again I think of DA Beckman's adage about choosing your battles carefully, a sound piece of advice but one to which I have difficulty adhering. Little things tend to annoy the hell out of me and become stones in my shoe, constantly at the forefront of my attention. I decide that the best course of action is to let it drop. With that, I thank Stengel and make my way to Arigga's office.

I knock at the door and enter. Arigga is sitting behind his expansive desk; Terhovian is on a wing chair, his jacket buttoned, his hands lying on the armrests. Both he and Arigga look tense and serious.

I look from one to the other and say, "I take exception to this *ex parte* meeting."

Among my many talents is a particular knack for shooting myself in the foot despite the best intentions, often without my even realizing it is going to happen. Something about engaging my mouth without first putting my brain in gear.

Arigga looks at me for a moment, then creases up his face and flicks his hand to the side. "Oh, relax, Milano; the hell's a matter with you?" He aims an elbow toward Terhovian. "Two old guys shooting the shit, haven't seen each other in months?"

Neither of them looks like one of two great buddies catching up on old times. There is no easy camaraderie in evidence, no slouched and relaxed postures that might indicate idle passing of gossip. Then again, these two are not hail-fellow-well-met types to begin with.

I give the judge a look that is meant to be fraught with meaning, trying to convey that I will be no pushover in these proceedings. Maybe calling him out on a technicality at the very start is not such a bad idea, I tell myself, and then I do let it drop.

I walk to the straight-backed chair directly in front of the desk, unbutton my jacket, and sit down. I ask Terhovian how his son is doing, taking a chance that the rumors about the drug problems are true. He seems visibly startled by the question, then tells me he is doing very well, better than hoped.

"It hasn't been an easy time. And it has taken a lot of mine, I can tell you." He tries to smile at his minor play on words, but there is real pain in his eyes, a good deal more than there should be if things were really going all that well. I suddenly feel ashamed for my glib chastisement of his breach of procedural etiquette, realizing that this troubled soul does not need yet another worry, especially over something so inconsequential.

Terhovian has often struck me as one of those driven, Jekyll-and-Hyde kind of savants you frequently find in the legal world. In the arenas of advocacy jurisprudence, be that a courtroom or a deposition or a hearing, they can stun you with their erudition and eloquence, alternating easily between quiet but damning probing and thunderous oratory brimming with righteous indignation. Their case could be hurtling over an abyss but every mannerism will be communicating that they are seconds away from victory.

Outside the judicial setting, it's another story. Often tongue-tied in social situations, unwilling to involve themselves in confrontations as minor as correcting a restaurant bill, many of these revered litigators have personal lives that lie in ruins around them as they sit, mystified and helpless, wondering in later years what could possibly have gone wrong. I think it is the lack of rules, of regulations and standards and prescriptive doctrine for every conceivable situation, like those you find in the law. The newest, freshest, poorest lawyer can take on an entire suite of high-powered corporate attorneys, all of whom are following the same procedures and operating according to the same laws, and he knows that, generally, if he is right, he stands a chance of prevailing. But in the world of everyday human social intercourse, no such expectation is reasonable. You can begin arguing with the mechanic who just overcharged you for an unnecessary brake job and have all the forces of fact and logic on your side, but at some point he dangles your keys and says pay up or lose it, leaving your airtight thesis in the rubble of his intellectual indifference.

I suspect that something like this may have happened to Gus Terhovian: that while he dazzled them in the courtroom his home life crumbled, and he is desperately hoping that he can make up for all those lost years in just a few short months. However, that doesn't explain why he took on this case.

Arigga lets us talk without interrupting, not even jumping in when it has become clear that we've exhausted as many niceties as two combatants can exchange without the strain becoming too evident. I look at Terhovian and hold out a hand, palm up, then let it drop to my thigh. *So, what's on your mind?* He shifts his gaze to Arigga, who finally gets us to the business at hand.

"You feel you have a pretty strong case, Milano?"

The question catches me off guard. Arigga knows I won't be making any motions. This is Terhovian's show, and he should get the ball rolling. Why start with me?

"About as strong as it can get, your honor." That's all I plan to offer.

He nods, then Terhovian picks it up, his voice reverting back to its legal tenor. "How much do you know about your complainants' pasts?"

I jerk my head around, faster than I would have liked had the movement been entirely voluntary. "What are you talking about, Gus? That kind of thing isn't allowed in evidence in California!"

He knows that, of course, but my response doesn't seem to bother him. "I was just wondering," he says calmly, looking down at the floor, "if you ever asked Lisa Pierman if she was pregnant, out of wedlock."

The dizziness overtakes me so suddenly it is all I can do to just sit still, never mind formulating a coherent response. It's critical that I don't betray any surprise. "I believe my conversations with the complainants are privileged," I manage to get out. I want to get as much information as he has without letting on that I don't have the slightest goddamned idea what he is talking about. It will not do, especially in front of the judge, to reveal that the defense attorney knows more about the victims than I do. "Why are you asking me that? Where's its relevance?"

He refuses to elaborate. "I myself don't know anything of significance in this regard. I merely wanted to know if you asked her the question. As one might, given her, ah . . ." He looks up and rocks his head, as if searching for a polite word for a sordid concept ". . . her reputation, as it were."

Arigga glowers at me as I try to hold myself together, like this was something I should have told him. I force myself to concentrate as Terhovian goes on in his maddeningly calm style.

"Your biggest problem, as I see it," he says, as though he were a professor commenting on a student's preparation for a mock trial, "is that you have no corroborating witnesses."

My head is still reeling from the last blow, so it takes me a moment to try to integrate this one. In this attempt, I fail. "What the hell are you talking about?"

"The sisters, yes, I know." He leans back in the wing chair, rubbing his chin and gazing thoughtfully at the far wall, taking on the look of a friend and colleague who is concerned for my case and wishes only to be of help. "The claim is that they each watched the other's alleged violation. A most repugnant state of affairs, it is true."

There is no need for me to comment. It's only a baldly transparent jab, one he surely doesn't expect will get a rise out of me.

"However . . ." He tears his gaze from the distance and brings himself to sharp focus, slapping both his legs, pursing his lips and looking directly at me. "I am going to file a four-oh-two motion *in limine* to prevent each of the sisters from testifying on behalf of the other."

This instantly relieves my anxiety and makes me chuckle, the absurdity of his remark hastening my return to some semblance of an even keel. "That's rich, counselor. And just how do you plan to argue that one?"

He returns my expression of mirth with an amiable smile of his own, glad to be part of the merriment. "Well, Sal, both of these women claim to have been raped, which prejudices them against the defendant and increases the likelihood that they would lie to get a conviction."

"Yeah . . ." I turn my head slightly so I'm looking at him out of the corner of my eye. "You want to run that one by me slowly?"

"Certainly." If he heard the sarcasm in my voice, he doesn't let on. "Let us suppose that one of them had really been raped. Just hypothetically, all right?"

I wave away his feigned concern that I might take him literally. "Sure, hypothetically."

"Fine. And let us say the other one hadn't. Now: both of these women desperately want the perceived perpetrator put away, and they may not much care about the niceties of exactly how that comes about. Now, look—" He puts his hands to his chest. "Don't misunderstand me. Who could blame them?" He lays one hand back down and shakes an admonishing finger at me with the other. "But the problem is, this raises the possibility of at least one wrongful conviction, even though we mightn't be able to tell which one it was."

I have to smile at this. "So what you're telling me, even if your client really raped one of them, it would be a travesty of justice if he was convicted for the wrong one?"

"Ah! You understand perfectly! Because one of the victims would be lying!"

I'll go along with this for just a little while because it feels so good to get one up on this living legend. "But we're contending they were *both* raped, and we're going to prove it."

"Yes, yes, I quite understand, but you see . . ." He is all academic and helpful again. ". . . your only proof is their testimony. And it is my contention that this testimony is biased in the extreme. There is little question of it. Both sisters are claiming to have been raped. Would they not be prone to fabrication to assure a conviction?" He turns to Arigga. "Based on the case brought by the deputy district attorney, it seems apparent on the face of it that each of these women's testimony is incontestably tainted by their alleged experience with my client."

I feel better about our case already and glance impatiently at my watch. The morning is wearing on and I don't have any more time for this pathetic grasping at straws. "Hey, Gus, why don't you just go ahead and ask for a dismissal, throw the whole damned case out right now? Save us all a lot of time and bother."

Arigga ignores my feeble attempt at wit and says to Terhovian, "Are you making a motion to suppress?"

Terhovian spreads his hands and shrugs. "I am."

I look at the ceiling and exhale loudly. Arigga sticks out his lower lip. "Your response, Mr. Milano?"

"Is one required?"

Arigga sits up straight and rolls his leather chair closer to the desk. "He has made a motion, after all."

"Can't you just rule on it as a matter of law?"

"I'd like to hear your rebuttal."

"Sure. No problem." If Arigga wants to keep this completely kosher, I'm glad to play along. I open my attaché and withdraw a manila folder, holding it up in the air and then dropping it square on the desk. "First of all, who said anything about multiple rape charges? I don't see Diane Pierman's name anywhere on the information."

Arigga lets the document lie where I dropped it. "Aren't you planning to file additional charges?"

I am forced to admit that I might. "But we haven't perfected those yet."

"Then don't play games, Mr. Milano!" Arigga slaps his hand down on the desk. "Are you planning to file an additional rape charge for the other sister or not?"

I'm staring at him and have to force myself to respond, as calmly as I can. "We are planning to file an additional rape charge, yes."

"For the other sister?"

"Yes."

"Well." He sits back, takes off his glasses and begins wiping them with his tie. "That's better. Now that we're putting the bullshit aside, what is your response to defense counsel's motion?"

He's really going to make me do this. "Defense is arguing that there might be bias attached to each complainant's testimony. Maybe. But that is something for a jury to decide, as it always is. There is no precedent for the exclusion of damaging testimony by an involved eyewitness."

"An eyewitness who is also a victim," Terhovian throws in. "An alleged victim."

"Well if she's so goddamned *alleged*," I say, unable to keep the anger out of my voice, "then why would she be mad at your client?"

Terhovian remains unruffled. "Because, as I stated in my previous hypothetical, the other one may be a *real* victim, and this would incline her sister toward perjury."

"You telling me your client really raped one of them?"

"Don't be absurd."

I turn back to Arigga. I'm under no obligation to speak directly with Terhovian; argument is before and to the judge. "Like I said, there's no reason to preempt the jury's right to hear the testimony and let them decide. If defense counsel wants to try to impeach the testimony, let him."

"Yes, but I have a duty to see that raw emotionalism doesn't get in the way of a search for truth."

I don't believe I'm hearing this. "Fine. I'll split this into two trials and mention only one rape in each one of them." I sit back on my chair and fold my arms across my chest, an unfortunately juvenile display of petulance but one I can't help.

"No, you won't. The accused has the right to have such

tightly related cases tried together." Obviously, Arigga has already thought of that one. "I'm not going to let you test out your strategies in one trial and then readjust them in the second, not when the fact patterns in both are identical."

I feel myself slipping inexorably toward that chasm in which I make immature and uncontrollable errors of the most egregious sort, just because I'm mad and it feels good. "So what are you telling me, judge; I should drop all the charges?"

"No," Arigga answers, drawing out the word slowly as though this preposterous suggestion might have merited some serious consideration. "But you might consider dropping the rape charge, just go with kidnapping and a few other things."

He mistakes my shocked speechlessness for thoughtful deliberation and goes on. "Those might be shown to have happened for sure to both sisters, whereas rape can't. If I grant the motion to suppress, that is."

My father's best friend, a Jewish tailor and a Talmudic scholar with a shop across the street from the bakery, used to say that ten wise men cannot retrieve a stone thrown into a well by a single idiot. I feel that I am about to do something equally irrevocable, like ask this judge how he is enjoying his first trip to our galaxy. I am that close. It's so ridiculous I don't even know where to begin arguing. In my evolving state of confusion, I am unwilling to commit to anything. I just feel an overwhelming urge to get out of here, to breathe some fresh air, to consult with Marsha, to just think for a few uninterrupted minutes.

I clear my throat and nod, as though I were considering his suggestion. "I need to go off and make some decisions. A lot's gone on here." Not the least of which is Terhovian's bombshell concerning Lisa's impending motherhood.

Arigga narrows his eyes and regards me with disdain. "Now see here, Milano: you promised Judge Goldman a speedy trial when he denied bail!"

I have no choice but to admit we made this commitment.

"I don't take such promises lightly," he admonishes me sternly. "We got a crowded calendar and I don't like people willy-nilly clogging it up."

It's not your *goddamned calendar,* I want to tell him,

since he won't be the judge hearing the case—thank God—but some still-operative sense of self-preservation bids me hold my tongue.

Terhovian stirs in his seat. He's been silent for some minutes. "I am not troubled by this failure to come to a conclusion at this first meeting, your honor." He should be gloating but instead seems dispassionate, almost remote from these proceedings, and anxious to terminate them. "Might I suggest that the deputy DA go off and think about it, and we can meet again? Soon," he adds.

Arigga glares at me a moment longer and then sits back. "That okay with you, Mr. Milano?"

Like I have a choice. I rise to leave and make sure that Terhovian does so at the same time. I'm already late for a scheduled meeting of head deputies throughout the county, but I'm damned if I'll leave these two old cronies alone together again to smirk about how tough they're making my life.

What a joy to congregate with my brothers and sisters in the employ of the elected district attorney, especially as an election year approaches. Two hours spent in the company of a guest lecturer instructing us in how to conduct ourselves in the public eye in such a manner that the sensitivity of our boss is seen to drip down into the ranks. We are no longer to say "substance abuse" but "the abuse of alcohol and other drugs," so that we don't inadvertently convey the impression that alcohol is any less a drug than heroin. Do not refer to "youth at risk" for drugs or other things because the implication is that such risk is inherent in the subject, namely the youth. Rather, speak of "youth in high-risk environments," thus underscoring the current fashion that absolves all individuals of any responsibility for their actions. This morning over coffee I read in the *Times* about a guitarist for a major rock band who sued the group after the statute of limitations for doing so had expired, contending that he was unable to bring the case earlier because of debilitating childhood abuse that had rendered him passive. I thought that was funny as hell until I got to this meeting.

If my mood was dark and distracted before this political circle jerk, it is positively foul now. I don't even bother to check in for messages on my car phone on the way back to Santa Monica, preferring to stew in my vexation without disruption. I make my way through the lamentably necessary indignity of the metal detector that guards the front entrance to the county building. My badge sets it off as usual, and as usual, I'm waved through anyway, as are all recognized employees. Then it's up the stairs to our offices on the second floor. They are right next to those of the public defender: saves a lot of steps as we bargain over the lives of every felony defendant on the west side of town.

Marion is waiting for me as I stride into the anteroom outside my office. She stands quickly, takes my briefcase, helps me off with my jacket, and asks if I would like a cup of coffee. Marion and I are a wonderful team with deep mutual respect for each other's jobs, but it is impossible to describe how utterly out of character these actions of hers are.

"Oh, for Chrissakes, Marion—what could possibly be this wrong?"

"Sure you don't want that coffee? Bourbon on ice? Back rub?"

"No, just hit me with it."

I rub my face with both hands, hard, up and down several times, and go into my own office and sit down on one of the chairs facing my desk. Marion hands me a yellow message slip. It says *Call Marsha* and the urgent box is circled with red ink. I look up at Marion. "What." It is not a question but a demand to tell me what's going on.

She backs off and makes as if to run. "Rosamund is out on bail."

I stare at her stupidly.

Marion is in her late sixties, a grandmother six times over, a great-grandmother twice. She passed the mandatory retirement age several years ago, and I called in every chip I had to make it possible for her to stay. Not only is she the best partner I could possibly have, but I'm certain she would wither and die if forced to accede to the state's official opinion that she is no longer capable of being useful and productive.

"What the hell happened?" I manage to croak, ignoring her stab at lightening the blow.

She walks back in and sits down opposite me. "I got a call from one-oh-eight in superior while you were in the meeting downtown. They said hell or high water somebody better get down there, so I called Marsha. The rest you better get from her."

I slump back on my chair and stare again at the message slip. Marion gets up, goes out, and comes back a few seconds later with a cup of hot coffee, which I can tell by the smell she just brewed up fresh. "If you're thinking of jumping, just remember it's only two stories high," she says, heading for the door and closing it behind her. I hear some muffled words and then my phone rings. I take a deep breath and stretch across my desk to get it.

"She's on," Marion says, and then there is a click. She placed the call for me.

"You heard," Marsha says.

"I heard. So?"

"Arigga's clerk called. Terhovian wanted to make a new bail motion now that we're in superior, so I said fine, schedule it, and he said, it is scheduled, it's now, and I say, where's defense counsel? and he says, about eight feet away and if you don't get somebody down here to argue it, your guy is out the door."

"So you went."

"No, I told him to stuff it. Of course I went. I'm there about ten seconds and Arigga tells me it's unfair to deny bail completely. He says there's no record of violent crime, no examples of prior flight, so what amount am I seeking?"

"What the hell are you talking about? Did you even hear the—"

"Yeah, yeah, just listen for a second. So I say to him, 'Hold it, is there, like, a motion somewhere?' And he says, 'Yes, defense counsel has made a motion,' and I say, 'Great, do I get to hear it or what?' "

I think back to Arigga's conduct in our pretrial meeting just a few hours before. "How come you're not in jail on contempt?"

"Beats me. He gives me this look could freeze my testicles if I had any, but the room is full of people and I'm in the right on this one. So he tells Terhovian to make it again and Terhovian says, 'There is no record of violent crime, no examples of prior flight . . .' Arigga's exact words, for Pete's sake!"

More like the other way around. "Then what?"

She sighs audibly. "What the hell could I do, Sal? I take out the bail schedule and I start doubling everything on it in my mind, figuring we got some special circumstances here, same shit we gave 'em in muni court. 'A million dollars,' I say."

"And Terhovian doesn't even blink, right?"

"You ever seen him blink? 'And on what do you base this request, Madame Deputy?' he says to me. 'Madame deputy,' my black ass! 'Let's start with a hundred fifty thousand on kidnapping for purpose of felony sexual offense,' I say, and he holds up his own copy of the bail schedule, says it's only a hundred grand."

"He had the old one."

"Yeah! I hold up mine and tell Arigga there is a corrected version, 'drafted by you yourself, your honor,' and I hand it to Terhovian." She lets out a gleeful cackle but it quickly dies away. " 'Is that all, *Ms.* Jones?' he says." She pronounces "Ms." like it had seven zs, highlighting Arigga's apparent disdain for her little triumph.

As much as I appreciate her urge to vent, I need for her to get to the end of this. "So what'd you go for?"

"I threw in the rape, of course"—which is only good for fifty grand, she doesn't bother to remind me—"use of a firearm during a felonious sexual act and a bunch of other garbage, eventually got it up to half a mill, and demanded it be doubled. Terhovian says Rosamund may not have ties in the LA area but he does in Bakersfield, strong roots and all that crap . . ." Her voice trails off.

"What'd you say?"

She clears her throat. "I said, 'Strong roots in what, the Medellín cartel?' "

I try to stifle a laugh but am only half successful. It was a stupid thing for her to do. I know, because it's the kind of thing I might have done myself, and ought not to be encouraged. "So Arigga gave him what, the five hundred thou?"

"Uh-huh. He posted bond less than an hour later."

That part stuns me more than the rest. "Where in the

hell did he get that kind of scratch? Did you file a twelve-seventy-five?"

"While I was standing there." We have the right to discover the source of the funds, which is what a 1275 motion is supposed to do. Marsha tells me the money came from a professional bail bondsman.

"I figured that much. What else?"

"We're working on it. I asked Marty to check it out."

This will not happen quickly. While we also have the right to know what the defendant put up as collateral for the bond, it can be a long, drawn-out process. We have to call witnesses, which can include the bail bondsman himself. The purpose of the law is to ensure that the funds came from a lawful source, but I'm less interested in that than in knowing whether Rosamund is really being backed by a drug syndicate. There's a slight chance we might be able to use that against him, at least in a bail revocation hearing. We may not be able to get it into the actual trial.

"It could happen sooner than you think," Marsha is saying. "Marty's done this before. He goes to the bail guy and says, 'You want to take some time out from work and appear as a witness or you just want to tell me now and get it over with?' One way or the other the guy has to 'fess up, so he might as well just tell him."

"Unless there's serious muscle behind the money and he's scareder of them than of us."

"Let's let Marty worry about that." I don't want to hear the rest. However it turns out, there is nothing I can add that Marty will not already have thought of. Something else is troubling me more than that.

"Sal, you still there?"

My mind has begun to wander and her voice snaps me back. "Yeah."

"Sorry to hit you with it all at once like that. But that's how it hit me." She had misunderstood the reason for my side trip into outer space. My turn to hit her one.

"That's not it. You know the pretrial this morning?"

"Just gonna ask you about that. How'd it go?"

"I'll tell you later, but here's the thing: remember we promised Goldman a speedy trial, no delays?"

"Course I do."

"Arigga reminded me of that this morning, and I couldn't say anything because it was true. But the damned thing is—"

She doesn't wait for me to finish. "That was in return for Goldman denying bail."

"Right. But with Rosamund out on bail, who gives a shit about speed? The defendant isn't suffering; there's no denial of due process; Arigga's got no beef, right?"

"Yeah, so . . . ?"

"So I'll bet you anything that bastard knew Terhovian was going to make a new bail motion as soon as we got out of that meeting, and that he was going to release Rosamund a few hours later. And he went ahead and gave me shit about a fast trial anyway!"

Marsha isn't buying into my paranoia so fast. "How could he have known Terhovian was going to go for new bail?"

"Start with the fact that they were chatting each other up when I walked into chambers."

The reference to a highly improper *ex parte* conversation gets her attention. "You serious?"

"Completely."

"Did you say something?"

"Yeah. He rammed it back down my throat, like I was some kind of whiny school kid."

"Well this is just fucking swell, Sal. On top of everything else, the defense counsel is right up the judge's ass." It takes a bit to bring out the longshoreman in Marsha, and I have to remind myself that, of the two of us, it is my responsibility to see that our indignation does not carry us over some dangerous cliff. Both of us have already given vent to our frustration in front of the judge, and we're going to have to check this tendency if we're to bring this matter to a satisfactory conclusion.

There's a knock at my door and it opens, Marty's face peering at me inquiringly. I wave him in and he takes a seat in front of my desk. But I'm not through with this phone call yet. "There's one more thing, Marsha."

"There can't be."

I tell her about Terhovian's intimation that Lisa is wanton and pregnant, and Marsha is near speechless. "I think I'm gonna be sick," she groans, meaning it.

"Don't panic. Call her and ask her."

"I will. It's horseshit. I guarantee it." The wavering voice doesn't match the confident words.

There's no time to worry about that right now: we have a problem concerning the likelihood of Arigga, as improbable as it may sound, disallowing each of the sisters to testify on the other's behalf. I shudder at the thought of filing a pretrial appeal of such a decision to the appellate court and would much prefer to find a less visible and belligerent way out of the predicament.

"We still on for tomorrow?" Marsha asks. Today is December 22, a Thursday, and I sense some hopefulness in her voice that we might yet be able to take off the Friday before Christmas Sunday, but we cannot.

"No way around it. Maybe we can knock off by lunch."

There is little conviction in my voice as I say it and hang up. I take a deep breath and lean back in my chair, looking at Marty. "You got bad news, I don't want to hear it."

He shakes his head. "Nah. Just a story."

"I'm in no mood for stories."

"This one doesn't go with milk and cookies."

Vincent Rosamund sat uneasily on the vinyl chair. Then he stood up, paced back and forth a few steps, sat down again and lit another in an endless succession of filterless cigarettes. He glanced at his watch, hoping against hope that the minute hand had not advanced appreciably since the last time he'd looked at it, which was about a minute ago.

There was only one flight out of Maracaibo to Houston, a vestige of the days when that Texas city flew high on oil, and traffic between there and Venezuela had been thick with overfed tycoons making deals. Now the plane carried mostly drilling-rig roustabouts hustling any jobs they could find, and the little airport had fallen into disrepair, making it no place for a well-dressed guy like himself to be hanging out, especially not when he was carrying bags filled with $20 million of the purest possible heroin.

He'd driven nonstop from Bogota in order to avoid

landing in the U.S. on a flight that originated in Colombia and he was goddamned if he was going to sit in this shithole overnight because Enrico couldn't follow a simple plan. Of course, exactly what Vinny was going to do about it was unclear.

Four men walked in through the creaking double doors at the far end of the waiting area, and Vinny tensed reflexively at the sight of the three uniforms. They were talking and laughing, though, and the fourth man was Enrico, so Vinny forced himself to stay seated and tried not to look in their direction.

He uncrossed his legs as the group approached, then watched, disbelieving, as they passed him by, Enrico practically rubbing against his leg but not even glancing at him.

"Hey!" he started to say as he began to rise, but a single, murderous backward glance from his contact pushed him back into his seat and he turned his head away, jaw hanging open, not knowing what to do next. The four men disappeared around a corner.

Vinny blinked a few times, put his elbows on his knees and bent over with a grunt, then spotted the brown envelope on his carry-on that hadn't been there before. He picked it up and opened it to find a U.S. passport, its cover grimy and worn from heavy use. He opened it and found a picture, smiling brightly and innocently back at him, and flipped through the inside pages, which were covered with a multitude of customs stamps from around the world. He smiled and turned back to the picture, to the right of which was stamped his name beneath protective, forgery-proof plastic: Samuel Geoffrey Pendleton. Same name as on his airline tickets, driver's license and credit cards.

He slipped the passport into his jacket pocket, picked up the carry-on bag, headed for the gate and was soon settled into his coach seat. During the flight to Houston, he forced himself against all instinct to behave, and even refrained from annoying the flight attendants, normally one of his favorite in-flight activities.

* * *

He wished he'd dressed differently. Sitting in coach was a good touch, but here in baggage retrieval in Houston even his plain tan slacks and gray jacket stood out among the jeans, denim vests and cowboy hats. What the hell: no sense worrying about what he couldn't change. There was plenty of other stuff to worry about.

He walked away from the working stiffs crowded around the baggage carousel and made his way to a pay phone. He dialed a number using coins rather than a credit card, had a few words with somebody on the other end, then held a memo recorder up to the handset, smiling in satisfaction as he listened. It only took about ten seconds; then he hung up with no further conversation and went back to the carousel.

His single suitcase appeared after about fifteen minutes. He tried to be as casual as possible in picking it up and carrying it to the customs area, but his aplomb threatened to abandon him as he scanned the blue-uniformed officials manning the inspection workstations: the face he was looking for wasn't among them.

He took a few steps backward, as though he had forgotten something, and pretended to scan the carousel again, taking up a position where he could keep an eye on the inspection stations. He didn't have much time: if he appeared to keep a watchful eye on the carousel and then emerged without an additional bag, some pain-in-the-ass security type might get suspicious. He went back to the phone and pretended to make another call, then walked slowly back to his suitcase and looked out again. The guy he was looking for was just coming through the door, toothpick sticking out of his mouth, and he stood by a workstation as another official finished with a passenger. Then he took over the station, relieving the original blue uniform, and smiled at the next passenger. Vinny got in line for that station, turning down an offer from a leather-faced cowboy to join him in a shorter one.

Vinny watched carefully as Elroy "Lucky" Peterson

processed passengers through customs. He was at least sixty and had nearly forty years in the service. Another seventeen months and he'd retire on full pay. Vinny knew a lot about Lucky Peterson. He watched as the old man smiled at the passengers, made friendly conversation, and seemed almost apologetic whenever he decided he needed to look into a bag. Vinny couldn't discern a pattern to his decisions but knew with a near certainty his own bags were unlikely to escape scrutiny.

Finally, it was his turn. He dropped the carry-on onto the belt and then hoisted the suitcase up, trying to look as nonchalant and unconcerned as he could. "How you doin'?" he asked the customs man.

Peterson smiled. "Just fine, sir. And yourself?" He ignored the bags and took Vinny's customs declaration, looking it over as Vinny answered.

"Real good. Glad to be back home, know what I mean?"

"Yep, sure do. Nothing to declare, Mr. Pendleton?"

"No sir. Dirty underwear's about all," he chuckled, or tried to. Chuckling did not come easily to Vincent Rosamund.

"All righty, let's have a look at this'un here." Peterson tapped the top of the large suitcase.

Vinny made no move to open it. He leaned in close to Peterson and said quietly, "Rather you didn't have a look in there, Lucky."

Peterson's eyes grew wide at hearing his nickname from this total stranger. He blinked several times in confusion. "Come again?"

"Just kinda rather you let me pass on through, stamp whatever you gotta stamp."

"'Fraid I don't quite getcha. Can't do that, sir, you got to open this here—"

Vinny leaned in yet closer and tried to hold Peterson's eyes with his own. "Lemme make this real clear, Lucky. You got a granddaughter, cute little twelve-year-old. Name's Angela, right? They call her Ange."

Peterson's brow knit in confusion. "The hell are you talkin' about, Mister?"

"I'm talkin' about *we* got her now. I'm talkin' about, you let me through without raisin' a ruckus, and your son gets her back."

The old man's breathing speeded up, and a thin line of sweat began to form on his upper lip. "Bullshit," he managed to rasp.

"Bullshit?" Vinny liked this part, liked watching the awful fear in the man's eyes. "Me, I like that cute freckle she's got on her little apple dumpling tit. Lemme see now—" Vinny held his hands up in the air, forming cups with each one. He looked from one to the other, then wiggled the fingers of the right one. "That'd be the left, eh?" He dropped his hands and leaned in close again, waiting for a response.

"I said bullshit." This time there was less conviction in the man's voice.

Vinny pulled the memo recorder out of his jacket pocket and held it up to Peterson's ear, clicking it on with the volume low, and played back what he'd recorded off the phone ten minutes ago. At the sound of his granddaughter's hysteria-tinged, pleading voice, Peterson began to shake and leaned against the belt to steady himself.

Vinny pulled the machine away, loving the look of abject terror in the man's eyes. "And right now she's not getting her asthma medicine, so you smile—I said smile, goddammit!"

Peterson smiled as best he could.

"There you go. Now you take that envelope sticking out of the bag. That's it. Ten grand for your trouble, Lucky, and stamp my little piece of paper there. Okay, now we're getting square here."

Barely able to control his trembling fingers, Peterson handed the customs declaration back to Vinny.

"Good boy, Lucky. You be cool, and just keep doing your job until your shift ends, and if everything goes right, little Ange'll be home for dinner." He hoisted the carry-on onto his shoulder, then picked the suitcase up off the belt. "Anything goes wrong, anything at all, and I swear to Christ the little cunt comes back to you minus her right arm. You understand what I'm telling you?"

Peterson looked like he was going to pass out, but he nodded, unable even to throw in a last-ditch plea for his granddaughter's safety. He watched helplessly as "Mr. Pendleton" sauntered over to passport control, where he spent less than a minute having his passport number punched into the State Department's international computer system. It came back clean.

Vinny rented a car and drove it to Los Angeles, where he turned over the goods without ever having his face seen in a California airport.

I stared at Marty for a few seconds, disbelieving. "Where'd you get this?"

"Feds, strictly on the QT. You can't use it. Just wanted you to know what kind of boy you're dealing with. What was that you called him once . . . ?"

"A sociopath. How'd he get a clean passport?"

Marty sneers at my naiveté. "We're talking billions of dollars in this business, Sal, not just millions. My guess, he got it from some friggin' clerk right in the State Department."

I nod in understanding. "They're bringing in twenty million in pure H, that's what? Sixteen in profit?"

"Minimum. So they hand some low-level bureaucrat fifty grand to produce a clean passport, number in the system and everything, and it's more than the guy pulls down in a year. What's a few hundred Gs in expenses to Sylvester Pontanegro, he's making that kind of net? Rosamund gets maybe a hundred, plus all the snow he can trim."

A little bit out of each of fifty or so plasticine bags. Not a bad week's work. I shake my head, trying to clear it. "Pontanegro," I mutter reflectively, then say to Marty, "When'd this all happen?"

"He got back to LA the same day he raped the twins."

I squeeze my eyes shut and tilt my head back. "You mean he was in The Alley celebrating?"

"Probably. Did a few lines, thought he could take on the whole world and never get caught."

"Well, I guess it kind of explains why Pontanegro finds him so valuable, even if he acts like a cheap slimeball sometimes. How come a guy like him, that much juice upstairs, he deals blow in a bar?"

It isn't about the money, Marty explains to me. It's about a kind of social acceptance. For all his bravado and daring, Vincent Rosamund is still pond scum to the kind of people who frequent The Alley. Maybe he feels that by being a supplier to the tony set, he becomes a part of them. Who really knows what goes through the mind of a psychopath?

"The little girl okay?"

Marty shrugs. "If you don't count the nightmares. Peterson turned the money over as soon as he knew his granddaughter was safe, gave up all the details."

"So why don't the feds get Peterson in for an ID and have a go at Rosamund, too?"

"Too scared. For his grandkid. Says he'd rather spend the rest of his life in prison than cross those people."

I try to picture the terrified old man, turning in the money so he can't be accused of complicity but steadfastly refusing to make an identification out of raw fear of retribution from an organization that could pull something like that. "And this is typical Rosamund?"

"Nope. This was one of the milder ones. Usually he just blows stuff up. There's no question he's gonna get himself killed someday. Best favor you could do him, get a conviction and put him away where he'll be safe."

Sounds like a plan.

7

I usually enjoy working around the holidays. Things get a little slower, less frantic, many people take a few days off, and it's almost pleasant to come into the office. Mostly what we do are new arraignments, since shoppers laden with holiday spending money bring out the worst among the predatory elements, and arraignments are fairly routine affairs requiring little effort. People seem to be nicer around the county building as well. Thank God they only have to endure the strain for a few weeks each year.

Early on this Friday morning, at seven o'clock, we are going to have a case strategy meeting with all the players. Nestor Parnell, managing partner of Diane's law firm, Marchetti, Parnell & Kozinski, has invited us to his offices to get us out of the courthouse maelstrom so we can concentrate undisturbed. Diane has requested that Parnell be present, and I have no problem with that. I've known him since I came to California, and I like him very much. He's tried to recruit me to the firm many times, and it's becoming a running joke with us. The fact that he is one of the best-known criminal defense attorneys in town doesn't trouble me either: there is no friend like an enemy temporarily in your own camp. He's passed some oblique hints that he could round up support for a campaign if I chose to run, and I chided him for assuming that the support of prominent defense attorneys would stand a DA candidate in good stead. It would be like the Tobacco

Council endorsing someone for surgeon general: suspicious in the extreme.

I'm waiting in the outer lobby for Marsha and Marty. The receptionist has told me that Diane and Lisa are already inside. It gives me a chance to look around, to imagine what it must be like to work for an outfit like this.

My office in Santa Monica could charitably be described as functional. As head deputy, I'm one of the few prosecutors to rate a private office, but my furnishings consist primarily of what I was able to scrounge during my years coming up through the ranks, plus what of my predecessor's I retained when he moved over to the fed. My desk is a government-issue metal-top with hospital green sides, and my wooden roll-around desk chair is redeemed only by a fabric-cushion affair I found at a flea market. The two credenzas are in slightly different styles, one being neopenal, the other classical depression era. All in all, it looks like the kind of eclectic taste to be found in a college dorm furnished by the student's mother from the family basement on Long Island.

Things are a little bit different here at Marchetti, Parnell & Kozinski. The receptionist's chair alone easily cost more than everything in my office put together. Her wraparound desk sports no manufacturer's label anywhere because it was custom hand crafted, of mahogany, and it sits on the edge of a ten-by-fourteen Persian rug, which itself rests on a hardwood floor of dark cherry. The floor is offset by rich wainscoting of a deeply grained wood that looks like teak, all softly lit by recessed overhead lamps in brass fixtures. The two Chesterfield couches along the walls opposite the reception desk are of burgundy leather and sit under the obligatory corporate art, which in this case consists of a Hockney print and a Laddie John Dill stone and acrylic number.

There is a Christmas tree in the corner beyond the two couches. It's a beauty, a Douglas fir, and so perfectly symmetrical it could have been made by hand. As I draw nearer, I see that it was. The decorations are perfect, too, the colored glass globe ornaments evenly spaced both horizontally and vertically, garland strands arcing down gently between the branches, colored acrylic figures placed just so on every third branch. There is a small, candy-striped tag hanging off the lowest limb. I bend to read the calligraphic lettering, "Professionally trimmed by Santa's Little Helpers—Brentwood, CA" along with a phone number. In this position I notice that there are several dozen small boxed presents under the tree, and I wonder when they are to be opened, seeing that this is the last working day before the holiday. I turn to see the receptionist on the phone, facing the other direction, and I pick up one of the boxes, then another. They are all empty.

"Stealing Christmas presents again, are we?" I straighten up awkwardly, startled by the loud voice, which is Marsha's. Marty is with her, rubbing one forefinger over the other and clucking his tongue as they step off the elevator that opens right into the reception area. Then he stops to look around.

"Looks a lot like your offices, Sal."

"Yeah. Same number of walls and everything. Shall we?"

"Hang on a second." Marsha motions me over to the couches and we take seats sideways, facing each other, Marty standing in the middle.

"I spoke with Lisa," she says, then proceeds quickly as she sees my face begin to blanch. "When she was able to pick herself up off the floor, she told me that not only was she not pregnant, she's been working so hard she hasn't been with a man in over a year, not even a serious date. She gave me permission to speak to some of the people in her firm, and they said her involuntary celibacy was a running joke in the company. Her last birthday, one of the guys bakes up an angel food penis with ice cream balls, gives it to her at the party in the office. 'Looks vaguely familiar,' she says."

"You believe her?"

"Hunnerd percent." She looks up at Marty, who nods.

I slump back on the couch. "So what in the hell was Terhovian talking about?"

Marsha shakes her head. "Lisa has no idea how a rumor like that could possibly have gotten started. I also talked to the bartender at The Alley, said he's seen every type there is, and these two are about as lascivious as his grandmother."

"Tell you what I think," Marty says. "I think he was playing with your head, boy-o."

I see that now. "I think you're right."

Marty starts shrugging off his topcoat, really just the outer shell of an ancient London Fog, about the only kind of coat you need in Los Angeles. "You come into the meeting for some heavy-duty negotiating, the old fox throws a few wooden shoes into your machinery, shake you up before you start."

That is exactly what happened. "He did it in front of the judge, too."

"What I'm betting, he didn't say it so much as ask if it was true, am I right? Didn't commit himself?"

"Then you better straighten it out in front of the judge," Marsha says, not waiting for me to answer Marty's question because she can tell from my face that he's right, that I got badly snookered.

"Important thing is," Marty says, "we can get a hundred character witnesses to swear they're practically Snow White, so let 'em fling whatever shit they want at us."

Marsha pats my arm. "He's right. Christ, these two are even friendly with their old boyfriends. I get cavities just listening to them."

I'm barely listening, trying to get a grip on my anger. Not at Terhovian, for pulling a sophomoric stunt like that, but at myself for falling for it. I'm going to need a way to smack him back in front of the judge, make Arigga understand that he, too, was the dupe of a dubious dirty trick.

Or am I being unnecessarily vengeful and losing sight of the goal? It happened in front of the judge, not the jury. It doesn't count. Terhovian would never dare do such a thing in court because it would backfire badly, so why dwell on it? I am proud of this cool reasoning and ashamed of how little difference it makes in how I feel. If I had more self-possession, this anger would now be transmuting itself into an even greater desire to win this case rather than just a wish for some transitory revenge.

"Either of you read the paper this morning?" I ask.

Neither has, but Marsha has a copy in her briefcase. She takes it out and hands it to me, and I open it to the front page of the metro section and turn it around for them both to see, Marty bending down over Marsha's shoulder.

The lead headline reads, SUSPECT CHARGED IN RAPE OF PROMINENT WESTSIDE TWIN SISTERS. It is over Eleanor Torjan's byline.

Marsha reads it over again, her expression a mixture of disbelief and anger. A tone sounds from the receptionist's phone. Marsha looks up at me then back down at the headline, then back at me. "How the hell'd this happen, Sal? I thought—"

"Would you care to go in now?" the receptionist intones brightly, phone at her shoulder. Marsha appears not to hear her, but Marty holds up a forefinger at her, indicating she should wait, and throws his own questioning look at me.

"Through that door," the receptionist says, pointing. She is more concerned about the boss being kept waiting than deferring to Marty. "Turn right, last office at the end. And Merry Christmas."

"Merry Christmas," we all mumble as we exit the lobby area and begin shuffling our way down the long corridor.

Marsha is still holding the paper but now quickly stuffs it back into her bag as we spy Lisa sitting on a love seat up ahead. As we approach, we see that she has a newspaper in one trembling hand, the other holding a tissue to her face. She turns at the sound of our approach, tightens her fist so it crumples the edges of the paper, then turns away again.

"Lisa—" I start to say.

"You said you could keep this out, Sal!" There is anger and bitterness in her voice, which is choked and strained from recent crying.

"I tried as best I could." There's no sense explaining that I have no control over these things, that all I could do was call in some favors and extract some promises.

"What happened?" she whimpers, turning back to me, lifting the paper then dropping it back down heavily. I can see Marsha and Marty have the same question.

I reach for Lisa's hand and start to gently urge her up. "Let's go inside and I'll tell you." We walk through the open door into the anteroom, and the secretary points to Nestor Parnell's closed door. I knock and open it.

It is palatial, a "corner" office that is really at an apex

of the triangle-shaped building, on the forty-fifth floor. It affords a sweeping panorama that stretches practically from the desert all the way to the ocean and points north. Professionally decorated in dark-stained hardwoods, two oriental rugs, enough chairs and couches to seat ten comfortably without even using the six-place conference table in one corner, green baize wall covering and incandescent rather than fluorescent lights, it is every ambitious lawyer's dream of ultimate success. I could spend my life in this room.

Diane is on a straight-backed chair staring vacantly out the window to the sea, Parnell standing a few feet away from her, where he has just turned to see us. His face is grim as he walks forward to shake hands. "Milano."

"Hello, Nestor. Diane?"

She turns as Marty and Marsha make their greetings to Parnell, rises and walks forward, pointing toward the paper clutched in Lisa's hand. "Great start to the day, that."

Parnell motions everyone to seats on one side of the office. "What happened, Sal?"

"I got a call from Eleanor early this morning." Actually, it was late last night but as is my habit on occasion, I turned off the phone ringer in my bedroom and let the answering machine take over. If it were anything urgent, I would get a beeper message, and that I keep on the bed stand. I got Eleanor's message and retrieved the paper from outside the door before phoning her back.

"She told me it was going to run and I started to tear her head off, but she said she'd found out the *Daily News* was printing it this morning." It goes without saying that once any paper picks it up, she is no longer bound to our pact.

"How'd they get it?" Parnell asks.

"Well, they always had it; they just agreed to hold off for a while."

"What changed their minds?" Marsha wants to know.

"Have you read it?" I ask Parnell.

He nods. "Have to admit it's pretty fair." He looks over at Lisa. "Considering. They didn't mention your names."

"Yeah." Diane slaps the arm of her chair several times. "It could be any pair of twenty-nine-year-old twin sisters from the west side, one a lawyer, the other a caterer."

"The quote from Gus Terhovian, I mean." I reach for Marsha's bag, and she takes the paper out and hands it to me. I open to the continuation on page seven and start to read out loud, then think better of it and hand it to Parnell, pointing to a particular paragraph.

"This is a ridiculous case that never should have been brought," said noted defense attorney Gustave Terhovian, retained on behalf of the suspect. "If a woman can yell rape after every spat following casual and consensual sex, it makes a mockery of our legal system. It is unbelievable that the prosecutor would stoop to this kind of harassment because he doesn't like the looks of my client."

"Why no quotes from you?" Parnell asks when he has finished reading.

"She tried but couldn't get hold of me." I see a look of doubt creep into Parnell's eyes. "It's true; it was on my machine." I think I can sense Diane wondering where I spent the night, and it suddenly becomes important that I tell her I was home with the phone turned off. I likely would not have supplied a quote anyway, given the awful drubbing I got from Beckman the last time I ventured a choice observation or two to the press.

"You got any java?" Marty asks deftly, breaking the uncomfortable silence.

"Damn!" Parnell says, rising. "There was supposed to be a whole bunch of stuff. Let me go see."

"I'll go with you," I say. I don't like the idea of leaving the other four alone, but I want to talk to Parnell for a second.

We step into his secretary's office and close the door behind us. A steward is already rolling in a breakfast cart, but Parnell holds up his hand. "Thanks, Alonzo. I'll get it from here."

"They take it hard?" I ask when the steward is gone.

Parnell turns toward the door to his office, as if he could see through it. "I called Diane; she wanted to stay in bed and never get out. I told her to get the hell up and into the office."

"She doesn't look so good," I observe.

"Yeah, but that's mostly anger. Anger is good." He idly fingers the plastic wrapping on the breakfast cart. "Wish Lisa would come around a little. She's really bent out of shape."

"What's your role here, Parnell? I mean, I appreciate the nice digs and all—"

"Moral support," he says. "She's a valued colleague, could even run this place someday. And, frankly"—he looks at me without guile or sarcasm—"to make sure you handle this right."

I think I surprise the hell out of him when I tell him that I appreciate his help, and mean it. His features instantly soften and he backtracks from whatever speech he had prepared when he thought I was going to argue with him.

"Look, you're the prosecutor; I'm not going to interfere. That's not what I meant. I just figured, me being on the other side of the fence, maybe I could help you figure out—"

"Nestor, anything you can do, I'll be grateful. I just want the sonofabitch to go down."

I look carefully for his reaction to my emotional disparagement of a criminal defendant. Parnell has made a fortune defending such types as Rosamund and defending them in the press as well. I am curious how he will respond to assisting in a prosecution, how he feels when someone he cares about deeply is the victim of someone who could easily have been his client.

His eyes tell me that he is more acutely aware of the contradictions inherent in this situation than I am. And I know in that moment that, no matter how much help he is, no matter how much of an influence he has on our winning the case, nobody outside of our small circle will ever hear about it. My office will get all the credit because the last thing in this world Nestor Parnell wants is any notoriety associated with putting a defendant in jail. I also realize the depth of his commitment to Diane, placing his reputation in this much jeopardy, and I am sorry I tested it with my ill-considered and profane expression of venom. Then I wonder if he maybe has some kind of a thing for Diane, and then I wonder if I am doing too much damned wondering altogether.

"Sure could use some of that coffee. Go back in?"

His secretary rises to get the cart, but Parnell waves her away and starts pulling it himself. As it passes her, she swoops up a coffee carafe and pours some into her own china cup that has an inscription hand lettered on the side: IF YOU CAN'T FIND A LAWYER WHO KNOWS THE LAW, FIND ONE WHO KNOWS THE JUDGE.

In addition to the coffee, the cart is laden with three kinds of juices, a selection of sliced melons, strawberries, grapefruits and pineapples, and an assortment of pastries. The women all go for the fruits, and Marty practically inhales an almond croissant. Parnell, as I knew he would, takes nothing but a cup of coffee, only one in a great library of subtle power demonstrations, this one involving gustatorial largesse from the master, who does not eat with the serfs. Especially not prosecutors and their investigators.

"So where are we on this?" Parnell asks when he sees that we are through bustling with the breakfast cart.

While it is true that I value his help and we are presently on his geographical turf, it is still my show and I will handle this in the manner I see fit. There is no time for a full briefing. "I think everybody knows the basics and what's gone on so far, except for the first pretrial meeting, so let's not rehash it. What's facing us now is a monkey wrench Terhovian's gone and thrown into the machinery."

"Just one?" Marsha says, the remainder of a cantaloupe slice dangling from her fork.

"Don't worry, it's a lulu." I wet my throat with a long slug of decaf, then look at the cup. "Damn, this is good coffee."

"Bloody well ought to be," Lisa says. She has finished a small plate of strawberries and seems to be taking motherly joy in the appetites of everyone else.

Parnell smiles. "Guess who does all our food service."

"In that case . . ." Marty says, reaching for a raspberry danish.

"Like you needed another excuse," Marsha chides him.

Lisa is smiling broadly, pride in her cuisine quite evident. How do I convince a jury that this ingenuous woman gets her pleasure from the admiring comments of people eating her pastries, not from squalid trysts with repulsive criminals?

"Bottom line," I announce, "Terhovian made a motion to preclude Diane and Lisa from testifying about each other's complaints."

Diane jerks her head up and Lisa looks confused, but there is nothing in the legal arena that could amaze Parnell. "On what grounds?" he asks without betraying any surprise.

"That it's more prejudicial than probative." Meaning that its value in actually determining the defendant's guilt or innocence would be outweighed by its negative impact on the jury.

"He was serious?"

I nod, and Parnell says, "What else?"

"That's it."

He creases his brow. "What do you mean, that's it? No other motions?"

"Like I said, that was it. Except for trying to intimate that Lisa is a nymphomaniac with a bun in the oven." I deliberately word it strongly, to see how Lisa takes it. She will be one of our two star witnesses—I hope, given the topic at hand—and I need to know if we can count on her to hold together and help this case instead of hurt it. Now is as good a time as any to find out, here in an uncomfortable situation, with other people present.

Parnell looks over at her and raises an eyebrow. Lisa makes her eyes large, tightens her lips and gives him an *Oh, honestly!* look of childish exasperation. "Forget it," she says. "I haven't played slap-and-tickle since the earth cooled."

A loud laugh explodes out of Parnell, and Marty tries to chuckle around a mouthful of whatever else he has picked up since he polished off the danish. I smile as well and can understand their desire to positively reinforce Lisa's occasional flashes of levity, but her cycling between deep depression and clever, offhand wit troubles me. I'm no psychologist, but I know this isn't healthy.

"Don't worry about that, Nestor. It's a dead issue." I find myself talking to him rather than the others. I don't know if this is because we are in his office, or I am intimidated by his position, or somehow I feel he can be of the most help. Something about the man just seems to command respect, or at least deference. "Terhovian only did it to scramble my brains before making his motion." *And it worked, too,* I decline to add.

"Then what's the problem?" he asks dismissively.

"I told you. He made a four-oh-two motion to suppress."

He waves it away. "But it's ridiculous on its face. Why worry about it?"

"Because Arigga didn't throw it out on the spot."

Parnell regards me for a long second, then waves his hand again. "He's just toying with you, Sal, trying to soften you up to accept a plea bargain. Hell, the old fart doesn't want this to go to trial. His age, who needs the grief?"

"I don't think so, Nestor. You had to be there. I think he's really going to consider it. Terhovian got him to agree to break up the meeting so I could go off and think about it."

"But it's the dumbest thing I ever heard," Diane says.

"I'm not sure I get this," Lisa says. "Suppress our testimony? Don't I get to say what happened to me? Doesn't Diane?"

"Yes," Marsha says to her. "The problem is, you wouldn't get to say what happened to Diane, and she wouldn't get to say what happened to you."

"But why?"

"Yeah, why?" Marty adds. I haven't had a chance to fill him in prior to this meeting. Marty is not a lawyer but he has a lot of common sense, and this situation is violating it. I should think he would be used to it by now.

"What Terhovian is saying is, because of what happened to you guys, you each might be willing to lie for the other."

"But I don't have to lie," Lisa protests. "What happened, happened."

"I see where this is going," Diane says. "He's saying, suppose only one of us was really attacked?"

I am amazed that she latched on to that so fast, but my amazement quickly turns to dismay. If she was able to make that leap of logic so rapidly, maybe Terhovian's reasoning is not as specious as it first appeared.

"I don't believe this," Marty says.

Parnell has turned to stare out the window and now

swings his chair back around. "I still say it's bullshit. You could apply that reasoning to any case where there were multiple victims, some of whom were also witnesses."

There is a little brass plaque mounted on a block of wood sitting on Parnell's desk. I read it and then hold it up for him to see. It says: THERE IS RIGHT, THERE IS WRONG, AND THERE IS THE LAW. "You have to believe me, Nestor. Arigga is taking it seriously."

"Then you'll file an appeal," he says. "Maybe that old fox is just intimidating the judge. He can do that, you know: he's got a hell of a reversal record."

I shake my head. "I don't want to do that. Win or lose, I'll have Arigga so pissed off he'll sink the case just out of spite."

"I never got that impression from Arigga," Marsha says.

"You sure you're not still brooding over that Friehling case?" Parnell asks.

"Gimme some credit, f'Chrissakes. The sonofabitch busted my chops from the second I walked into the room." I tell them about Arigga's clearly evident inclination toward Terhovian, but I leave out the *ex parte* conversation, thinking it might really make me sound paranoid. "And another thing," I conclude, pointing to the newspaper on the chair next to Lisa. "I'd make book Terhovian gave that story to the press."

"That story's gonna make any sort of plea bargain damned difficult," Marsha says. "He has to have known that."

"Maybe he's just setting you up," Marty says. "Trying to put the screws to you as much as he can, then he offers a plea."

"No, I see what Sal's getting at." Parnell is nodding and rapping a knuckle on his desk. "If Gus wanted a plea, there's no way in hell he'd give the story to the paper. He'd want it as quiet as possible."

Diane leans back on her chair, thumbing her lip. "Are you telling me he wants to go to trial?"

I look at Parnell and turn up my hands. "That's what it sounds like to me."

He thinks for a moment longer, then looks over at me. "You really believe Arigga is going to give the motion serious consideration?"

"I'm certain of it."

He swings back toward the window and stares out. There is a marine layer to the west that is only now beginning to dissipate beneath the rising sun. The diffused light casts a pale orange glow on the walls inside the office.

"You're thinking Arigga could rule against us," I say to him, "that he could sink this case from the outset."

Parnell takes a deep breath and lets it out slowly. "If everything you're telling me is so," he says, not turning to face me, "I'd say there's a damned good chance."

Lisa looks from Parnell to her sister to me. "Sal? Are you saying we can't testify for each other?"

"Only if the judge grants Terhovian's motion."

"But he might?"

"He might."

"So we can still each tell our own stories, can't we?"

Yes, you can, and then it is your word against his, and he will go free. Everyone else in the room already knows this. "If he rules that way, it hurts our case, Lisa. A lot."

The silence that follows is long and uncomfortable. If we pursue our present course, we could lose this case before the trial even starts. It is even possible—

"You know," Parnell says, interrupting my thoughts, "if Gus gets this one, next thing he's going to do is demand that Arigga throw the whole thing out. For lack of evidence."

Just where my own thoughts were heading, but not exactly. "No, I think it'd still get to trial, because of Diane and Lisa's testimony. There's no way he can keep that out."

"Maybe. But what if Terhovian lets us put on our case and then moves to have the whole thing thrown out?"

Lisa shrinks back. I think we're beginning to scare her, that she feels the whole enterprise slipping from somewhere in the realm of common sense down into a through-the-looking-glass world she is not trained to comprehend. "They can do that? Without the jury?"

Diane sighs, and I know exactly why. She has pulled this move many times herself, including in the Friehling case, and now somebody might use it against her. "They can do that."

"Okay, people." Marsha straightens up on her chair, slapping a hand down on her ever present leather-bound writing tablet. "There's no way we can take that chance. We gotta change gears here."

"What if we argue that—" Parnell begins, but Marsha shakes her head and interrupts him.

"No. Arguing isn't going to do it. We can always lose the argument and then we're toast. We need a radical change in thinking here. Something that'll neutralize Terhovian's bullshit."

"Like what?" Diane asks.

"Like, if I knew, I would've told you already." There is nothing mean in the way she says this.

"But there's nothing we can do unless we change the charges," Diane counters.

Marsha stares at her, regards her curiously, then begins chewing her lip. I hope everybody stays quiet for the few seconds it takes whatever is brewing in the back of her brain to bubble up to the surface.

"I got an idea." She turns to me, uncaps her pen and begins tapping it on the yellow writing paper on her lap. "What if you dismiss the complaint involving Diane, completely and with prejudice."

"What's that mean, with prejudice?" Lisa asks.

"It means we can never file again, no matter what." I don't want to get into a legal tutorial now, and turn back to Marsha. "Okay, we drop it; then . . . ?"

"We pin the whole case on Lisa's testimony, backed up by Diane's. Arigga can't exclude Diane because there's no bias."

"Of course it's biased," Marty says. "Complaint or not, she still got—she was a victim, too, wasn't she?"

Marsha turns to address Diane directly. "You don't even mention what happened to you, at least not the last part." She is referring to the actual rape, which nobody feels like naming out loud. "Far as everybody's concerned, you're a witness, not a victim."

"But what if the other guy brings it up?" Lisa asks. "Terhovian?"

"He wouldn't dare." Parnell catches on quickly. "He'd have to be an idiot to prejudice the jury against his client that way, bringing up something like that."

"It's better than that," Marsha says, growing even more excited. "Their whole shtick is that everything was consensual, that Diane and Lisa went with Rosamund willingly." She sits back, a canary-eating smile on her face. "What's he gonna say now, that the witness is prejudiced because his client raped her?"

She said the word, and if anyone is startled, it doesn't show, not in light of the beautiful dilemma Marsha's strategy creates for the defense.

"Of course!" Parnell slaps the side of his head. "How could they bring anything else up if nothing forcible is supposed to have happened?" He looks admiringly at Marsha. "You looking for a higher-paying job? Nice offices, an understanding boss . . . ?"

"Back off," I tell him, openly delighted that something may finally be breaking our way.

Marsha jerks a thumb in my direction. "He made it possible," she says to Parnell.

I look at her, puzzled, and she turns to explain. "You only filed charges on Lisa's behalf. No official court paper even mentions Diane."

I shake it off. "Good Lord, that's just because I was paranoid about getting it all right."

"Well, whatever. The good news is, we don't have to withdraw any charges, and the defense can't claim they ever existed. It doesn't wind up looking like a cheap trick."

It is a positively brilliant strategy, at least from a purely technical perspective. But there is still an issue, and I address myself to Diane.

"What do you think?"

As I expected, her enthusiasm is not as great as Parnell's and Marsha's. She tilts her head to one side and lifts a shoulder. It looks like grudging rather than eager acquiescence.

"What's the problem here?" Parnell asks.

He is so used to spending his time getting criminals off the hook, he doesn't quite comprehend the feelings of their victims, so I try to help him understand. "The problem is, someone gets denied her fair share of justice." Only Lisa's case would be heard, and no mention would ever be made of Diane's own victimization.

"You think this'll work?" Diane asks Parnell.

"Sounds good to me," he says, "although nothing in this game is foolproof. But I think this is as close as it can get."

She nods absently, then seems to come to a decision. "Then it doesn't matter. I'm not interested in a lot of symbolic crap; I just want the bastard to go down, hard. I don't much care how." She leans over to take Lisa's hand. "Do you?"

Lisa shakes her head. "Can I take a break for a few minutes?"

"What do you want, a bathroom pass?" Marsha says loudly, jerking her head toward the door.

Lisa tries to laugh and gets up, striding quickly out of the room. Diane looks at her as she leaves. "I'm worried about her," she says when her sister is gone.

"How come?" Marty asks.

"She seems to be holding up well enough, but it's all on the come, waiting for Rosamund to get locked away somewhere for a long time. Like it's all she's living for."

Marsha sneaks a knowing glance at me. Diane's analysis applies to herself as well, we know. Her expression of concern for Lisa is a projection of her own fears that have focused to the pinpoint called Rosamund's incarceration.

"What we need to do," I tell Diane, "is get the hell out of pretrial as quickly as we can. Once we're in trial, we have a new judge"—I make a wiping motion with my hands—"Arigga's out of our hair permanently. I've got to believe the trial judge is going to be a lot more fair."

I can see she is becoming convinced. It is not really her call, but I need her to be completely committed to following this through and to see to it that Lisa does the same. Marty knows it as well and takes a backdoor approach.

"Hey, Sal, what *about* a plea bargain?"

"No way." I watch Diane's face as she answers for me. "If Terhovian's gone this far, he won't settle for a lot of hard time, and Rosamund's got to go away big-time." She turns to look at the door through which Lisa exited moments before and shakes her head. "I already told you that."

"Let's everybody hang on a second, here." We all turn to Marty. "How do we know what he's gonna settle for? Maybe this defense attorney is playing hardball on account of he knows his client's up against heavy time." He's referring to prison sentences measured in decades rather than years. "Sounds to me like we're all rushin' to trial here, and trials are risky, right? Why don't you go offer him something?"

Parnell is not used to being lectured by a cop, even if that cop is really a DA's investigator, but he does respect street smarts when he sees them. "What would you suggest?"

Marty shrugs and looks at Diane. "How 'bout ten years?"

Diane frowns. "He'd be out in five, maybe four."

"Nuh-uh." Marty shakes his head. "He does it all. That's the deal."

"Ten years." Everybody realizes that Diane is speaking for Lisa as well now, but somehow nobody feels the need to verify that this is all right. "Doesn't sound like a lot."

"Yeah?" Marty will not give up easily. "Imagine a guy, he went to jail when you got your first kiss in high school."

Diane looks at him slyly. "How do you know when I got my first kiss?"

"I'm guessing sixteen. And the guy just gets out now. That strike you as long enough? And I'm talkin' hard time, not some damned country club."

The math is a little off, but I can see that Diane is really trying to visualize what that much time in a prison cell must be like.

"That's against maybe no time," I prod her.

"Are you telling me that'd be okay with you?"

I have to admit that, given the circumstances, putting Rosamund away for a decade has its attractions.

Diane leans over toward Parnell. "What do you think?"

He looks at me. "I think you should offer it to him."

Diane nods. "If he turns it down, we still have Marsha's strategy for trial. What've we got to lose?"

Marty jerks a finger toward the door. "This gonna be okay with Lisa?"

"I'll make it okay." Diane takes a deep breath. "Why don't you make the call now, Sal?"

"There's a spare office three doors down on the left," Parnell says, rising. He leans over his desk to hit an intercom button. "Val, would you show Mr. Milano to Barry's office, please? He's going to use the phone."

There is no sign of Lisa as I head into the corridor. I ask Parnell's secretary, and she tells me Lisa wanted to walk outside the building for a few minutes and said she would be right back.

Whoever "Barry" is, his office is about half the size of Parnell's, which still makes it about four times bigger than mine. I settle into the big leather executive chair behind his desk and gather my thoughts before placing the call.

"Bernacchi, Klippel and Daniels?" the switchboard operator answers with an upward inflection, as if she were seeking confirmation of it.

I ask for Gustave Terhovian. "Sir, he's on another line. May I have him call you back? It'll only be a minute."

"Then I'll just wait."

She hesitates for a second. "It would really be better if he calls you back. Can I have your number, please?"

It occurs to me that Terhovian is not really in the office but probably at home. The arrangement must be that the operator calls him and gives him the message, and then he calls back. "Hang on just a second," I tell her, then put her on hold and ring Parnell's secretary. "Tell me, if somebody calls the number in this office, does it go through the switchboard or just ring directly in here?"

"Goes straight to that office," she answers. "It's a private line."

"Thanks." I hit the first button and give Terhovian's receptionist the number and hang up. It wouldn't do for him to know I'm calling from a private law firm.

Waiting for him to call back gives me time to consider Terhovian's situation: still on some kind of leave and yet he agreed to take on this difficult case. An old war horse trying to prove he still has what it takes, despite illness and age? That would make him a dangerous adversary, particularly if this is the only case he's working on. Usually, I can exploit an attorney's enormous caseload burden by holding out the hope of some brief respite if the client cops to a plea. Less than two minutes later, the phone rings.

"How are you, Milano?"

"I'm fine, Gus. You?"

"No complaints. How can I help you?"

"Maybe we can help each other." No more preamble than this is necessary. "I think it might be better all around, for your client as well as the complainants, if we let you cop to a plea on this one."

I bite my tongue at how this came out. I was concentrating so hard on making it sound like we were doing him a favor that I inadvertently pluralized "complainant." If we go to trial, there will be only one. I have little time to consider whether he has noticed because his answer comes out of left field.

"I don't think so, Sal."

"What are you talking about? You haven't even heard the deal yet!"

"It carries jail time, doesn't it?"

"Of course it does!" Less than a minute into the conversation and already I'm having trouble keeping aggravation out of my voice, which contrasts noticeably with Terhovian's own even modulation.

"Then forget it."

"What is it with you, Gus? Do you honestly believe you're going to keep Rosamund from doing any time at all?"

"Sal, do yourself a favor and drop this one. I'm telling you for your own good."

"My own good? What the hell is that supposed to mean? I'm gonna put your guy away for a lot damned longer than the deal I was gonna offer! Why don't you do *yourself* a favor and listen to it?"

"Sal . . ." His voice trails off, but not before a certain despondency comes through. For one speaking such confident words, he doesn't sound as happy as he should.

"What?" I ask him, hoping he senses my irritation.

There is a long pause. "Nothing."

"C'mon, what? Let's try to do something here, dammit!"

"Nothing." Another pause, almost like he is considering some alternative.

I try a different tack. "You're obligated to at least pass the offer along to your client. You have no choice."

"See you in court, Sal." He gives me his permission to make an *ex parte* call to Arigga to fill him in; then there is a quiet click. He has hung up.

I stare stupidly at the phone in my hand. I haven't told Terhovian that we would be altering our charging strategy, as per Marsha's idea, but that is his problem: I am not the one who hung up. He will find it out in plenty of time, though, according to the rules of the court.

I dial Judge Arigga's number by heart. His clerk answers on the fourth ring and tells me Arigga is busy but I should hang on for a moment. A few seconds later I hear his voice.

"I'm in the middle of a hearing, Milano. What is it?"

I fill him in on what transpired with Terhovian, and he interrupts to tell me that he would prefer not to see a trial.

"Me neither," I say amiably and collegially, like we are thinking along the same lines and I couldn't agree with him more, "but the guy wouldn't deal."

"Maybe that's because you're making unreasonable offers."

So much for collegiality. "I never even got to the deal, your honor. He wouldn't listen."

He *harumphs* loudly, just to let me know that, despite the facts, this is somehow my fault. "You sure you know what you're doing, Milano? You sure you want to press this?"

Despite my best intentions and the rationalizing disclaimers from both Marsha and Nestor Parnell concerning my opinion of Judge Arigga, I find myself really beginning to hate this guy. "You telling me I should drop it?"

"No, no," he says quickly, "that's up to you. I'm just saying, is all . . ."

"Saying what?" I want to see if I can fit a size twelve, triple-E in my mouth all at once.

"Don't sass me, Milano. You got anything else?" It fits, all right.

I should tell him that we will be altering our charges, but I don't want to talk to him anymore right now, so I ring off as politely as I can stomach. I will tell him later, and he will see to it that the defense has enough time to prepare. I sit alone for a moment, trying to get myself ready to go back into Parnell's office.

Everybody looks at me expectantly as I come through the door. I can tell that nothing much beyond small talk has been going on in my absence.

"Looks like we're going to trial," I say, then recount the details of my conversation with Terhovian. Parnell gets a faraway look in his eyes again, trying to figure out what all this means. I think analysis paralysis is starting to set in, and apparently Marsha does, too.

"Listen," she says, getting up and walking toward the conference table on the other side of the office. She plants her feet firmly, one hand on the conference table, the other jabbing at the air as she speaks. "I think we only have one decision to make here, and that's whether we think there's any chance of Arigga getting away with the motion to prevent Diane and Lisa from testifying for each other. That's it. If we can convince ourselves Arigga won't grant it, we stay the course. If not, we withhold charges involving Diane and bet the whole match on Lisa. It's that simple."

It *is* that simple. Thinking back over the last hour, all we have really been talking about is the likelihood of the judge granting Terhovian's motion to prevent the sisters from testifying for each other. All the rest has been peripheral. Marsha lets it sink in and then presses Parnell.

"You first, Nestor. What do you think?"

I can see that it's a strain to stop himself from launching another round of free-flowing speculation, but Marsha's assertion of leadership has its intended effect. "Well, if everything Milano is saying about how those two have been behaving is true, I would have to conclude that there is great risk of Arigga suppressing the testimony."

An absolutely masterful shifting of responsibility to my shoulders, but his assessment is accurate. The only evidence anybody in this room has that Judge Arigga would approve a patently ridiculous motion like Terhovian's is my say-so, and I have not even mentioned the pleasant little phone chat with Arigga that just followed the one with Terhovian. Parnell has merely pointed out that, given

Marsha's nutshell summarization of the issue, there is no other conclusion that can be drawn.

"I'd have to agree," Diane says.

Of course, there is no basis for me to come to a different conclusion. I nod and then look around. "What about Lisa?"

"It'll be okay," Diane reassures us again.

"So that's it, then." Parnell slaps his hand on his desk. He may not be happy that Marsha is the one who powered us to a decision, but I think he's glad that there is now a clear course of action. It lets him go into his customary general-manager-of-the-universe routine, but I let him go on because his advice is sound.

"Diane, you and Lisa need to refuse all requests for interviews, a blanket 'no comment' on everything, you got it?"

"Should I do the trial?" Marsha wonders out loud to no one in particular, obviously wanting Parnell's opinion but reluctant to sound him out in front of me. "That way, Sal can testify about Rosamund's behavior in the bar." If I'm on the prosecution team, my testifying could get the whole DA's office disqualified, and we'd have to retain private counsel to continue the case.

Parnell shakes his head and looks at me. "I think the head deputy should handle it personally. The bar thing is a minor point, and besides, McConagle was there, too, and he can testify, right?"

"Lookin' forward to it," Marty says.

I tell Marsha I want her at the prosecution table as co-counsel. This is as much her show as mine—the whole strategy is now hers, after all—and I have a feeling her creativity, and even her mere presence, will do me a lot of good.

Parnell asks for my assessment of the case.

"We've got two highly credible witnesses," I begin, "versus a demonstrable scumbag who we can imply was at The Alley that night pushing drugs. There's nothing in Diane or Lisa's backgrounds to even hint at the kind of lifestyle patterns that would comport with going off for a ménage à trois with a stranger, and half the regulars at the bar, all upstanding citizens, are willing to testify to that if we need them." We can only bring in witnesses to vouch for character if the opposition attempts to impugn it. "Ter-hovian will never find a witness willing to say otherwise unless he invents one, which he would never do."

"Don't be so sure," Parnell says.

"There's nothing I can do about that, Nestor." There never is, except to investigate and discredit the phony witness. I look at Diane and wish Lisa were in the room to absorb some of the confidence I am trying to convey. "You and your sister are going to be great on the stand. You ask me, I'm willing to bet Terhovian comes begging for a plea before we rest." Marsha is nodding as I speak, but Parnell is very still, just listening. He asked the question so now I wait for his reaction.

"I think you have it covered very well," he says, which gives me an additional comforting feeling, surprising considering the general level of self-confidence I had to start with. It probably has to do with a need for some outside confirmation that I would not be behaving any differently if I had no personal interest in the case. "I have to agree that arguing with Arigga is fruitless, and you'll be a lot better off after the trial starts and he's out of the way."

There is nothing left to do here. We're going to trial and the rest is entirely in Marsha's and my court. I lead the way as we leave and see Lisa sitting on the same couch as when we arrived. She is rereading the *LA Times* article but is dry-eyed now. I tell her we're done and that Diane will go over the details with her later. I find it disconcerting how alike the two of them look. I almost feel silly talking to her, as though I just got finished doing so inside the office. It's easier when the two are together.

"How does it look?" she asks anxiously, and her relief is immediately apparent when I answer.

"It looks very good, Lisa. We're going to go with your complaint and leave Diane's out of it. That way, you can both testify."

She nods. She is not as intrigued with the legal maneuverings as the rest of us are, and assumes that Diane will clarify everything for her later and tell her what she needs to do. For now, it is enough for her that all of this assembled talent feels very confident about the strength of our case. "And a settlement? What about that?"

I don't bother to correct her usage of a civil law term in place of *plea bargain.* "I tried to offer him ten years," I say, and she jerks her head around to Diane. "Don't worry," I quickly add. "They didn't go for it."

"Good," she says sharply.

I look at Diane, and she shakes her head very slightly. *Leave it alone,* she's telling me. She doesn't want me to tell Lisa that we would likely accept such a sentence if they offered it. She will handle that with her sister another time.

We shake hands all around, and Diane offers to walk me to my car. I tell Marsha I will see her back in the office, and we all leave, giving each other cheerless holiday greetings.

When Diane and I are alone on the first level of the underground parking garage, she slows us down and says, "I wanted to apologize." I look at her blankly. "For making you uncomfortable on the pier the other night."

"What do you mean?" I ask as innocently as I can, knowing full well what she means.

She looks away, embarrassed. She didn't expect me to make her say it in words. "You know, about bringing up your interest in me. That whole thing."

"Ah." I want to say this without stammering. "It's okay. Really." What an eloquent reply I managed to muster up.

"How come you never followed through? I mean, I'm not saying you should; I was just, you know . . . wondering."

I am flattered to near speechlessness, but my self-image and personal brand of paranoia force me to ask myself if there is really reciprocal interest or if this is some sort of attempt on her part to pull me in because she thinks that I am now the only man who might pay attention to her going forward, that I am maybe the best she can hope for. I am instantly ashamed of this thought and mumble something ludicrous about professional distance and decorum and can tell that she sees through it right away. Thankfully, she doesn't press against my discomfort.

I look at her out of the corner of my eye. She is beautiful. She is one of the smartest, sweetest, most poised and self-possessed women I have ever met. I would be lying if

I didn't admit that my heart leaped with joy every time our investigation came up with more evidence that Diane Pierman was about as far from an easy pickup as one could get, that she'd had only two serious relationships and is still good friends with both of those men.

Is it possible that Diane, right here and now, is making a first move toward me? I want to find out very badly. My problem is that if I say something based on that assumption and she denies it, even laughs at me—or, far worse, is solicitous and understanding and tries to soothe my feelings, as if I were a helpless puppy that just got run over by a truck—I will sink into the very concrete in embarrassment.

I look at her again and decide she is worth taking that chance. There is no doubt in my mind that once all of this is over, my feelings for her will only have intensified and I would be happy to grow old with her, to see her every morning until the day I no longer awaken.

And that is why I say nothing. Despite the temptation of the moment, I need to know for certain if she is reacting honestly to me and not merely clinging to the symbol of her salvation. If it really is me, I'll worry later about how to deal with my expressed concern about professional distance and why, for some mysterious reason, it no longer applies. Hell, I'm a lawyer; I can handle that one.

I stop and turn toward her. Her eyes are wide open in the dim light, and there is nothing desperate in them. All else aside, my desire to both protect and avenge her is stronger than I would have guessed, but I am a public official and it is vital that I steer clear of her on a personal level until this is all over. Even as I stand here I can easily see myself slipping into a plea bargain mode that gives away the courthouse just so we can end this thing and start something new. The thought frightens me, but I am redeemed by the need to impress her, to put Vincent Rosamund in jail for such a long time that I look like the Lone Ranger and the Terminator rolled into one.

Diane smiles as I am thinking of all of this, like she's reading my thoughts. "I said I didn't want to make you uncomfortable," she says, "and here I am doing it."

"Maybe just a little." The thought occurs to me that maybe Diane is the one afraid of being embarrassed, afraid that maybe I don't feel anything for her and am trying to tell her this without hurting her feelings. This is unfair, especially considering that she is braver than I, she being the one who took the first step. I don't know if her feelings for me are genuine or not, but of one thing I'm certain: right now *she* thinks they're real, and only when the case is resolved will she be able to examine them honestly and know for sure. And that is the only condition under which I want her.

"I'm going to do everything I can to put this guy away, Diane, and to do it as quickly as possible. Then . . ."

She cocks her head to one side. "Then . . . ?"

"Then, I'm going to take you out to dinner."

She tilts her head farther sideways and raises one eyebrow.

"Then, maybe dancing . . ."

The other eyebrow.

And then home and then to Niagara Falls and a couple of babies and a great little house on the beach. . . . "What is this, a cross-examination?"

She laughs, a gentle sound. "Just wanted to see what you look like when you squirm."

"So how do I look?"

She looks down at the ground and then away. "This is not a good time, is it?"

It is not. "Listen, let me concentrate on this trial. I don't think there's anything more important right now, do you?"

She shakes her head in reluctant agreement without looking up.

"What I need is for you to stay together, and keep your sister together, and help me nail this bastard for good. Afterward, we'll all get drunk for two days, we'll have a blowout and declare the whole matter officially dead. All of it."

I raise her chin with one finger. "Is it a deal?"

Her eyes are brimming. I know the pattern, have seen it in other victims with no visible scars: periods of deep depression as events replay themselves in their minds, spells of elation as they convince themselves that it could have been worse, a few stretches of heavy guilt as they wonder what they might have done that could have changed what happened, the entire manic-depressive syndrome of creeping self-destruction, the victim unaware of the price being exacted with each turbulent cycle.

She nods without speaking, leans forward to quickly kiss my cheek, then turns away abruptly and quickly walks back toward the elevators. I feel a small electric spark tingling on my face where her lips were and reach up to touch it without considering how corny that would look to an outside observer. The spot feels warm. The faint whiff of her perfume infiltrating my nostrils feels like it's diffusing throughout my whole body.

Once I'm out on the street, I call Marsha's car phone and tell her to put through the paperwork dismissing Diane's criminal complaint, setting in motion the process of the DA's office declining to prosecute. I tell her that she should call Terhovian and get over to Arigga's court with him, let the judge know what is going on and request a trial date.

"A trial date? What if Terhovian has more motions?" I can tell she's reaching the Overland exit on the Santa Monica Freeway because the reception is getting fuzzy. It's a dead spot on the cellular system.

"He won't." I'm sure of this. There is nothing left he can do, and I'm still convinced that he wants to go to trial as quickly as Arigga. Between the two of them, I would predict that we conclude the pretrial meetings this afternoon. We might even have a date and judge in the next couple of weeks.

Arigga doesn't set the dates or choose the judge. Once the pretrials are over, the case goes to Judge Douglas Nyqvist, who is the supervising judge of the superior court in Santa Monica. He will assign it based on availability and experience, and I can only hope that the next free judge is someone we can count on to be fair and rational.

"Okay," Marsha says as the static starts to drown her out. "I'll see you on Tuesday. Have a merry—" The cellular line goes prematurely dead with a familiarly annoying rasp of static.

Monday the 26th has come with merciful speed. Christmas depresses me, as I am so far from my family and so lamentably single. As always at this time of year, I find myself ruminating on my life in New York, what a shitty place it was and how I didn't realize it while I was growing up there. The whole city is a dysfunctional human zoo, a Noah's Ark of every known depravity, hopelessly trapped atop an Ararat of asphalt and toxic muck.

The first-time visitor to New York mistakes noise for energy and filth for character, and is like a child who visits Alcatraz and thinks prison might be fun. In fact, a good deal that is thought to be wonderful about the city is a vestigial perception of happier days, dragged reluctantly into today and projected onto a rotting slag heap of dying dreams and progressively more insupportable deceptions.

The New Yorker has raised interpersonal contention to a fine art, making it the subject of a type of lighthearted humor that is at extreme variance with the brutal reality of cultivated hostility. It is like joking about tuberculosis or disembowelment. There is even a delicatessen in midtown that is famous for the invective the proprietor heaps on the customers. The theater of abuse, not the food, is the primary attraction, a Monty Python sketch come to real life. I blame the city for my father's death almost as much as the people who killed him.

But, oh my, does that city know how to throw a great Christmas. It owns the holiday, more so even than Bethlehem itself. I grew up taking for granted that Christmas actually took place in Rockefeller Center and that everything else, even the tree at home, was an imitation in tribute. The lights, the brilliant red and green decorations, ice-skaters, chestnut peddlers, roving carolers, the gigantic Norwegian spruce and crowds of beautifully dressed people and cops on horseback and department store windows to rival any Broadway stage set—that was Christmas for sure, set to music coming from everywhere at once, like cosmic background radiation, infusing the crisp, clear air. Everybody was nicer, even the traditionally surly doormen and taxicab drivers, and if it had to do more with the heaviest tipping season of the year than a religious holiday, what does a little kid know about that?

Here, in southern California, Christmas is a bad joke played on transplanted New Yorkers after it is too late for them to do anything about it. The temperature is often in the eighties, and palm trees and people skateboarding in red Santa suits does not quite do it for me. There is little sense of holiday tradition here; the city of Santa Monica has even done away with Santa and his elves on the decorative posters it displays around town, replacing them with King Neptune surrounded by dolphins, an admirable ecological sentiment perhaps but, like so many things are here, hopelessly inappropriate and cheerless.

I'm sitting alone in the living room of my beachfront condominium, a beautiful place I bought at the absolute height of the California real estate madness, scant seconds before the market began the precipitous plunge that no one believed was possible, rivaling that of Johnstown's after the flood. I spent the day with a group of friends keeping alive somewhat of a tradition we started a few years ago. We met here a little after five this morning and went across the street to the beach, zipped tightly into winter wetsuits, and surfed for about two hours, beginning in darkness and continuing while the sun came up. Surfing is not the same as it was in the old days: "localism" has become the norm in many locations, an interesting phenomenon in which the regulars claim a prime surfing spot as their own and not only harass outsiders verbally but throw rocks at their cars or even physically attack them in the water. That a gang mentality like that can invade even such a bastion of camaraderie as surfing ought not to surprise me in these times, but it does. In many ways, Los Angeles is not unlike New York.

I'm not much of an athlete—and that's phrasing it charitably—but can surf fairly well because it is more about balance and coordination than strength or endurance. I got picked on a lot as a kid, and school yard confrontations were the nightmares of my childhood. Many were the times I stood, red-faced and seething with helpless rage, while tougher boys, never alone but always in packs, used me as an outlet for their own egotistical fulfillment, often in front of the girls in my class. I spent an inappropriate number of hours plotting revenge horrifically out of all proportion to their actual transgressions. None of my plans were ever executed, of course, and my anger toward injustice accumulated rather than abated, gradually generalizing away from grade-school bullies and toward more socially worthy targets. It wouldn't take much psychiatric insight to determine that each violent criminal I put away represents merely one more unlanded sock in the mouth to one of those sneering, slack-jawed, nascent Capones of the fifth grade.

This morning the air was so clear we could see the snow-covered San Bernardino Mountains from the water. A few of the local surfers unfortunate enough to fail to recognize police out of uniform started right in with their usual shenanigans, purposely nearly running one of my deputies through with a sharp-pointed surfboard. I admit ashamedly to a deep visceral thrill when Pat Salerno forcefully hauled the perpetrator out of the water and, in full view of around fifty people, proceeded to pat him down with extraordinary thoroughness, an interesting proposition when the subject is wearing naught but a skintight wetsuit.

Around seven-thirty we came back to my place for coffee, doughnuts and showers, and by nine we had a four-car caravan heading up to the very mountains we could see from the water. By noon we were on the ski slopes near Big Bear. Where else on this planet can you spend the day after Christmas surfing in the morning and skiing in the afternoon?

Now I'm alone, pleasantly exhausted, trying to concentrate on enjoying one of my illegal, genuine Havana Cohiba torpedoes and a glass of Strega and forgetting about the case against Vincent Rosamund as much as I can. There is little left to do except prepare witnesses. We will be fully ready to go to trial, and there is no reason why I should eat myself alive over it when I could spend quality time eating myself alive over other things. Like, why am I alone, and what is Diane Pierman doing at this moment? My carefree bachelor life is the envy of many of my married friends, but all I really want out of life is to know that there is someone at home I can hug and kiss whenever I want to, who loves me without conditions. I don't need great sex as much as I need to be able to brush my teeth next to someone doing the same without it feeling like an illicit morning after.

Just as Diane's face pops into my head, the phone rings, destroying the stillness and making me jump. A small thrill runs through me at the thought that it could actually be her, calling because of some inexplicable psychic urge that resulted from my ineffectually repressed desire.

It's Nestor Parnell. I hope my disappointment is not evident.

"How was your Christmas?" he asks.

"Fine," I answer warily. He didn't call to check on my holiday. He tells me I might want to sit down for this, and I do.

"I just came from dinner at a friend's house, a federal judge. One of the other guests was Doug Nyqvist."

Head of the court, and the man who is going to set the room and date for the trial. "How is old Doug?" I ask irreverently.

Parnell ignores the implied disrespect, which is just a joke. I like Nyqvist, everybody does.

He snuffles and clears his throat. "He told me Constantin Arigga is going to handle your trial."

I have heard about how all the blood can drain out of your head as a result of a shock but thought it only a colorful expression. Now I feel that there is nothing but air inside mine, and it's difficult for me to focus my eyes, as if there is insufficient pressure left to make them work.

"Sal? You there, pal?"

"Yeah, I'm here."

"Near as I can tell without pressing the guy too much"—it wouldn't do for Nyqvist to know Parnell has been consulting to the prosecution—"Arigga requested the case. Told Nyqvist he could clear the decks and get it started on time, second week in February."

"He requested it?" I seem capable only of simple, open-ended questions, and prefer to let Parnell do all the talking. "Why?"

"He says the issues are highly complex, and he is very familiar with them from handling the pretrial meetings. He told Nyqvist that it's going to be very high-profile, very public, and if there's a conviction, it's no doubt going to be appealed. He said he could keep it cleaner than anybody else, so it'd reflect better on the whole court."

We prattle on for a few more minutes, but my mind cannot proceed beyond the fact that Constantin Arigga is going to be the judge in this trial.

It is the worst possible news I can imagine.

8

The gauntlet of reporters outside the courtroom is not as bad as it might have been. There has been some diminution in the public mind about this case, which has been overshadowed not by another earthquake or a war but by the expansion L.A. Stars winning the Super Bowl, an occurrence that threw most of southern California into a frenzy that has still not completely abated. I doubt the repeal of Prohibition was accompanied by this much extended celebration.

Also, there are no recognizable names involved in the case. As has become tradition of late, the names of rape victims are not reported. This is to protect their privacy. No such protection is afforded the accused, however, despite the core precept that says he is innocent until proven guilty. It makes all the self-aggrandizing chest-thumping by the media for this isolated forbearance in the case of rape victims all the more insufferable for its blatant hypocrisy. Needless to say, though, in this case I'm glad of it.

The reporters know who Lisa and Diane are, of course, and are disappointed when they don't show up. There is no requirement for them to be here today. There are no plaintiffs in a criminal case, just complainants, defendants and material witnesses. The people of the state of California are the plaintiffs and I am their lawyer. Diane and Lisa need only be here for their own testimony, and all we'll be doing today is selecting the jury. That will be a difficult process, and there is no chance that we will start our case before tomorrow, at the very earliest.

I spoke with Gustave Terhovian earlier this morning, and we agreed to be polite but close-mouthed to the press. When I didn't bring up the matter of his quote to the *LA Times,* he did. "I assumed you were going to give them something equally hyperbolic," he said, "so I fired off what I thought would be an equalizing shot." He was lying. I had a deal with Eleanor Torjan, and there is no way she would have solicited a statement from Terhovian unless she thought the story was going to break in another paper first. I let it go for now because I want it as quiet as possible from here on in, and if I confront him with his dissembling, we will have no deal. I still don't understand his rationale for exposing it in the first place.

We have a few minutes until Judge Arigga makes his entrance. As this is somewhat of a special assignment for him, we're not in his customary courtroom but are borrowing someone else's. It is a standard trial room. There are about seventy spectator seats, four rows deep, divided into three sections separated by two aisles. The group of seats on the left are just on the other side of the bar from the jury box, which contains fourteen office-type chairs comfortably padded in a bright blue that is out of place in the otherwise muted room. A thick Plexiglas partition mounted on the bar and extending about six feet in the air separates the jurors from the spectators in the left section.

The judge's podium is elevated at the front of the room, with a witness box at his right and the clerk, bailiff and court reporter stations to his left. There's a door just behind and to the left of the podium, the entrance to chambers, and another door behind the bailiff that leads to a corridor through which defendants still in custody may be escorted from a small holding cell. There is a good deal of wood paneling on the walls, and the floor is of tiled linoleum, giving the whole place the look of a suburban playroom.

We're all milling around waiting for the judge. I barely recognize the man talking to Eleanor Torjan at first. Vincent Rosamund, sporting a haircut trimmed well above his ears, is wearing a conservative gray suit of American cut, full shouldered and with little tapering at the waist.

Nicely offsetting his white shirt with plain cuffs is a rep tie, probably loaned to him from Terhovian's collection of menswear from the Jonathan Club, one of the oldest and stuffiest in town. I push up on my toes to get a glimpse of his shoes, and I'm astonished to see a pair of wingtips. The overall sartorial impression is that of a successful stock broker with a Wharton MBA.

I recognize several other reporters, all cooling their heels while Eleanor scoops them by talking to Rosamund and taking notes. Free on bail, Rosamund can come and go as he pleases, but he is not free of bailiff Drew Stengel's watchful glare, and it makes him uncomfortable. Marsha is laying out papers on the defense table and waves to somebody in the gallery. I turn to see that it's Nestor Parnell, accompanied by several other attorneys from Diane's law firm. Priscilla Fields, the rape counselor, has taken a seat near the back of the right section, and Marty McConagle and Pat Salerno are sitting together in the third row. Nearly all the other seats in that section are taken as well, as are most of those in the left. The middle is completely empty: that's where the prospective jurors will be sitting.

At the defense table, Gustave Terhovian is sitting alone, and for him, it looks ostentatious. He is normally surrounded by associates from his firm as well as a handful of expensive jury selection consultants, independent paid specialists whose job it is to subvert the underpinnings of the jury system by making certain that the panel of the defendant's peers is as biased toward his case as possible. In their marketing literature, these people don't even make a pretense of trying to find a fair and impartial jury.

But today Terhovian is alone. It's strange to see him without the usual phalanx of sycophantic assistants. Is it possible that this case is such a loser that the firm of Bernacchi, Klippel and Daniels is not even backing him up, perhaps instructed not to do so by the people behind Rosamund who don't want to throw good money after the bad they have already used for his bail? I feel sorry for Gus, looking small, frail and vulnerable behind the large table. I hope we can end this quickly.

Terhovian knows he needs only one solid juror on his side to stonewall and cause a mistrial, so he will be looking for someone not only sympathetic to the defendant but strong enough to stick to his guns in the face of eleven other angry jurors bent on conviction and dying to get out of here already.

The clerk calls the court to order and Judge Arigga strides in, looking neither Terhovian nor me in the eye. He seems hell-bent on quickly getting through the preliminaries and inside of twenty minutes has fifty prospective jurors filling up the middle section of the spectator gallery. The first task is to qualify them for time. The estimate is that this trial could take as long as three weeks, and he needs to make sure that only those people who can go the distance get selected. He takes a deep breath, knowing what is coming next, and says, "Are there any of you who could not be present for the three weeks of the estimated trial length?"

About forty hands shoot up into the air. Arigga tightens his lips and exhales through his nose. "Okay, let's hear it." He points to a man in the first row who had his hand up. "You first. What's your excuse?"

The man rises. "I'm on my last day of jury duty. I'm only supposed to be here ten days and—"

"You're only supposed to be on *call* for ten days. If you get on a jury, you stay the duration. Any other hardship you want to tell me about?"

The guy didn't have time to think up anything else, certain he was going to get away with the first excuse. After nine days of hanging around waiting with nothing better to do than talk to other jurors, he should have learned better. He shakes his head and sits down.

"Next?"

An older woman stands up. "Your honor, my employer thinks I'm gone for only ten days. They're not gonna—"

"Who do you work for, ma'am?"

"North American Rockwell."

"Your employer will understand. I guarantee it." He's right. Nearly all of the big employers in the greater LA area, including every one of the aerospace firms, have policies dictated by their public relations office that make magnanimous allowances for things that enhance their appearance of civic-mindedness. The court has a book on

each employer that tells the judge exactly what those policies are. I would estimate that fully half this jury pool has
jobs in defense firms, large banks, municipal govern-
ments and the like. Few will be able to use employment
policy as an excuse.

A better class of excuses starts to spew out of the
remaining potential jurors: *I own my own business and it
can't run without me. I'm being sued and due in court in
three days. I have two small children and can't afford the
baby-sitter. I'm a writer on a deadline, I have a vacation
planned and it's pre-paid, my wife is sick, my mother
is dying, I'm an accountant and have to close the
quarter.* . . .

At the end, only eighteen prospectives are left, but it's a
larger number than I would have guessed. Arigga brings
in fifty more and the whole process starts over again, and
this time we get twelve, then again and we get another
twelve. Interestingly, these same people, who fought like
hell to get out of jury duty, will now as prospective jurors
turn around and fight with equal fervor to sit on a case.

We're going to need sixteen jurors for the trial: twelve
primaries and four alternates. Each side gets ten peremptory challenges, meaning that we are allowed to knock
people off the jury without stating a reason. We also have
an unlimited number of excuses for cause, in which we
can exclude jurors if we can demonstrate that they might
be biased against our side. These need to be approved by
the judge.

Terhovian and I submitted proposed juror questionnaires to Arigga several days ago and received the written
answers yesterday. Arigga himself will handle the questioning of the jurors in open court, and he doesn't have to
allow us to ask any questions of our own. But Arigga's
clerk informed Terhovian and me in advance that we
would be able to ask questions and that each side would
have a total of an hour in which to do so, used however
we want. We could spend the whole hour on a single juror
or spend a minute each with sixty of them, but once our
cumulative hour was up, that would be the end of it. It's
the same way a chess match is conducted and is just
another one of those quirky little bits of cleverness that
only adds more uncertainty and crapshooting to a process

that is supposed to be geared toward finding out the truth. Okay, maybe not the truth, but at least an acceptable level of human certainty.

I question the first juror, a black woman sixty years old. She has obviously taken a good deal of care in her appearance, which tells me that she takes the jury process and her civic duty seriously. You have to be very careful with jurors like this because peremptory challenges used to be an absolute right but this is no longer the case: excuse more than one minority juror and you had better be prepared to explain to the judge exactly why.

I don't think it's an issue here. All the odds are on my side in this case anyway. Nobody has sympathy for rapists, and the defendant is white, one of the few times that will be a liability for him rather than an asset.

I'm ninety-nine percent sure I'll go with this lady, and I use a few minutes mainly to establish some rapport with her, to get her on my side from the outset.

"Have you ever served on a jury before, Mrs. Curtis?"

"Yes, sir. Two times."

"That's great, you already know how much fun it is."

She smiles broadly, glad to be in on a private joke with one of the privileged individuals controlling the proceedings.

"Tell me, you have any kids?"

"Yes, three, and grandchildren, too."

"Really?"

She nods. "Two girls, eleven and seventeen."

"Good kids?"

"Oh, yessir, very good kids, good in school and everything."

Two girls. It doesn't get much better than this. "I have no doubt of that, Mrs. Curtis. No doubts whatsoever. Have you ever had any problems with the law, or with attorneys, anything like that?"

She hesitates. "This one time, my sister had some problems with the rent, you know. This sheriff came to the house, came with a lawyer, said they was gonna throw her out, but I lent her the money and it was okay." She shrugs. "That was it."

I nod in sympathy. "You think you can reach a fair

decision in this case," I ask quietly and seriously, "based only on what you hear in this courtroom?"

"Yes, I can. Absolutely." She wants to sit on this panel, badly. Wants to show me she can be the trooper and the citizen I want.

I stare at her for a long few seconds, like I am absorbing her words and thinking them over carefully. Then I nod slightly and turn to the judge. "Your honor, this juror is acceptable to the people." I didn't have to make this announcement right now. I can wait and do it anytime, but it locks Mrs. Curtis in tight. I give her one last look; she's beaming with pride. Let Terhovian knock her off and he will earn the enmity of everybody else in the room.

He rises, stares at her for a few moments, and then spreads his hands and smiles. He waits until she smiles back, then addresses himself to Arigga. "Defense passes for cause and accepts Mrs. Curtis."

A good move on his part. Her relief is apparent and she now has two friends. Sides are even.

It goes on like this for a while with half a dozen more people. There are not many factual questions we need to ask; most of it has been covered on the questionnaire. *Are there any police officers in your family? Do you know anyone who has been the victim of a sexual assault? Ever been in trouble with the law?* We are more concerned with trying to get a feel for things that don't come out on paper, any signs of hostility or sympathy.

Terhovian thinks he may have two on his side, young, swaggering males for whom this whole process seems to be a joke and to whom rape may not be considered such a bad crime. Thankfully, they are both white, and I wait until we have fifteen acceptable jurors before rising to excuse them both, glancing at Terhovian to see if he looks dismayed. He seems unmoved, and we complete the selection a few minutes later with an unemployed day-care worker.

I wind up with just what I want, basically a group of good citizens, mostly minorities, with two, maybe three strong personalities that might be able to ramrod the weaker ones through to a conviction if there is some reluctance. I don't need anything special, as I might if our case were weak.

It's three o'clock, and everyone is surprised that we managed to impanel a jury in a single day. Terhovian only exercised four peremptories, as against my eight. All of the sixteen for-cause excuses were done by Arigga himself based on the written responses or his own questioning.

He decides to recess until tomorrow morning, and I breathe a great sigh of relief: I wasn't ready with my opening and would've had to wing part of it and stall the rest. Arigga lectures the jury with the standard admonition not to discuss the case with anyone, including each other, and to report any attempts to do so on the part of participants in this case. I instruct Marsha to get hold of Diane and Lisa and tell them to be ready to go tomorrow.

Terhovian has hustled Rosamund out quickly, keeping him away from the press. I got the sense that he wasn't pleased that his client talked to a reporter prior to the start of court today. I catch up with Eleanor in the hallway and ask her how her conversation with him went.

"You know," she says, "for such a street-savvy hustler, he sure as hell doesn't have a very good idea of how much trouble he's in. He's like one of those overconfident wise-guys you see at New York mob trials, joking around like nothing much important was happening."

"You get a statement?"

She nods, tilts her head and shows me what is written on the last page of her notepad:

I think we need to put this behind us and let the healing begin.

I'm going to relish the day this contemptible animal goes down.

9

I feel exactly the way I had hoped to feel this morning, relaxed and eager. I learned long ago that there is nothing more useful in preparation for a challenging day as a solid night's sleep. No last-minute cramming, no frantic rehearsals, no panicked self-doubt as to strategy. I went to the movies, alone, a nonstop action picture that would keep my mind occupied. The film had already been out for weeks, and I usually like to see movies on the day they open, but I saved this one for the evening before the actual presentation of our case. It made me forget about the trial.

Diane and Lisa sit together in the front row of Judge Arigga's borrowed courtroom, an empty seat on either side of them. They look forlorn, alone, mutually protective. Nestor Parnell and several of his firm's associates are three rows back. Marty McConagle is sitting next to Pat Salerno, who is in uniform. She's on duty and will be a witness later in the week.

One thing I'll say for Arigga, he takes the jury system seriously, has even written philosophical articles on it for legal journals. He turns to the jury now and delivers a variation of his standard lecture.

"Ladies and gentlemen, you are the most important body in this room, more so even than the attorneys or me. With all of the legal machinery, all the lawyers, judges, police, legislators, courthouses, you name it, there is nobody here but you good citizens who will make the ultimate decision on the guilt or innocence of this defendant. It is a powerful, profound responsibility, one you must take with extreme seriousness. Rarely will you be called upon by your fellow citizens to undertake a task so important, not just for what it means to this trial and this defendant and these victims, but for what it means to our society. Your government has the power to make war, raise taxes, even change the course of rivers. But when it comes to deciding the fate of someone accused of a crime, the bigshots step back and put it in the hands of people like yourselves, and there is no power in this country that can make you do other than what you feel is right.

"This is done because it works. Sure, there are mistakes, but basically jurors do their jobs and do them well, and that is why the system has survived as long as it has. And as long as jurors continue to do their jobs well"— here, Arigga pauses and stares long and hard at them— "the system is safe and the people can continue to rely on it as one of their most cherished rights." There are answering nods from the jury box, the main twelve plus the alternates, sixteen citizens who were moaning and whining about jury duty only a few days before suddenly invigorated and motivated by the sobering realization that they are direct participants in a cornerstone of western civilization.

Arigga fits his bifocals on his nose and looks down at the papers before him. Terhovian and I both submitted standard jury instruction suggestions from a state handbook. Where we agreed, Arigga will use these as submitted. Where we differed, the judge conducted a telephone conference call and we sorted it out, largely by dint of Arigga's commanded resolutions.

"The defendant, Vincent Rosamund, has been charged with a number of crimes under the California Penal Code. These include kidnapping to commit certain sex crimes, forcible rape, drawing or exhibiting a firearm in the presence of a motor vehicle occupant, felony indecent exposure and sexual battery. There are also some other factors to be considered, such as the use of a firearm in the commission of a felony. I am going to explain each of these to you, but there are some things I want to go over first."

He turns away from the papers and takes off his

glasses, looking at the jury again. "The single most important thing is that the burden of proof is on the people, not the defendant. Now, I know you've heard this phrase a million times, mostly on *Perry Mason* and in the movies, right?" He flashes a smile for the first time, and the jurors smile back, some giggling nervously. He has made a more important point than they realize: while we are taught in school about history and math and biology and personal hygiene and basketball, there are no courses on that great body of statute and regulation that governs nearly every facet of our daily lives, the law. With the exception of trained attorneys, virtually every citizen in the country gets his or her knowledge about the law from television. One of the hardest jobs of a trial judge is washing away in a few minutes a lifetime of accumulated misconceptions.

"I want you to be real clear on what it means. It means that, as of this moment, Vincent Rosamund is an innocent man. Were there to be no trial, if everything were to stop at this moment and the future was based on how things are right now, Mr. Rosamund walks out the door a free man. The only way that changes is if the people, represented by the prosecutor, Mr. Milano, prove that Mr. Rosamund committed one or more of the crimes with which he is charged. If they do that, then you, the jury, will change his status from innocent to guilty. Mr. Rosamund does not have to prove anything. He is presumed innocent. If the people fail to prove he is otherwise, he must stay innocent and you must declare him to be so.

"This is not to say that his lawyer, Mr. Terhovian, will stay silent as the prosecution puts on its case. Far from it. Mr. Terhovian will do everything he can to show that the people are *not* proving their case. He may do that by cross-examining the state's witnesses. He may call some of his own witnesses. He may call Mr. Rosamund himself to testify.

"Or, he may do nothing at all. He may just sit there and listen and do nothing. That does not mean that the people made their case. Only you can decide that. But you have to decide it beyond a reasonable doubt, another phrase you may have heard, and let's talk about that for a second." He looks back at the papers on his desk.

"Reasonable doubt is not a mere possible doubt, because everything relating to human affairs, and depending on moral evidence, is open to some possible or imaginary doubt. It is that state of the case which, after the entire comparison and consideration of all the evidence, leaves the minds of the jurors in that condition that they cannot say they feel an abiding conviction, to a moral certainty, of the truth of the charge."

He looks up again. "I'm just reading straight from this book here and you have no idea what the hell that means, right?" Loud laughs from everybody. "I know from the questionnaires that some of you have sat on juries in civil cases. You were told to decide the case based on a preponderance of the evidence. But the standard in a criminal case is much higher. What I just read to you means, in English, that you can't just think it's *possible* the defendant did it, you have to be firmly convinced, otherwise you must find him innocent. If there is another scenario that fits the facts and would exonerate him, you must find him innocent. It's that simple . . . although it'll get more complicated later, trust me." It elicits another nervous giggle from the jurors. They're enjoying this. They're sharing some personal time with a respected jurist and feel that they have been admitted as full members into a secret society of people better and smarter than they. What they want more than anything else is to please this judge, to make him think they are going to do a good job, and then solicit his approval when they render a verdict.

Arigga takes some time to discuss each of the charges, defining them and explaining what constitutes proof of their commission. Then he talks about the differences between direct and circumstantial evidence. He's doing all of this now so that the jurors will be vigilant when they listen to testimony and can make some judgments about what to believe and what to discredit. It's easier than allowing them to form conclusions in their minds and then have to rethink them later, when they discover that the law is often at variance with their own notions of right and wrong. Later, before they are sent off to deliberate, he'll repeat much of it, but that will be a refresher to help them sort out their thinking.

"You must accept and follow the law as I state it to

you, whether or not you agree with the law. If anything concerning the law said by the attorneys in their arguments or at any other time during the trial conflicts with my instructions on the law, you must follow my instructions. Statements made by the attorneys during the trial are not evidence. However, if both attorneys have agreed to a fact, you must regard that fact as conclusively proved. If an objection to a question is sustained, don't guess what the answer might have been and don't speculate as to the reason for the objection.

"You must decide all questions of fact from the evidence received in this trial and not from any other source. Forget everything you have heard about this case in the newspapers and on television; the only thing that counts is what you hear in this courtroom."

He gives them one last, penetrating look and then calls on me to make my opening statement. It catches me off guard because usually, in a case like this, the judge's opening statement is lengthier, and there are several questions from the jury.

I half turn to Marsha as I gather together my notes, so she can look me over. My relationship with the jury is about to change dramatically. Yesterday, during selection, I was the inquisitor, the one who sat in judgment of their fitness to serve. Even those who didn't want to be on jury duty, who did everything they could to avoid service, subconsciously got caught up in the general desire to please the attorneys, to be found acceptable. Jurors excused during the *voir dire* exhibited various levels of discomfort, their faces and mannerisms reflecting everything from embarrassment to hostility even though, for many of them, the reasons for their dismissal were obvious and nonpejorative: this one had a cousin who was raped, that one's brother is a policeman. . . .

But now all of that has changed. I'm no longer their judge; they are mine. Their seats on the panel are assured, and I'm no longer asking the questions: I'm doing the supplicating, the imploring, asking them to believe my side of the case and enter the verdict I want. The power of the jury is enormous—they are free to completely ignore the law, disregard the facts, and essentially enter any judgment they wish, no matter the degree to which it contradicts logic or statute. Everything I do during the course of this trial is focused solely on them, the twelve people in front of me. Every gesture I make, every inflection of my voice, every question, motion, objection, are all geared toward ensuring that these people, amateurs with virtually no knowledge of criminal law, come out of the jury room with a verdict of guilty. I can't count on the judge for this, because even though he has the right to pronounce the defendant innocent any time he wants to, even after the jury finds him guilty, the opposite is not possible: he cannot direct a verdict of guilty because that would be a denial of the defendant's right to a trial by a jury of his peers.

So I have Marsha look me over. I'm going to walk over and chat with the jurors, which is how I think of my opening statement, and I want them concentrating on me, on my words, on the conviction beneath them. I know that if my tie is askew or there is an errant thread of saliva on my lip or a blot of mustard on my lapel or a nose hair sticking out, they will home in on that like a laser-guided missile and never hear a word I say. It's human nature, this propensity in the face of the profound to be distracted by the trivial, and it has happened to me at least once before: I was dying like a bad comedian on amateur night, unable to make eye contact with half the jurors, convinced I was going down in flames, only later while splashing cold water on my face in the rest room to discover an ink spot on the side of my nose.

Marsha silently pronounces me presentable, and I stand and saunter over to the jury box. I'm going to pummel them with the message that there is nothing subtle, tricky or delicate about the case against Vincent Rosamund. A law professor of mine used to say, "If the facts are on your side, argue the facts. If the facts are against you, argue the law." In this case, the facts are solidly on our side, and I don't need any sophistry or arcane technicalities to put it over.

"It's very simple, ladies and gentlemen. Couldn't be simpler." My voice is not dramatic or overwrought with self-righteous indignation. Instead, it is offhand and casual, as though my point were so obvious it barely needed to be said out loud. "A beautiful young woman, a professional of outstanding and unblemished character, who escaped from Communist Russia as a child and came to this country to find the American dream—this fine lady who did nothing more than step out of a restaurant one evening with her sister to drive home after a hard day's work, finds her tires slashed"—I pause to back away from the jury box and move toward the defense table, where I point at Rosamund—"and meets up with this piece of street trash." The harsh language underscores the contrast between the type of person Lisa is and the subspecies Rosamund represents, and I can see it has a slightly startling effect on several jurors. Terhovian could easily object—after all, it is not my intent to prove that Rosamund is literally "street trash"— but I don't think he will: it's generally a bad idea to interrupt during the opposition's opening because it makes you appear worried and unsure of your case. Better to sit, looking bored and disdainful, as though nothing the other side says can hurt you.

"And let me tell you what this punk did to Lisa Pierman, the hopeful daughter of a family of hopeful refugees." Meaningful glances to the four jurors I know have daughters of their own. I tone my voice down, as though even to speak of this requires muted and respectful modulation. "He puts a gun in her face. One squeeze of his finger and she is dead. He forces Lisa and her sister Diane into his black Cadillac." I mention the car because I want them to know he isn't some put-upon lowlife in economic distress. I also wonder again if Terhovian is going to object, since I mention Diane and there are no charges in connection with her, but it would be a bad objection: even though Rosamund is not charged with doing anything to Diane, I'm still free to bring out any facts relevant to Lisa's complaint. Terhovian stays quiet.

"While Diane drives, he begins pawing Lisa in the backseat. All the while he has the gun pointed at her, jamming it painfully into her face, threatening to blow her head off if she resists." I pause and stand up straighter. "And then he rapes her."

Most of the jurors glance at Lisa at this point. She has begun crying quietly, tears visible on both cheeks, her head resting on Diane's shoulder. I let them look, let them imagine the magnitude of the outrage, let them project onto Lisa's face the images of their own daughters or friends or loved ones.

"You will hear from Diane Pierman, who will describe for you the events of that evening in detail." I want to start my case with a complete accounting of the details, to satisfy the jury's morbid but understandable curiosity and settle them down. I can then methodically flesh things out and drive home the solidity of the evidence. Having two sets of direct testimony, one from the victim and the other from an eyewitness, is a golden opportunity to open with a complete story, go through details in the middle, and close with a new, wrenching recounting. I could put Lisa on first, but there are some reasons I don't want to do that. Diane has courtroom experience and will do a better job of laying things out methodically, cautiously and in detail. Second—and I feel bad about it—Lisa will probably crack on the stand, and that powerful emotionalism, the devastating effect this whole episode has had on her, is the thing I want to leave the jury with just before our side rests.

"You will hear from witnesses in the restaurant who saw Vincent Rosamund make an obscene gesture at Lisa. One of those witnesses is an experienced and decorated investigator in the district attorney's office with whom the defendant tried to pick a fight that night. You will also hear from a police officer who picked up the sisters in the woods where this animal left them after he was through with them."

I walk back to the jury box. "And, finally, you will hear from Lisa herself. And when you have heard it all, you will wonder why we are even here, why we are wasting your time with this trial, when there is no doubt whatsoever about the defendant's guilt." I shrug, to tell the jury that this imposition on their time is not my fault. But I'm not done. There are two more points I have to make.

"Now understand something: the defense may try to convince you that there was no kidnapping, no assault, no gun and no rape. Vincent Rosamund could get up on the stand and tell you that Lisa Pierman, who owns her own successful business, and her twin sister Diane, a criminal defense attorney with a prestigious firm right here in town, that both of these women came out of a restaurant where they are well-known, hopped into a car with a complete stranger, drove happily into the woods and had sex with him in the backseat and on the cold ground, then sent him off so they could be left alone in the middle of nowhere in the dead of night."

There is no obligation on the part of the defendant to testify, but I know Terhovian has to put Rosamund on the stand to refute Diane's and Lisa's testimony. Otherwise, what they say will stand as undisputed fact.

"It's a ridiculous story, but they have to come up with something, and you will make up your own minds, and that choice will be easy." I wave it away with a flip of my hand—not even worth my breath to bring it up. "One last thing . . ." I say, looking stern and serious. There is little doubt as to what is going on in the juror's minds. They expected to be hearing about two rapes and two complete sets of charges, and all they are hearing is one. The confusion is obvious, and I need to orient their thinking early on.

"Judge Arigga told you to forget everything you think you know about the law. He will explain to you what the law requires of you in rendering your decision. That's very important and I know you understand that." If Terhovian tries to make the case that the sisters humiliated his client and there was some revenge involved, the jurors need to know that this provides no excuse in the eyes of the law. However, in order to do that, the defense would have to admit that there was coercive rather than consensual sex, and of course they won't do that, but I'm taking no chances.

"He also instructed you to ignore everything you have heard on television or read about in newspapers. Now I gotta tell you . . ." I smile and look down, shaking my head in amusement. "There have been more lies, rumors and just plain garbage in the newspapers than I could possibly tell you." I get some knowing smiles from a couple of jurors, but mostly what I sense is withering hostility from the reporters seated in the back of the gallery, Eleanor Torjan the most formidable of the bunch. I will suffer from that for a few weeks, but I not only have to get the jury away from wondering why there is only a single case instead of two, I have to discredit Terhovian's inflammatory statement to the *Times* alleging that the claims of rape were a sham following a spat.

"That's the nice thing about trials," I continue. "There are rules designed to keep the baloney down and let the truth rise to the top. So there are things you may hear in this room that are different from what you read about, and in this room"—I pause and slap my hand on the wooden rail in front of the witness box and glance at Terhovian for a second—"in this room, statements are made under oath." Terhovian has not reacted to my little barb at all. He's slouching in his chair, idly twirling a pencil, scratching at his neck, looking at his watch every once in a while.

I look back at the jury. "Together, we'll put this animal behind bars where he can't do this kind of thing to innocent people anymore." I chose these words carefully, a veiled implication that this is not Rosamund's first offense, but I have no proof and cannot bring it up formally. I also skate past the fact that the jury's job is to bring in a conviction, not incarcerate the defendant; that's up to the judge.

After a last look at the jury, I walk back to our table and sit down. Marsha puts a hand on my arm and squeezes as she smiles at me.

"Mr. Terhovian?" Judge Arigga says, bidding the defense to its opening statement.

"Please the court, defense reserves opening statement, your honor," Terhovian says without rising.

Marsha and I exchange looks. I didn't expect this. I thought for sure Terhovian would present the jury with their defense in advance: yes, his client drove into the woods and had sex with the twins but everything was consensual. There was no gun, no threats, etc. After all, I reasoned, our case has no surprises in it, so why would Terhovian wait to see how it goes and then make a statement?

"He's gonna set them up for Rosamund's testimony just before he goes on," Marsha leans over to whisper to me, "tell them what to listen for, tell them what to think while he's speaking. That's what's gonna stay fresh in their minds." She straightens up and purses her lips. "Could be a good move." She's making sure I don't get complacent, telling me that somewhere in the cold pumice of Terhovian's senior years a memory of fiery lava may still burn.

I see her point, but right now I have to concentrate because I wasn't prepared to get started so quickly. I was counting on at least a twenty-minute statement from Terhovian, time I could have used to gather my mental horses before dropping headlong into the fray. No problem, though: two minutes into it and I'll settle down and relax.

"Call your first witness, Mr. Milano."

"People call Ms. Diane Pierman."

She is the picture of poise and self-possession as she walks to the stand. Dressed demurely in business clothes of neutral gray, she is neither whore nor ice queen, just a very pretty girl next door. Her voice is steady as she is sworn in and states her name for the record, and she trains her eyes on me as we begin.

"Ms. Pierman, you are the sister of the complainant, Lisa Pierman, are you not?"

"Yes, sir. Twin sister."

"No kidding." Ordinarily, I wouldn't crack a joke here because I'm trying to create a solemn scene, develop some apprehension before I take Diane and the jury down a hellish path into the Piermans' nightmare. However, I don't want to give the impression that we've rehearsed this testimony, so this bit of seeming spontaneity not only amuses the jury but makes it appear as though she's hearing these questions for the first time. It's not true, of course: we even rehearsed the joke, and the response from the jury tells me it was a good idea.

"You aren't native to this country, are you?"

"No, sir. We came here as children when my parents fled the old Soviet Union."

"Your parents were political refugees?"

Diane nods. "My father spoke out against the Communists, wrote articles and things like that. The authorities made our lives very difficult, and so my father smuggled us all out."

I take Diane through the basics of her education, her law degree, stressing her high levels of achievement and how hard she has worked. I can't mention her sexual history: if I don't bring it up, Terhovian can't either. But the picture I'm painting is one of a woman too ambitious and hardworking and grounded in basic values to be suspected of a wanton lifestyle.

"You're a criminal defense attorney, is that correct?"

She nods, then says, "Yes," remembering that the court reporter cannot record gestures, only the spoken word. "I thought, this is my way of giving something back, for the persecution my parents suffered."

Terhovian rises, and in a voice thick with exasperation, says, "Objection, your honor."

It seems to snap Arigga out of the focus he had been applying to Diane's testimony. "Grounds, counselor?"

"Relevance, your honor. What's all of this got to do with the case in point?"

Arigga turns to me and raises his eyebrows. I'm prepared for this and amazed only that it took Terhovian this long. "Merely establishing the credibility of the witness prior to her critical testimony, your honor. Our primary evidence of these crimes, in addition to testimony of the victim, is this eyewitness. To the extent her recounting of the events in question conflicts with that of the defendant"—I look at Rosamund, hoping to underscore the relative credibility of his eventual story when contrasted with Diane's—"I feel it is highly relevant to lay the groundwork for why the jury should believe her."

I can see that the jury has taken to Diane and is fascinated with her, so I am delighted when Terhovian says sarcastically, "Well, the defense will stipulate to this fairy-tale story if it means we can move on." The jurors don't see it as a fairy-tale story because it's the same dream that many of them have had, for themselves and their children. I believe I have succeeded in highlighting the point that Diane and Lisa are immigrants, as many of the jurors are, and they don't look kindly on Terhovian's denigration of things they hold dear.

Besides, I know that Arigga will not sustain the objection. Witness credibility is not something you can blithely stipulate, like somebody really fired the gun or really was in that motel. It's not a question of fact but of feeling, and I have the right to let the jury form a positive opinion about a witness whose credibility the defense will attempt to impugn.

"Overruled," Arigga says, "but do hurry along, Mr. Milano."

"Certainly," I answer amiably. There's no need to dwell on this any longer; I've made the points I wanted to make, and I begin the core of my questioning without delay.

"Ms. Pierman, on the evening of this past November twenty-first, can you tell us where you were?"

"Yes. I left work at approximately seven and went to meet my sister."

"Your sister Lisa?" I point her out as I ask this question.

"Yes. She's my only sister."

"And where did you go to meet her?"

"At a place called The Alley."

"That's on Montana Avenue?"

"Yes."

"What kind of place is that?"

"You mean—"

"Uh, like, is it a seedy tavern, say?"

"Oh, no, not at all. It's a restaurant, a very nice place, a little on the expensive side. A lot of people from the west side go there: doctors, lawyers, other professionals. Like you, Mr. Milano."

That gets another nice laugh from the jury, and I smile sheepishly, although Diane and I have rehearsed this well. Juries generally like me, and I figured that including me among the regular clientele of the restaurant will solicit their positive perception of the place. Neither of us refers to it as a bar, although I am sure Terhovian will on his cross-examination.

"I see. And you've been there before?"

"Many times."

"Had business meetings there?"

"Quite often."

"So you're known by management, by the people working there."

"Yes."

I'm being methodical, careful, to an almost extreme degree. I don't want any distracting objections while I establish that The Alley is a respectable watering hole favored by respectable people, and that these respectable people know Diane and Lisa well, have had occasion to observe them, and can laugh off any suggestion that they go there to get dates because in fact they have reputations as being unapproachable in that kind of setting. Among the witnesses Marsha will call later to corroborate these observations is Marty McConagle, the owner of the restaurant, two partners from Diane's firm, a world-famous cardiac surgeon from UCLA and, if I feel necessary, one or two movie stars of international repute who are regular customers of Lisa's catering business. These last would only be a desperation move, though, since we are trying to attract as little additional notoriety as possible.

After a few more questions along these lines, I start to narrow the scope. "Ms. Pierman, did you have occasion that evening to observe the defendant in the restaurant?"

She looks at Rosamund, who returns her glance without hesitation. She turns quickly back to me. "Yes, I did."

"And how did that come about?"

"He was banging his hands on the bar—"

"Banging his hands?"

"Yes, like he was playing drums or something."

"I see. Please continue."

"It was annoying everybody—"

At this point she hesitates. Her answer was planned purposely so that Terhovian would object to it as speculative, on the basis that Diane could not possibly know that Rosamund was annoying anybody else unless she could read their minds. Arigga would then strike the remark and order the jury to disregard it, and the trivial victory would be more embarrassing than helpful to the defense.

But Terhovian doesn't say a word, doesn't even move, and Diane stumbles for a second to retrieve her line of thought.

"—and I looked at him. I can tell you, he was dressed a good deal different than he is today."

Another gnat for Terhovian, this time to demonstrate that Rosamund cleaned himself up for court, that he doesn't always sport conservative blue suits with rep ties and a neat haircut. Arigga might strike the remark as irrelevant but the jury would hear it anyway. Again Terhovian doesn't object. I look over to make sure he is awake.

"You looked at him, uh-huh. And what, if anything did he do?"

"He looked directly back at me, stuck his tongue out and wiggled it back and forth."

"I see." I look over at the jury to make sure they did, too. Ordinarily, this gesture would not seem such a big deal, but we have been so careful to cast Diane in a chaste light that they can easily make the connection as to the inappropriateness of Rosamund's action. "And what did you do then?"

"I went over to the buffet to be with my sister. She's a professional caterer and is always checking out everybody else's food. I wanted to get out of his line of sight."

"And then?"

"And then, he picked a fight at the bar."

"Objection!" Finally, at long last, Terhovian takes the bait and decides to participate.

"Grounds?" asks Arigga.

"Speculation, your honor. She just testified that she walked out of my client's line of sight. Now, how does she know he picked a fight?"

Arigga looks down at Diane over the tops of his bifocals. "Ms. Pierman, can you explain?"

Diane shrugs. "I just figured."

"Remark is stricken. Jury will disregard. Ms. Pierman, please restrict your comments only to those things which you directly observed, not which you were told by somebody else or are guessing at."

"Sorry." Diane looks down at her shoes and looks genuinely apologetic, but it is, of course, all a sham. Diane is a lawyer and knows well what the hearsay rules are, but we have managed to plant in the jury's mind the notion that Rosamund is a troublemaker.

"What did you yourself observe?" I ask in accordance with Arigga's directive.

"There was some kind of commotion at the bar; I couldn't tell exactly what it was. But when I looked, Marty McConagle, he's an investigator in the DA's office, Mr. McConagle was squaring off with the defendant."

"Squaring off?"

"They were standing facing each other, having some

words. The defendant looked angry and his face was getting red—"

"Objection!" Terhovian interrupts. "Your honor, how does the witness know that my client was angry—"

"Your honor," I say before Terhovian can finish. "The witness testified that he *looked* angry, that she saw his face grow red. These were her own direct observations and conclusions based on those observations. The jury can believe her or not, as they see fit, but she can testify to what she saw."

It's a simple rule of evidence and Arigga overrules Terhovian's objection, telling Diane she may continue.

"Mr. McConagle was standing between you and the defendant."

"Just a second," Arigga says and turns to the jury. "You should understand that Deputy District Attorney Milano was present in the bar on the night of this alleged incident. He will not be testifying, however, although others may testify that he was present." He turns back to me. If he senses my annoyance at his use of the word "bar," he doesn't show it. We have discussed my involvement in the altercation at The Alley in pretrial and agreed he would say something to the jury only if it came up. "You may proceed."

"You say Mr. McConagle was standing between Mr. Rosamund and me," I say to Diane.

"Actually," she says, "I thought he was defending you."

"Your honor," Terhovian begins, but Diane puts her hand up.

"Sorry. I have no way to know that."

"Jury will disregard," Arigga says laconically. Diane and I never discussed this point, and it's a bit of a blow to my manhood, but I was never any kind of a fighter anyway—too short, too out of shape and too inexperienced—and any time Marty McConagle wants to interpose himself between me and somebody wishing to do me bodily harm, well, there will be no objections from me.

"Anyway," Diane continues, "a couple of seconds later the defendant turned around and walked out of the bar, with half the place staring at him."

We have made no mention of the teasing trick Diane

and Lisa played on Rosamund before he tried to pick a fight with me. If Terhovian brings it up, perhaps to try to show the jury that the twins deliberately tempted Rosamund, I will characterize it in redirect as an attempt to humiliate him, not seduce him. Then Terhovian would have no choice but to try to show that Rosamund's subsequent actions might be justified in light of his public emasculation and if he does that, he has as much admitted that forcible rather than consensual sex took place. Terhovian will know all this and never bring it up himself, which is why I know it's safe for us to omit mention of the teasing.

"What happened then?"

Diane moves her hands, which had been resting on the arms of her chair, and folds them in her lap. I'm not sure but it seems as though her shoulders are pulling in toward each other. "Nothing much right away. We stayed in the restaurant maybe another hour or so."

She stops. I wait a second and then ask her to please go on.

"Lisa and I left."

"Are you sure of the time?"

She nods. The court reporter is about to ask her to make a verbal answer, but Diane then speaks and the reporter can tell from the context that her affirmative nod is superfluous and she lets it go. Some reporters are downright compulsive about getting everything on the record, but this one is savvy about exercising a little discretion. "There's an employee there"—she doesn't say *bartender*—"who comes on at nine. He'd only been there a few minutes when we left."

The employee is on our witness list, as are seven other patrons who will make the time Diane and Lisa left to within five minutes. This is important: establishing that the sisters were in the restaurant for over an hour after Rosamund left will show that he was lying in wait for them, that it was not a chance encounter. Maybe we can't prove that he cut up Lisa's tires, but we can imply that their meeting in the parking lot was no accident.

"Then you went out to the parking lot—" I instantly regret saying this. I am getting anxious and that always makes me prone to impatient carelessness.

"Objection," Terhovian says calmly. "Leading the witness."

"Sorry, your honor; I'll rephrase. What happened then?"

"We went out to the parking lot." Diane smiles, as do several members of the jury, amused by what appears to be an unnecessarily pedantic interpretation of the rules of examination.

I smile as well. Let the jury see that I have a sense of humor and can take a joke at my own expense. There's an art to playing to the jury. Terhovian and I will be up and down in an endlessly repetitious cycle of examination, cross-examination and redirect. After a while, the jury will undergo a kind of Pavlovian conditioning regarding what to expect depending on who is up. I want them to get used to the fact that every time they see me, something interesting is coming. Not a lot of tedious hammering and chipping away and going over the same thing a thousand times, no wild fishing expeditions in an attempt to trip witnesses up over some trivial detail of no consequence. Let Terhovian induce that response. I want the jury to feel that whenever they see me, they are going to be—dare I say it?—*entertained*. By a nice guy with a self-deprecating sense of humor who is not out to embarrass or humiliate anybody.

"What happened then?" Technically, I should be saying "What, if anything, happened then?" but I don't think Terhovian will object. He knows how to work a jury as well and doesn't want to incur their annoyance by bombarding us with petty objections.

"The defendant was waiting for us."

Bad wording.

"Objection!" Terhovian says loudly.

Arigga doesn't even bother to ask for grounds, it's so obvious. "Sustained. Jury will disregard that last remark." He turns to Diane and gives her a comically reproving look. "Ms. Pierman." One jurist to another: *you should know better.*

"The defendant was in the parking lot." Much better. There's no way Diane could know if Rosamund was waiting or just happened to be there.

"And then?"

Her shoulders pull in even closer, as do her elbows. She seems to shrink even as I look at her. Rosamund has fixed her with a piercing glare, a bald attempt to intimidate her which, to my surprise, seems to be working. I scratch my tie. I told Diane when we were preparing that anytime I did that, I wanted her to look at me, and only me, that it was a signal that Rosamund was getting to her.

"We noticed that two of the tires on Lisa's car had been slashed—"

"Objection," Terhovian says. "Witness is not an expert on tires. Does she mean that they were flat?"

"I prefer to ask the witness my own questions," I say to Arigga, "if defense counsel doesn't mind."

Arigga doesn't bother to rule on the objection but addresses himself to Diane. "Tell us what you saw, Ms. Pierman."

She looks directly at Terhovian. "There was a deep cut about six inches long, just above where the tire sits on the road. Same exact cut on both tires. Same length, same position. Identical." She looks up at Arigga. "They were slashed."

Terhovian sits down and makes a dismissive hand wave at Diane, as if to say, *Who cares, anyway?*

A small triumph for Diane, and it pumps up her confidence, which shows as she continues her testimony under my controlling guidance. She describes in detail how Rosamund threatened them with a gun, forced them into his car and drove off. There are some details we leave out, specifically so that Terhovian will jump on them in cross; when he does, we will supply the missing pieces that will only strengthen our case and make his look worse.

Now Rosamund has made them stop the car. He gets out and climbs into the backseat with Lisa, orders Diane to drive on. He jams the 9 millimeter automatic against Lisa's face, and Diane hears her gasp in mortal dread of the fearsome weapon. Later I will hold my pointed finger against a juror's cheek and try to get them to understand how it really feels to have the means of your complete destruction a hair's breadth away, aimed somewhere near your eye. Rosamund starts telling Lisa to do things, Diane can barely see the road through her tears, Rosamund's voice grows deeper and more menacing, his breathing becomes raspy and labored, he gets more careless and aggressive with the gun, Diane knows because she can hear squeals of pain from her sister . . .

There's a stir in the back of the courtroom. Diane notices and pauses, then looks down at her feet. Arigga looks out across the room, and I turn to follow his eyes. Nestor Parnell and the group of associate attorneys from Diane's law firm have risen from their seats and are quietly stepping through their row toward the center aisle. One by one they turn toward the large double doors at the rear of the courtroom and make their way to the corridor outside. Parnell turns to cast a supportive look at Diane and then he, too, leaves the courtroom.

It is a gesture of consummate grace and style. They know that Diane is getting to the more sordid parts of her story, a piece of the tale that is embarrassing to an extent unfathomable to most people, particularly males. Our system of criminal justice does little to protect the hapless victim from a morbidly curious public and instead gives the accused the right to hear allegations in open court. Only in rare cases will a judge seal a courtroom from the public's inalienable right to know.

Arigga asks Diane if she would like a break, and she responds quickly and forcefully that she would rather not. She's like a first-time parachute jumper standing at the open door of the plane, wind screaming past her ears as she gets ready to step out into space: let her come back in for a minute and she'll never go near that door again. She has to close her eyes and do it now. Perhaps it will not be so bad once the free fall has begun.

Diane pauses to gather herself several times during the subsequent recounting. The struggle to keep from crying is evident in her voice and every gesture, from clenching her jaws together periodically to keep her mouth from quivering, to looking up at the ceiling so no tears would leave her eyes. She looks at Lisa frequently, and I'm pleased to see that her sister has tapped into some inner reserve of strength and is transmitting it to Diane. Right now, for the purposes of this trial, it is really Lisa's story Diane is telling, and Lisa is telling her, *If I can be strong as I hear this, you can be strong as you tell it.* Diane's resultant evenhanded presentation makes a deep impression on the jury, and on everyone else in the courtroom.

Even Terhovian. He hasn't interrupted once, not even when it might have been appropriate, such as when Diane surmised about things happening in the backseat that she couldn't see. It's difficult for me to tell why this is so. A smart defense attorney will sometimes let an eyewitness go on so as not to incur the enmity of a sympathetic and engrossed jury. But in this case, Terhovian himself seems to be caught up in Diane's description of events.

I was hoping he would object. It's one of the traps I set, but he is not taking the bait, so I'm forced to bring it out myself, the coup de grâce of this piece of testimony.

"Ms. Pierman, are you merely guessing about what was going on?"

"No, I am not."

"And why is that?"

She looks at Rosamund full on, and the hatred written across her face is unmistakable. "Because he made me move the rearview mirror so I could watch him. Watch him rape my sister."

There are audible gasps from several jurors. Two have dropped their heads and a few others cast murderous looks at Rosamund, who is slouching in his seat and apparently trying to suppress a smirk.

I don't take Diane beyond witnessing Lisa's violation in the mirror. I can't bring up the subject of Diane's own rape not only because it is technically irrelevant but because it would confuse the jurors, who would spend the rest of the trial wondering why there were no charges brought on Diane's behalf. In fact, they might even be tempted to conclude that, because there were no charges, it is possible Diane did consent to having sex with Rosamund. Obviously, Terhovian is not going to bring it up either, so it will not be an issue on cross-examination.

But I do have her mention that Rosamund used a condom. If I don't, Terhovian will, as though this were proof of consent. Then I ask a question whose answer is sure to bring an objection, but I want it in the jurors' minds.

"Do you know why he used a condom?"

"He didn't want to leave any traces."

Terhovian pops to his feet immediately, telling Arigga that there are no facts in evidence to support this conclusion. Arigga sustains the objection and has the remark stricken. Later, when Terhovian asks the examining physician if there are any signs of rape, I will begin making a case for Rosamund taking pains to hide his crime.

It's time to begin wrapping up. The key details have been played out, and I can sense Diane's developing fatigue, but more important, I want Terhovian to begin his cross-examination this afternoon. I don't want to recess until tomorrow morning or even take a break.

"What happened when Rosamund was through with Lisa?" I phrase it in that manner to heighten the perception of Lisa's being used.

"He left us in the woods and drove away. He told us if we said anything to anybody, he'd hunt us down like animals and kill us both." It is a final shock to the jury's sensibilities, a reminder that this was not just a rapist and kidnapper we were dealing with here, but a man not above taking the lives of innocent people.

A few more questions to bring out the phone call to Pat Salerno and I turn Diane over to Terhovian, genuinely curious about how he is going to handle this. It was a good move, leaving time for him to begin his cross. Diane has deeply impressed the jury not only with the viciousness of Rosamund's actions but with her own honesty and integrity. Let Terhovian struggle to overcome that without giving it a chance to dissipate overnight in the minds of the jurors.

Terhovian thinks for only a second before standing up quickly and kicking back his chair. He doesn't ask for a recess or even a short break. He doesn't ask Diane if she would like a glass of water or if she feels able to go on. He buttons his suit jacket with one hand and takes several steps toward the witness box and before I'm even fully down on my seat asks, in a loud, clear, commanding voice, "Ms. Pierman, did Vincent Rosamund rape you on the night of November twenty-first?"

I hear a sharp intake of breath from Marsha and a collective gasp throughout the courtroom. I myself feel like I have been punched in the chest, and I drop heavily and clumsily onto my seat. Another half second and an excited yammering rises from the spectator section, and Arigga bangs his gavel several times, hard, shouting above the hubbub, "Order! I'll have order in this court or I'll clear it!" There is no doubting his resolve in this regard, and quiet is restored immediately.

Diane's eyes have grown wide, and her mouth is hanging open. She's looking at me, and there is a frantic tinge to her features. Terhovian has jammed his hands into his back pockets and is leaning backward, staring intently at Diane, waiting for an answer. Marsha is jabbing me in the ribs, making no attempt to hide it, until I jump up and say, "Objection!"

Arigga is still looking around the room to make sure everyone is keeping still, and eventually he gets around to me. "On what grounds, Mr. Milano?"

What grounds, indeed? "Relevance," I say, and it comes out more weakly than I had intended. I'm in an internal frenzy trying to figure out what in the holy hell this madman of a defense attorney could possibly be doing. Has he gone completely insane, or is there something coldly sinister but perfectly rational here I'm not getting?

"Surely the prosecution is not serious," Terhovian says to Arigga, smiling and looking at me as a kindergarten teacher looks at a child who produced nineteen from two plus two. Then his face gets hard, and he turns back to Arigga.

"Your honor," he says, taking his hands from his pockets and resting the fingers of his right hand on the defense table, pointing the other directly at me, "the prosecution has deliberately withheld a vital piece of evidence from this court, evidence that goes directly to the state of mind of this key witness!"

"What evidence?" I demand.

"Evidence that there is bias in this witness's testimony against my client!"

I look at him like he really has gone crazy, then at Arigga and back again. "Of course there's bias! For Chrissakes, your client raped her sister right in front of her!"

Terhovian's head started shaking halfway through my statement. "Maybe, maybe not, but how can the jury be expected to rely on the testimony of someone who has been raped by my client?"

There is not a sound in the courtroom. All eyes are on Terhovian, as they would be on the lead actor in a play who suddenly begins reciting the wrong script. Even the lay public can see that he has stumbled down a minefield from which there is no recovery, and my confusion is turning to fear, because Arigga may have no choice but to declare a mistrial based on incompetent counsel. Until that time, however, I'm under an obligation to press my own case forward, so I say to the judge, and I say it loudly, "Your honor, do I understand that defense counsel is admitting that his client raped Diane Pierman?"

Arigga looks from me to Terhovian. There is no need for him to repeat the question nor to tell Terhovian he needs to answer it. Because of his mistake, which is on the record, it becomes the only question of issue at this moment and one he must deal with as best he can.

If he is embarrassed or flustered or regretful or worried, he doesn't show it. He simply looks at me and then looks at Arigga and he says, "Defense will stipulate that Vincent Rosamund committed rape against the person of Diane Pierman."

I can't take my eyes off him to gauge Marsha's reaction to his having gone completely and publicly berserk.

He is not finished speaking. "Further, I would strongly urge the consideration of sanctions against the prosecutor's office, and Mr. Milano in particular, for deliberately trying to conceal this information from the jury!"

There is dead silence in the courtroom. There are certainly a number of people in the room who are wondering why Terhovian would throw his own client to the dogs like that, admit he committed a felony, hang him out to dry in public. The lawyers and those involved in the pretrial hearings know that there is more to the story. We have already agreed to dismiss charges against Rosamund for his crimes against Diane; it was part of our strategy in nailing the case involving Lisa, the way we got around Terhovian's objection to each victim testifying for the other. Those charges were dismissed with prejudice, meaning that we can never press them again.

So in a technical sense, Terhovian's startling admission that Rosamund committed rape can't hurt him.

However, it is now a matter of record that Rosamund had forcible rather than consensual sex with Diane, which means he was lying during the police interrogation, and it surely seals his fate with respect to the charges connected with Lisa. I have to think, and do it fast, and alone, because I can see on Marsha's face she is as blown away as I am. How do I handle—

"Mr. Milano," I hear Arigga say, "you have made an objection to defense counsel's question to your witness. Do you have anything to add before I rule?"

I have forgotten the exact question and the nature of my objection. "May I have the reporter read back the question, please?" I ask, trying not to stammer.

Arigga shows no annoyance at my momentary lapse. This is an important trial, and he doesn't want anything on the record that might show him not giving both sides every consideration. He nods to the reporter, and she reaches back behind her machine into the Plexiglas box that catches the folded strip of recording paper, runs her finger down the scrambled shorthand code that only she can read, and locates the correct spot. "Mr. Terhovian: Ms. Pierman, did Vincent Rosamund rape you on the night of November twenty-first? Mr. Milano: Objection. Judge Arigga: On what grounds, Mr. Milano? Mr. Milano: Relevance." Then she looks at me to make sure I heard, then at Arigga, who nods again. She drops the strip back into the box and puts her hands back on the keyboard. Arigga turns back to me, waiting for an answer.

I have no choice. Even though I would like to confer with Marsha and try to figure out what's going on, there is no time, no opportunity. All I can do is shake my head without even looking at the judge.

Arigga says, "Objection overruled. Witness may answer the question."

Diane is looking at me, but there is not a thing I can do.

"Ms. Pierman," Terhovian asks impatiently, "did my client rape you or not?"

She looks down for a second, then up, her chin high. "Yes," she says, simply.

Terhovian nods and jumps right into his next, clearly

planned move. "Your honor, at this time, defense requests that all of this witness's testimony be stricken."

Is that all? That whole performance was an attempt to get Diane's testimony excluded on a 402 motion to suppress evidence? Surely Terhovian doesn't think it can work, that this is enough to win his case!

"Sidebar!" Marsha is on her feet, not waiting to see if I'm back in control. I'm not sure myself. Something in the back of my mind is trying to make itself known to me, but I can't see it through the haze fogging my brain.

It is good that we are going to do this out of earshot of the entire court. If Terhovian is going to go down in flames, better to let him preserve his dignity. There is now little doubt that Arigga has to declare a mistrial. As the three of us approach the bench, the court reporter picks up her machine and heads for us, but Arigga holds up a hand and she stops. "Do we really need this on the record?" he asks, looking at me.

"No objection." I'm grateful he is trying to spare Terhovian the humiliation, at least the human part of me is. I have another motivation in keeping this off the record, though: incompetent counsel is grounds for an appeal should the defendant be found guilty. When Rosamund's new lawyer—and I have no doubt he will get a new lawyer if this trial continues—when that lawyer looks through the record and discovers the errors Terhovian has made, he will have little trouble getting the appellate court to grant a new trial. So one of the stranger tasks I have now is to cover for Terhovian, make him look good, prevent him from making mistakes which, while they might bolster my case in the short term, will certainly make it harder for the conviction to stick later.

Arigga waves the reporter away. Marsha wastes no time and takes it upon herself to get things moving, and she asks Terhovian, "Why didn't you make the motion *in limine* before trial?"

Terhovian stays silent. I'm not sure the question even registered.

Arigga picks up the thread. "Yes, Gus," he says, more gently than Marsha, "why wait until trial to do it?"

Terhovian at least pays Arigga enough deference to

acknowledge the question, but he only shrugs his shoulders noncommittally. He's under no obligation to explain his reasoning to the judge. He has made a motion, and if Arigga wants more information before ruling on it, he can ask for it. Depending on how, or if, Terhovian responds, he may or may not win. In this case, of course, he has no prayer of prevailing but he ought to at least argue his side.

This tickling in the back of my head is really starting to bother me. I'm having trouble concentrating, and I think this is beginning to worry Marsha, who perhaps is starting to think I'm becoming as unglued as Terhovian. I would really like to talk to somebody because I'm looking at Terhovian and there is not a doubt in my mind that he is in full possession of all his faculties, every bit as sane as I and a damned sight more poised and confident. My thoughts are starting to triangulate in on some target I can't quite see yet, and I can hear Marsha talking to me. I believe she has spent the last several seconds talking to me, her back turned to Terhovian and Arigga.

"Let's object on procedural grounds," she is whispering to me loudly. "Sal? We'll recess to file briefs and buy some time to figure out how to handle this. Sal!"

Arigga is looking at me strangely. Terhovian is looking at his shoes. And then it hits me.

"You must be out of your fucking mind," I say directly to Terhovian, ignoring both Marsha and Arigga, who I have forgotten are even there. "Taking a chance like that with your client! This is gonna blow up right in your face!"

Not the slightest sign from Terhovian that anything I said registered. Arigga should already be chastising me severely for carrying on this private conversation right in front of him without including him, but he's not reacting either. I know exactly what Terhovian is doing, what he has done, and there is no way he can pull it off and I sense Arigga sees it, too, but he isn't taking Terhovian to task for it, and I decide I better take it seriously although I have no time to explain it to Marsha, who is as confused as I have ever seen her.

"Your honor, what defense counsel has done is not only underhanded and unethical, not only in violation of the spirit of the rules of procedure, it is not in the best interests of his client." I'm back in the game now, fully alert and focused. Marsha sees this right off, and although she doesn't quite grasp what's going on, she's relieved and glad to let me handle it.

That is as far as I get. Arigga's eyes have narrowed and his teeth are clenched. "I would appreciate it if you would let me decide what's unethical in my own court, Mr. Milano."

I start to say something, but before I even get a syllable out he says, "Understood?" in a loud voice that can likely be heard in the first several rows behind the bar.

I'm not worried, only mildly embarrassed in front of one of my deputies. Arigga is trying to regain control, to save some face, because he knows he has to rule against Terhovian but he will be damned if he lets it look like I intimidated him into doing it. I wish I could take a moment to fill Marsha in on what Terhovian, with many years of brutal legal infighting under his belt, has tried to do by skating the outer edges of the law and how badly he is going to fail.

Terhovian wants to prevent anything Diane says from being considered in this trial. He could easily have made his argument in the pretrial hearings. Had he done so and won the point, it would have given me the opportunity to reconsider our strategy, perhaps alter the charges, add some, dismiss a few others. Had he failed, he would have had ample time to reconsider his own strategy, maybe made some different motions, tried some new technical tactics. But once this trial began, something automatically happened that was irretrievable and absolute under the American system of jurisprudence.

Under the law, it is flat out impossible to try a person a second time for a crime of which he has been acquitted. Once a jury finds him innocent or a judge dismisses charges, even if he then jumps up from the defense table and confesses everything right there in the courtroom, he is free to walk out the door. Trying him again is called *double jeopardy* and it is prohibited, with virtually no exceptions.

However, the question arises, at what point is the defendant officially "in jeopardy"? Where is the line which, once crossed, can never be crossed again?

In California, jeopardy is presumed to attach when the jury is sworn in. From that point on, there is no going back. Unless there is a mistrial beforehand, if the prosecution fails to convict, they have lost forever.

What Terhovian has done is to wait until Rosamund was in jeopardy before making his motion to suppress Diane's testimony. Now if he wins his point, our side has no opportunity to change gears. We cannot realistically alter the charges, we cannot bring new ones on Diane's behalf because we already gave up that right, and if we blow it, Rosamund can never be tried for these crimes again. If Arigga excludes Diane's testimony, all I have left is Lisa's word against Rosamund's, with little or no physical evidence. Our case would go from being open-and-shut to being difficult and uncertain. If Terhovian gets away with this, we are in trouble.

But I already know he will not get away with it. He has taken a great and terrible risk with his client at stake. He has no way to know in advance if Arigga will rule favorably on his motion. Had he made the motion in pretrial, he would have had a chance to regroup if things didn't go his way. He might even have been able to plea bargain or simply change his strategy. But if he loses now, he is dead in the water because there is a trial under way and he has rested his entire case on this one tactic. And he will lose it because his motion to exclude Diane's testimony is based on a silly and ridiculous contention that even an undergraduate prelaw major would laugh at. How is it possible that someone like Gustave Terhovian could base his entire defense on this maneuver?

Arigga has leaned back on his seat, although he's still glaring at me. I sense this more than see it because I can't take my eyes off Terhovian. He looks so in control, so serene, and it's starting to scare the hell out of me. He is not even mounting an impassioned argument on Rosamund's behalf, the least he could do for the client he has just effectively convicted single-handedly.

He's still looking at his shoes and I turn to see Arigga, who appears to have forgotten about me. He is stroking his chin, having turned his attention to Terhovian now, and there is something very wrong with this picture, and it occurs to me in a moment of pure terror that the judge might be thinking seriously about Terhovian's motion, and then I realize that he is. This, of course, is a complete impossibility, and for reasons I would only be able to explain much later, my mind shoots back several weeks, and I picture myself walking into an empty courtroom for a scheduled meeting, seeing the bailiff, strolling over . . .

Without thinking, with no planning or any thought at all of my own self-preservation, I turn to Arigga and fire off the single most ill-considered remark of my entire legal career: "Your honor, I want to know what you and Mr. Terhovian discussed before I came into your chambers for the first pretrial meeting."

For the first time since we approached the bench, Terhovian turns his head and looks at me, his jaw hanging partway open. Marsha seems to physically wilt somewhere off to my side, or maybe she just moved off slightly to escape the aura of imminent doom with which I have just surrounded myself. Arigga is too shocked to speak, and his breathing has speeded up. His hands grip the edges of the wooden bench top, and his knuckles are turning white. I notice all this because there is really nothing to do until the shock waves subside. Finally, Arigga seems to find his voice and some semblance of control, although it appears to me he is fighting to restrain himself from tearing off my head.

"I want you to know, Mr. Milano, that I take very seriously defense counsel's suggestion that you be sanctioned before the bar."

I stand as still as I can. Anything I say now will only hurt me worse. It turns out that even doing nothing at all makes Arigga angry. What could I reasonably expect after I implied that he colluded with the defense?

"I find myself inclined to grant defense counsel's motion," he says, and that gets my attention. I jerk my head up, and I believe he is pleased that he has finally gotten to me where it hurts. I feel myself start to panic at the thought that this judge I've just insulted might actually grant this insane motion, and at the thought that my insolent and accusatory demand might have tipped him over into doing it. Marsha is useless at this point, and I have to do something. When in doubt, ask questions.

"Are you seriously considering this motion?" I ask, as respectfully as I can.

"I am considering it," he answers, which tells me nothing: I should have phrased the question differently. "Do you have anything to add?" he asks me.

Arigga knows he can't grant the motion, but he and I have gotten ourselves to the point where we have polarized the problem such that one of us must come out the winner and the other the loser. Somehow, I have to defuse this situation and let Arigga save face. I have to mount an argument, an airtight legal one that he can nod at, mumble about and eventually say, I, Judge Arigga, and not you, Mr. Prosecutor, have reached a conclusion that is fitting and proper under the circumstances. But where do you start to argue when someone tells you in all earnestness that two plus two do not necessarily equal four?

"Your honor," I begin, my voice dense with respect and deference, "whether Diane Pierman's testimony is tainted with bias is something the jury should be allowed to decide for themselves. I did not improperly withhold the fact of her rape, and in any event, it is beside the point. They know it now. If anything, the dramatic manner in which it was revealed hurts my case, not defense counsel's, at least according to his own logic. Let Mr. Terhovian argue to the jury that my attempt to withhold this information from them proves that Diane Pierman is biased and maybe even lying. I can live with him saying that."

"But," Arigga counters, his anger apparently mollified somewhat, "part of my job is to keep unlawfully prejudicial material away from the jury, not burden them with the complexity of sorting out the legality or relevance of evidence when they deliberate. Everything they hear should be properly given, and they can decide what they do or do not believe."

Am I really hearing this? "Quite so," I say, fighting to keep exasperation out of my voice, to make this sound like a reasonable debate between mutually respectful and amiable adversaries, "but consider, for example, testimony given by the victim of a land fraud scheme. Let's say the case was brought by a different party, and this witness was not involved in the transaction in question but is only testifying about what happened to him under similar circumstances. Clearly, this is a biased witness: he wants the defrauders to go away for a long time. But there is no bar to that testimony, right? The jury can decide if he is lying in order to ensure a conviction."

Arigga mulls this over, then says that, in this case, it was my own decision to drop the charges involving Diane. Now that the defense has admitted in open court the commission of a terrible crime against her, it casts a very large pall over her testimony: would she not in fact do or say most anything to ensure the conviction of the man who raped her, regardless of whether the rape against her sister actually occurred? Is there not a reasonable presumption of perjured testimony?

That's it. I have had it. I feel like an idiot even having this discussion, and I am not about to listen to any more specious, pseudo-academic bilge that lends more credibility to the issue than it deserves. If I keep this up, Arigga is going to convince himself that there really is some merit to all of this. Worse, everything being said is off the record because the court reporter is not taking anything down, so where is my evidence when I file an action to have this lunatic removed from the bench? "For Chrissakes, your honor, let the goddamned jury decide for themselves! It's what we pay them for!"

"I told you once," he barks at me, regaining his earlier ire with surprising suddenness, "I'll decide what they hear! And watch your language in my court!"

"Your honor, if you grant this motion, I have nothing left!"

"Not so," he says, "not so. You'll have the sister's testimony. She is the victim, and I am sure she will be very compelling."

Not good enough. I will not have this. "Prosecution would like leave to file an emergency appeal," I declare firmly.

"On what grounds?" Terhovian says out of nowhere. He has been so quiet I wasn't even sure he was paying attention. "There have been no errors of procedure, no compromise or breach in the presentation of evidence, except against my client for which, by the way, all is now forgiven." Very magnanimous: it's the legal equivalent of a football team that just scored a touchdown declining a penalty assessed against the other side.

"Your honor—" I start to say, ignoring Terhovian, but Arigga cuts me off.

"File an appeal against what?" he asks me, all innocence now. "I haven't even made my ruling yet." He spreads his hands and holds them out toward me. "Now, do you have anything else to add?"

Better to leave bad enough alone. We have both had our say, and I believe Arigga has gotten himself to the point where he can do the right thing and look like he is the one in control. "Nothing, your honor."

"Fine." He nods his head, waves us back to our tables, and looks out toward the back rows. "Court is recessed for ten minutes to allow consideration of defense counsel's motion." He is going to go off for a few minutes, pretend to consider all the ramifications, and come back with a ruling that is entirely his own, one he can separate from any notion that he is succumbing to pressure from me. Bottom line, I don't have a problem with that. Let it be entirely his decision, let him be king of the court, as long as we can get back on track and move this thing along.

He bangs his gavel and rises, as do we all, then leaves for chambers. Terhovian and Rosamund are hustled out a side door near the front of the room. As the rear doors open, Nestor Parnell, having heard the commotion, comes back in and makes his way through the crowd of people in the center aisle, standing in the second row behind Diane and Lisa, where he is soon joined by Marty McConagle and Pat Salerno. Marsha and I lean against the bar so we can talk to them.

"The hell is going on, Sal?" Marty asks me.

As briefly as I can, I explain to everybody what Terhovian is trying to do. Summarizing like I am doing, it seems less complicated than it did as it was happening.

"I can't believe Arigga is taking this seriously," Diane says. She's been before him many times and thought she knew how his mind worked, but this doesn't fit with anything in her experience of him.

Parnell is equally confused. "It's not even a matter of

judicial discretion. It's bad law If your side tried to pull something like that, the defense would get an appeal no questions asked."

He knows, of course, that there is no appeal from an acquittal. The prosecution gets one shot and that's the end of it. "What happened, I think I may have gone and pissed him off," I confess.

"Diplomatic you were not," Marsha says, not unkindly. It's obvious to both of us how cool and professional Terhovian came off while I was ranting and insulting the judge. "I bet he cools down in chambers and handles it right. But I gotta ask you something." All eyes turn to her. "What was that question about what they were talking about in chambers?"

Parnell has a quizzical look so I explain. "Three weeks ago, the first pretrial hearing? I show up in court and the bailiff tells me Terhovian is already in Arigga's chambers."

His eyebrows rise up high. "An *ex parte* conversation? In a case like this?" He shakes his head. "Not right."

I nod in agreement. "So I say something and Arigga tells me they were just shooting the shit, haven't seen each other in months, don't get testy about it."

"So what you said to Arigga just now," Marsha says, "you implied there's some collusion going on."

"I wanted to imply that," I say. "I wanted him to think it smelled fishy, like maybe he knew in advance this motion was coming, so he'd realize how bad it looks and kill it immediately. You think I went too far?"

Marsha shrugs. "Just because the judge wanted to strangle you with his bare hands, what makes you think you went too far?"

Everyone laughs but Lisa, whose face is scrunched up in concentration and worry. "Why the recess? If it's so obvious, what's he need to go off and think for?"

Pat Salerno offers a possibility. "Maybe he hadda go pee?"

Now Parnell is the only one not laughing. "It's a good question, Milano. Why the break?"

"Best I can figure," I begin, looking back toward the bench as though Arigga's mind were on display there for me to read, "he got mad at me, thought I was being arrogant. So if he upholds my objection so soon after I tick him off, he loses face. Like I railroaded him or something."

Parnell is nodding now. "So this way he gets to go off and look judicial."

"But what if he grants it?" Diane asks plaintively. "What if he throws out my testimony?"

"We still have mine, don't we?" Lisa says. "Don't I still get to tell my story?"

"Absolutely," Marsha assures her. "But he won't grant it. The whole sorry mess just underscores how desperate the defense is getting."

I agree. "My guess, once he loses his motion, Terhovian is going to ask for a recess to discuss a plea bargain. We get this nonsense out of the way, he's got squat to work with. He's going to have to try to cop a plea."

"Does that mean Rosamund'll get off easy?" Lisa asks.

"Nuh-uh," I tell her. "We let him cop a plea, it's going to have to be a winter—"

"—like mid-February in Antarctica," Marsha adds.

"Right, or we go to the end of trial and put him away until his slick-ass hair turns gray." We shouldn't be using our private, in-house slang in front of Diane and Parnell. We try to keep these kinds of expressions in the family so we don't offend defense attorneys, and also for ethical reasons: we're supposed to be seeking justice, not victory, and plea bargains are supposed to be worked out for reasons that are in the public interest. In this instance, our personal satisfaction at a "winter" plea is more evident than any sense of civic obligation we might harbor.

While we're waiting, Parnell asks what is next. "We're going to call up some witnesses from the restaurant," I tell him, "and that includes you, Marty. Might even get to it this afternoon, so stick around."

"No problem."

Diane leans back to say something private to Parnell, but I hear it clearly. "Thank you for stepping out."

He nods. "How'd you do?"

Diane looks at me, knowing I'm eavesdropping. "She was terrific," I say, meaning it. "Wasn't a person on that jury didn't believe every word."

* * *

The side door opens, and Terhovian and Rosamund walk in without looking at us. The door behind the bench opens and Arigga strides in. Drew Stengel, the bailiff, calls us to rise and to order. Arigga takes up his gavel and bangs it even as he's sitting down, waits a second for silence and for everyone to be seated, looks at his notes and says, "Court grants defense motion to exclude witness's testimony as unfairly prejudicial."

With no further preamble he turns to the jury and begins instructing them, taking no notice of the shock waves radiating outward from the epicenter at our table and rippling across the spectator section. "Ladies and gentlemen, you are to completely disregard everything you have heard from Diane Pierman. As far as you are concerned, she never took the stand, never—"

Marsha doesn't even wait for me this time, is already on her feet shouting over Arigga's voice. "Your honor! Prosecution requests a recess so we can file an emergency appeal in the appellate court!"

"Denied," he says without raising his voice or even looking away from the jury but just continuing his instructions where he left off. "Never said a word in open—"

Marsha will not let it be. "We demand the right, your honor! We can get it in before the day is—"

"I said denied!" Arigga yells at her, taking up his gavel like a weapon.

"On what basis?" she asks heatedly.

"No errors of procedure, no compromise or breach in the presentation of evidence—"

The exact words Terhovian used not twenty minutes ago.

"—no nothing. Your request is denied, so sit down!" He is pointing the gavel at Marsha now.

I yank her sleeve and pull her down onto her seat. There will be no change of heart from Arigga, and Marsha is only inviting a contempt citation. Some weird kind of calm and control has come over me despite the blow Arigga has delivered to my well-cultivated sense of reality. I'm not sure of its source, but I think it has something to do with the fact that no matter how faultless I might appear in losing a case that is going to hell because a burned-out judge has gone off the deep end, I'm still under a moral obligation to do whatever I can to salvage it. I don't think it will be too difficult.

I turn away from Arigga and lean into Marsha, my mouth next to her ear. "Stay quiet, don't panic." I look at my watch: it's a little after one o'clock. "Next break, I'm going to run down to my office, get hold of Laurie." Laurie Ballard is the head of the Appeals Division of the DA's office. "She'll get an appellate judge to stand by when we recess this afternoon. You, me, even Nestor Parnell, we'll all drive down there together and file an emergency appeal, get a writ of prohibition to get this fucking circus stopped." Such a writ is rare and extraordinary, and was designed for when there is no other means of redress for the wrong about to be inflicted by the act of a court below the appellate level.

If I get the writ, which is a virtual certainty—Nestor Parnell will back me up in front of the appeals judge as I describe Arigga's flawed ruling—his honor's career will likely suffer. He will know this: if we press him for leave to file for the writ, he may become entirely unhinged. I would prefer to just get through the day, head downtown and get it done without his foreknowledge.

Marsha has calmed down listening to what I'm saying. Arigga is still talking to the jury, telling them that, in the eyes of the law, Diane Pierman does not even exist. I tell Marsha, just let's get through the rest of this session, that it doesn't matter what happens because we will get Arigga recused on the basis of manifest senility or some-such. Just don't let's do anything stupid in the meantime.

While I'm saying all of this to her, huddled close and progressively less mindful of what is occurring around us, I realize that Arigga has finished his instructions and it is Gustave Terhovian who is doing the talking. I missed the beginning but I hear the last part and it sounds like he has said, ". . . dismissal of all charges against my client."

Sounding foolish, I blurt out, "What? What did he say? I didn't get that."

Terhovian looks at me for a moment, as if he is considering whether I am even worth his repeating what I ought to have been paying attention to, then decides to honor me with the graciousness of a repetition. "Since there is no longer any significant evidence to convict my client beyond a reasonable doubt, all charges against him should be dismissed, immediately and with prejudice."

This little gem helps me recover my equanimity in a hurry. "Excuse me, counselor," I say, unable to keep the sarcasm out of my voice, "but isn't this just a tad early for such a motion, considering that we still haven't heard the victim's direct testimony?" I turn to Judge Arigga. "As you yourself pointed out during our sidebar?"

"Not true." Terhovian says this, not Arigga. The judge is watching, not speaking. *What's not true?* I wonder, and look at Terhovian, who turns to address his remarks to the judge.

"Your honor, the jury has been irreparably sullied by the knowledge of Diane Pierman's rape, a fact that the prosecution tried to hide. There is no way to close that barn door. We cannot truly expect that this jury of honorable men and women is really going to simply forget the fact that my client raped Lisa Pierman's sister."

He pauses, waiting for a reaction. Arigga provides a good one, nodding thoughtfully, like Terhovian wrote the script himself.

"I am fearful," Terhovian goes on, "that even if the prosecution fails to prove conclusively that Vincent Rosamund kidnapped and raped Lisa Pierman, this jury might bring in a verdict of guilty nonetheless, simply out of sympathy for Diane Pierman. They know she was kidnapped. They know she was raped. We admitted that. They know that, for some reason, my client was not charged with those crimes."

He spreads his hands in an expansive gesture of the most innocent supplication. "They might see a need to punish my client for those acknowledged crimes, even though they are not the subject of this trial. And, as I am sure has not escaped your honor's notice, there is reason to believe that Lisa Pierman's testimony itself is subject to enormous bias. After all, is it inconceivable that she might perjure herself in order to ensure the conviction of the man who admitted violating her sister, even if she herself was not a victim?" He drops his hands to his sides, pauses, and bangs his fist on the top of the defense table. "And that would be a most grievous miscarriage of justice, an unspeakable abomination in the eyes of the law!"

Everyone in the courtroom is hanging on his every word. His impassioned speech is mesmerizing. Even Marsha is drawn into his act, and it is time to break this spell.

"Oh, Jesus Christ, Gus!" I say in the most dismissive and cynical tone I can muster. "Are you serious here or what?"

He doesn't respond. There is no need for him to do so: he has been addressing the judge, not me, but now I have everyone's attention, which Marsha proceeds to wreck by standing up with her own remarks.

"Your honor, defense counsel seems to forget we have other witnesses besides Lisa Pierman, like the people who were also in the restaurant that night."

I step in front of her angrily. "You crazy, too?" I say only loud enough for her to hear. "Are you that ready to give up Lisa's testimony on this flimsy bullshit premise?"

"You have something to say, Ms. Jones?" Arigga says. We ignore him.

"Of course not!" she hisses back to me. "I'm just trying to keep this trial going for two more hours so we can get the hell out of here and file for an emergency writ!"

She leans in even closer and turns her head sideways in case Arigga can read her lips. "Do you realize how close this freaking maniac is to dismissing all the charges?"

"Ms. Jones!" Arigga yells angrily, and Marsha finally steps away from me so he can see her. "Did any of these other witnesses see the alleged kidnapping, or the alleged rape, or the alleged assault?"

I can see she is tempted to say yes, they did, but that is too transparent and would never work. According to Diane's testimony and her statements to Pat Salerno and the counselors, sworn statements that we presented during the preliminary hearings, there was nobody else present. Marsha is forced to admit that to Arigga.

"Uh-huh," he says, warming to it. "Uh-huh. Do any of these alleged witnesses have anything of substance to offer other than the subjective appraisal of an insult allegedly made by the defendant in a bar?"

"No, your honor," Marsha says, gritting her teeth, "but there is a wealth of circumstantial—"

"I am not interested in circumstantial anything, Ms.

Jones!" Arigga admonishes her sternly. "A man's reputation and freedom are at stake here!"

I feel a whirlpool forming at my feet. It really *is* Arigga who is cracking up, after all, not Terhovian. The canny defense attorney merely figured it out before I did and played it for all it was worth. For some reason I cannot even begin to guess at, Arigga wants this trial to end, now, and if Terhovian can get him to dismiss all the charges against his client, Rosamund walks out a free man. There is absolutely no appeal available to the prosecution, even if Arigga is disbarred or committed to a psychiatric institution this very afternoon.

Terhovian is pressing it for all it is worth. "Your honor, even if you allow Lisa Pierman to testify, it is her word against my client's, and surely Mr. Milano can never prove his case beyond a reasonable doubt. So why subject Vincent Rosamund to the rigors of a trial the prosecution cannot hope to win?"

It's all flowing down into a black hole. We are helpless before Arigga's unfathomable inclination to side with Terhovian and end this trial in Rosamund's favor. We have to stall, somehow get out of this court and over to the appellate court before Arigga does something irrevocable. Perhaps I can appeal to his vanity, give him a way out that doesn't make him look like a fool. The emergency appeal route won't work: he will get reversed and probably reprimanded as well.

"Your honor, if it please the court, prosecution moves for a mistrial on the grounds of compounded procedural errors." These grounds don't actually exist, but it sounds good, and there is no mechanism for questioning a judge on why he granted a mistrial, so it's safe.

Terhovian will not let it go. "Defense opposes the motion, your honor. The admission of the crimes against the person of Diane Pierman took place in open court. In what venue does the prosecution now assume that my client, an admitted rapist, could possibly get a fair trial?"

Arigga appears to contemplate this seriously, and I can only stare at him, incredulous, as Terhovian's motion hangs like a sword of Damocles over our heads, the threads fraying and flying apart even as we watch. I'm out of ideas. I turn to Marsha, to Parnell, and I get nothing back, only empty and useless astonishment. Arigga makes a steeple of his hands and rests his chin on his fingertips, purses his lips, looks upward and scratches the bottom of his chin, all the signs that some serious and carefully considered decision-making is going on.

Pissing him off is no longer a concern of mine. "Your honor, prosecution demands a recess so that we may appeal to the Second District! There are no grounds upon which you may deny this request!"

Not a movement of his head, not a flick of his eyeballs. It's as though I don't exist. Terhovian is motionless.

"Your honor?"

Nothing.

Arigga clears his throat, pushes his glasses up higher on his nose with one finger, folds his arms on his desk and leans forward. "I have carefully considered the arguments from both the defense and the prosecution," he begins, and I feel as though I have been thrown from an airplane, free-falling through empty space on a collision course with jagged rocks far below me. If Arigga were simply going to overrule Terhovian's motion to dismiss, he would have done it without a lengthy and pompous preamble and simply allowed the trial to continue. This preparatory speech can mean only one thing: he's going to rule against us.

"Your honor!" I interrupt, in a voice so loud it startles the jurors and probably some people behind me in the audience. "There is a prosecution demand before you, and we are waiting for a ruling!"

He ignores me completely. This can't be happening. He hasn't skipped a beat, is still talking, reading from some scraps of paper in front of him. "According to California penal code section eleven-eighteen-point-one, the court, on motion of the defendant, shall order the entry of a judgment of acquittal of the offenses charged if the evidence then before the court is insufficient to sustain a conviction of such offenses on appeal."

"You left a few words out!" I interrupt again. "I believe the section says you do that only after the close of evidence!" Thus my sarcastic comment to Terhovian about the motion being early: it cannot be made before we finish our case, and we are far from finished.

No reaction from Arigga. "I am forced by logic and the law to conclude that, absent the obviously prejudicial testimony of Diane Pierman, and with no other substantive witnesses but the victim, and with no physical evidence of sufficient weight or merit—"

"Your honor, *goddammit,* we're not finished with our case!"

"—the prosecution cannot hope to prove its case beyond a reasonable doubt, and the legal system ought not to subject Vincent Rosamund to the rigors of a trial the prosecution cannot hope to win."

Again, Terhovian's exact words. I am amazed at how articulate and poised Arigga appears even as he parrots the most appalling legal gibberish.

Is he so enraged at me that he's deliberately trying to aggravate me by pretending I'm not even here? I walk out from behind our table and head for the bench, intending to put myself right in his face where he can't ignore me. Bailiff Drew Stengel steps out protectively in anticipation of stopping me if necessary, but I take little heed, except to halt my forward motion so he doesn't interfere. I raise my voice so Arigga's cannot be heard above it. I am nearly yelling.

"It is not the prosecution's responsibility to make the defense's case! I was under no obligation to bring up Diane's rape and you damned well know it! This trial was about Lisa's violation, not Diane's, and there is no reason for me to impugn my own client's testimony, and besides, you can't grant an eleven-eighteen motion before we're finished!" I start mouthing off about miscarriages of justice and judicial impropriety and every other cliché of outrage I can conjure up on short notice and now I'm really yelling, temper lost, insulting Arigga without any regard for his power to find me in contempt and suddenly I notice that *he* notices and he slams his hand down on the bench and screams, "Enough!" so loud it bounces forcefully off the rear walls, bringing me to an instant halt.

He's up out of his seat again, gavel in his trembling hand, pointing it at me. I see that he is not in as much control as I thought. His features are contorted, his face is red and there is more than anger here, but I can't tell what it is. "I told you once and I'm telling you again, counselor; I took defense counsel's request for sanctions against you seriously!"

Terhovian has not said a word in some minutes. The twins are both near catatonic, and Marty is out of his seat, Pat Salerno holding him back. I start up again about emergency appeals or a mistrial, and Arigga swings the gavel around to Drew Stengel.

"Bailiff," he says, his voice now softly modulated but full of unmistakable menace, "if Mr. Milano opens his mouth one more time, cuff him and get him the hell out of my court and into a cell. Don't wait for my order, just do it!"

He turns back to see if I have finally quieted down, and I have. I cannot look at Diane or Lisa. I have failed them miserably and I don't even know why. Arigga's hand on the gavel looks like the trigger mechanism of an atomic bomb, the charge already lit, the implosion already traveling inward to the core. I watch the gavel start to rise, and I see Arigga's lips begin to form words. I sense rather than see movement among the spectators, reporters scribbling frantically without really understanding what's going on, people leaning into each other trying to make sense of it all. The gavel is still rising and words are coming from the judge and I have to concentrate very hard to make them out. I'm vaguely conscious of looking like a blubbering, slack-jawed idiot but I can't help myself and I feel everybody staring at me and then Arigga says, "The state having failed to make a *prima facie* case of sufficient merit to send to the jury, and failing to convince the court that it will be able to do so if allowed to continue . . ." The gavel has ceased its upward travel and hangs, poised, a suborbital rocket at the peak of its trajectory. ". . . all charges against the defendant Vincent Rosamund are hereby dismissed." The gavel is motionless for another brief instant and then reverses direction, accelerating as it falls until it finally slams into the small circle of wood that protects the top of the bench from repeated blows, the sound of the bang radiating out to the far corners of the room, reflecting back to where I am standing and piercing my heart until I want to cry out in pain. I barely hear as Arigga continues: "The defendant is free to go and his bond is to be returned forthwith. The jury is excused with the thanks of the court."

There is a moment's hesitation and then pandemonium in the courtroom, and Marty has enough presence to summon Drew Stengel and his assistant to keep the reporters away from the twins, who are stunned and disbelieving. It is all I can do to force myself to go to them, to watch Lisa as she looks from me to Parnell to Diane and back again, her face all panicked and questioning and frightened. "He let him go?" she asks nobody in particular in a small, weak voice.

Diane is staring straight ahead, her eyes focused distantly. She blinks at the sound of Lisa's voice and turns to her sister, not touching her or making any move to comfort her. "He let him go," she says, her voice flat and dead.

Lisa looks up to me. "Can't we appeal?"

"No," says Parnell from behind her, and she turns to look at him. "We can't. Acquittals are absolute." Parnell then addresses me. "You can get Arigga removed from the bench, that's for goddamned sure, but . . ." Back to Lisa again. "He's a free man, Lisa. He walks." There is no way to soften this message, and he pays Lisa the courtesy of giving it to her straight.

He doesn't bother to fill in the details of all the bad news, doesn't bother to explain the concept of corollary estoppel: because of the dismissal of all the charges and our pretrial agreement not to press charges on Diane's behalf, in the eyes of the law neither Lisa's nor Diane's violation ever took place. So even if we could come up with additional charges against Rosamund, which is doubtful considering we threw the book at him already, we would have no evidence. The kidnapping, the threats, the use of a firearm, his sexual crimes, none of that could be brought up at trial, and thus we could never make the charges stick. He is truly free, truly vindicated. It is only now starting to sink into Lisa. Diane already comprehends it fully.

At the next table, Terhovian is gathering up his papers. I watch as Rosamund offers him his hand, but Terhovian refuses to take it or even look at him. Instead, he glances with acute discomfort in our direction before heading for the back door and leaving the courtroom, without even the standard, obligatory acknowledgment to me of a battle well fought. It is I who should, by tradition, have walked over to him, gamely swallowing my defeat, offering congratulations like a Grosse Pointe blue blood freshly trounced at tennis—*Well struck, Bigsley*—but it was strikingly obvious to the both of us, through some mysterious but unmistakable mental conveyance, that this would have been distastefully unbefitting.

Lisa is on the edge of hysteria. Diane's reaction is more worrisome: she seems to have gone into herself somewhere and is staring vacantly ahead, not even paying attention to Lisa anymore. Priscilla Fields, the rape therapist who had been so helpful earlier, tries to approach Diane, who turns to her slowly and holds up a hand, as if telling her that she is the last thing in the world she needs or wants right now. Priscilla persists—she has seen this sort of thing before—but Diane warns her in threatening tones to back off.

Diane turns to Lisa and takes her arm, telling her in a commanding voice to get up. Against the press of reporters breaking through the barrier the bailiffs are trying to maintain, Diane turns to me and says with icy calm, "Get us out of here."

I motion for Drew to take us through the bailiff's door, and he urges us past the insistent throng, placing himself between us and Vincent Rosamund, whom we can plainly hear talking to reporters.

"True justice was done here today," he is saying. "True justice."

"Hold it a minute!" Eleanor Torjan flings at him over the heads of rival reporters. "The case was dismissed on a technicality. Didn't you admit to raping Diane Pierman?"

Rosamund waves it away with the back of his hand. "Just a legal maneuver, don'tcha get it? Frigid bitch loved it." He cackles smugly, whether out of relief or true evil I cannot tell. "Christ, it was practically a mercy fuck, y'know what I'm sayin' here?"

Diane hears it and stops in her tracks but still looks straight ahead. I shove her gently forward, past the swirls and eddies of human bodies, through the door, across the hall and down the stairs, through a staging area where two startled deputies look up at our entourage, and, finally, out into the ludicrously inappropriate bright light of a California afternoon.

PART
TWO

10

The winter sun raining heat down onto the desert floor is so bright it can't even be discerned as a disk in the sky. It's more like an indistinct smear somewhere above, the glow from an industrial-size furnace with the door left open, flames licking out and searing the surroundings to near incandescence.

This is hard desert, arid and implacable for most of its considerable extent, yet I'm standing on a field of brilliant green grass, date palms lining the left edge, a half-acre pond on the right, the sound of a small waterfall coming from somewhere ahead and to the left. This entire region sits above a rich aquifer fed from the north, and it takes very little to bring the water to the surface and work such magical transformations as this, the eighteenth hole of the Indian Wells golf course in Palm Springs, where I stand at ten o'clock in the morning, the Monday after the Thursday on which Vincent Rosamund's trial came skidding to an ignominious and surrealistic halt. I'm playing alone, having secured that privilege by beginning before dawn, as I have each of the past two days. I came to wring myself out in the oppressive heat, having sunk into an almost clinical depression following the dismissal of the charges, hoping that a bit of isolated introspection in a physically hostile environment might allow me to regain some perspective.

How could I possibly have fucked this up so badly?

Hanging around the office Friday—a big mistake—

caused me to go into one of my periodic funks, a mid-life career crisis of the first magnitude. Even the consoling remarks by the more thoughtful of my colleagues who bothered to stop by had the wrong effect on me, not bolstering my damaged confidence but underscoring the blow just suffered by my painstakingly constructed aura of invincibility. I tortured myself with an excruciatingly detailed analysis of every move I made in this case until I realized, not for the first time, that procedural machinations, legal maneuvering and case strategizing have a good deal to do with brilliant lawyers, competitive egos, legislative caprice and the jurisprudential fads and fashions of the day but precious little to do with the reasoned dispensation of justice. Everybody just wants to win, even if the intricately bizarre, Rube Goldberg construction of rules oftentimes renders victory hollow or defeat inevitable.

At times like these, when I'm in danger of flying off the top of the morose scale, I even find myself questioning some of the constitutionally based axioms that we all take for granted as among the most glittering conceptual jewels of our society, such as the prohibition against compelling someone to testify against himself. How many times have I been in court where the defendant is the only person in the room who knows for sure if he committed the crime and he is the only person in the room I cannot question about it? Vincent Rosamund knew for certain whether he did what the Pierman twins allege he did, and he was able to sit in the courtroom in full view of his accusers and those tasked with assessing his guilt and say nothing, held tightly against the warm, soft, comforting bosom of the Fifth Amendment while his victims shivered, naked, in the cold of its indifference to them.

Many such concepts have their genesis in truly worthy objectives, such as that of not repressing the right of the people to dissent. But in modern times, such splendid notions have been exploited largely by common criminals, the original precepts subverted into unrecognizability. Rights have been elevated to such an exalted position of nobility that the concomitant obligations have gotten lost in the noise. Something tells me the founding fathers did not have Vincent Rosamund in mind when they penned the Bill of Rights.

Late Thursday night, after my brain had stopped reeling long enough for me to think a bit more clearly about things but before anybody could stop me, I prepared a complaint against Judge Arigga to be filed with the Judicial Conduct Committee of the state bar association. I gave him both barrels, alleging gross misconduct, incompetence, malfeasance, dereliction of duty and a host of equally egregious-sounding charges, venting every ounce of my considerable rage on the seven pages it took to lay it all out on my word processor, burning up the eighty-thousand-word electronic thesaurus in the process. Then I printed it out and stuck the paper in my desk drawer, forcing myself against all instinct to adhere to one of my most ironclad life rules: a minimum of twelve hours between whatever it is that pisses me off and whatever it is I do about it. Circumstances permitting, of course: I wish I'd had that luxury in the courtroom when I felt Arigga rocketing out of control, but I didn't, and my resultant loss of temper may have cost us the trial. I wonder how that would look if I run for DA and my opponent, probably Gerard Beckman, trots it out for the world to see. Not to worry: I'd have about as much chance of winning a DA election now as Alan Dershowitz.

I pulled out the printout early Friday morning, read the first half page and threw it all away. I started over, forgoing the computer and using a pad of paper and a splendid DuPont fountain pen I got as a birthday present. I knew that this method would achieve what I failed to accomplish on the computer, a certain economy of language necessitated by the inability to instantly cut, paste, move, rearrange, emphasize and otherwise embellish what ought to be flat and emotionless text. What I needed to do was to strip out of the words any hint of anger, frustration or the desire for revenge and render the narrative studied and businesslike, a totally objective and professional assessment that merited serious attention by virtue of its calm and reasoned analysis. If I were clever enough, the towering significance of what I was trying to convey would be underscored by deliberate understatement and restraint. *If you would be so kind and it isn't too much trouble, sir, please take note of the torpedo presently two hundred yards to starboard headed in our direction. . . .*

Marion typed it—one look at my face and she assumed, correctly, that I was not to be questioned about it—and I filed it before my first cup of coffee. Superior court justices are elected by the people, not appointed, so it isn't easy to get one removed. Of course, the people have no idea who any of these candidates are: a slate is proposed and automatically voted in by the six or seven percent of the voters who actually bother to punch those sections of the ballot, there being no alternatives presented. But there are ways to get the bad ones out, and I have taken the first step.

My father's friend, the tailor, used to say that if you're going to go after the king, you'd better make damned sure you kill him. If Arigga doesn't go down, I'll have an enemy for as long as I'm a prosecutor, which will likely not extend more than a few days beyond his vindication, at least not in California and maybe not anywhere. Marsha came in to commiserate and looked over Marion's shoulder as she typed, then asked me to think real hard about what I was doing—*pick your battles carefully* yet again. She wonders if maybe Arigga didn't just have a particular bug up his butt, as she put it, one which we might even be able to understand, and would be back to normal by Monday. I countered that if he had a particular bug up his butt, you would expect that it would relate to his only daughter and a desire to keep rapists off the streets, so there has to be more to it than that.

By that afternoon, I had to get out of town. The stampede of people climbing over each other to make me look bad had already begun, with Beckman leading the charge. At first I treated it as a natural reaction, people in the legal community reflexively protecting a judge and the elected DA, but in truth I knew better. The prevailing sentiment seemed to be that I should have filed an emergency appeal during the pretrials and gotten this all sorted out when it was still fixable, rather than embarking on a creative but risky strategy that depended for its success on the court's acceptance of its radical premises. In retrospect, it is difficult to explain why I didn't file such an appeal. I am even having difficulty explaining it to myself. Marsha, having designed the alternate strategy, has gallantly tried to absorb some of the blame, but I won't let her do that: she was just dealing with my obstinacy as best she could and has no culpability whatsoever.

I simply had a very strong feeling at the time about what it would take to secure a conviction without unnecessarily muddying the waters with a messy and risky pretrial appeal. Now I will have to reexamine my thinking, and this is the thing that is scaring me more than anything else: what makes me such a good prosecutor—just ask anybody—is an unerring instinct that has rarely failed me in the past and never with such disastrous results. It has shaken my confidence badly. Couple that with losing my temper and insulting a judge in open court and it is a wonder that I am not already prosecuting speeding tickets in Encino. Run for DA? I might as well run for pope. It may look bad, my skittering away to the desert, but I was in such a bleak mental state that I didn't trust myself to talk to my grocer, much less the press or Gerard Beckman. My supportive boss. His quoted sound bite was something along the lines of, "This is an outrage, and I'm going to get to the bottom of it, starting with my own office. But I take full responsibility." He even made himself look manly by immediately "taking responsibility." Responsibility for what? For how one of his people screwed up, obviously. How much more blatantly could he have hung me out to dry?

I'm feeling very sorry for myself. Even Eleanor Torjan called to berate me for embarrassing her by letting her print a story saying that there were two rape charges. I reminded her that she wasn't supposed to have printed that story at all, so where was my obligation to see that it was accurate, but the logic of this was lost on her.

I ranted on for a while longer about the more important issues of justice and retribution, but I don't think Eleanor was particularly enamored of my extemporaneous treatise, and I have no idea which pieces of it wound up in print. That's the real power of the press, not in fabrication but in editing, serving up carefully apportioned dollops of the larger truth to whatever purpose the reporter and editor feel appropriate.

Christ, I'm in a bad mood. I'm torturing myself with these thoughts under a blistering sun, struggling around the course and taking it all out on a hapless and defenseless golf ball that responds in kind with a series of physically impossible hops, corkscrews, hooks and dribbles that make my usual forty-handicap game look graceful by comparison. I was even nasty to the range marshal on the par-five sixteenth, an unpaid retiree who fishes your ball out of the lake in front of the green for no other reward than a few seconds of pleasant conversation, this time concerning a helicopter that had landed near the clubhouse about twenty minutes ago. I told him to keep the damned ball, then bounced my cart over the retaining curb to the seventeenth without even finishing the hole, tripled the stupid par-three, and headed for eighteen, promptly dropping my tee shot onto the street on the other side of the out-of-bounds fence.

I'm beyond caring about this round and place a new ball in the middle of the fairway just to avoid any more aggravation. I'm about 225 yards from the green and as I look over there to line up my shot, I see somebody standing next to the cart path. It's probably a greenskeeper, since he's dressed from head to foot, too experienced to expose any skin to this sun. He is politely awaiting my shot, keeping still so as not to disturb my concentration, which he has no way of knowing is nonexistent. Nevertheless, now that I have an audience, I try to focus on the fundamentals, forgoing a fairway wood for a three-iron which, from a purely statistical point of view, I have a better chance of hitting cleanly.

I'm not sure why I love this sport, but I think it has something to do with the occasional stroke in which every single element of a horrendously complicated game blends together in a single perfect moment, a transcendent unity of mind, body, ball, club and environment that is as sublime as it is effortless. No matter how badly I play, every once in a while such a shot reminds me that there is no reason why I can't play better, that if I can whack a beauty once in a while, I ought to be able to do it more often. It may be luck, but as Ben Hogan himself put it, the more I practice, the luckier I get. Maybe the reason so many lawyers play golf is that it's an almost perfect metaphor for the life of the litigator, endless plodding and duffed shots relieved by the rare epiphany timed to appear at just the precise moment that will make you come back for more.

On the other hand, I once played a round with a famous pro who afterward gave me some sage advice: "Son," he said, "I want you to lay off completely for three weeks, then quit the game for good."

I know that I'm supposed to swing easy to hit hard, but what the hell, it's the last hole: I wind up and I can tell from the backswing that I'm in the groove, so I uncork with everything I have and watch, blissfully, as the ball rockets upward and into the distance following a sweet, pure click. It starts out headed for the right side of the green, just where the fully clad man is standing, but as it begins to lose some of its purely ballistic momentum and the spinning dimples bite into the air, it arcs gracefully to the left and drops onto the front of the green, rolling slightly uphill and coming to rest less than fifteen feet from the flag. My eye is on the man, and I think I see him nod in approval. As nonchalantly as I can, I place the club back into the bag, crack one or two knuckles and get into the cart. Nothing to this game.

As I drive up on the cart path, the figure turns fully toward me and I have to blink a few times. Marty McConagle looks for all the world like being here is the most natural thing imaginable. I have a few seconds to compose myself into similar nonsurprise, and I drive up to within a few feet of him. He's wearing a tie, loosened, but no jacket.

"Nice shot," he says calmly. Sweat glistens on his upper lip.

I shrug, looking over at the ball as if for the first time. "Not too bad. Could've kept it a bit lower."

"Uh-huh." He waits until I get my putter and begin walking onto the green. "You mean like that piece'a shit you just plopped onto Highway One-eleven?"

"Saw that, did you?"

"Saw it? Nearly took out a red Mercedes. Good thing I'm not in uniform."

I leave the flag in and stand over the ball, lining up the

putt. I give it something extra for the uphill lie, and it hits the flag, hard. It would have gone at least ten feet past if the pin hadn't stopped it, but now it's less than a foot away.

"Was me, I'd call it in," Marty says. He's about fifty feet away, but it's so deathly still out here that he speaks barely above a whisper and I can hear him plainly.

"Nope," I say, and pull out the flag, a stout display of sportsmanship. I tap the ball in, pick it up and replace the stick.

As I head back toward Marty, he's nodding his approval of my honesty and says, "So what's that give you?"

I pretend to count on my fingers and then tell him, "About a hundred and thirty."

He grins at the joke with bearish good humor, and it is then that I see he doesn't look so good: pale, drawn, disheveled, as if he hasn't slept in days. His eyes are pained and troubled, and I see that it's taken him some effort to play along with my little game for a few minutes and contain within himself whatever reason he had for coming out here.

He gets into the cart, taking the wheel; I put away the putter and get in on the other side. He drives us up about fifty feet until we're beside the artificial waterfall, stops and sets the brake, then turns to me.

"Vinny Rosamund's dead," he says.

I draw back in surprise and raise my eyebrows as this sinks in, Marty staying quiet.

"Can't honestly say this strikes me as bad news, big guy," I say after a few moments. "How'd he die?"

"One of the Pierman twins shot him."

My breath catches in my throat, and I can't quite manage the next question so he answers it without my asking.

"We don't know which one."

"What do you mean, you don't know?"

"I mean, we don't know, and they're not saying."

It is one in an endless succession of chi-chi eating establishments of surpassing pretense, initially popularized by a review in the *LA Times* that would rival any pre-Renaissance religious paean for sheer overuse of extolling prose, once overcrowded with swarms of beautiful people less interested in gustatory bliss than in scoring another notch on their silver spoons before the place closed, which it surely would inside of six months. Tawqinah boasts not only a deliberately unpronounceable name, an unlisted telephone number and eighteen varieties of tap water but such things as striped bass imported from New Zealand, despite the fact that the best such fish in the world can be caught barely a Frisbee toss from its own front door.

It's the kind of place to eat in once so you could say you did, forever after begging off with quibbling criticisms about the veiny radicchio or thready ratatouille, thereby saving yourself a repeat experience of gagging at the prices and going home hungry after a full meal. Those on expense accounts—studio executives, sports promoters, foreign diplomats and members of various county commissions—lingered longer, but by now, most everybody has figured out that this particular emperor has few clothes indeed and has moved on to worship at the mesquite grills of other chefs who command reverence equaling that of a venerated tenor. Now Tawqinah is populated primarily by people pretending to be rich who are trying diligently to impress other people who are pretending not to be impressed by people who are rich, a futile game with paradoxical rules whose only winners are the restaurant's investors.

Tonight the place is less than a quarter full. The power table is occupied, at least the one on the far corner most distant from the maître d's podium. There are half a dozen power tables, and the big trick for the maître d' is to memorize to whom he has told which one was really the power table, so he doesn't get them mixed up on repeat visits. You can get a power table by being the chairman of Paramount or a recent Oscar winner (major categories only, please) or by slipping a fifty to the maître d', which is how Vincent Rosamund got his table tonight. A hundred would have gotten him the one closer to the window by the front door, as well as an expansive and sincere hug and warm greetings in front of the whole restaurant from said maître d', whom he has never laid eyes on before. The raven-haired beauty on his arm had remained cool and aloof as they were escorted to your usual table, m'sieur, led by the maître d' because Vinny had no idea where his usual table was, this being his first visit. The fifty had been passed earlier this afternoon when Vinny stopped in to make the reservation, because he didn't have the unlisted number either.

Vinny had blanched at the menu, but it had nothing to do with the prices. It was simply that he didn't understand French. This was beside the point, anyway, since he would not have understood anything that was written there had he been born and raised right in the Second Arrondissement. He slapped his menu closed with a flourish and suggested to his companion—Veronique, or something close to that, he couldn't quite remember—that his old friend Bernhard choose the dinner items for them. The maître d', whose name was in actuality Gerhard, was only too happy to oblige. Vincent silently hoped that he wouldn't choose anything too unfamiliar and disgusting, although even that would be preferable to something he didn't know how to eat in the first place, like one of those absurd little green swatches you could never tell if you were supposed to eat or just admire.

It seems awfully expensive, Veronique had said generously, after Vinny had dispatched Gerhard/Bernhard and it was too late to do anything about how expensive it was. It's a kind of celebration, he had answered. Of what? Had a little trouble with the law, he had answered, got off (snap) just like that. What kind of trouble? she had asked, wide-eyed with admiration and curiosity. Ah, you know . . . the usual, making her think it was some enormous drug deal that it took a wad of cash to fix. Probably not a good idea to let her know he had beaten a double-rape charge, through a combination of his own cleverness in how he had committed the crime and the wily machinations of his syndicate-supplied attorney. He leered at her, thinking, let's hope I don't have to get away with it again too soon. Before long, they are daintily dipping into their appetizers, she fairly certain that the long, stringy things on top are edible, he less sure that breaking through the crust and scooping out the insides was correct and proper, both not quite confident about the red-green goop in the shape of a yin-yang upon which the whole concoction rested.

The front door opens, causing the bartender to start because he hadn't noticed any action at the valet stand. A single woman enters. She's wearing an oversize, black Los Angeles Stars sweatshirt over ordinary blue jeans. The bartender starts to frown in disapproval, then thinks better of it: maybe this is the latest thing in fashionable evening wear, who knows? She's also wearing dark sunglasses, completely normal despite the lateness of the hour, and a long scarf that covers her neck and the lower part of her face.

"Can I help you, madame?" Gerhard asks politely, suspending his disdain until he can ascertain whether this is a somebody or an interloper.

"Just meeting a friend," she answers, not breaking stride as she moves past the podium and into the dining area. She casts her eyes about briefly and makes a left turn, heading for the far corner opposite the bar.

Vincent takes no notice until she is only ten or so feet away, then looks up in annoyance, no recognition on his face. The woman reaches underneath the sweatshirt and withdraws a .45 automatic pistol, holding it straight out and gripping it with both hands, one wrapped firmly around the grip, the other clasping the trigger hand from below. Her feet are planted a shoulder's width apart.

"Hey . . ." Vinny drops the whatever-it-is onto his plate and raises both hands about neck high.

The woman points the gun at the table behind them and says, "You might want to move over a bit."

A young couple scrambles frantically off to the sides, freezing when the woman unwraps the bottom hand and holds it up for them to stop. Then she points the gun at Veronique and wiggles the barrel until the redhead gets the message and also moves away. She gives no such directions to Vinny, who raises his hands a little higher and says, "Hey!" again, only louder this time, as the woman replaces the steadying hand under the grip and points the barrel at him once again.

With little further ado she squeezes the trigger. The explosion from the large-caliber bullet is shocking in the enclosed space, almost painful. Everybody winces in response, and it thus takes them a moment to realize that several hundred grains of heavy metal have entered the chest of the young man in the shark-gray suit, expanding several times in size before leaving through his back, taking a fair-sized chunk of his innards with it.

The sound is still reverberating around the room but nobody is moving, all of them too terrified to do anything but sit still and pray that the nice young man was the intended target, which would mean that this was not a random shooting, which would mean they might survive if they didn't do anything stupid. Most of them are too unsophisticated in firearms to know that there aren't enough rounds in a .45 to do them all, which is a pretty good clue that there is some focus to this woman's madness. Besides, she is wearing dark glasses and a scarf, which means she doesn't have to kill them all as potential witnesses if they just stay still. The thing on the floor that used to be human makes a few wet, sucking sounds and dies.

Veronique figures out that some of Vincent's blood and some other stuff she cannot identify has splattered her white leather outfit and barely notices that the woman is speaking to her. "Wh-what?" she stammers.

"I said, I just did you a big favor."

The woman gives a last glance in Vinny's direction. He is splayed out indecorously along the wall against which he was thrown by the force of the bullet. The pressure inside his chest was so large that his eyes bug out slightly and blood trickles from his ears.

The woman turns and walks rapidly back toward the door. Lest any of the braver potential heroes in the room get any smart ideas, she whirls suddenly and points the gun once more, this time in the general direction of several diners. Having a loaded weapon pointed at you is one of the most acutely uncomfortable feelings imaginable, and this action disabuses them all of any fancy notions regarding heroism in her capture, although they do notice that her abrupt movement has caused the scarf to drop from her face. Moments later, she is out the door and gone, just another body in the sea of strollers along Santa Monica's promenade, many of whom are moving in to see what the ruckus is about but barely notice her as she exits.

Nobody moves for about a minute, even though most of them have enough presence of mind to think that somebody ought to call somebody. But what if she decides to turn around and see if anybody is making a phone call? The valet parkers are long gone, having departed as soon as the shot was fired: for $4.25 an hour, they generally eschew altruistic intervention on behalf of people who can afford to eat in places like this.

It is a full two minutes before the bartender makes the call to 911, another two before he gets through, another three before the operator feels she has wrung enough useless details out of him to warrant a call to the Santa Monica PD, and two more before word is radioed to a pair of bicycle-mounted SMPD patrolmen who were only two blocks away from the restaurant to begin with. It is about five more minutes before they can start taking statements because they first need to calm down three hysterical patrons whose distress has nothing to do with the shooting but with the fact that their companions for the evening are not their spouses but other people's or, in one case, of the same rather than opposite sex, normally not a big deal but awkward for a priest.

Eventually it all gets sorted out, and word is dispatched to the detective bureau and DA's office about thirty minutes later.

11

We're still sitting by the waterfall, Marty and I. The sun has risen higher in the sky, and impossibly, it's grown even hotter. There isn't a breath of wind, no birds on the wing or even singing in the trees, not a squirrel or lizard in sight; it's as though the heat has crushed even the omnipresent insects beneath its weight. The only sound other than the waterfall since Marty last spoke was the rattle of a pair of golf carts from the foursome that was well behind me, heading for the clubhouse and a few tall, cool ones after skipping the eighteenth. We didn't turn our heads to say hello as they passed, and they were too hot to care.

I reach for the squeeze bottle resting in the cup holder mounted to the right of the steering wheel. Now grown warm, it's full of erg, an electrolyte replacement fluid used by endurance athletes. If I keep slugging at it the heat never really bothers me. I take a long draft and offer some to Marty, who waves it away.

"Make you feel better," I tell him.

He reaches into his pocket for a cigarette. "Couple people a few blocks away from the Promenade, they saw a woman fitting the clothing description get into a green Lexus and drive off."

Lisa's car. "They ID the face?"

He shakes his head. "Got the height and weight right. No license number 'cuz there wasn't any reason to note it down."

"Then why'd they notice at all?"

Marty lights the cigarette and inhales deeply, blowing the smoke out over the pond in front of the waterfall. It forms a light blue cloud and then hangs there, undisturbed, dissipating slowly but in no hurry to go anywhere. "It was parked in a handicapped zone, flashers blinking."

Like someone left it for only a few minutes. Like they had to run a quick errand and were hoping nobody would notice a lapse of the new social etiquette. "Not exactly a heat of passion kind of thing, huh?"

Marty grunts and takes another drag. I bet he's not wearing any sunscreen, either. I'm slathered in two layers of waterproof, sweatproof number thirty, a veritable suit of armor. A cart with a lone rider comes at us from the other side, the direction of the clubhouse. I recognize one of the attendants as he pulls up.

"You guys all right?" he asks amiably.

"Yeah," I tell him as I stand up and step out. "Just hanging out for a couple minutes."

"No problem." He gets out himself and walks to the back of his cart, reaches into the plastic ice chest mounted on the fender and pulls out a container of fresh ice water. He tosses it to me without warning, and I have to scramble but I catch it. "Just keep drinking. You should see two of the guys just came in."

I thank him and he drives off, probably hoping he can force some fluids on the macho types still out there who think playing without taking any water is some kind of test of manhood. I dump about half the container into my squeeze bottle and hand the rest to Marty. "Don't be a schmuck."

He relents, polishes the whole thing off in one long slug and sets the bottle down in the cup holder. "Happy?"

"Delirious. Then what?"

He pulls out a handkerchief and runs it over his brow, then dips it in the pond, wrings it out and wipes the back of his neck. "Took the cops less than twenty minutes to put it all together, and they dispatch a car to Lisa's house."

"Who?"

"Pappas." Of course. "They show up, Diane answers the door, Lisa's sitting in the living room."

"What are they doing?"

He knows why I ask. "Nothing. Not watching television, not reading the paper . . . nothing."

Just waiting for the police to show up. "What're they wearing?"

"Other stuff. Not what the shooter wore."

"So what's Pappas do?"

Marty shifts in the seat, leans forward and grabs the back of his shirt, pulling and wiggling it to unstick it from his sweaty back. "You know Pappas, he knows when to bullshit, when not. He tells them, look, somebody fitting your description capped Vincent Rosamund; you wanna tell me which one'a you did it?"

"And they stay quiet."

"Natch. So Pappas asks them to identify themselves, then he tells Diane she's under arrest and starts to read her her rights."

Starts to read, he said. "But she does what . . . ?"

"She asks him, what probable cause does he have, and Dan tells her, we're familiar with the fact pattern in your previous encounter with the victim, and the witnesses' description of the shooter fits your description. And then she says—"

"Uh-oh."

Marty nods. "She says, how do you know you got the right one?"

I take a swig from my squeeze bottle. The erg is now diluted but at least it's cold. I should have kept it in the ice chest on the back of the cart, but I didn't much feel like moving around while we were talking.

"But Pappas was ready for that," Marty continues. "He says, I don't have to know, I only have to reasonably suspect, and I got a fifty-fifty chance of being right. And she says—you're gonna love this, she's a smart broad—she says, it's only fifty-fifty if you're sure it was one of us; otherwise it's a lot less, isn't it?"

I have to smile at this, but I can guess what Dan's response was. "And he says, well, I got good news and I got bad news: the good news, I don't need fifty-fifty; the bad news is, you're under arrest."

Now it's Marty's turn to smile. "Somethin' like that. Then he turns around and does the whole thing all over again with Lisa. He asks them, where'd they put the gun, but they both keep their mouths shut."

"Diane's doing. It's the right move." I'm being objective and analytical so Marty won't see I'm dying. I think he knows already. Why else come all the way out to this inferno instead of phoning?

"Dan had 'em taken downtown in separate cars. By that time a search warrant arrived."

"Who signed it?"

"I don't know. It make a difference?"

"Don't know. What'd they find?"

"A Stars sweatshirt hanging in the closet, but no piece."

"A Stars sweatshirt. Shit."

Marty takes a final hit on the cigarette and looks for a place to stub it out. Everything is so pristine, so unnaturally clean, he can't bring himself to toss it, although I can tell he was close to throwing it in the pond. He twirls out the ash and tobacco and puts the filter in his pocket, military-style. "Patty Salerno called me soon's she found out. I got the skinny and came out to find you."

He reaches down to a black lever mounted below the seat and flips it to reverse, then backs the cart away from the wall before shifting again and heading us toward the clubhouse.

"Wouldn'ta come, I'd a'known it was so fucking hot."

Yes, he would have.

We drive back to LA together in my car. Marty flew out in the helicopter I noticed landing somewhere in front of the hotel, courtesy of another one of his countless buddies, this time a San Bernardino County medevac pilot usually assigned to yanking wayward hikers and campers out of the canyons in the rugged mountains just to the north. The variety of geography in southern California never fails to astound me. The long drive back is like a symphony, starting in the quiet and relaxed exposition of the desert with opening notes of muted colors, reaching a coda in the cool limitlessness of the Pacific Ocean. The temptation to jump in and swim forever is strong.

It's about two in the afternoon, and we're waiting on the pier for Marsha Jones to show up. I don't want to go near the office just yet. A homeless man on crutches approaches us. I recognize him from the distance because of his slicked-back hair and deeply chiseled features, so I'm not surprised at his perpetually red-rimmed and watery eyes, the signs of a chronic drunk.

"Felix. What happened to your leg?"

"Broke it." His speech slurs almost into unrecognizability. "Just t'row me off the pier, okay? Don' wanna live no more."

The cast is at least two weeks old, peeling at the edges and crusted with filth. His technique on the crutches is wobbly. I notice that they are of two different types and sizes, even though both are adjustable.

Marty notices, too. "Siddown, Felix. Gimme those."

Felix complies, and Marty starts to unloosen a screw on one of the crutches.

"Hey, Mis'a Depitty Dee-yay, gimme a buck, I can git a hah dog."

"Where you going to get a hot dog for a buck, Felix?"

"Don' worry, I get it."

"You mean you'll drink it, you dumb rummy," Marty says without malice.

"Fuggin' cop, whyn't you min' yer own bidness?"

"How many times I gotta tell ya, Felix: I'm not a cop."

I can see Marsha at the top of the ramp leading to Ocean Avenue as I walk across the boardwalk. I buy a hot dog and drown it in mustard and onions, then bring it back to where Marty has finished adjusting the crutch, and hand it to Felix.

"The fug izzis?" he asks me, looking quizzically at his hand.

"It's a hot dog. You said you wanted a hot dog."

He shakes his head and looks at Marty. "He's almos' dumb as you, cop."

"Eat it," Marty tells him, and hands back the crutch. He stands over Felix and makes sure he starts eating the hot dog. Serious alcoholics without money often forgo food because an empty stomach helps them get drunk faster. Felix is a Vietnam vet who did two years north of Da Nang only to return home and find both his wife and his old job gone, and a citizenry acutely embarrassed by his very existence.

We leave him munching disconsolately on the hot dog and head toward Marsha, who hasn't spotted us yet. She's walking more slowly than her usual purposeful stride, and her mouth is set in a tight line. I suspect she's not sure how I took the news and may be anxious about seeing me.

"Hey!" Marty calls out, and she looks around to try to localize his voice, finding me first.

"How was the desert?" she asks as she approaches.

"Hot," I answer, "but not as much as if I'd stayed here." She nods in understanding. "You check your machine?"

"No."

"Tape's probably full by now anyway. I was more than glad to field phone calls from every asshole on the planet trying to get 'hold of you, though." She pauses for a moment. "Don't mention it."

"Thanks," I tell her. "Beckman?"

She shakes her head. "He doesn't work weekends. You'll hear from him today."

Great. My boss beating me about the head and shoulders, trying to save face in an election year, ought to put a pleasant cap on my day. "Anybody seen them yet?" I'm referring to Diane and Lisa.

"Nope. Waiting for you. Had any lunch?"

"Not hungry." The sight of Felix's hot dog nearly made me gag. I ask Marty if he needs to eat.

"It can wait. We better go do this."

I turn to look out toward the end of the pier. It's an unseasonably warm day, and a light haze hangs in the air. Seagulls are wheeling around in the sky over the fishing platform, looking out for errant pieces of bait they can steal. I envy them, looping around in the air and not giving a shit about anything but their next meal.

The police station is five minutes and half a world away from the pier. Nestor Parnell is walking up from the parking lot just as we round the northeast corner of the building. I suspend any comment because Eleanor Torjan bears down on us from out of nowhere at the same time.

"Sal!"

"Eleanor. What took you so long?"

"Don't get snotty: I'm still mad at you." Which is how I know she really isn't. She has her portable tape recorder out, microphone in hand. "Are you going to press charges against the twins?"

The question throws me. "Are you serious?" I answer, and point to the recorder, making a downward waving motion with my hand. She clicks it off and we have a deal: no direct quotes in exchange for more candid responses. She pulls a pen and writing pad out of her handbag. "Why wouldn't I press charges?" I ask her back.

"Because they were raped and the guy got off on a technicality. What, it's such a stupid question?"

"Are you telling me for sure they were raped and for sure one of them shot Rosamund?"

"Well, didn't she?"

"How the hell should I know?"

"Oh, for Chrissakes, Milano!"

"Eleanor, you're a reporter, not a psychic. How's it possible you already brought in a guilty verdict and I haven't even asked them any questions yet, tell me."

I have a real way with public relations sometimes, but what the hell: my political ambitions are in the Dumpster anyway. Like I told Diane on the pier weeks ago, I needed one big triumph to justify putting my name on the ballot for DA. What I got instead was one giant, very public shellacking. And who, outside of a small handful of friends, is going to believe that it wasn't my fault, that the judge went cuckoo at the worst possible moment?

And Eleanor *is* asking a dumb question, although it isn't any dumber than a lot of people might ask in similar circumstances.

"So you're going to prosecute."

"I'm going to prosecute."

"On what charges?"

"I don't know yet. I don't have enough background. One shouldn't leap to conclusions before one has the data."

"Oh, shouldn't one?" She regrets the sarcasm right away, not out of conscience but because I still represent a good data source for her. "Cut me a little slack, Sal. What's going on? Jones?"

Marsha looks to me for permission, and I nod. "Diane and Lisa Pierman have been arrested on suspicion of homicide," she tells Eleanor, who has flipped the tape recorder back on. There was no reason not to, as Marsha will stick largely to the public record, at least for now. "A woman fitting their description shot and killed Vincent Rosamund in a restaurant last night. We don't have a specific suspicion as to which one was the shooter—"

"Are they talking?" Eleanor interrupts.

"They're standing on their Miranda rights, and—"

"Who's representing them?" Eleanor breaks in again.

"We don't yet—"

Nestor Parnell steps forward and puts his hand out, palm down. "Might I suggest we table this for the time being?" I had forgotten he was standing there.

"Who're you?" Eleanor demands, but Parnell has me by the arm and is steering me inside the station. I offer no resistance because I'm grateful for him getting us away from Eleanor without making it look like we're retreating. Marsha gives her a helpless shrug and follows us in, Marty close behind. I wonder irrationally if Parnell knew anything in advance of the shooting.

Parnell's face is full of concern and shock. "What the hell was that all about? What's going on?"

"What are you doing here, Nestor?"

He looks around and then leans in close, his voice low. "I got a call from the night switchboard, said Diane called and I should get here no delay. That's it. That's all I know."

He is unshaven, and his tie looks like he put it on while driving. His face is lacking some of the self-possession it usually carries; I think it disappeared during Marsha's brief conversation with the reporter. He really doesn't have a clue.

"One of them shot Rosamund?" he asks tentatively, almost as if he is afraid to say the words, forgetting even to throw in the obligatory "allegedly."

"Would appear so," I answer.

He glances from Marsha to me. "Which one?" He inclines his head back toward where Eleanor is still standing, fuming. "I mean, really." Like we didn't tell Eleanor but it's okay to tell him. I realize we have something in common: we're both fervently hoping it wasn't Diane.

"We really don't know," Marty tells him. "They both fit the description, obviously, and they're really not talking."

"You going to represent them?" I ask him.

He shrugs, still bewildered. "Probably that's why Diane called, but I don't know if it's her, both of them—I don't know . . ." His voice trails off. I can't tell if it's in reaction to the circumstances or because he just realized, as I did, that we might wind up on opposite sides of a nasty trial before too long, and maybe we should be careful in what we say.

Officer Pat Salerno comes out from the corridor to the left of the reception windows and into the lobby. She recognizes Parnell from the trial and walks over.

"Diane wanted to know, can you represent her at least at the arraignment, and do you want to see her?"

Parnell shifts quickly into professional mode. "What about Lisa?"

She lifts a shoulder and drops it. "Hasn't said anything."

"Can I see her?"

"Uh, she didn't request you, so you can't demand it. . . ."

Parnell cocks his head and furrows up his brow, an exaggerated gesture bidding Officer Salerno to get real.

I jump in for her. "I'll ask her, okay?"

"Thanks," Parnell says. "Gotta go see a client." He heads for the right-hand corridor without waiting for a response, and Pat steps in closer.

"We swabbed 'em both for gunshot residue, and the sweatshirt's already on its way to the lab."

"Where'd you do the swab?" Marsha asks.

"At the house," Pat answers, evoking an approving nod from Marsha.

Marty clears his throat loudly. "What say we go see Lisa?" He means, before a lawyer does it first.

"Maybe it should be me," Marsha suggests.

I veto the idea. This may be our only real shot at Lisa, and I want an experienced interrogator with me. "I'll handle it with Marty. Why don't you stand guard here in case anybody else shows up. We won't be long."

If Marsha is miffed, she doesn't show it, just looks over toward Eleanor and says, "Do I get a gun?"

Doreen Sumara is on duty again but this time there isn't even an attempt at banter with Marty as he checks his gun in a locker and we go through the great iron door into the jail. She leads us to a small, nearly bare conference room and a few seconds later a jailer brings Lisa in. She's wearing jeans and a sweater with tennis shoes but no jewelry or anything to hold her hair together. The shoes have no laces. Her eyes are bloodshot and she looks scared and anxious. The jailer points her toward a plastic seat, and she sits down, looking at her hands.

"You okay, Lisa?"

The sound of my voice startles her, and she jerks her head up, looking back and forth between Marty and me.

"You need anything?" I ask.

She shakes her head, then looks back at her hands, which she is twisting together in her lap. Lisa Pierman has never seen the inside of a jail except on television and never thought she would, either.

Marty coughs and scratches his chest, then gets up and takes off his jacket. I notice that his face is a little red from his brief time in the desert sun only this morning. He deliberately exaggerates his movements, trying to make things seem a little less unnatural to Lisa, a little less strained, like it's okay to be yourself here: there's no need to minimize movement and sound.

"You mind we ask you a couple questions?" he says lightly.

Lisa hesitates, then says, "Diane told me not to say anything."

"Fine, no problem." Marty rubs the back of his head. "But hey, you already said something right there, so all bets are off, am I right?" He laughs loudly at his joke, and Lisa tries to smile politely in return. "So when did Diane tell you not to say anything?" he asks amiably, trying to communicate to Lisa that he's only making polite conversation to start things off, that this is not an important question. I know that if she answers it wrong it could be grounds for premeditated murder.

She thinks for a second. "Before."

Marty nods vigorously, encouraging her. "Before what?"

"Before it all happened."

"Okay, I see. I get it. You mean before Rosamund was shot or before you were arrested . . . what?"

I've let this go on long enough without interfering, but if Lisa's constitutional rights are violated, there isn't going to be any case so I have to break in, much as I don't want to.

"Lisa, you know you have the right to remain silent, don't you?"

She looks away from Marty and toward me. I can sense him giving me a look that could freeze motor oil, but there's nothing I can do. And it suddenly further occurs to me that, Diane being a lawyer, her conversations with her sister might even be considered privileged. I don't bring up that point, though.

"Anything you say can and will be held against you in court. You have the right to an attorney and if you can't afford one, the court will provide one for you. You got that?"

"I understand."

"Good. Go ahead and answer Marty's question if you want to."

"I want a lawyer."

Before all the words leave her mouth, the door opens and Nestor Parnell's head comes through it.

"Did you ask her?" he says to me.

Shit! "Ah, Nes, I forgot! Swear to God, it wasn't on—"

"Diane sent me to represent you if you want," he says to Lisa before I even get a chance to finish apologizing. I did promise to ask if she wanted Parnell as her attorney, and I did completely forget. No way is he going to believe that.

"Yes, please," Lisa tells him.

Parnell looks back at Marty and me, not pleasantly. "This meeting is over until I've had a chance to confer with my client."

I make a show of rising immediately and without

argument. "Please believe me, Nestor; I just plain forgot and we didn't get into—"

"Yeah, I know." He stands up straighter and steps aside, making room for us to exit.

It's only Monday. I haven't even been to the office yet.

12

There is a popular misconception about the law, that the trial process is about a search for the truth, as though the truth were some kind of objective creature hiding within its dark cave and our job is to ferret it out and hold it up for the world to see, then let the consequences flow from our discovery.

In fact, the law is frequently about not the search for, but rather the *creation* of, truth. It is something we declare, not something we unearth. This is especially so when all the facts are known and only their interpretation is in doubt. Two brothers kill their parents, claiming they were continually abused at their hands and had no choice. A robber puts duct tape on a woman's mouth, not realizing she has a simple head cold and cannot breathe through her nose; she dies an agonizing death. A motorist is distracted by a bird and runs a stop sign, taking out a family of four. In all of these cases no facts are in dispute, but what is the defendants' culpability? Do their trials reveal the truth or do they merely manufacture an official answer?

It's Tuesday morning and Marsha and I are handling the arraignments in front of Judge Ephraim Goldman. I haven't yet decided who will undertake the actual trial work, but it seems expedient for the two of us to get this preliminary procedure out of the way, since we're the most familiar with the facts. It's also a good excuse to stay away from the office. Marion will handle as much of the administrivia as she can and when she can't, will yell for me.

The press, needless to say, is according this case the attention due a world war or a presidential infidelity scandal. I wouldn't even make a pretext of trying to put a lid on this one. There are teams of reporters, on-camera people covering the arraignment itself and background investigators looking under rocks for "angles," a polite euphemism for details guaranteed to titillate, stun or otherwise provide fodder for gossip. I wouldn't have a problem with this except that in the minds of the public many of these details, culled by the media from a mountain of equally relevant data, are the only ones they hear and often become more important than they really are. Before this day is out, it is very likely that Diane and Lisa Pierman will be painted as symbols of virtue most perfect, nuns-without-portfolio, while Vincent Rosamund will be cast as Lucifer incarnate. Marsha thought it might be just the opposite, but I took the bet, relying on unassailable logic: if the twins are depicted as malicious temptresses and Rosamund as an innocent, there really is no story, because then it's just straightforward murder with non-controversial prosecution. The way I see it, my office had better gird for some heavy battering regarding our pursuit of the case.

I risk a backward glance at the assembled reporters. There is Eleanor Torjan, of course, an essentially competent journalist of vaulting ambition, who is where she is only after years of relentlessly pounding her editors for the choicest assignments, the highly visible stories that ensure prominent bylines. Then there is Ernie Borjano, from the *Daily News*. Ernie's father was an obsessive disciplinarian who made life for his three kids almost unbearable, to the point where Ernie's brother was eventually institutionalized. In the early '70s, Ernie became a notorious campus radical at UC Berkeley, railing loudly against university patriarchs, campus recruiters from big business and faculty department heads with the effrontery to tell him how he ought to be educated. His favorite news stories involve alleged government corruption and abuses of authority by law enforcement. Marissa Gitcheson from AP lost a sister to a heroin overdose and writes periodic

features on the LA County Board of Education's dismal
track record in policing students' lockers to uncover drug
stashes, while Garson Toomey from the *Sun* covers legislative initiatives he believes allow government authorities too much latitude in invading citizen privacy.

It seems inevitable that I am going to suffer for what
the papers will print about the present situation. Torjan is
annoyed with me for what she perceives as my leading
her astray regarding the nature of the charges against Vincent Rosamund. From my perspective, there was no story
yet, as we had agreed, so there was no need to keep her
apprised of case strategy minute by minute. But she has
the pen, and the minds of two million readers. To Ernie
Borjano I am an authority figure of the worst sort, and as
far as Marissa Gitcheson is concerned, I am the incompetent who busted her dead sister's dope supplier but
couldn't make the charges stick: I wonder if she remembers that Ernie, now sitting two rows away from her,
praised the dismissal as a victory for privacy from gov-
ernmental intrusion. I can hardly wait for each of them to
remove my viscera and smear them across the pages of
their respective publications. None of their readers will be
aware of any of the personal motivations behind the spins
their stories carry.

As is typical for high-profile cases, procedures have
changed somewhat today. The Piermans will be arraigned
alone rather than along with a batch of other prisoners.
They have both been held in the Santa Monica jail under a
suicide watch, which basically involves a twenty-four-
hour camera aimed into their cells. Nestor Parnell didn't
object: he knows one of them killed Rosamund, and he
therefore knows that some profound psychological alter-
ation had to have taken place, one that could easily meta-
morphose into an equally profound depression and make
suicide a real possibility. He didn't say any of this, of
course, but he did tacitly approve of the suicide watch.

Diane and Lisa are brought in together, and quiet falls over
the courtroom. Marsha and I are sitting at the prosecution
table, Parnell across from us at the defense table. He has
an associate I don't recognize, but Marsha tells me he is
also from their firm. As Goldman enters the courtroom, we

all rise respectfully, an interesting, anachronistic throwback to another era but a tradition I like because it helps to set an atmosphere of respect for the bench, to remind everybody who is really in charge: not actually the judge but the law as personified by the judge.

Goldman calls the case and Parnell rises. "Nestor Parnell for the defendants, your honor, assisted by Scott Nikrum."

"Both of them?" Goldman asks. It would be unusual for a single defense attorney to represent two co-defendants. The potential for conflict is too great, for example if one of them decides to make a deal to give the other one up.

"Just for the arraignment for now," Parnell explains. "Both of them are pleading not guilty anyway." *Nobody is giving anybody up,* he's telling the judge.

Goldman nods and looks at the papers in front of him, then at Diane and Lisa, who are sitting in the front row of the jury box. He makes a motion to marshal Brad Kamen, who walks the sisters over to the defense table, where two extra chairs have been set, and removes their cuffs after they are seated.

"Diane Pierman and Lisa Pierman—" Goldman begins but as soon as he does, Parnell and I are both on our feet. Goldman hears the chairs scraping back and looks up in amusement. "Already?"

I speak first. "Your honor, we'd like to handle these separately, if it please the court."

Parnell whips his head around to look at me. There is surprise on his face as Goldman asks him, "Defense?"

Parnell looks back at him. "Defense has no objection," he says, then sits back down. He was going to make the same request. Each of us discovering that the other feels it would be beneficial to his case to keep the arraignments separate worries us both.

Goldman shrugs. "If it's good enough for you guys . . ." He lectures the twins on their rights as Kamen brings Lisa back to the jury box, then separates out one sheaf of papers and starts reading. "Diane Pierman, you are charged with murder in the first degree as regards the death of one Vincent Rosamund on February nineteenth, conspiracy to commit murder, criminal solicitation, unlawful possession of a firearm . . ." He ticks down a list of progressively lesser charges, and then says, "How do you plead to these charges?"

Parnell rises, nudging Diane on the elbow so she stands as well. "Not guilty on all counts, your honor," he announces.

Goldman grunts and looks at his calendar. "Preliminary hearing is set for March seventh. I'll hear motions on bail." Parnell doesn't object to the judge exceeding the ten-day rule: he can use the time to prepare.

"People request bail be denied," I say as I rise. I have barely glanced at Diane since she entered the courtroom, which is the first time I've seen her since the end of Rosamund's trial. As far as I can tell, she has been avoiding my eyes with equal effort. I have little doubt that there are at least a few people in this room who are watching both of us for any signs of mutual recognition, so I am consciously adopting the most professional, dispassionate demeanor I can muster. The knot in my belly is so tight and my legs so weak that I barely trust myself to stand, and I keep clearing my throat before I speak. Handling this proceeding myself is a terrible mistake. I have no business being here. I don't know if I can pull it off.

"Grounds?"

"This is a capital crime. The defendant is charged with a cold-blooded, clearly premeditated killing—"

Parnell stands before I finish. "There is nothing in this defendant's background to indicate that she is either a public danger or a flight risk."

"That's my point, your honor," I insist, "if counsel would let me finish. There is nothing in her background to suggest this kind of behavior, which leads us to believe that she is under great psychological stress and ought to remain in custody until trial." In my peripheral vision I saw Diane turn toward me as I was speaking. It was just a change in reflected light from the soft brown of her dark hair to the pale flesh of her face, but I know she is looking at me. I know others know she is looking at me. I need to keep talking, but Parnell has exploited my hesitation and jumped in.

"That is a fatuous argument, your honor. It takes as its premise that my client committed the crime with which she is charged, and the prosecution has no way of knowing she pulled the trigger."

"Are you admitting one of them did?" I ask quickly.

"Don't be absurd. I'm asking a hypothetical question here: how can you charge two people with the same crime, a crime that can only have been committed by one person?"

Goldman is letting us go on uninterrupted. As long as we remain civil and give each other a chance to speak, and as long as we stick to germane comments, there is no need for him to say anything, and his ego is well enough in check that he feels no need to assert himself. He only looks from one to the other, stroking his chin. Now he is looking at me.

"I'm not charging both of them," I say to him. "I'm only charging one of them. And a charge is not the same as proof at trial. It is based on a reasonable suspicion, and we have extremely convincing grounds for believing that someone fitting Diane Pierman's description shot and killed Vincent Rosamund on February nineteenth. Part of your honor's decision on bail is based on the likelihood of the people prevailing at trial, and in this case that likelihood is at least fifty-fifty, which is a lot higher than most, and a lot higher than we need to justify denial of bail."

Parnell smiles and shakes his head, as though amused at my inability to see the obvious. "It is only fifty-fifty if you can even prove one of the twins did it, never mind which one"—just what Diane argued to Dan Pappas when she was arrested: who is in charge of their case, she or Parnell?—"and you have given us precious little to believe that you can. This case is completely dependent on eyewitnesses and even if, and I'm speaking hypothetically again, even if some of them think the perpetrator looked like one of these defendants, not one of them will be able to tell us which one." He turns his whole body toward me. "I'd say your odds were considerably less than fifty-fifty. Closer to zero."

"What are you asking for, counselor?" Goldman asks him.

"Release on own recognizance, your honor. My client has never been in trouble with the law, never even gotten a traffic ticket, as far as I know. She is in every respect a model citizen, with strong roots in this community. In fact, she is an attorney, an associate in my own firm. She represents no flight risk whatsoever and no harm to either herself or others."

"Why did you approve of the suicide watch?" I ask him. Goldman doesn't object—his surprised look tells me he was unaware of the conditions under which Diane was being held—but looks to Parnell for an answer. Parnell didn't like his speech being interrupted, and he certainly didn't like being put on the spot like this. He turns back to me and puts a hand on his hip.

"First of all, I didn't 'approve' anything. It wasn't my decision, and it wasn't my place to interfere with normal procedure in the jail. Second of all"—at this, he turns back to Goldman—"nobody could gauge the depth of Diane and Lisa's public humiliation owing to their totally mistaken and ill-advised arrest. When ordinary, law-abiding citizens are suddenly thrust, with no provocation, into radically unjust and inhumane situations, situations with which they have no prior familiarity, it is impossible to predict the psychological effect. That is why I didn't object to the suicide watch."

And thus am I hoist with mine own petard, having broken the first rule of trial lawyering: never ask a question to which you don't know the answer in advance. Now it's too late for me to give up. "No prior familiarity? For Pete's sake, counselor, your client's a defense attorney, she spends half her time in jails!"

"Never on the other side of the bars," he counters easily, then addresses Goldman. "There is no flight risk, your honor. Might I remind the court that both Diane and Lisa were waiting quietly for the police to arrive and could easily have fled at that time if they wanted to. But they didn't."

Parnell should have kept quiet while he still had me good. I'm back on my feet in a New York second. "A question, please?"

Goldman nods his permission and I turn toward Parnell. "So let me ask you this, counselor: how come these model citizens just happened to be waiting around for the police to come and arrest them one night?"

It's a zinger of a challenge. Marsha is beaming at me,

leaning forward on her chair and waiting to hear Parnell's response. I'm feeling pretty smug until I chance a glance at Diane and see that she is not attempting to hide that she is looking at me full on. Her face is a mixture of dismay, confusion and pleading: *Why are you doing this to me!*

I don't believe her eyes are asking me why I'm prosecuting her. She has to have expected that. What she wants to know is why I seem to be taking such apparent glee in it. Mere days ago we danced around the edges of a serious relationship, and now I'm blasting her from all sides, trying to get bail denied and tricking her attorney into inadvertent implication. *What has happened here?* Her confusion can only be a pale imitation of my own. I'm starting to feel sick again.

Goldman intrudes to spare Parnell potential embarrassment at my question. "Gentlemen, this is a bail hearing, not a trial. You don't have to start cross-examining each other."

Parnell holds up a hand. "I don't mind answering that question. Mr. Milano"—he assumes a scholarly air—"assume for a moment that one of them is indeed guilty."

I don't answer but he takes my silence for assent to his hypothetical. "She didn't run, did she? She stayed put. So if one is guilty, they have already demonstrated that there is no risk of flight. And if neither of them is guilty, there is no need to keep them in jail at all, correct?"

Again, I stay quiet, and he concludes by addressing Goldman. "QED, your honor. There are no circumstances under which it makes any sense to continue their incarceration, as I'm sure the deputy DA must agree."

"You have anything to add?" Goldman asks me.

Diane is still looking at me, her eyes asking questions I cannot answer. If I go balls to the wall on these motions, I'm a cad and a heel. If I don't, I'm not doing my job.

"If these women conspired to commit this murder, they likely didn't feel there was risk of either prosecution or conviction. As facts and evidence develop, they may feel differently and *become* flight risks."

Goldman takes a moment to think about this, then looks at Diane. "Ms. Pierman."

Diane rises. "Yes, your honor?"

"What assurances do I have that it is safe to release you on your own recognizance?"

"I'm innocent of these charges, your honor." She answers in a surprisingly strong voice, probably bolstered by the judge's question. If he's asking it at all, he is on the verge of granting an OR release. "I'm not going anywhere until that innocence is firmly established. I plan to resume my duties in the firm and remain in the area as long as this matter is pending."

It is convincing, sincere and professional. Even I almost believe it, at least the part about her not running.

Goldman looks back to his papers and then announces, "Defendant is released on her own recognizance and is hereby ordered to appear at the preliminary hearing on March seventh. Mr. Parnell, I am holding you personally responsible for any failure on Ms. Pierman's part to return for court-ordered appearances, understood?" He can't really do that, but what he's telling Parnell is that he's going to be really mad if she skips and, somehow, will make him suffer for it. He's also telling Diane that if she fails to reappear, she will be causing her lawyer and friend a great deal of grief.

"Perfectly, your honor. Thank you."

"Call the next case, Ms. Lisa Pierman." He waits as Diane is brought back to the jury box and Lisa is escorted to the defense table. He recites the charges against her, which are identical to those against Diane. She pleads innocent and a preliminary hearing is set for the same date as Diane's, and Goldman calls for motions on bail. I rise and request bail be denied, he asks for grounds and I tell him, then Parnell requests an OR release, and Goldman says, "Okay, okay, hold it a second."

He leans back and drums his fingers on the bench. "Bottom line, are we facing the same set of arguments here?"

Parnell and I look at each other. "Probably," he starts, and I say, "Not exactly."

"Not exactly, how?" Goldman wants to know.

This time, I won't look at Lisa as I posture for the record, uselessly, as I know in advance. "Lisa Pierman doesn't work in defense counsel's law firm. Is he going to take responsibility for her return as well?"

"Ms. Pierman owns her own business; she is well known to me; she isn't going anywhere," Parnell says.

It's a formality and I let it go. I'm on the record with my request, even though I'm fairly certain neither of the sisters is a risk. Not entirely certain, though: my argument concerning their questionable psychological state following such a radical behavioral departure is a valid one. Goldman orders Lisa's OR release but Parnell isn't finished.

"Your honor, at this time defense requests that the preliminary hearings be separated, so these two cases don't get confused."

I'm on my feet immediately. "People object. There are elements of conspiracy here that are so tightly related that two hearings and two subsequent trials would greatly inhibit the prosecution's case, but a single trial will in no way damage the defense. Conspiracy is central to our set of charges, your honor, and separating these matters makes no sense."

It's a no-brainer, Goldman rules in our favor, and it is over. This time, I'm the first one out of the courtroom. Diane and Lisa are free to go, and I don't want to see either of them. I'm too sick at heart to face even Marsha, who has remained mostly silent throughout the entire arraignment. I'm not sure it would be such a great idea for a subordinate to be subjected to the anguish and confusion her boss is wrestling with right now.

13

One of the things I miss most about New York is the seasons. With some exceptions, southern California might as well be under a stadium dome, the climate is so maddeningly consistent. People preparing for outdoor affairs don't fret about the weather like we used to in the east; there's no such thing as a "rain date." The distinction separating a nice day from a lousy day to an Angeleno is below the perceptual threshold of a New Yorker.

One of the exceptions is the three-month "winter," a laughable misnomer to anyone accustomed to real atmospheric differentiation. Winter is the rainy season, at least along the coast. When we're not experiencing one of our multiyear droughts, it really can rain, sometimes quite heavily, although thunderstorms are a rarity. Rain here is more dangerous than in regions where it falls throughout the year: roads become treacherous when months of accumulated grease and oil are suddenly squeezed upward by the heavier water, mud slides and floods result from the arid ground's inability to quickly absorb rainfall, and people unused to the curtailment of their activities develop cabin fever with alarming rapidity, making them surly and unpredictable.

I love it when it rains. It's a blessed relief from the tedious constancy of all that sunshine, and I find the dark skies and pattering sounds comforting and even romantic as long as I don't dwell on the half-dozen virtually untraceable leaks in my beachfront condo, leaks heretofore unnoticed owing to three years of relentless drought since I bought the place. The builder, who earlier raved about how well the building stood up to a large earthquake, now claims the same quake, an act of God and therefore not his responsibility, caused the leaks in his heretofore unimpregnable structure. The builder was originally from Bensonhurst, where logic like that helped him through his adolescence. He should have become a lawyer.

"Who you gonna give this one to?"

I was lost in the rivulets running down my window, the glass blurry from evaporated ocean water spray, and Marsha's question snaps me out of it. "Haven't decided yet."

It is the Pierman case, and that I would be giving it to somebody else isn't even an issue, Marsha and I having handled the Rosamund case, in which Diane and Lisa were complainants. Now they are defendants. That might be construed as a conflict of interest. I guess. Maybe not. I haven't bothered to think it through: I'm too busy with other thoughts.

Uppermost among these is why I dove into the arraignment with such avidity and fervor. Forty-eight hours ago, these women were my friends. A week ago, my life was wrapped around their salvation. But two hours ago, as I arraigned them for murder, I found myself unholstering my heaviest ordnance in an effort to get them denied bail, even though I knew there was no risk of them taking flight. I told myself it was my professional responsibility, that I wanted to avoid any appearance of favoritism, but the fact is I wanted to land on them as hard as I could. At least Diane. Why?

At least Diane. It's so obvious.

Perhaps it's true, as the twins and the therapists felt, that Diane and Lisa might never have truly gotten over their shock and anger, but were they not at least getting on with their lives? Now, no matter how it all turns out, those two lives are surely ruined. They will either go to prison, or if they get off, every man they ever come into contact with—every woman, too, for that matter—will know that they are capable of killing, or arranging to kill, someone with whom they had a problem. Of course, the first time it was a cold-blooded rapist, but how would one know for what lesser offense, or perceived offense, they were willing to do it again? And isn't it supposed to get easier after your first one, as everyone who has ever read a mob or spy novel knows?

But that's their business. I'm clean. So why am I so mad at them? At Diane?

"Shouldn't be a major problem," Marsha is saying. "I figure, one of them on murder one, the other on solicitation, both of 'em on conspiracy, obstruction, reckless endangerment—"

I look up at that last one.

"She fired a gun in the presence of innocent bystanders," Marsha explains. "Waved it around and pointed it at them on her way out."

"Might as well throw in threat of great bodily harm and intimidation." What is killing me is that Diane knowingly took a piece of me with her when she willingly threw her own life away. She'd as much as hinted at a life of domestic bliss for the two of us, a tailor-made match between two previously reticent colleagues, and now she's gone and put a bullet through the whole silver-framed picture. Without even a thought for me, not a trace of consideration for how I might feel about it. How could she do this to me?

"Major problem is, we need to be able to show which one did it." Maybe it wasn't Diane. Maybe I can nail Lisa and get Diane off. I wonder if I have any business being in this business at all.

Marsha looks at her watch. "We have gunshot residue swabs, remember? I tried to rush it through the lab, but it's not a real emergency and they're backed up."

This being only Tuesday, Scientific Services is probably not even finished going through Saturday night's batch, which is typically larger than the rest of the week's put together. What Marsha is telling me is that, with eye-witnesses to testify that it was at least one of the twins, and the gunshot residue test telling us who pulled the trigger, we have a solid case to prosecute.

"You know," she says, "I knew that their feelings about Rosamund ran deep, but I underestimated how much they were pinning on the outcome of the trial."

"That supposed to make me feel better?"

"Listen," she says in a curt tone, "when you're through feeling sorry for yourself, give a thought to me, what do you say? I'm thc one listened to them four hours straight the morning after; how do you think *I* feel?"

"You're right. Sorry." She thinks my self-flagellation involves losing the trial. She doesn't know how much more it is. Are we both that self-centered all the time, thinking of everything only in terms of how it affects us?

We're interrupted by a knock on the door. It opens and Marion leans in. "Sultan of Swat is here," she whispers, jerking a thumb back over her shoulder.

Marsha smiles. "Well there, that oughta take your mind off things for a while."

"Jesus, what else today? Marion, tell her I'm in the middle of—"

"She says she'll wait." *As long as it takes,* her look tells me.

Marsha gets up and starts gathering her papers. "Prelim's in ten days. It's a walkover but you gotta make a decision—today—on who handles it."

"I know that. But forget the prelim; we're gonna get a grand jury indictment."

She pauses, then shrugs. "Good idea." She turns and walks to the door. As Marion steps aside to let her pass, she says, "But you gotta decide today anyway."

"Hey Jones, you want my goddamned job or what?"

"Not on your life, Sal."

Marion looks at me inquiringly, and I slump back in my seat, nodding at her. "Might as well. Do the phone call thing in about twenty minutes."

"I'll set an alarm." She steps back into the anteroom.

Moments later the doorway is filled with the form of Ernestine Denier, a highly visible and vocal member of the Santa Monica City Council, wanting to speak with me privately. I wave her in. Her giant pink pup tent of a muumuu nearly brushes both sides of the doorway as she enters. She's carrying her usual macramé pocketbook and stack of disheveled papers poking out of an overstuffed vinyl portfolio.

Ernestine is an overweight, badly dressed, generally unkempt woman with a rapier tongue and affected intensity that is as tiring as it is obvious. She has a general reputation as a loudmouth pain in the ass wedded to a few hundred strongly held political beliefs, spearheading many of the initiatives of a vocal group of suburban liberals who fancy themselves to be modern radicals. Most of what they do is symbolic and divisive, accomplishing little actual social good beyond making profoundly important points. Ernestine can drop phrases like "ethnically diverse, multicultural empowerment" into polite conversation with a straight face, and is the type of official who likes to pounce on ordinary citizens speaking before the council when they use masculine pronouns to refer to the general population, often disorienting them to the point where they forget the point they were trying to make in the first place.

But I've discovered that in private, when not compelled to posture for her worshipful constituents and knowing I'm not buying into her symbolic displays of assertive enlightenment, Ernestine is a bright, canny human being, a delightful conversationalist well versed in a staggering variety of subjects, with a great sense of humor, often directed at herself. She is also a recovered heroin addict and alcoholic, nine years clean and five years sober, a rare feat that wins my undying admiration no matter how much she might annoy me. I wave to a chair facing my desk, and she squeezes herself into it as best she can.

"It's always a delight to see you, Ernestine."

"You're so full of shit, Milano."

"One of my most endearing qualities, I'm told. I'm surprised it took you this long to show up." I know why she's here.

"This long? It's only Tuesday."

"Like I said . . ."

She plunks the stack of papers on my desk, drops her pocketbook to the floor and leans back on the chair. Drops of rain fall from the ends of her short hair onto the shoulders of the pink dress. "So what's it going to be, Mr. DA: are you going to prosecute Diane and Lisa Pierman?"

I drop my head forward and look up at her. "Now, what do you think?"

"That's what I figured." She drags the back of her pudgy forearm across her brow, then wipes the arm on her dress. "I must tell you, I'm sensing the beginning of a groundswell of support for the Piermans."

I can't stifle a laugh. "It's only Tuesday and we got a groundswell already?" We both know that a *groundswell* means that she's spoken to two other people and intends to crank up a new urgent cause.

"Ah, Sally, you know how fast the people can move when matters of sufficient gravity warrant their attention."

"Matters of sufficient gravity, yeah."

She leans forward on the chair, and her forearms land with a heavy thud on my desk. "Don't pretend you don't know what I'm talking about, Milano. This is as clear-cut a case of justice denied as I have ever seen."

I decide it's best to stay silent for the time being, see where this is going. Besides, I agree with her observation so there's no need to argue.

"That pig was released on egregious technicalities, the same kind of crap that goes on all the time against women."

Now it's time to argue. "Good Lord, councilwoman! Those are the exact kinds of technicalities that were put into place to protect people like you!"

"Nonsense."

"It isn't nonsense. Rules about testifying, about illegally seized evidence, reading people their rights even though they've been read to them the last three hundred times they were arrested ... people are getting off on those kinds of technicalities by the carload."

She smiles. "You're starting to believe your own marketing, Sal. All the public really knows about is the big-money cases. Then they see a lot of fancy defense footwork and think everybody's getting off on technicalities." The smile disappears. "But who are you trying to kid? Maybe one out of a thousand can afford a private lawyer. The rest? Your office railroads them into accepting whatever it is *you* tell them to take, and they have no way to fight because their PD's are carrying a hundred other cases." She leans back, relaxed in her conviction. "You guys have all the power and you call all the shots. So you need to get hit once in a while by somebody who can afford real justice."

She's more right than even she imagines, but this is no

time to be gallant. For all I know she's wearing a wire. "But the downtrodden always have people like you, don't they, Ernestine? You paraded all over LA three years ago to get some guy on death row released because he wrote poetry. You said there was a technical error in his indictment. So who do you think you're kidding?"

"The guy didn't deserve to fry, so we used every means possible to get him out. The hell is wrong with that?"

I get angry, and I'm not sure it has to do with this particular conversation. "If Rosamund's brother turned around and put a bullet in Diane Pierman, you'd be in here screaming for his balls!"

"Well, for heaven's sake, Sal, what the hell got into you today?"

She sits up straight.

What, indeed? I rub my tired eyes with my thumbs. "Why are you here, Ernestine?"

"Sorry?"

"Why are you here?" I normally try to stop myself from getting sucked into this kind of discussion with her, and I think my intensity may be surprising her.

She idly fingers some pages sticking out of the stack she laid on my desk. "I don't think the Pierman twins deserve to be persecuted for this."

"They're not going to be persecuted; they're going to be prosecuted."

"Same thing. I think there's going to be a great hue and cry, and it'll likely extend beyond city boundaries. Maybe even become like a national thing."

Swell. "Are you threatening me?"

"How can I threaten you? You're the establishment."

"So what does that make you: Exxon? You're the one was elected by the people, not me. I'm just a hired gun doing his job."

"It's your decision. You go ahead with this thing, you should be prepared for the consequences."

"Let me ask you something, Ernestine. You discuss this with Diane or Lisa? You ask them if they want to become national celebrities as a result of their being raped?"

She waves it away. "This issue is too important to concern itself with the wishes of its victims."

I am a county employee, domiciled in Santa Monica only because that's where the county's westside facility is located. I am no more beholden to a city council member than I am to any other ordinary citizen, although I do try to do my bit for good community relations. But Ernestine's brand of titanic arrogance has to be more than I am obligated to bear, even after surviving the elected DA's mandatory course work on sensitivity and understanding. "By whose standards?" I ask her, as calmly as I can.

She smiles indulgently. "You're a small thinker, Mr. Deputy. Is it so hard to understand that sometimes the cause is bigger than the individual?" The smile vanishes. "And if you're so damned concerned about these women, why are you prosecuting them?"

"Because they broke the law—"

"Allegedly broke the law."

"Allegedly, my foot. And if you're so hepped up on street justice for women, how come you didn't try to defend that mother up north who killed her son's accused molester?" I remember it clearly because it was one of the few times she and I were on the same side of an issue.

"C'mon, Sal, that was different, too! She popped the guy before the trial. For all she knew he might've been convicted and put away for twenty years! She was just after visceral revenge, not justice."

I nod to suck her into thinking I agree with her. "So you're telling me the Pierman sister who pulled the trigger was answering to a higher calling? She believed it was, like, her civic duty to see that justice was done? Or did she just want to put a bullet into the sonofabitch?"

She's smart, Ernestine is, very smart. Unlike some of her fellow sojourners in the Great Causes, she finds it difficult to ignore logic. Some of the people she hangs out with can look you square in the eye and argue the most specious inanities, toeing the party line as though that in itself constituted clear thought. But Ernestine can't do that. If you get her up against a logical wall, you can see it in her eyes. "What difference does it make, ultimately?" she asks. "This guy got what he deserved, didn't he?"

"I don't know." A thought pops up out of nowhere. "He committed rape: did he deserve to die for it?"

"Of course."

"Of course. Right. Well, I think the guy who spray-painted my wall deserves to die, and all he got was a fifty-dollar fine. Should I go out and shoot him? Maybe I should shoot you for jaywalking."

She purses her lips and makes a spluttering sound. "You're just being facetious. You know that's different."

"No, I don't. If you allow everybody to make their own decisions about applying punishment, then nobody is safe. You can't have it both ways, Ernestine. You can't kill Vincent Rosamund because he committed rape and then let the murderers go because you decide it's okay."

"But oughtn't the law to be tempered with a little compassion once in a while? If you just enforce it to the letter, you assume it takes into account all circumstances, and you know that isn't true!"

"Obviously. And we make those decisions all the time. We decline to prosecute an incredibly large percentage of the cases brought to us by the police." I don't add that most of those are dropped because of difficulties with making the case, not any sense of righteous compassion. "But I'm a strong believer in the rule of law."

"Extreme law is often extreme injustice." She's quoting from *The Self-Tormenter,* thinking I don't know where it comes from.

I smile and shake my head. "You know, when you start doing that, I know I'm winning."

"Bullshit. Winning what?"

"The argument. When you start spouting quotes as though they were inarguable truths, I know you're running out of gas. Believe me, for every drop of wisdom from Terence I can give you seven from Machiavelli that are equally irrelevant, so if you want to talk, talk. Don't quote." I can see the picket signs now, pithy and inventive little literary references all done up on identical pieces of oak tag in identical handwriting, stapled onto identical wooden sticks to be carried around by the spontaneous crowd.

She rubs her eyes now, long and hard, and speaks before she removes her hands. "Don't you have any sympathy for them at all, Sal?"

Do I have sympathy? I'm the sorry sonofabitch whose

strategy got the charges against Rosamund dismissed; doesn't she realize that?

I suddenly feel very alone. Ernestine's question is too enormous for me to attempt an answer, especially to her, and I don't have anybody I can pour my heart out to. Maybe I should go to a psychiatrist; not that I need the therapy, but just to be able to unload on another human unfettered by complex social protocols. I've learned in talking through cases with colleagues that the point of the discussion is not really to express your opinions but to form them, that the act of trying to convince somebody else of something is in reality a secret mechanism to perfect the framing of your ideas. If I only had somebody to talk to. . . .

But, of course, of late my fantasies had been running to idyllic pictures of Diane Pierman being that someone, the two of us in a verdant backyard somewhere spilling our souls out to each other. I sneak a glance at Ernestine while she fiddles with some papers in the stack she dumped on my desk. Do I have sympathy? How can I tell her that my feelings for the twins are vast and painful, my remorse for Rosamund's death nonexistent? But I represent the law enforcement community: if I rise up and say it's all right to kill for revenge, especially in the absence of a judicial finding of guilt, I am granting every citizen license to take out whomever they choose for whatever reason they choose.

Without warning a wave of fatigue sweeps over me. I'm tired of these pseudo-intellectual head games with Ernestine, but I'm also tired of everything else, somehow. This case is not about some abstract cause, some disembodied symbols floating around in the cultural ether; it's about real human lives. It's about *my* life, dammit!

I don't tell Ernestine any of this. I remember who I am and where I am. "Let me remind you that it's possible that Vincent Rosamund didn't rape the Piermans, that what he said was true. And now we'll never know, will we, because he's dead."

"But we might not have known anyway," she counters, "since the charges against him were dismissed. He walked, and that would have been the end of that, right?"

Again I have to hold my tongue. I'd like to tell her what

I know to be true: that Diane and Lisa were popular figures in the community, that every cop in southern California would have had his eye on Rosamund, a known drug dealer and troublemaker, and inside of six weeks would have busted him for something, somewhere, and would have gotten it tried in some court other than Arigga's. If I tell her that, though, she'll run screaming to the press that she was right all along, that abuse of authority is rampant in government, that the complaints of people branded as radicals are not the paranoid rantings they're always portrayed to be. In many ways, she'd be right. I think maybe a paranoiac is simply someone who knows all the facts.

I start to formulate some suitably innocuous reply when we're interrupted by a knock on the door. I look at my watch: just about twenty minutes since Ernestine arrived. Good ol' Marion, right on the money. The door opens and she walks in, handing me a pink note slip. "DA's in the conference room?" I ask after reading it, and Marion nods.

I give Ernestine a helpless shrug. "Boss wants to see me."

She looks skeptical but lets it pass. "Do give him my best. He backing you on this?"

"Of course." I have no idea if he is or not.

She gathers up her papers and bag and stands up. "Will you keep me posted?"

I rise as well. "No."

She laughs. "Who's gonna handle it?"

"Don't know yet. It'll all be on the public record."

"Thanks a lot. We'll be seeing each other again on this, Milano."

As soon as she's out the door, I wink at my secretary. "Perfect timing, Marion. Thanks."

I turn to go back to my desk, and she taps me on the shoulder. "It's no joke, Sal. He's really here."

"You serious?"

"Yup."

I take a deep breath and look around to see if I should be picking up or hiding anything, then I stop. What difference does it make? "Okay, show him in."

Marion shakes her head. "You go to see the principal, young man; he doesn't come to see you. He's waiting in the conference room."

She reaches for my jacket but I wave it off. "How's he look?"

"The usual. Surly, mad, impatient."

"You get him coffee?" I ask as I pick up a yellow pad and my own cup.

"Didn't want any. And he's alone."

The conference room is about thirty feet down from my corner office. As I walk through the corridor, I get a number of knowing looks from the deputy DAs ranging from apprehensive, covert glances to outright smirks to expressions of sympathy. My mutually hostile relationship with the DA is a poorly kept secret indeed, despite my halfhearted denials. It's difficult to hide my irritation at the switch in my stature from mature, confident leader to cowed subordinate every time he shows up.

Gerard Beckman is a politician first and a lawyer second. Richard Nixon was one of his personal heroes, and I think a good deal of his personal style derives from that worship. Whereas most people would wear a jacket in public and loosen up in private, Beckman does the opposite: he likes to be photographed with his sleeves rolled up and tie undone because it makes him look hands-on but he's acutely uncomfortable like that, so when he retreats from the public eye, he puts the jacket on and buttons it. Sitting at the conference table—just sitting; no papers, nothing to read, not fiddling with anything in his hands—he looks ready for a formal portrait.

Beckman is just under six feet tall, light complexioned and gifted, as he would probably consider it, with angular features, thin lips and ears pressed flat against his head. His hair is crinkly, much like Henry Kissinger's, and I think it embarrasses him, which is why he wears it so short. Or maybe because he thinks it gives him some kind of military look, in keeping with his political proclivities. He is wearing one in a vast wardrobe of banker suits, this particular number a dark blue with pinstripes, a plain white shirt with a button-down collar and a nondescript tie. His shoes are those heavy, clunking black wingtips with thick soles so favored by senior businessmen and their sycophantic entourages who try to emulate them.

He looks up as I enter but doesn't stand or offer his

hand. I close the door behind me and head for a seat facing him on the other side of the long, narrow table. "Gerry, how are you?"

"Fine. You?" He doesn't even seem to take note of the fact that I'm not wearing a jacket and my sleeves are rolled up. Bad sign.

I nod. I have a feeling this is all the preamble there's going to be. I sit down and drop my yellow pad on the table. I'm no sooner seated than he starts right in.

"What're you going to do, Milano?"

I turn up a hand then let it flop back down onto the table. "Business as usual. Assign the case, put some investigators on it, handle it like any other case."

Beckman folds his hands together and glares at me. "I don't give a shit about the goddamned case; I'm asking what you're gonna do about the election. You going to run against me or not?"

I need a second to shift gears. He's worried about the election, about my possible role in it. *That's* why he blasted me in the press. "Where'd you hear that?"

"I didn't get where I am by being stupid. So what about it?"

"No, I'm not." It's an honest answer and it takes him aback. He doesn't look like he was prepared for that.

"Uh-huh." He's buying time to rescript the scene he probably wrote in his head on the way over here. "But you thought about it, right? Talked to some people?"

"Some people talked to me."

"And you told them no, just like you're telling me?"

"I told them it was an interesting idea. No commitments."

"What makes it so interesting?"

"Listen, Gerry, I don't think this is a proper—"

"Let me worry about what's proper here, okay? I'm still running things, last time I looked, right?"

He's waiting for a response, but I won't be humiliated into answering a rhetorical question like—Marion's simile comes back to me—a schoolboy in front of the principal. I stare Beckman down.

"So you considered it," he says. "Why?"

"Because I could do a better job." I fight the urge to

look around the room to get a glimpse of the idiot who just said that to my boss.

Beckman is nodding and he suddenly looks relaxed, even amused. The gloves are off so the strain of dancing around has been relieved. "A better job, I see. Like you did on the Rosamund case?"

"We had a bad judge and you know it."

"Yeah, so you've been saying." He leans back on his chair and crosses one leg over the other. "And you're going after him, too, is that right?"

"That's right."

He is nodding again and seems to be considering something. "Nice way to cover your ass, Milano. Lose a sure thing and then light out after a respected jurist because he didn't rule your way?" The upward inflection at the end makes it a question.

"It was more than that."

"Horseshit!" he yells, leaning forward and slamming a fist onto the table, startling me. "You were unprepared! Holy shit, you didn't even know what the charges were until practically the day before the trial, you left out half the complaints because of some half-assed, college-god-damned-law-review strategy—"

"Arigga wasn't going to let either of them testify!" Now it's my turn to raise my voice and lean forward; we'd be nose to nose but for the intervening conference table.

"How do you know that!" Beckman is jabbing the air between us with his forefinger. "How-do-you-know-that! You never let him make the fucking ruling!"

I grit my teeth and speak through compressed lips, slowly and distinctly, fighting to stay calm. "It was my best professional guess that he was going to suppress both sisters as witnesses."

"Your guess?" He gives me an incredulous look and his voice drops several decibels while rising in pitch. "What kind of crap is that?" He raises his hands in exaggerated confusion and looks around the room as though seeking support for his disbelief. "Why didn't you let him make his ruling and then change the charges, or file an appeal, or any of the half-dozen other things you could have done?"

Why? Damned good question. Because I was hoping to force a plea? Because I didn't want to file a pretrial appeal and have Arigga mad at me for the rest of my career? Because I thought I could pull off a precedent-setting maneuver and get my name in the law journals? "But I was right, wasn't I." I lean back as well. "Arigga threw out Diane's testimony during trial so he would have done the same thing in pretrial if I'd waited for that ruling."

"Bullshit again." He's still speaking quietly. Confidently. "He did it at trial because you tried to hide the other broad's rape from the jury. Everybody in this whole goddamned state knew there were two rapes so where do you come off with this cheap grandstanding, Milano? Did you think you were going to get a write-up in some law journal for this brilliant legal thinking?" He purses his lips, looks down at his shoes and picks at some imaginary lint on his pants as he shakes his head. "You blew the case, is what you did, and now you're trying to railroad a decent judge to cover your ass." He looks up at me, folds his hands on the table, and leans forward. "*You* fucked it up, Milano, not Arigga. You did it all by yourself."

Beckman is torn between his delight that I botched the case and eliminated myself as a political opponent on the one hand, and the problem he is going to have accounting for the apparent malfeasance of one of his subordinates on the other. Either way, he gets to berate me all he wants. But I don't have to sit here and eat it.

"So what are you going to do, Gerry?"

The question seems to surprise him, as I intended. "What am *I* going to do?"

"Yeah. You going to resign? Or just wait and forfeit the election?"

A short laugh explodes out of him. "Excuse me? What the hell are you talking about?"

I try to look like it's obvious, that I'm surprised he doesn't know what I'm talking about. "You told the *Times* you take full responsibility. So what's that mean?"

"It means just what it says."

"It means nothing. What did you mean, you take responsibility? If it's your fault, what's your punishment?"

He's getting annoyed. "I have no idea what you're talking about."

"What I'm talking about is hack politicians like you always *taking responsibility* and then suffering no consequences for it. Me, I'm suffering plenty. I'm out of the running, everybody thinks I should turn in my law degree for a refund, I'm sunk. But it happened on your watch, you said so yourself, you're *responsible:* so what's your punishment?"

He knows exactly what I'm talking about but won't admit it. He tried to slip behind a tired management cliché and I wouldn't let him.

He grows still, menacing. "You're setting me up, aren't you?"

Now *I'm* confused. "Setting you up?"

"Sure you're going to run, you lying sonofabitch! You're gonna make it look like this was all my fault, and then you're going to run against me." He's snarling now. "I was right in the first place: you're going after Arigga to save your own sorry hide!"

It's an intriguing thought, but then I'd be like him and that will never happen. Or maybe it will. I wonder if Gerard Beckman was ever like *me,* whatever that is. "Don't be ridiculous."

"What happens now? With the case." He's not buying my denial. He thinks he's figured it all out and it doesn't merit further discussion. "It's still in your office."

"I told you: handle it like any other case. Get an investigation going, assign it to one of my deputies . . ."

"Assign, nothing." A smile slowly grows on his face. "You're handling this one yourself."

"No, I'm not."

"Uh-huh. And why is that?"

"It's a conflict." We both take note of the stammer in my voice as the words come out. Beckman is enough of a coyote to spot the weakness and go for it.

"And why is it a conflict, exactly?"

"I represented them in the Rosamund trial."

"No, you represented the people."

"I was privy to conversations and interviews with the complainants."

"Well then, I certainly hope you shared all of that with defense counsel, as Prop One-fifteen requires. Are you telling me you held something back, in violation of judicial procedure?"

"I was a witness in the case myself."

"Then why didn't you testify?"

Beckman isn't enough of a lawyer to be thinking of these answers that quickly. That means he's gone all over this before, probably with a bunch of people who are very good at this sort of thing. "The appearance of a conflict," I remind him, "is as important as a real one when it comes to maintaining public credibility in our office. People are going to look at this funny."

"No they aren't," he says evenly. "I want you to prosecute this personally. Anything else would look like we're not taking this seriously enough. Besides, you already opened your big mouth half a dozen times before about how citizens shouldn't take the law into their own hands, remember? Got up on your high, goddamned horse and preached to the people. How's it going to look if you walk away from this one?"

He can't be serious with this! "I'm not walking away! I'm still the head deputy, still responsible. I don't need to prosecute it personally!"

"You take full *responsibility*, is that it?" he says, drawing out my own words with merry sarcasm.

He doesn't bother to wait for a reply, which is just as well, since I have none. "You *will* do it!" he says forcefully. "You're still working for me, pal, remember? You do it and do it balls to the wall or you'll be handling public indecency cases in Van Nuys by month's end if I don't fire your ass first for insubordination as well as incompetence, and what do you think that'll do to your little campaign, huh?"

He's on a roll now, a freight train roaring down a hillside. "You fucking well better win it, too, like you shoulda won the last one. And don't bellyache to me about Arigga, either, speaking of which, who the hell are you to file a judicial complaint against him without talking to me first?"

Beckman just gained the upper hand in this conversation. We both know it. "I figured, it's an election year, you might not want to create waves."

He laughs again, with real amusement this time. "Yeah.

More like it's an election year and *you* want to create waves, isn't that it?"

"The man's a lunatic. He doesn't deserve to be on the bench and I told you: I'm not running!"

"Right. Clear as mud. Well"—he stands up, strains his arms backward and stretches—"you better put those girls away, pal. And don't look so glum: there is a certain poetic justice here, isn't there?"

He's enjoying himself now. He's even smiling at me as he goes to the door and opens it, exchanging a few pleasantries with the people hovering outside, knowing that he scored big in this round. He has no idea that this is a case involving real human beings, not just names on a police report. He has no idea—how could he, after all?—about my hopelessly passionate nonrelationship with Diane Pierman and how agonizing this is all going to be.

Beckman was right: he didn't get where he is by being stupid. He got there by being smart in a crafty, mean-spirited, blithely manipulative manner, as evidenced by the way he just casually and ingeniously screwed me. He doesn't have to fire me; he doesn't have to embarrass me; he doesn't really have to involve himself in any risky way at all. By giving me this case he has ensured my ruination as surely as if I had been caught lobbing incendiary devices at City Hall.

If I go at this case with my customary zeal, it will appear to the public as though I'm pursuing some special vendetta against two popular citizens. They won't realize that that's the way I go after every case. I will be vilified and loathed throughout the county by the populace at large, denounced by every editorialist and second-guessed by every attorney. But if I pussyfoot and ease up on the prosecution, I will be accused of malfeasance, dereliction of duty and bias.

And what if Beckman is right, that I single-handedly blew the Rosamund case with a cockamamie strategy and a bald-faced show of unrestrained anger and contempt at Judge Arigga?

Diane's face floats in front of me, my mind reaching out for some comfort in the maelstrom and, finding none, creating it for me. Her face is as she was, as I pictured her, before all this began. Everything about her is warm, inviting, dreamlike. Is it all lost to me? Is there no way to salvage some small bit of happiness for the two of us?

Jesus H. Christ: I never even laid a hand on the woman and she's ruining my life.

14

It's beginning to look like we're in for another season of drought. The teasing showers we had in February never made it past the end of the month, and there is talk of reinstituting the water rationing policies that were developed during the devastating six-year dry spell that ended only last year with equally devastating flooding and mudslides.

Southern California's special brand of children are blissfully unaware of this, as I can see as I pedal my way up Ocean Avenue. It's the eighth of March and everywhere along this famous bluff park overlooking the Pacific people are walking, jogging, biking, picnicking, in-line skating or tossing Frisbees, and doing so in a wide array of clothing ranging all the way from military camouflage to thong bikinis not much more substantial than dental floss. The sun glinting off the ocean is so bright it hurts to look at it, and the warmth radiating upward from the asphalt is offset somewhat by the cool breeze that rustles the palm fronds overhead. Just another boring day in paradise.

Running alongside me as I gasp my way up the barely perceptible incline in my lowest gear is Miguel Dominguez, one of my deputy DAs who specializes in gang-related homicides. I've met his mother and know that, whatever Miguel might have been tempted by during his barrio days to deter him from the track that eventually led him to my office, she more than made up for as only a strong parent can. The first time Miguel put one of his childhood friends away for twenty-to-life, he spent the next morning in church fervently thanking whatever deity he prays to for giving him that mother.

He's in training for the Los Angeles Marathon less than ten days away, now in what he calls his "taper period" when he decreases his mileage until three days before the event, when he stops altogether. Then he sits or lies down as much as possible and drinks water. By the morning of the race, every muscle in his legs is aching to get up and run. I wonder, if I trained like he does, would I look like him as well? Trim, compact, graceful? I doubt it: it's all in the genes, definitely, so there's no sense my trying. First rule of athletics: pick your parents carefully.

So I'm chugging along as best I can on my forty-pound mountain bike while all around me hardbodies are flexing their muscles in a disgustingly shameful display of their fitness that I, for sure, wouldn't dream of doing if I looked like they do. I sneak a glance at Miguel: he hasn't even broken a sweat yet.

Back in another lifetime a century ago—actually more like six weeks—when I was considering running for DA, a judge I play golf with got me a meeting with a media consultant. He set up a very realistic mock interview in a fully equipped television studio and videotaped me as I pretended to be on the air being grilled by journalists. After several hours of fielding some tough questions and feeling pretty smug about my performance, the consultant presented me with his evaluation: "Milano," he said, shaking his head and scratching his ear in befuddlement, "you're too short, too fat and too ugly."

I kind of knew all that but felt compelled to defend myself anyway and began to mount a pitiably pathetic rejoinder, protesting that I didn't feel myself particularly too far gone along any of those three axes, when he held up his hands. "You're not," he agreed unconvincingly, "as I stand here and look at you. But you photograph like shit." He waited until I looked appropriately crestfallen and stopped trying to argue with him, then told me not to worry about it. He wasn't telling me not to run, just how to align a campaign to show off my better attributes, of which physical presence wasn't one. "You're smart, your people love you and you have a terrific track record in court." That was before the Rosamund trial. Before the Pierman case.

I've got a strategy meeting with Marsha and Marty this afternoon and I need to get some idea of whether this "twins defense" can really work. I had heard that when Miguel was with another office he had gotten involved in a similar case involving two gang members. He said he'd tell me all about it if I wanted to bike along while he ran.

"Heard you gave up on the grand jury," he says easily. My speedometer reads eight miles per hour.

"Yeah," I answer between breaths. "Seemed a bit of a risk. Unnecessary."

"Uh-huh." I've fallen a few feet behind and he slows down so I can catch up. "What I heard, Beckman made you do it."

Are there no secrets left at all? "Oh, really?"

Miguel's hands are chest high as he runs, and he flips one up casually. "Way I heard it, case could go downtown if the grand jury indicts. This way, it stays here." He turns his head and grins at me. "Stays with you."

True. Beckman found out I had scheduled a grand jury hearing and put a quick stop to it. So we had the preliminary in municipal court yesterday and it was a walkover, as expected. As Miguel observed, my last tactic to try to get the case moved to another office never even got off the ground. Diane and Lisa will be tried in superior court and yours truly is the prosecutor.

We've reached the top of Ocean Avenue, and mercifully, Miguel stops for a drink of water from the fountain a few steps away from the totem pole marking Inspiration Point. He's careful not to let his mouth come in contact with anything but the barely bubbling water, cognizant of the fact that fountains along this stretch serve as washbasins for the homeless population and toilets for the pigeons. I dismount to stretch my legs, but before I even get the kickstand down, Miguel is off again, turning onto San Vicente and running up the steepening grade as though it didn't exist.

This beautiful, tree-lined street is one of the most popular running spots on the west side. The wide, grassy traffic divider has two well-worn tracks where countless thousands of runners have carved out separate east and west lanes. On any given day, you can see everything from weekend joggers all the way up to Olympic marathoners working out here. You can also see a distressing number of them getting hit by cars as the two mainstays of southern California culture, fitness and automobiles, meet in jarring discordance. I catch up to Miguel near Third Street, having noticed that about half the runners who pass him in the opposite direction wave in recognition.

"You put in any time in the office at all anymore?" I ask as I pull alongside.

"I knew this was a mistake," he replies. "Next time we'll meet on a golf course."

"So tell me about these guys. They really pull this off?"

He nods. "Oh yeah. Arthur and Eddie Chisworth, two of the meanest and smartest sons-a-bitches you ever saw."

"Marimba Keys, right?" One of the most notorious street gangs in LA history.

Miguel whistles and shakes one hand like he was drying it off. "The worst. They were identical twins and worked at making it as identical as possible. If Eddie gained five pounds pigging out on junk food, he either went to the gym and worked it off or Arthur bulked up. They cut their hair the same, they didn't wear any jewelry anybody could tell apart . . . listen, Eddie got this scar on his cheek, in a knife fight? About two inches long?"

"A scar? But—"

Miguel held up a hand. "Two days later, Arthur carved his own face to make a match. Even used the same knife, so the legend goes."

All of this was hardly a demonstration of brotherly love, Miguel is quick to point out. The only time these two fought more fiercely than when they defended each other was when they were going at each other. No, the reason was a pure scam. Every time one of them stuck up a convenience store or carjacked a Mercedes or administered some street justice to a slow-paying junkie, the other stayed safe and out of sight. If the first one got busted, the other one showed up at the arraignment with their lawyer and used the arresting officer's inability to tell them apart as their sole defense.

"And it worked?" I ask.

"Almost every time. What're you gonna do? They stand on the fifth, cops can't swear to anything—even if they did, a simple test in court would show them up as liars—and they walk."

We're back to the water fountain at the totem pole. This time Miguel doesn't bolt as soon as he's finished drinking. He's looking out over the top of the bluff, across Santa Monica Bay toward Palos Verdes. His old neighborhood is somewhere to the left of the hilltop that rises out of the middle of the peninsula. Beyond it, to the south, is Orange County, where all of this took place. "Who's your judge?" he says finally.

"Harriet Genet." There's still some laboring to my breathing. Miguel nods knowingly. Genet is a protégée of Judges Nyqvist and Goldman both. She's a top-notch jurist, and there will be no surprises, just fair dealing for both sides. I take a sip of water and let my breathing settle down before I speak again.

"How'd it end?"

Miguel continues to look out over the bay. "One of 'em died. Killed in prison."

"Prison? How . . . ?"

He bends down to take a last slug from the fountain, straightens up, and does a couple of calf raises. "Smart cop caught Eddie shaking down a newsie, cuffed him to himself and didn't take 'em off until the arraignment. Judge says, 'Which one is he?' and the cop says, 'I don't give a damn what his name is,' and he holds up his hand, still cuffed to Eddie, and he says, 'This's the sumbitch, pure and simple.' "

Miguel looks at me. "Elsewise, they might still be pulling it off today." He gives me a half salute with two fingers, turns and takes off.

"Great," I mutter disconsolately as he quickly recedes into the distance. I've got two more miles left to get back to the office. My butt is sore and my back hurts; I briefly consider calling a cab and abandoning the bike—it would last less than thirty seconds out in the open without a chain, maybe three minutes with one—but prudence wins out and I remount. I can't even see Miguel anymore.

* * *

I may have Marsha's attention, but Marty's eyes keep darting to the counter. I can practically see him salivating in Pavlovian response to the delicacies being carved up in full view, visible even from our private table along the opposite wall. Saburo Kumito's knife flashes in a hypnotic display of the skills he has honed during his twenty-three years as a master sushi chef. We usually like to sit at the counter and watch the action, but today we needed to meet privately, and Kumito is always accommodating. He has even trained his assistants to avoid calling attention to us with the traditional shouts of greeting as we walk in the door.

Marsha is probably no less hungry than Marty—it's almost two o'clock, owing to my lunchtime ride with Miguel Dominguez—but I've just told her about Beckman's order that I handle the case personally. I've avoided the matter in the two weeks since he and I had our little chat in the hope that I might be able to change his mind after the preliminaries, when he cooled down a little, but he wouldn't even take my calls. I'm hoping maybe Marsha has an idea about how to get me out of this.

"He's right," she says after only a second or two.

"Right about what?" Marty asks in one of the brief intervals when he's not watching Kumito. I introduced Marty to sushi about two years ago when we were interviewing potential witnesses in the mid-Wilshire district. He gagged at first but quickly developed a taste. Only the cost keeps him from eating it seven times a week instead of only two or three, but today it's on the county. I figured, as long as I'm in this much trouble, might as well go out swinging a heavy expense account.

Marsha raps a knuckle on the side of his head. "Pay attention. Sally's going to handle the Pierman case himself."

"Says who?"

"Says Beckman," I answer.

"He's right." Having thus pronounced, Marty looks back at the counter and makes a hurry-up motion to Kumito, who frowns but otherwise ignores him.

"What's with you two?" I demand. "I was expecting a little support here."

Marsha lifts the wooden bowl of miso soup and takes a slurping sip. "You don't handle this one yourself, you're as much telling the world it's not as important as the Rosamund case, or that you're letting your personal feelings get in the way."

The last part of that throws me. What does Marsha know, or think she knows? "What personal feelings?"

"Going after a dirtbag like Rosamund is easy. Doesn't take much courage. But prosecuting Diane and Lisa Pierman? Knowing all the shit you're gonna get?" She sets the little bowl down. "And on the other hand, are you going to be zealous enough about two well-off, white, middle-class professional chicks? There's an integrity issue here."

Kumito has finished arranging the tray and is coming around the counter toward us, relieving Marty's anxiety enough for him to rejoin the conversation. "Besides, you shot your mouth off how many times about justice and due process, how you gonna back off now just 'cuz it hits close to home?"

"You guys are a fat lot of help."

Kumito has arrived and sets down the food with a flourish, then stands there beaming, waiting for us to dive into his creations. He never does anything straightforward. If he serves a piece of radish it comes with several dozen tiny knife cuts, and when he presses it with his finger in front of you, it magically spreads out into a perfectly symmetrical flower. Even the pickled ginger condiment is shaped like an ocean wave rolling across the plate.

We all sit and stare at him until he gets the message and the smile leaves his face. He turns with a grunt and flaps a dismissive hand at us as he leaves. We know he will keep the tables on either side of us open the whole time we're here, to ensure our privacy.

"The hell happened to ladies first?" Marsha asks as Marty picks up a piece of yellowtail wrapped around a finger of rice and dips it into a shallow bowl of soy sauce.

"First off, you ain't no lady." He takes a small bite and closes his eyes in pleasure. The only time I ever see Marty eat slowly is when he eats sushi. I think it's because it enables him to eat twice as much. "Second, I'm starving."

After the first round is concluded and we call Kumito over for a new order, we get down to business. "So far," Marty begins, "they haven't given a single statement to the police or agreed to say anything, even off the record." That is their Fifth Amendment right, and a jury will not be allowed to take that into consideration as evidence of guilt. "Pappas thinks Diane's calling the shots on that one but probably her lawyer agrees."

"What's that tell us?" I ask.

"That Parnell may not put on a defense," Marsha opines. "The sisters won't testify. He'll beat the shit out of our witnesses on cross and rest his case on reasonable doubt."

"No doubt counting on the sympathies of the jury, which'll rest squarely with the twins," I finish. The defense is under no obligation to call witnesses of their own or do anything to defend themselves. If Parnell thinks we can't prove our charges, he can wait until the end and just tell the jury why he thinks we failed to do so. If there is enough reasonable doubt in our case, the jury has to acquit. Of course, Parnell is free to cross-examine our witnesses and try to trip them up or damage their credibility.

Having gotten rid of his opening hunger pangs, Marty is fully back in the conversation. "I'll tell you this: we're gonna have a helluva time making a tight case unless we figure out who really pulled the trigger and prove it."

"Conspiracy and solicitation carry the same penalties as the actual act," Marsha argues. "It's the same as if the conspirator pulled the trigger herself."

Marty is shaking his head. "That's not the point. What I'm saying, what's the jury gonna think, you can't even tell them which one did it but you're smart enough to know it was a conspiracy?" *C'mon,* says his sneer.

I agree. "I think we're going to have some trouble even showing that one of them did it, never mind which one."

"Are you serious?" Marsha asks. "Woulda thought that was a slam dunk."

She's not as up on recent developments as Marty and I, so I fill her in. Patrons in the restaurant caught only a fleeting glimpse of the killer's face. While there is little doubt in their minds who it was, or at least that it was one of the two sisters, we've been having some trouble getting any one of them to stand up and say it without a shadow of a doubt. Half a dozen of them identified photos correctly, but each felt bound to tell us that they might not be able to make a positive ID without adding the small caveat that they could be mistaken. Stress of the moment, questionable lighting, partially covered face and so forth. "And then there's the matter of the gun," I add.

"As in, we don't have one," Marty clarifies.

"That part worries me more than the ID," Marsha says. "The motivation is so clear in this case, all we need for eyewitnesses to testify is that the shooter could easily have been one of the Piermans."

I hold up a hand palm down and rock it back and forth. "Not enough. We need something better than that."

"The gun thing is a real problem," Marty says. "We traced through state records, and there's no gun purchased under the name Pierman since they started keeping records."

"Big surprise," Marsha says sarcastically. She knows, as we all do, that the gun registration and waiting period laws are a bad joke played on the people by their elected leaders so everybody will think they're doing something positive. But the laws only cover purchases from licensed dealers. You can buy a gun in another state or from a perfectly legitimate unlicensed dealer or at a gun show or from your next-door neighbor with no waiting period or registration requirement at all. A recent "guns for concert tickets" campaign in Los Angeles was a source of much amusement in our office, having netted about three hundred weapons out of the millions known to exist, and they were mostly inoperable war relics or rusted antiques the owners had forgotten they even had. Interviewed by a newspaper about a party being thrown for the genius who came up with the idea, Miguel Dominguez came in for much heat when he inquired as to how many Bloods and Crips traded in their AK-47 assault rifles for free passes to Disneyland.

"We know a couple things, don't we?" I ask Marty. "One of the people at the restaurant knows guns; he said it was a forty- five."

Marty rubs the side of his nose. He's getting hungry again. "Yeah. And it was a forty-five slug they took out of Rosamund. Unfortunately—"

I interrupt to address Marsha. "You haven't heard about this yet. You're gonna love it."

Marty sighs deeply. "We thought we had a lock on the shooter because Diane's sweatshirt tested positive for gunshot residue."

Marsha whips her head from Marty to me. I hold up a hand and tell her not to get excited: there's more. Just then Kumito arrives with round two of our lunch and stands there waiting for us to dig in. This time the whole plate looks like a giant flower, with sushi petals arranged around stems made of dill leaves, the whole thing sprouting out of a pickled ginger earth and topped with round, green buds of the viciously hot wasabi paste.

"Hey, Kumito-san," Marty says. "You want me to eat it or photograph it?"

"You're such a plebeian," Kumito says in perfect English with flawless diction. "Swear I don't know why I allow you in my place."

" 'Cuz I'm puttin' your kids through college, that's why," Marty calls to him as he leaves. Without Marty and the dozens of cops and investigators he's dragged to the restaurant, Kumito's business would be down at least twenty percent. Marty picks up a piece of octopus that Kumito liberally smeared with sweet sauce and topped with sesame seeds the way he likes it, and bites into it.

"Unfortunately," he continues while chewing on the rubbery concoction, "Diane and Lisa were in the Santa Monica Gun Club a day before the murder, target shooting with a forty-five automatic." He pops the other half of the tako in his mouth and watches the shocked expression on Marsha's face.

She turns to me and then back to Marty. "They were firing a forty-five? The day before they did Rosamund?"

Marty and I stay silent, letting it sink it. Marsha blinks several times. "Well, gee whiz, fellas: sounds a tad incriminating to me, n'est-ce pas?"

"Did to us, too," Marty says.

"Until we found the manager of the gun club on Parnell's preliminary witness list," I add.

Now Marsha is really confused. "On Parnell's list? Why the hell would he do that?"

"Because," I answer, taking a sip of tea, "it explains away the gunshot residue on Diane's sweatshirt. All he has to do is get the manager to testify that he saw the twins shooting guns, and that's the end of the residue angle."

"But in order to do that, he has to call a witness. I thought you were figuring he wasn't going to put on a defense at all."

I shake my head. "*I* have to put the manager on."

"You! But why on earth . . . ?"

"Because if I don't, Parnell will, and he'll make it look like the prosecution was deliberately withholding a key piece of evidence that might exonerate his clients. The only reason the manager is on Parnell's list is in case I'm stupid enough not to mention it." Like I didn't mention the second rape in the Rosamund case. It's no fun having Parnell on the other side.

Marsha slumps back, the delectables on the plate in front of her forgotten. Marty eyes them covetously. "Gonna look a little funny, you calling the guy up just to spoil your case."

"No. I have another reason. Parnell will say the session at the club easily explains away the positive gunshot residue test, but the jury's going to have to be wondering why a prominent lawyer and a successful caterer just happened to be shooting off a forty-five-caliber automatic handgun the day before their unjustly released attacker was murdered with an identical weapon." I take another sip of tea. "We're going to contend that they were practicing for the killing."

"The manager was sure it was them?" Marsha asks, then thinks better of it. "Yeah, like two gorgeous, mirror-image white chicks walk into his place every day. Wait a minute, how does he remember it was a forty-five?"

"I spoke to him the day after," Marty says, motioning to the eel on Marsha's plate. She nods and he picks it up. "He checks every gun coming into the place before anybody's allowed to shoot. Quick inspection to make sure the gun isn't so screwed up it might misfire and hurt somebody. He also checks the ammo to make sure it's legitimate. The twins didn't have any and he sold them some rounds."

"How much?" she asks.

"Couple hundred."

"Jeez, so their clothes were covered with residue."

"Yup." He polishes off the eel and wipes his hands on a now-cold wet towel. "But I got another angle with the gun. Long shot. Lab's working on it now."

"We got a lot of circumstantial evidence," I tell her, "but none of it gives us much help in figuring out who pulled the trigger, and I gotta agree with Marty: without that, we're weak."

Marsha thinks about it for a few seconds, idly rearranging ginger slices with a chopstick. "Maybe our thinking's a bit too linear here. Need to come at it from the side somehow."

The last time Marsha came at it from the side, we lost the Rosamund trial. But it doesn't mean her thinking wasn't sound, just my execution of it. I ask her what she means.

"What if we just go after one of them and see how we do?"

She leaves it hanging in the air, waiting for comment. Marty sees the problem right away. "Gonna make us look pretty stupid, we pick the wrong one."

"Nuh-uh." Marsha shakes her head. "It all gets squared away in pretrial, before we get to the jury. Who cares if we look stupid there?"

She's right. All the tricks we play on people we're trying to put away, we're now playing on people we like. We wait to hear her start to flesh it out.

"Let's say we pick Lisa. It was her car was driven to the scene and her house where they were waiting when the police showed up. Let's hit her hard and see if Diane lets her take the fall. Play it like Solomon and the baby. If it was really Diane and we scare her enough, maybe she'll confess."

"Naahh . . ." Marty rumbles a long note as he crinkles up his eyes. "I don't like it. They gotta know a jury isn't gonna hang 'em based on a car could easily have been driven by either of 'em. We rest it on that, we're goners."

Marsha picks up a piece of shrimp, considers it glumly and then hands it to Marty, whose emotions rarely interfere with his ability to eat. Marsha slumps back on her seat and says, "Unless we come up with something to differentiate them, the judge may not even let this go to trial at all."

I'm not ready to quit, or to let them quit either. "Is it possible for us to go to trial without knowing in advance how we're going to do that?"

"Foolin' around before the trial is one thing," Marty says, licking some stray soy sauce from his fingertips. "Once we're out in the open and on the record, you risk lookin' like a major asshole." *A risk you can hardly afford,* he politely declines to add. "But I got another idea." He scarfs down the other half of the shrimp, then lifts his empty teacup so Kumito can see it, and taps the side with his finger.

"Lemme ask you something," he starts, setting down the cup. I can tell he's focusing because he forgot to bitch about how Japanese teacups never have handles and how the hell is somebody supposed to pick one up when it's hot. "The shooter and the other one, what sentences do they get?"

"Haven't given it too much thought," I answer, "but we're talking murder one so that's twenty-five to life right there—"

"Okay, and the other one?"

"What other one?"

"The one who didn't shoot. What about her?"

"I'm talking about both of them, Marty. Marsha just told you: in California it doesn't make a difference who pulled the trigger. An accessory before the fact is no different from the principal."

"Yeah, if you can *prove* it was 'before the fact,' but what I'm asking, suppose you can't. What does she get?"

I look at Marsha. She's more up on those details than I am. "Let's see, uh, harboring a fugitive, obstruction of justice . . ."

"Destruction of evidence," I add. "If she dumped the gun."

"I don't know," Marsha says. "Let's say five, maybe ten years. What about it?"

Kumito arrives with a fresh cup of tea for Marty and a platter of oranges, strawberries and honeydew cut up and arranged like a giraffe lying sideways on the plate. Kumito points to two raisins that form its eyes. "I was gonna put these under its ass," he tells Marty, "but then there wouldn't have been any left for your friends to eat."

"Very funny," Marty answers, slurping some tea. "Least it woulda washed out the taste of this roadkill you been feeding me."

"Could tell you hated it," Kumito says, giving him the bill and walking away. Marty hands it to me. For the life of me I could never figure out how Kumito figures prices. I've come in here alone and gotten a twenty-five-dollar tab, and other times the three of us will gorge ourselves for thirty bucks. I suppose it all evens out in the end.

"So what's this brilliant flash of yours?" Marsha asks Marty.

He grows serious as he lays out his thoughts. "Why don't we charge one of them with murder and *both* of them with all the rest of the stuff? I bet we can at least show that one of them did the shooting, never mind which, and the other has to have conspired. We sock 'em with everything we got during trial, and then in the middle"—he sits up straight—"we drop the murder charge."

He pauses and Marsha and I both see it. "Then we try to get the jury to convict them both on conspiracy?" she asks.

"Exactly. The deal is, we settle for nailing them both on the small stuff, because sure as hell they both deserve at least that, and we agree to give up the big nuts murder rap. The jury doesn't have a reasonable doubt problem because neither sister can possibly get more of a sentence than she deserves. Less, maybe, but not more."

It's an intriguing notion, almost like having the jury participate in a plea bargain, but I voice a concern that there's got to be a technicality somewhere that disallows this strategy, however logical it may be. Marty questions it, but as usual, there's right, there's wrong, and then there's the law.

"Look at it this way," I tell him. "You got little blue markers on the freeway that are exactly a mile apart. Now let's say you got a helicopter overhead watching some car, and the pilot's got a stopwatch and he times the car going from one marker to the next in fifty-five seconds."

Marsha looks at me skeptically, but Marty used to be a cop and he knows where I'm heading with this, so I turn to Marsha. "It means the guy's doing sixty-five miles an hour. Now that's a more accurate measurement than if a cop is right behind the guy, watching his own speedometer. But can you convict the driver?"

"No?" Marsha asks.

"Nope," Marty tells her. "Evidence isn't 'direct.' And what Sal is telling me, we may not be able to convict the twins without knowing which was which."

I hold up a hand. "Maybe."

Marsha was right: maybe it is time to switch mental gears but perhaps in an entirely different direction altogether. It occurs to me that we're getting collectively depressed over a situation that may not exist.

"You know, we've been operating under the assumption that Parnell is banking on our inability to identify and prove the shooter."

Marsha folds her arms across her chest. "Sounds like a reasonable assumption. . . ."

"Maybe. But isn't it possible that he'll actually put on a full-bore defense to try to demonstrate that the killing was justified?"

Marsha thinks this over for a second, and some small spark seems to reignite her eyes. "If that's true," she says, picking up the thread, "one of the sisters is going to have to admit pulling the trigger."

"Why?" Marty asks.

"Because," I answer, "how can you claim the homicide was justified if you haven't admitted doing the homicide in the first place?"

"Ahhh . . ."

We go on like this for another twenty minutes, having fun and confusing ourselves, but something is nagging at me, something from earlier in the conversation about the twins' constitutional protection against being forced to incriminate themselves. We shouldn't have dropped that line of reasoning so quickly.

I can feel the first beginnings of an idea starting to cook somewhere in that deep place in my mind that only makes itself known to me when it's good and ready.

15

The last time I was in Nestor Parnell's office, we were on the same side. I found myself feeling a good deal more charitable about the ostentatiously self-aggrandizing display that constituted his office. Now all of these expensive trappings appear to be exactly what they are, symbols of a never-ending struggle with his deep-seated insecurities and a desperate need for the external validation he believes will drive them away. It is all part of the same clinical symptomatology that fuels his ambition and makes him want to win at all costs.

As opposed to purer motivations, like mine.

I'm here with Marty. I called Parnell and asked if I could meet with his client, Lisa Pierman. It went without saying that such a meeting would include her attorney as well. We're sitting at the small conference table in the far corner of Parnell's office, a more formal and businesslike setting than the last time we were here, arrayed around the couch and comfortable chairs. Then, I was fighting for Diane and her sister, being gallant and sympathetic, a knight chivalrous coming to their rescue. Now there is no breakfast cart full of fruits and pastries, only cups of coffee. Lisa looks confused, dazed and vacant. Her fingernails are cut short and have no polish.

It appears from the expression on Parnell's face that there are to be no opening niceties, so Marty gets right to the point. I prefer him to do most of the talking so that I can come in and propose variations without us losing too much negotiating leverage, the good guy–bad guy thing.

"We're trying to seek an accommodation here," he says. We wait to see if Parnell has any objection to Marty's participation: the authority to deal is mine, not Marty's.

Parnell seems not to notice. "What kind of accommodation?" he asks noncommittally.

Marty turns to Lisa. "We believe Diane was the triggerman."

A cloud passes over Lisa's face. Her eyes narrow slightly and her brows crease just a touch but she stays silent: she is probably under instructions from Parnell not to say anything without his prompting.

"We want you to identify her as the killer," Marty continues, and now Parnell jumps in.

"Hold it, hold it." He bends forward slowly, not as though to communicate interest but only to buy a few seconds to think. "Even if Diane did what you say she did— and I'm speaking purely hypothetically here—" He waits for answering nods from Marty and me, which he gets. "Even if that were the case, Lisa's admitting it might implicate her as a co-conspirator or accomplice. She has a Fifth Amendment right against self-incrimination." He sits back once again, the front legs of his chair rising off the ground. "Assuming, of course, that there is anything to admit in the first place, which I'm not saying there is."

"Understood." Marty has his eyes half closed and is shaking his head before Parnell finishes his sentence. "No problem." He looks at Lisa again. "We know Diane pulled the trigger. She needs to pay for that, so . . ." He drops against the back of his chair and puts both hands on the table, palms down. "We're offering you complete immunity from the charges of aiding and abetting, and any and all other charges that might accrue as the result of your being an accomplice to Diane in any way connected with this incident."

This was the essence of the idea that began to unfold in my mind in the restaurant. If we offer one sister immunity from prosecution for conspiracy, only the actual triggerman can plead the fifth: the other one no longer runs the risk of self-incrimination because the immunity already gives her all the protection she needs, so she has no choice but to testify.

The only question that remained for us was, which one do we offer the immunity to? Maybe both?

No. We agreed to offer immunity to only one sister, Lisa, if she fingers Diane. Obviously, we don't expect her to give up her sister, but if Lisa was the triggerman, she might confess so that we don't wrongly go after Diane. If she doesn't confess, and refuses to give up Diane, we bear down on Diane with murder charges.

But what if we picked wrong? What if Lisa did do the shooting and we prosecute Diane for it? That's where the Solomon idea comes in: we'll pursue the case against Diane, and pursue it hard, and if Lisa isn't driven to a confession, we'll have to assume we picked correctly and Diane was the murderer.

Marsha had doubts about whether the judge would go for it. I plan to tell Harriet Genet as little as possible, except to assure her that our case may be creative but it is not frivolous. There's little doubt that she will acquiesce to this attempted bargain: otherwise, she might have to dismiss the case and let a murderer go free.

And now Marty has put Lisa up against a wall by telling her she's off the hook if she identifies Diane as the triggerman. There is a loud *thump* as the legs of Parnell's chair slam back into the ground. He quickly tells Lisa to stay silent. He pulls his yellow legal pad closer to him and uncaps his fat Mont Blanc fountain pen.

"This offer of immunity," he says. "Does that include immunity from the murder charge as well?"

I try to hide my amazement at this question, and I can feel Marty doing the same, each of us trying not to sneak any glances at the other. Parnell has just let slip an astonishing piece of information.

If he knew Lisa was the killer, he wouldn't be asking me if her immunity applied to a murder charge. It is too obvious an admission that she did it and that she needs immunity from the murder charge. And if he knew Diane did it, Lisa wouldn't need the immunity in the first place and he wouldn't have asked.

I can hear Marty exhale softly as he comes to the same

realization that I just did: *Parnell doesn't know which sister did it.*

I tell Parnell that there will be no immunity from the murder charges. He continues to stare at me, and I add, "Are you serious, Nestor? Why on earth would I offer immunity from murder if the whole point is to nail the murderer!"

He isn't thrown by my rhetorical question. "You just got finished saying it was Diane who did the shooting, so what difference does it make if you grant Lisa immunity?"

"If it was Diane," I shoot back, "what does Lisa need it for?"

He shrugs, as if it were obvious. "Just in case you decide to go after Lisa later anyway."

That's not it. I know what he's thinking. He doesn't know if Lisa shot Rosamund or not, but if he gets her blanket immunity from all the charges, he gets at least one of his clients off scot-free and then he'd have only Diane to worry about. I tell him the offer doesn't include the murder charge.

But Parnell dwells on that only for an instant because he's just remembered what we've all known all along, and what renders this little charade of Marty's and mine suspect. I can see it in his eyes, and I feel a small spot of sweat in my lower back threatening to become a trickle. Does Marty see it, too?

Parnell turns to Lisa and smiles. "Would you mind excusing us for a second? Gonna talk just among us lawyers." He pats her hand solicitously, and she gets up without saying a word and leaves.

As soon as the door is closed behind her, the smile leaves Parnell's face. He regards Marty and me with a mixture of distaste and suspicion. "Do either of you two seriously believe one of these women would turn on her sister?"

I panic for a second. I may have underestimated Parnell, and our complicated little house of cards is threatening to collapse. He may be getting dangerously close to figuring out what Marty and I are *really* doing. What I'm fervently hoping he hasn't figured out, though, is that I don't really care if Lisa takes the offer. As a matter of fact, I don't even want her answer right now.

I ignore his question and tell him that this is too important a decision to be made in haste. "Think about it. Take your time. The offer is open until I withdraw it, even after the trial starts."

He knows I'm up to something, but he still doesn't know what, although he's correct in his observation that we wouldn't really expect one of the Piermans to betray the other.

"Have you made a similar offer to Diane behind my back?" he asks.

It's a good question, but I'm relieved because he's on the wrong track. I leap on the chance to change the subject so Marty and I can get the hell out of his office as quickly as possible.

"I did no such thing," I tell him, sounding as offended as I can. "Like I said, we know Diane did it and she's not going to be offered anything."

"Did *he*?" Parnell asks, jerking a thumb at Marty.

I rise, all indignation and hurt professional pride. "We're not playing games here, Nestor. Nobody offered Diane immunity." I motion to Marty and he gets up, and we both head for the door.

Parnell looks like he's wondering if he made a mistake in insulting me, that maybe he's blown the opportunity to get at least Lisa off if she wasn't the shooter, a fifty-fifty chance. "You say the offer stays open?"

I've got a hand on the doorknob, and I answer without looking back. "Until I say it's withdrawn." I open the door, Marty and I both step through, and he pulls it closed behind us.

Lisa is sitting on the couch in the secretary's anteroom. I nod curtly and Marty and I stride away rapidly. I can hear the door to Parnell's office click open as Lisa reenters, probably anxious to hear what went on.

When we're out of the secretary's earshot, Marty exhales with a loud whistle and whispers hoarsely, "Fuck *me*!"

I pull out a handkerchief and run it across my forehead. "That was a little too close for my blood pressure."

"Think he figured it out? Think we're okay?"

I nod my head hopefully, but my mind is elsewhere, going back over the conversation in Parnell's office. I know now with dismaying conviction that it really was Diane who pulled the trigger. It might even be possible that Lisa didn't know about it in advance, and I can feel the canvas of what might have been my life unraveling at the edges.

16

Wednesday, April 26.

The trial begins today.

I can hardly believe it. We made our offer of immunity to Lisa Pierman in Nestor Parnell's office on March 22, and that was the last time anyone from my office spoke with either of them. We exchanged documents, witness lists and interview transcripts through Judge Harriet Genet's office without ever having to see each other.

I haven't seen Diane, either, except once in a bakery on Wilshire. My hand was on the door handle when I saw her through the glass, talking with the counterman. Her face was somber, and even when she managed a polite smile in response to his broad grin, it never reached her eyes, and a haze of sadness seemed to surround her. She was wearing a coat of some soft material in the damp chill of an April morning, and there seemed to be more makeup on her face than usual, especially the patently artificial rosy hue on her cheeks, a futile attempt to hide the pallor beneath. Her step as she turned to leave was not crisp and purposeful but hesitant and unwilling, and I quickly turned from the door and stepped behind a dumpster, hoping she was headed for the street side rather than the alleyway. I noticed Lisa's green Lexus parked in a red zone, then saw Diane get in on the passenger's side. Bending lower, I could see Lisa behind the wheel and then they were gone. I wondered what Diane's days must be like, how many times each hour she looks up from her desk to gaze out the window and wonder what the rest of her life is going to be like. I know she spends most of her time in the office because it would be unseemly and disruptive for a lawyer accused of murder, even if technically innocent until proven otherwise, to be arguing cases in court. I wonder what Diane spent her childhood thinking her life was going to be like at this point, in contrast to how it turned out.

I almost got married once. It was back in New York, to a nice Italian girl named Angela. It had little to do with love but rather with inertia, the accumulated momentum of my old-country upbringing propelling me toward a traditional marriage that would have been safe, secure and acceptable rather than loving, exciting or fulfilling. Angela would have wound up as professional breeding stock, dutifully servicing me three nights a week, spending countless hours snapping gum and prattling on with others of her ilk whose only ambition was to end up like their mothers. I know this to be the fact because that's exactly the way she did wind up just a few short years after I woke up one morning, took a careful look at my future and called it off. She went on to marry a friend of mine whose eventual beer belly, gambling habit and macho, dominating parochialism perfectly complemented Angela's expectations of wedded bliss. Not a day goes by that I don't consciously thank whatever deities intervened on my behalf.

Those same deities, of course, brought me to this day and hour in my life. Court was supposed to begin in twenty minutes, but I've requested a meeting with Judge Genet and I have a few moments to myself. From the second-story lobby window overlooking the front plaza of the Santa Monica County Building, I can see a small crowd of demonstrators marching in a circle, Ernestine Denier standing to one side with a bullhorn organizing the chanting conga line. True to her word, Ernestine and her troops have stirred up a hornet's nest of publicity in defense of the Piermans. Miguel Dominguez, who has been spending some time in the law offices of Marchetti, Parnell & Kozinski trying to negotiate a plea bargain on an unrelated case, learned from some friends on the staff there that Diane and Lisa are angered and shamed so badly they don't even want to leave their homes to go to work.

I have spoken with Ernestine about this. She has made the case a political cause célèbre about rape and the difficulty of getting a conviction, so that a woman's only alternative is to mete out her own justice. They also believe that victims whose fact patterns support these contentions have an obligation and a duty to their sisters to come out into the open, regardless of their willingness to do so. Exposing them against their will not only makes the situations more public, it supports the corollary belief that too many of these crimes go unreported or are only halfheartedly prosecuted. All part of Ernestine's "the cause is more important than the victims" philosophy.

The marchers carry signs of such disparate sentiments that it is difficult to pin down the basic premise. One subcontingent seems to be pressing for more laws protecting women, more specifically that the Santa Monica City Council require that landlords spend a minimum percentage of collected rents on enhancing security for female tenants in their buildings. Another bunch carries signs protesting the new master plan for the city's civic center, demanding an early death for the project because the increased traffic will lead to greater crimes against women. Ernestine, needless to say, is also chairman of CATCH, the Committee to Abandon This Civic Hell, although this is the first I've heard it is because of danger to women: I thought they just hated developers.

Priscilla Fields of the rape center, while disavowing any connection with Ernestine or her minions, did urge me to investigate Judge Arigga, believing that what he did, or allowed to happen, was unconscionable. I told her that, while I'd already started that process, frankly there is nothing in his background, even rumors, to indicate that he has ever been anything but fair and professional with female colleagues, so bias toward the defendant on that score was unlikely. I don't bother to mention that the one other time Arigga ruined my day, he did so in favor of a female attorney. The defendant was Peter Friehling and his lawyer was Diane Pierman. I agreed with Priscilla that a travesty occurred in the Rosamund case without admitting my private pain over whether I shared complicity in bringing it about via my temper tantrums in court. I think I sounded like a self-interested politician as I spoke with her.

"Salvatoré!"

I turn away from the window and see Deputy Sheriff Drew Stengel heading toward me. He's pointing back over his shoulder with his thumb. "Judge is ready."

"What judge?"

"How many judges you got a meeting with today?"

"Genet?"

"Of course, Genet." He draws alongside me and looks at the goings-on below. "Sultan of Swat again. What's it about today?"

"My case. What're you doing in Genet's court?"

"She's using Arigga's. It's bigger."

"Where's he?"

"Took some time off. You ready?"

We turn and begin walking down the hall together. "Since when?"

"Couple weeks now. Goldman's handling master calendar, so I think the old boy's taking it easy. Didn't look so good lately anyway. Think maybe he's fixin' to retire."

I'm sure the complaint I filed didn't help matters any. What do I do if he does retire: pursue the case anyway, try to stick him with a black mark on his way out? Or just let him go quietly and accomplish my expressed goal of getting him off the bench?

I can't think about this now. I clap Drew on the shoulder. "You go on ahead. I gotta take a leak." He nods and heads down the hall as I veer into a corridor and try to refocus on the Pierman matter.

We have already started to figure out some elements of Parnell's strategy. He is not going to plead temporary insanity because he'd have to admit his clients did the crime, identify the triggerman and put her on the stand. Since he still has two clients instead of one, that tells me he isn't doing that: it would create a conflict of interest because one would have to come forth as the shooter.

I also don't think he will go for justifiable homicide and throw the case on the jury's sympathies: under the law he cannot win, and it is too risky to suppose twelve jurors will agree to ignore the law and vote his way, even though that is their right. First, they are intimidated by the judge, second by the public and third—I hope—by their own good consciences and sense of civic duty. Besides, again, Parnell would have to put both sisters on the stand in order to make that point. So I have a strong feeling that he is simply not going to put on any defense at all, and maintain his clients' innocence by virtue of reasonable doubt about my case.

It was based on that assumption that I decided to call for this meeting just before the start of trial. Marsha is waiting for me outside Harriet Genet's chambers. These are behind her own courtroom, some forty feet down from Arigga's where the case will be heard.

"Have a nice pee?" Marsha asks.

"I've had better. Am I late?"

She shakes her head. "Saw a strange face go in, though."

"Who?"

"I said it was strange, how should I know who? But I got a feeling . . ."

I hesitate, my hand on the doorknob. "A second attorney."

Marsha purses her lips and shrugs; she guessed the same.

"Damn." I take my hand off the knob. "It's a good move. Wonder why he waited this long."

"Just to screw us up a little," Marsha says. "Does it change anything much?"

Genet denied Parnell's early motion to divide this case into two separate trials but there's nothing she can do about two separate attorneys. All defendants have the right to choose their own lawyers, and it's common for each defendant in a case to have a separate one. In this case, it's a particularly apt strategy because it'll allow the defense the chance to try to separate Diane's and Lisa's cases in the juror's minds.

Marsha has said something to me but I was too lost in thought to hear it, so I ask her to repeat it.

"You don't suppose one of them is going to give up the other, do you?"

I shake my head forcefully. "Parnell's just trying to keep the two cases separate so he can emphasize our inability to identify the shooter. It makes it easier for him to argue against the fact that one of them must have done it."

"How?"

"If he keeps them separate, he never has to talk about both of them at once."

Marsha nods in understanding. "Each lawyer just says, it wasn't my client, and lets it go at that."

"Right. So who do you figure is representing who?"

She thinks it's obvious. "Parnell's gonna take Diane. Same firm, they're friends . . ."

"Buck says you're wrong."

"You're on."

When we go in, Parnell stands to shake hands with both of us and introduces us to Janine Ericsson, an attorney from Culver City. She is quite young, I would guess no more than late twenties at the outside. She is dressed like a newly minted MBA going out on job interviews with Fortune 500 companies: blue skirt, white silk blouse with the obligatory built-in fluffy tie, a smart beige jacket, sensible heels and an expensive leather schoolbag-style attaché, probably a graduation gift from her family. She is even shorter than I and of stocky build, her dark brown hair cut into a very professional nondescript style with layers in the back. She gives me the expected overly firm handshake and a too-bright smile that betrays both her discomfort and excitement at participating in this high-profile case, probably the heaviest thing she has ever handled. I instantly peg her as window decoration in Parnell's strategy rather than a bona fide presence in her own right.

Her smile falters slightly when she shakes hands with Marsha, a striking black woman five inches taller than she, who moves around the small office with the practiced insouciance of the truly initiated. Marsha doesn't look like an MBA: today, for some reason I can only guess at, she's wearing a full-length dashiki and boots that look like thongs wrapped around her feet and ankles, the whole getup set off by enormous silver earrings depicting warriors poised to throw spears and overly large, round, wire-rimmed glasses. She doesn't do it to show off; she does it because she likes it and doesn't much give a damn what anybody else thinks. That kind of nonconforming self-possession in a woman throws Ericsson a little, and I can hardly wait to see what happens when Marsha starts talking during the meeting.

Parnell looks her up and down. "Full battle regalia?"

"Going to war, aren't we?" Marsha answers amiably. She looks from Parnell to Janine and back again. "Who's whose?"

"I'm representing Diane Pierman," Ericsson says assertively.

Marsha dips her head and looks at me. *Right again, smart-ass.*

It's the only thing that makes sense: giving Diane to Ericsson eliminates the appearance of personal bias on Parnell's part that might have arisen from he and Diane being in the same firm. It's a minor cosmetic consideration but of no consequence to the actual conduct of the defense, since I'm sure Parnell will be calling all the shots for both sisters anyway.

I needed this meeting because I have a tricky problem. In order for me to prove beyond a reasonable doubt that the Piermans killed Vincent Rosamund, I need to be able to establish a motive. Certainly no one is going to believe that two women like these decided to commit murder for the hell of it. The motive is obvious: revenge for the unpunished crime Rosamund perpetrated on them. However, I have already seen what the effect the telling of that tale has had on a jury—I watched their faces during the Rosamund trial. They not only were prepared to convict him, any one of those twelve people would have been glad to throw him off a building as well. So the problem is, if I let those same feelings arise in the jurors in the Piermans' trial, they might acquit both sisters out of pure sympathy. My challenge is to engineer things to get the rapes mentioned just enough to establish a motive but not enough to move the jury to too high a level of sympathy.

Stengel walks into the room and asks if we're all ready, then knocks on a door behind and to the left of the large desk at the back wall. Judge Harriet Genet opens the door and comes in. Unlike Arigga "shooting the shit" with Gustave Terhovian during the Rosamund pretrials, Genet has a well-developed sense of protocol and wouldn't engage in such an *ex parte* conversation.

"Thanks, Drew," she says to the bailiff as he leaves through the main door.

"How's he doing?" I ask her.

"Stengel? A treasure. I'm thinking of hiring him as a personal bodyguard." She moves her eyebrows up and down a few times and looks at the door with a leer, getting a laugh from us all. Genet is about fifty-five but looks ten years younger than that, despite three grown children. She has a wonderfully self-deprecating sense of humor, but God help the green attorney who mistakes it for any lack of seriousness about her job.

She turns her attention to Marsha and gives her the once over. "What is this, like Marcus Garvey Day or something? Can I borrow those earrings sometime?"

Marsha nods her head. "If you think you could hold 'em up."

"You meet the new mouthpiece?" she says to me, inclining her head toward Janine Ericsson.

"I have. No objections."

"Gee, that's a relief." Like I had any grounds to object. "You up to speed on the case?" she asks Ericsson.

"Yes, your honor." Ericsson fumbles with her attaché momentarily, as if she thinks she ought to do something to demonstrate that she's sufficiently acquainted with the case files to represent Diane, then realizes nothing further is required, and is momentarily embarrassed as she settles down, the rest of us staring at her. Marsha and I want to increase her discomfort as much as possible while Parnell is anxious to relieve it.

"We've been over it in detail, your honor," he says, smiling supportively at his new co-counsel. "Ms. Ericsson is completely familiar with all aspects of the case and has spent many hours with her client."

"Good." Genet plops down onto her chair, her petite frame hardly making a sound as she hits the cushion. She wears her hair pulled back into a bun, but it doesn't look as severe as it sounds. It reveals a pretty, round face with widely spaced, almond-shaped eyes; she prides herself on never having worn glasses. "Then we're not going to hear any delaying bullshit on account of new counsel, are we."

It is a statement, not a question, and the mild profanity delivered so unself-consciously causes Ericsson to look up in surprise. She is the only one who does.

"No bullshit, ma'am," Parnell answers. "At least on that point."

That elicits another laugh from the attorneys, and Genet's eyes crinkle up in amusement as well. I pull a yellow pad out of my attaché. Genet folds her hands primly on the desktop and looks at me. "So, Milano, it's your dime. . . ."

I nod and flip my yellow pad to the second page. I always leave the top sheet blank to discourage prying eyes. "Prosecution moves to exclude any mention of rape from this trial, your honor."

Parnell gasps audibly and sits bolt upright. He starts to sputter something—he doesn't really know what to say but is too flabbergasted to just stay silent—and Genet holds up a hand to quiet him down.

"You want to wrap a few more words around that, counselor?" she asks me.

"Certainly." Now that I have gotten Parnell's attention, I relax into my prepared speech. "It is our understanding that Mr. Parnell and, presumably, Ms. Ericsson as well, are not arguing justifiable homicide, and so the alleged rapes are completely irrelevant in this trial and ought not to be mentioned."

"You don't think they're relevant," Genet parrots back to me, a trace of sarcasm evident in her voice.

"Of course not. And besides"—I indicate the defense team of Parnell and Ericsson—"how can they get them into testimony if they're not even willing to admit that one of their clients pulled the trigger? What relevance do the rapes have if their clients never committed homicide in the first place?"

It is, of course, a completely airtight argument that cannot be countered, but Parnell tries anyway.

"How does the prosecutor know we won't be arguing justifiable homicide? I might do that, but I can only make that decision once I see how his case goes."

Genet thinks about that for a few seconds, and I don't interfere with her thought processes. There is no need and besides, it's better for me if she thinks things through and comes to her own, inevitable conclusions without my having to supply them.

"But how are you going to get the rapes in without testimony from your clients?" she asks finally. "If you put them on the stand, they automatically give up all their Fifth Amendment rights and Mr. Milano here"—she points at me—"can cross-examine them freely."

Parnell is shaking his head, hard, even before Genet is finished speaking. "I don't have to put them on the stand to get the rapes in. There's an official police record, rape counselors, a physician . . . Jesus Christ, the prosecutor himself said there was a rape!"

I ignore this last remark. "All that stuff is hearsay without the sisters' testimony because"—this is where I have to fight to keep my voice steady—"in the eyes of the law, Vincent Rosamund was innocent: all charges against him were thrown out during trial for lack of evidence." My calm demeanor and unflappable style in this exchange surprise even me. I feel like Gustave Terhovian must have felt when he was tearing me into little pieces in front of Judge Arigga. I feel good. Great, in fact. I'm going to hang Diane and Lisa and I'm getting high off of it. "Surely we're not going to retry a closed case . . . ?" I add.

Parnell continues to protest ineffectually, but I interrupt after letting him go on a few seconds longer. "Look, Nestor, it doesn't make a difference. Even if you find a way around the hearsay problem, you're still going to have to put them on the stand."

He stops to catch his breath. "Why?"

"Because," I answer confidently, turning back to Genet, "justifiable homicide depends on the state of mind of the killer. The defense can't talk about their clients' state of mind without putting them on the stand, and they can't put them on the stand without identifying which one was the shooter."

I let that sink in. I'm glad I rehearsed all of this in advance, so that I could move smoothly through the words in such a manner that my conclusions seem incontrovertible and self-evident, like I was developing them on the spot by the force of their own internal consistency and logic. "So, unless we know in advance that the defense will do that, we demand that the rapes be excluded because it will only be a tactic to unfairly win the sympathy of the jury without any testimony from the sisters. Like I said"—I look at Parnell and lean back on my seat—"the issue of rape is completely irrelevant if the defense is contending neither of their clients shot Vincent Rosamund."

Genet's features have sobered considerably since our lighthearted banter of only a few minutes ago. The impact of my motion is not lost on her. She asks Parnell if it is indeed his contention that the sisters are innocent of the acts charged, regardless of any supposed justification for them that might exist.

Now it is his turn to present the tactics *he* has prepared for *us*. "Which sister are you referring to?" he asks coyly.

Genet doesn't quite get it and tentatively ventures, "Both . . . ?"

"Can't answer that, your honor," Parnell says. "Far as I'm concerned, there are two cases here, and I can only answer for my own client, Lisa Pierman."

Genet nods with a trace of sarcastic amusement, going along with the game. "O-kaay . . ." she says, dragging the word out, then she turns to Ericsson. "Let's start with Diane Pierman."

Ericsson is startled to be so suddenly thrust into the discussion, but she recovers quickly. "Diane is maintaining her innocence," she says, then looks to Parnell for approval. He makes no reaction, probably hoping Ericsson carries off the charade of her representation of Diane better at the trial than she appears to be doing now.

"And Lisa?" Genet asks Parnell.

"My client is maintaining her innocence." This must be a sort of rehearsal for their closing arguments to the jury at the end of the trial. There is no mention of the twins as a single unit. Each attorney is making a separate case for their client, trying to bypass the logic that insists at least one of them is guilty. Parnell would have loved two separate trials, but Genet correctly ruled that out. Their challenge now is to try to separate the cases in the minds of the jurors and show that, in each case, there is reasonable doubt as to identity and, therefore, guilt.

Parnell pretends to study me for a moment. All of us

are trying to perpetuate the illusion that our remarks are spontaneous and our arguments therefore obvious, rather than having been carefully thought out over many weeks and rehearsed endlessly prior to this day. Accordingly, Parnell seems to come to an on-the-spot decision.

"You know," he says, turning back to Judge Genet, "I may even decline to put on a defense altogether after I hear the prosecution's case. Way I look at it"—he shifts around in his chair, getting comfortable, conveying the impression that he might as well relax since this case is as good as won; he holds his thumb up in the air to start ticking off points—"the prosecution has no positive ID that it was even one of the twins because none of the restaurant patrons are absolutely positive about the face they think they saw. Second—"

"Scuse me," I interrupt. "Are you talking about your client now or both defendants?" It's a deliberate jab at his case separation strategy, which he seems to have forgotten momentarily.

"I'm talking about the case in general," he says with annoyance.

"You mean the *cases*," I respond, emphasizing the plural.

He ignores me and continues, another finger now in the air. "Second, they have no differentiating information that would point to one of the sisters rather than the other as the triggerman. And finally"—he puts up another finger and turns to me for the dramatic finish—"you have no murder weapon. Correct me if I'm wrong, counselor, but without the gun, you have no physical evidence to link the shooting to either of the twins in the first place."

Parnell leans back in his chair and tries not to look baldly triumphant, but Ericsson has a self-satisfied look on her face, as though she were a contributory participant in Parnell's brilliant thesis. Marsha and I keep still, despite Genet's bid for me to counter Parnell's argument, which she makes by raising an eyebrow and lifting her hands questioningly. I just stare back at her and shrug, a gesture that tells her the conclusion is self-evident. My faith in her insight and intelligence is rewarded as she addresses Parnell a few moments later.

"Well. If what you're saying is true, Mr. Parnell, and

you are contending innocence by reason of lack of evidence, then of what relevance are the rapes?"

Parnell stares back at her, stunned by how he has shot himself in the foot because he has forgotten my original motion, which led us to this point in the first place.

Genet mistakes his chagrin for noncomprehension and explains further. "What's the point of mentioning the rapes if you're saying your clients didn't shoot Rosamund?"

But Parnell understood it the first time and has now effectively made it impossible for himself to argue the point any further. He barely hears Genet as she makes her ruling.

"It's only proper for me to grant prosecution's motion, but . . ." She scratches her head, concern on her face. "I've gotta say *something* to the jury, Sal, on account of all the publicity. They'll know the background, and it's silly for us to think they can just ignore it all."

This is the moment I have been engineering for weeks, and I try to look thoughtful and sympathetic with Genet's concern as I offer a proposal. "That's a good point." I see Parnell perk up out of the corner of my eye. "How about this: why don't both sides simply stipulate that the rapes were alleged to have occurred, without going into any more detail than that?"

It is a conciliatory, seemingly magnanimous gesture on my part, a great concession that demonstrates my willingness to do the right thing and let this trial proceed on its true merits without standing on a lot of nit-picking technicalities. Genet looks at Parnell and he has no choice but to agree. As a matter of courtesy, Genet solicits Ericsson's approval as well, and she simply follows Parnell's lead and nods.

It is a giant, walloping setback for the defense, and I can feel waves of relief and admiration emanating from Marsha like radar beams aimed at me. I can hardly believe how we managed to finesse this critical element of our case.

We needed the rapes to be in this trial. Without them, we could show no rational reason why the twins would want to kill Vincent Rosamund and would have a much weaker case. With them, I have the complete inventory of elements required for every crime: motive, means and opportunity, but I have robbed Parnell of the ability to trot out the sordid details and gain sympathy for the twins. In the minds of the jurors, there may be doubts as to how bad, or even how real, those rapes really were, since the stipulated statement Genet gives to the jury will refer to them only as "alleged" and unproven in a court of law.

"That about do it?" Genet asks.

"That's it for us," I answer. I called for the meeting, so it would surprise me if Parnell had any other motions, unless he came up with something in the last few minutes as a result of our maneuvers.

"We're okay," he says.

"Then let's get this show on the road," Genet says, ushering us out of her chambers and telling us we'll start in half an hour. Parnell doesn't say anything to me as he and Ericsson leave, but this doesn't surprise me: I just beat him good and he can't be liking it much.

Marsha and I head back to our offices, and she sets a slow pace so she can talk to me. "Don't get too smug about that, Sal."

"About what?"

"About what you think you just did to Parnell in there."

"What I think I did?" I'm not following her.

We come alongside one of the large windows lining the outer corridors where the courtrooms are, and she stops to lean against it, facing me. "Parnell's a smart lawyer. More than smart. No way he lets himself get into a fix like that."

"He just did, didn't he?"

She shakes her head. "I don't think so." She smiles and waves as two secretaries from our office pass by. I don't turn to acknowledge them, trying to fathom what Marsha is driving at.

"You're telling me Diane is calling the shots," I finally conclude, and she nods.

"We tested a critical assumption and won," she explains. "The defense is going to base its case on our inability to identify which twin has the Tony, right?" I agree. "Well, if it were me defending," she goes on, "I wouldn't want the rapes mentioned at all. Without them, the prosecution can't demonstrate a motive, and who's going to believe one of the Piermans decided to go on a random shooting spree?"

"Then why did he freak out when I motioned to get the rapes excluded?"

"Because," she answers, growing conviction evident in her posture and voice, "Diane wants them mentioned. She needs for the world to know that this was a revenge killing. Sure, she'd like to be acquitted on this identification technicality, but she needs for everyone to know the truth, that they're not dangerous murderers and that they took Rosamund out because, as they used to say in the Old West, he needed killing."

She's so obviously right it doesn't bear argument, but there are pieces of it I don't fully grasp. "Why would Parnell object to that?"

"Because he's a lawyer, Sal. He's like us; he thinks the only reality that exists is the one inside in the courtroom, that what goes on out in the world doesn't count."

She can tell from my expression I don't get it, so she explains. "He just wants them to go free. He doesn't care how, or what anybody thinks about it; he just wants them to walk, just like Terhovian wanted Rosamund to walk. He's not concerned about how the world perceives them. In his eyes, if the law says they're innocent, that ought to be good enough for everybody, with no second-guessing. Without the rapes being mentioned, he's got a good shot at getting them off because not only can't we identify the shooter, we can't even show a motive."

"So you're telling me, the reason I got the rapes mentioned at all is because that's the way Diane wanted it?" It doesn't require an answer: the only reason my phenomenally brilliant pretrial strategy worked is because Diane Pierman wouldn't let her lawyer do his job.

"If Parnell had been in charge," she says, "he would have agreed to your motion to exclude the rapes and been out of those chambers like a bat out of hell before you had a chance to change your mind."

We both let that sink in for a while; then I grab a piece of material on the sleeve of her dashiki. "I shoulda fired your ass the first time you showed up in one of these things."

"Wish you had. Coulda made more off the wrongful

termination suit than my laughable salary." She takes my arm and leads me down the corridor. "There is some good news here, you know."

"What's that?"

"Anytime you got a client interfering with her attorney, there's opportunity to trip them up during trial. You know what they say . . ."

I do. *A defendant that handles his own case has an asshole for a client and a schmuck for a lawyer.* Prosecutors love it when a criminal defendant goes *pro per,* acting as his own attorney.

We grab two cups of coffee in the break room at our offices and sit down in a small conference room to gather ourselves before proceeding to court. There's something else on my mind, and it fits in with Marsha's analysis of how the defense is handling its case.

"Under similar circumstances," I begin, "I'd probably do just what Parnell is doing, base the case on the prosecution's failure to identify the gunman, but I might have tried something else to begin with."

"Like what?"

I take a sip of coffee and wince as the hot liquid hits my tongue. "I would have tried to get a reduced sentence for the gunman and a dismissal of the conspiracy charges against the other one, if the shooter agreed to confess."

Marsha thinks this over. "But his way, he might get them both off."

"Key word is 'might.' Parnell has to be scared to death right now."

That's because we have planted in his mind the notion that we're going to base the identification of the shooter on some forensic evidence, maybe the relative amounts of gunpowder residue on the sisters' clothing, maybe arguing that Diane had a greater amount and therefore had more recently fired a weapon. It's the argument I implied when we got this case past the preliminary hearing and into superior court for trial.

Marsha shoots me a look. We both know that if we get to that point, we're dead. I have no expert witness who will testify to such evidence because it's complete bullshit.

* * *

There is a crush of reporters and ordinary citizens in the corridor as Marsha and I make our way to the courtroom. Several of the protesters I recognize from my second-story observation of the demonstration are there, glaring at me with the kind of anger only freshly converted prose-lytizers seem to be able to muster up, and on a moment's notice.

We'll be starting off with *voir dire,* questioning prospective jurors. Judge Genet doesn't like to play games with this process and will be allowing Parnell and me a lot of leeway in asking our own direct questions so long as we stick to the topic and don't go on too many newly unconstitutionalized fishing expeditions.

During jury selection, I know I need to stack the seats with male chauvinist pigs who feel a brutal death was too stiff a price to pay for rape, and a contested rape at that. Parnell, of course, will be looking for ardent feminists. We will both be in contravention of Supreme Court directives regarding jury discrimination, but there's no real way to catch us at it. I wonder which is a greater perversion in the search for truth, that the Supreme Court can presume to tell us how to pick a jury or the way we actually do it?

As Marsha and I *no comment* our way past the reporters and enter the courtroom through the rear double doors, I see Diane and Lisa sitting side by side at the defense table, flanked protectively by Nestor Parnell and Janine Ericsson. I stride confidently to the prosecution table and make no effort to avoid eye contact, but Diane's presence has a sudden, disquieting effect on me. I realize in a flash that, once again, during our background maneuvering, she had been transmogrified in my mind from a human being into just another inanimate element of a case strategy. It's a necessary distancing technique to allow me to concentrate on business without getting confused.

But here, in court, in this suddenly small room, as I walk past the defense table I catch a faint whiff of her perfume—or think I do—and the rest of the courtroom instantly recedes to a distant pinpoint so that only she is left, filling my vision like a giant hologram. It catches me off guard and I feel my chest constrict, making it difficult to breathe. My fingers momentarily lose their grip on my trial notes and a sheet of paper flutters to the floor. As I reflexively reach for it several others fall out, and I have to sidestep quickly and almost lose my balance, stumbling into the side of the table.

"Easy . . ." Marsha's voice comes from behind me, one hand on the small of my back, the other near the floor retrieving the fallen pages. The back of the courtroom swells back into focus and I blink to clear my eyes.

"Sorry," I mutter, feeling light-headed and disoriented. Diane is wearing a demure skirt and a cashmere sweater, her soft hair pulled to the side so it drops onto one shoulder, held by a single ribbon that gives her an air of schoolgirl innocence. Following my uncoordinated stumble she turned to me at last, and she is still looking at me. Her pupils are large, bottomless wells, and if I accomplish nothing else today, I need to keep myself from falling down into them. Minutes ago, in chambers, I scored a major tactical coup, and now I drop onto my seat, wondering what the hell I'm trying to do, why I am even here. I can't sort any of this out, I don't know how to feel or how to behave or what I'm supposed to do, and it's starting to scare the hell out of me. I have to win this case, but doing so will be like a trapped coyote chewing off its own leg. What pieces of me will be left behind? How badly will I maul a woman who I fantasized about marrying scant weeks ago? I feel panic rising like acid in my throat. I take a sip of water from the glass Marsha has just poured, pulling an ice cube into my mouth and biting down on it, hard, until it cracks into several pieces. I close my eyes, turn toward Diane and open them. Thank God, thank God she has turned her attention elsewhere.

Jury selection starts off routinely; I drift into autopilot and allow the soothing rhythms of the courtroom to calm me. My natural instincts take over, and I find myself once again able to focus selectively, concentrating on those elements of the procedure that are important, trusting Marsha to alert me if anything sneaks up out of left field. The first hours pass without incident, and I'm now questioning juror twelve. She has a stocky build, short-cropped, slightly graying hair and unflattering glasses. She wears no makeup, is forty-seven and has never been married. Juror twelve is every inch the stereotypical "dyke feminist," which is what Marsha has just written on a piece of yellow paper and turned so I can read it. All of Marsha's myriad political sensibilities are out the window when she is in court trying to win a case. She sees this juror as the kind who feels castration is too kind a punishment for any male that even looks at a woman cross-eyed. Marsha goes back to her notes, full well expecting me to exercise a peremptory challenge and excuse this juror without wasting any more time.

But I keep asking questions. "What do you do for a living, ma'am?"

"I own a bookstore."

Marsha rolls her eyes heavenward.

"I see. Alone?"

"No, I have a partner." She hesitates, then says, "A female," in a defiant tone. I see Marsha circling her note to me over and over in heavy pencil, wondering why I'm bothering to toy with this one. Parnell is shaking his head in amusement, and Janine Ericsson is pretending to be absorbed in important note-taking.

"Have you read about this case?" I ask juror twelve.

"Of course. It's impossible not to."

"Have you formed any opinions about the case?"

"Sure, tons of them. How could one honestly answer otherwise?"

"So tell me: how would that affect your ability to serve as an impartial juror?"

She blinks several times. I doubt she expected to get this far. "I believe in the rule of law." She turns to the judge. "I also know that anyone who believes what the newspapers feed us is guilty of surrendering her free will to any causist with an agenda, and that the only thing that counts is what is presented in court under the rules of evidence and procedure."

Marsha perks up at this but Parnell is still smiling, knowing that I will excuse this juror and am only having a little fun. But something in her voice and manner, something about the sincerity of her tone leads me to believe that she can be trusted, not to side with me but to listen and think and set aside her own biases. I look at her for a long time, and she senses the appraisal taking place. I watch for signs that this is important to her, and when I think I see them, I look over at the judge and pronounce, "People pass for cause and accept this juror, your honor."

Parnell looks up, startled. He hasn't been paying close attention and wonders what it is I have seen. I can tell he is getting ready to exercise a peremptory, but he doesn't trust himself and he lets it go. I know I have a friend on the jury now, because she feels that I have seen something beyond the exterior trappings, which she undoubtedly wishes more people who meet her would do. She knows that to bring in a verdict against my case would almost be a betrayal of that trust. Let her think whatever the hell she wants as long as she is on my side. Unfortunately, that is only one friend, and I need twelve to secure a conviction. Parnell can get away with a single strong one to hold out for acquittal and hang up the jury.

We ask no questions regarding the death penalty. The prosecution has claimed no special circumstances to warrant capital punishment, and I am sure Parnell could prevail on mitigating circumstances during the penalty phase of the trial: if the twins were to be found guilty, there would be no need for Parnell to hide the fact of the shooting, and he could tell the whole story and go for sympathy unconstrained by the kinds of logical contradictions I pointed out in chambers this morning. So we have not asked for the death penalty.

And so it goes, for the rest of that day and into the following morning. Janine Ericsson asks very few of her own questions, and I find myself continuing to think of Parnell as the attorney for both sisters. Both Parnell and I make it a point to make eye contact and smile at each juror we pronounce acceptable, as though we have conferred some judicial imprimatur and placed each in a special state of grace. It's an interesting phenomenon of human nature, considering that most of the prospective jurors probably fought like hell to get out of jury duty in the first place.

The panel is finally seated and sworn in midmorning of the third day, April 28, and even though it's a Friday, Genet starts the trial, wasting no time in doing so. I was praying that she would wait until after the weekend, but there is no real reason to do so. Perhaps it's better this way, to step off the plane, ripcord tightly in hand, rather than have an extra three days—and nights—to brood about it.

First order of the day is the judge's instructions to the jury. She gets through the preliminaries quickly, knowing that they're waiting for the real heart of what she has to tell them. She puts aside her notes and the instruction forms to which Parnell, Ericsson and I have agreed and folds her hands in front of her, turning to the jury.

"The issues in this trial are very simple, although the process by which you will have to decide them is not. I say the issues are simple and you must be thinking, well, they sure didn't *sound* simple when I read about them in the newspapers!"

The jurors giggle nervously, not sure if it's okay to laugh in court, and the judge's smile tells them it's perfectly acceptable. At least when she's the one cracking the jokes. Then her face grows serious again.

"I want you to be sure you don't make things more complicated than they are by confusing what you hear in this court with what you might have read about in the papers or seen on television. Those things don't count. People were not under oath, no rules of procedure or evidence were followed, and the reporters are a lot more interested in boosting their ratings than they are in delivering objective news. Now"—she lifts a pencil and taps the eraser on the bench top—"we'd all be kidding ourselves not to acknowledge that a rape, or two rapes, have been alleged to have occurred, perpetrated against these defendants by the man they were charged with shooting." She waves a hand at the defense table as she speaks but doesn't turn away from the jury. "Whether those rapes occurred or not has never been settled in a court of law and is in fact completely irrelevant to this case.

"What *is* relevant is *a,* whether a murder, as defined by law, took place, and *b,* if so, to what degree, if any, were the defendants involved, and *c,* is one or both of them guilty according to the letter of the law. Those are three separate questions that need to be answered, and it is up to the prosecution to answer them and prove the defendants' guilt. This is what we mean by 'burden of proof.' The defendants are not required to defend themselves. All they have to do is sit there. As a matter of fact, if their attorneys feel the prosecutor has not made his case beyond a reasonable doubt, he may just simply sit there and say nothing." Genet, too, has lapsed into assuming Parnell is handling both cases, and she did so midsentence. She doesn't appear to have noticed, but Ericsson did, stiffening as the words came out. Genet's voice takes on a stern edge.

"You, the jurors, must decide the question of guilt based on only two things: the evidence you hear in court, and the law as I will explain it to you. You must leave your biases and personal feelings about the law at home. The only judgments you should be making are whether you believe the witnesses and the evidence, and what conclusion do they lead you to, *according to the law*."

She seems to relax on her chair and rubs the side of her nose casually. "There's been a lot of publicity about this case, but I've been listening to the *voir dire* and I am fully convinced that each of you is intelligent and properly motivated to do what's right according to my instructions. I have a great deal of faith in this panel's ability to produce correct verdicts, and I will do everything I can to help you get there. So if you have any questions at all during the course of the trial, don't be afraid to ask. If you're uncomfortable doing that in open court"—she points to Drew Stengel—"send a message to me with the bailiff." She looks at Stengel and then back at the jury. "He's big but he's a pussycat."

That draws a laugh, a red-faced Stengel grinning widest of all. In her own way, Genet is trying to win friends on the jury in order to impress them with the seriousness of the task ahead and to get them to behave responsibly. It was a competent and forceful lecture, but I only heard about half of it because I'm up next and I was busy trying to squeeze Diane's face out of my mind by sheer force of will.

"Your opening statement, Mr. Milano," the judge commands. I can feel the slipstream whistling past my ears, the hard earth looming before me several miles below. I know I'll be all right after the initial launch, but it is not a helpful thought at this moment.

Marsha, the judge, the bailiffs, other attorneys in the room, the clerks and some of the reporters have all seen me before, many times. If I do anything out of the ordinary, soft-pedal in the slightest or alter the style with which they're all familiar, they will know it in an instant. And that style has always been hell-bent for leather, treating every trial as though it were the Lindbergh kidnapping.

I take my time gathering up my notes and making my way to the lectern. I want some more time to pass between Genet's lighthearted reference to Stengel and my somber message. I riffle through the pages in my hand as I set them on the lectern: I'm a good public speaker but I always rely on notes. I put the whole opening in my word processor and printed it out in extra large type so I wouldn't have to squint.

"The judge is correct," I improvise immediately, in a low voice, forcing the jurors to concentrate if they're to hear my every word. We're just beginning; later, when they're bored with the unexpectedly tedious proceedings, it will be difficult at times to get their attention, but now they strain to make sure they don't miss a single critical syllable. A trial, contrary to popular myth and to paraphrase an old adage about flying, consists of interminable hours of sheer boredom punctuated by rare moments of excitement.

"This is a simple matter. There is only one real issue. On Sunday, February nineteenth, Diane Pierman walked into a popular westside restaurant called Tawqinah, stepped up to a man eating his dinner and minding his own business, and shot him through the heart with a forty-five-caliber automatic pistol. She then turned around and left, walked several blocks, got into a late-model green Lexus and drove away." There's more to it than that, such as brandishing the weapon at restaurant patrons, but I want to keep this as simple as possible for now.

"Ms. Pierman's life was not in any immediate danger from this man, nor does she contend that it was. In fact, she hasn't contended anything, which is her right. We have a host of completely reliable witnesses who will describe the shooting in detail to you. They were right there when it happened."

I turn to look at Diane and Lisa for the first time, and as expected, it doesn't trouble me at all. I'm fully into my trial mentality now, a state of almost transcendental focus and intensity, and the twins have been transformed in my mind from human beings to defendants. From this point on, I'm unstoppable, a priest vehemently and passionately exhorting his parishioners to adhere to a canon he himself doubts.

"Diane's sister Lisa knew she was going to do this and willingly participated in a conspiracy not only to commit the murder but to try to confuse law enforcement authorities as to which of the two of them pulled the trigger. This is an obstruction of justice." I turn back to the jury. "You know what that is? Well, the judge will give you the technical definition, but it's when somebody tries to interfere with the processes that keep all of us safe."

I abandon the lectern and my notes and walk over to the jury, leaning on the rail in front of the first row of the box. I'm almost done and can wing the rest.

"Lisa loaned Diane her car, and after the shooting, stayed with her so that when the police found them, they wouldn't know who pulled the trigger. You see, they figured that if nobody could tell them apart, there would be no way to convict them. So not only did they try to fool the police"—I look into as many of their individual faces as I can in a few seconds—"they're trying to fool you, too. If they can trick you into thinking that there's no way to identify the triggerman, then you won't be able to find them guilty because you can't be sure who's who. Now, under the law, they're both equally guilty no matter who fired, so you might think, well, what the heck, let's just convict them both." I smile at this glib turn of phrase and most of them smile back. "But the law won't let you do that. The law wants you to be positive, beyond a reasonable doubt. And if we can't tell you who pulled the trigger, the law says you must be suspicious of what we tell you the conspirator did. After all, how can we be sure of who did what if we don't even know which is which?"

I slap my hand on the railing and walk away, as though having effectively nuked my own case. When I'm back at the lectern, I finger my note pages and start to stack them up, preparing to leave. "So the only real issue is who did the shooting and we're going to tell you that and there won't be any doubt." I wait for the stirring behind me in the audience, hoping the jury notices what a dramatic statement I just made. "We'll use sensitive forensics and other evidence to prove conclusively that it was Diane Pierman, and you will have no trouble convicting her of premeditated murder, conspiracy and obstruction of justice, and you will have no trouble convicting Lisa Pierman of criminal solicitation, obstruction of justice, conspiracy, and aiding and abetting a felony."

I pick up the papers and head back to my seat. I stand behind the table and look at the jury again. "Like the judge said, it's a simple case, and you will have a very simple job to do. Thank you."

I sit down and Marsha squeezes my knee under the table. "Masterful," she whispers to me, and I reach for the glass of ice water, trying not to dwell on the tears I saw forming in Diane's eyes as I came around the table. I feel faint again and drink the whole glass, wishing it were something stronger.

"Mr. Parnell?" the judge says.

Parnell smiles and shakes his head, standing up but seeming to do so reluctantly. He speaks as he walks toward the jury box, scratching the back of his head in befuddlement.

"Ladies and gentlemen, frankly I have no idea what the devil we're doing here." He turns to our table and waves a hand at us. "What on earth are these people talking about? Look, this is America, right? We have certain rules here that were drawn up to stop authorities from persecuting innocent people. Some of those rules are complicated but some are real simple, like, it would really be nice if you had some *evidence* before you tried to convict somebody?" He makes it sound like a question, emphasizing the sarcasm.

"There's no evidence in this case! Those reliable eyewitnesses the district attorney told you about aren't as reliable as he'd like to think. They're telling you about some forty-five-caliber handgun, and they don't even have the murder weapon! Now, I represent Lisa Pierman, the alleged conspirator. She's sitting home one night with her sister when police come through the door and arrest her. Conspiracy? Aiding and abetting a felony? For heaven's sake, how does the prosecution think they're going to show that my client conspired to kill some guy when all she's guilty of was sitting home when he was shot! And oh, by the way . . ."

He walks to the defense table and stands in front of it. "In case the prosecution later tries to make the case that it was my client at the scene, let me point out that there's at least one person in the world who bears more than a slight resemblance to her?" That sarcastic inflection again, and he points over his shoulder at Diane with his thumb and the jury laughs along with him. Then he walks back to the jury box and his features grow sober.

"In all seriousness, ladies and gentlemen, the rules of law are important. The prosecution must prove beyond a reasonable doubt that my client, Lisa Pierman, participated in a conspiracy. The entire burden of that proof is on the prosecution. I'll tell you what reasonable doubt means: it means that if there's another explanation that fits the facts and exonerates my client, you have to acquit her. And that's going to be easy because there is not a single, solitary shred of evidence that she did anything at all in connection with the victim's death." He pounds the railing in cadence with every syllable. "None. So like the judge said"—he pushes back from the rail and stands up straight—"it's real simple."

It was a powerful and forceful opening. It's easy to see how the jury was drawn into Parnell's deep conviction. I wonder how Ericsson will do on Diane's behalf, that being a tougher defense case. Parnell was right: it is going to be very difficult to show conspiracy on Lisa's part without some convincing physical evidence. Showing that one of them shot Rosamund is easier.

Ericsson is clearly nervous, but she's a trooper and obviously determined not to be intimidated. Marsha sneaks a knowing smile at me.

"I'm not going to take up more of your time than is necessary," she begins, walking briskly to the lectern. "My client, Diane Pierman, is charged with murder. That's a very serious charge and it requires some very serious proof. Not a guess, not a maybe or a likely or a could be. It has to be *proved*! Beyond a reasonable doubt! Not somebody that *could* have been Diane Pierman, or looked like her or was the same height or wore the same perfume or whatever the hell else the prosecution dreams up. They have to prove it was her. Definitively. No doubts. Because if it *could* have been somebody else, then the law demands that you assume it *was* somebody else. It's not a gray area so don't let anybody confuse you with a mountain of trivial nonsense. If you don't know for an absolute certainty that Diane Pierman pulled the trigger, you have to let her go. That's the law."

She turns from the lectern, casts a cynical look at Marsha and me, then says, "And ladies and gentleman, I absolutely guarantee you that they can't prove she did it because no matter how you slice it"—she turns to them one last time—"there's just no evidence." With that she goes to her seat and sits down.

Marsha turns to me wide-eyed and covers her mouth with her hand, whispering, "Holy shit!" through her fingers.

I'm still staring at Ericsson, wondering if she wants a job as a prosecutor when this is all over. Genet looks at the clock on the wall behind us.

"We will adjourn until Monday morning," she announces, "at which time the prosecution will call its first witness." A great rustling rises up from the back as people prepare to leave, but Genet gavels them all to silence, then gives the jury the standard admonition regarding discussing the case with anybody or among themselves. She also forbids them, in strong terms, to read about the trial in the newspapers or watch anything about it on television.

"Everything you need to know about the trial happened in the courtroom right in front of your own eyes. You already know more about it than any reporter does. So if you were to learn anything new on the television, it's automatically wrong."

She bangs her gavel twice. "We're adjourned, so *now* you can all bolt out of here."

And they do, the reporters taking up stations outside the door and forming a gauntlet that we all have to run through like some fraternity hell-night hazing. I have only "No comment" to throw at them, and I told Marsha to do the same. Parnell, no doubt, will have plenty to say, since public sympathy is a cornerstone of his defense, but I don't care.

Eleanor Torjan follows me all the way to my office, but I'm steadfast in my refusal to say anything to her. Finally I tell her that what the judge said was right, that nothing is going on that she couldn't hear for herself in the court-room, so what does she want from me? She doesn't take it well.

I plan to spend this afternoon and most of the weekend clearing paperwork off my desk and trying to forget about the trial as much as I can. I'm fully prepared, and there's nothing more I can do except start second-guessing myself and screw things up.

17

We're back in court Monday. Last night I took two over-the-counter sleeping pills and this morning drank three cups of coffee, the real stuff, not decaf. I haven't had a cup of regular coffee in years so it did the trick, as I knew it would, countering the lingering aftereffects of the pills. I'm so wired you could plug a small household appliance into me and it would run.

There wasn't a prayer of getting any natural sleep, given the jumble of thoughts racing through my mind. The better I do my job, the worse I make myself feel, like a master carpenter convicted of murder and forced to build his own gallows in order to make sure it gets done right.

Our case really starts today, and it isn't long before I let my autopilot take over once again, drifting into it via some sort of self-hypnosis I don't quite understand. It is as though I were two people, one emotional, insecure and unreliable, the other an automaton that always seems to know the right thing to do at any given moment. I could easily drive myself schizophrenic by blaming everything on the android part, as though I have nothing to do with whatever he does. It's an inviting temptation, despite the inevitable pathology.

Diane is again dressed conservatively and wearing little makeup, but she has never looked more beautiful, more vulnerable—

"Your witness, Mr. Milano?"

Judge Genet's questioning tone makes me wonder if this is the second time she has called me and I never heard the first. I try not to jerk my head around, and pretend that all is well. "Prosecution calls Phillip Mavidian," I announce in my best, most easygoing voice.

Mavidian is a former psychologist who chucked his entire practice to go into the restaurant business. As far as I know, he has never told anybody where he came up with the name "Tawqinah," but I suspect he made it up out of thin air to sound trendy, like "Sergio Valenti" or "rich Corinthian leather."

He does not look happy. His business was already on the slide when the shooting occurred, and he has not bothered to reopen the doors since that night. When questioned by the police, he jokingly bemoaned the fact that somebody on the order of a Columbo or a Gambino wasn't shot in his joint instead of some wannabe, wiseguy rapist, which would do nothing to boost his traffic like Joey Gallo did for Umberto's Clam Bar in lower New York.

Mavidian is sworn in and under my questioning states that he is the owner of the restaurant and was tending bar on February 19. I ask well-bounded, precise questions and try to bring out as much detail as possible. We've gone over this, and I don't want Parnell tripping him up on details that may in fact be inconsequential but might make him look less than reliable. So far, he's described a woman walking through the door wearing a Stars sweatshirt and blue jeans, her face partially covered with a long scarf.

"What happened then?"

He shifts in his seat and looks at the jury. "She walked past the bar and looked around for a couple seconds."

"Looked where?"

"In the dining area."

"Did she say anything to you?"

"No. I figured she was looking for somebody."

I wait for a possible challenge from the defense, and Janine Ericsson doesn't disappoint me. "Objection!" She stands up, pushing her chair back with an audible scraping sound. "How does the witness know what was in the defendant's mind?"

Even better than I thought. "Are you telling us that the woman Mr. Mavidian saw is your client?" I ask Ericsson.

She looks at me in shock but recovers quickly. "You know what I meant. How does the witness know what was in the *woman's* mind?"

Genet is trying to stifle a giggle at Ericsson's gaffe and my attempt to exploit it. "I'd appreciate it if you both would direct your comments to me," she manages to say with a straight face. "Mr. Milano?"

"The witness never said a word about what was in the woman's mind, your honor. He said he *assumed* she was looking for somebody. That was going on in *his* mind, which he is entitled to testify about." The maître d' will say later that Diane actually said she was looking for a friend.

She nods. "Overruled. Witness may continue."

I motion for Mavidian to go on. "So she spots this guy—" he begins.

"What guy?"

"The guy that was shot."

"What do you mean, she spots him?" I ask before Ericsson objects again and ruins the flow of the story.

"She's looking around, she looks at this guy, and then she's not looking around anymore." He holds up his hands and his eyebrows: *that clear enough?*

"Okay. Then what?"

"Then, she walks over to where he's sitting and she pulls a gun out of her handbag. She says something to somebody at the next table over—I couldn't hear what—she points the gun at the guy, and she shoots him."

"I see. Did the victim say anything to the woman?"

"Yeah. He said, 'Hey.' "

"That's it? Just 'Hey'?"

"Yep."

"He didn't threaten her?"

"Nope."

"Didn't move toward her or make any aggressive gestures?"

"Nope."

"When did he say, 'Hey'?"

"After she pulled the piece out and pointed it at him."

"So he didn't say a word to her before she pointed a gun at him, is that correct?"

"That's correct."

"He didn't do anything to this woman or make any movements or gestures that would lead her to believe he was going to harm her."

"Objection!" Parnell and Ericsson shout simultaneously.

"Mr. Parnell?" Genet asks.

"Leading the witness, your honor."

"Sorry," I say. "I'll rephrase—"

"Hold it," Genet says because Ericsson is still standing. "Ms. Ericsson?"

"How does this witness know what might lead that woman to believe anything?" She's trying to blunt the effect of my question.

Now it's my turn to respond. "I believe I can entertain both those objections if I rephrase."

"Then do so."

"Mr. Mavidian: did the victim do anything at all from the time the woman walked in to the time she pulled a gun on him?"

He thinks for a minute. "He just ate."

"That's it?"

"That's it." And that should take care of any claims of self-defense or provocation that might be used to excuse the murder.

I turn to face Parnell and Ericsson but don't say anything, a silent challenge, and they both sit down.

Genet doesn't like the private byplay. "Any further questions, Mr. Milano?"

"Yes, your honor." I step to the side, toward the jury box, giving the witness a clear look at the defense table. "Mr. Mavidian, did you get a look at the woman's face?"

He nods. "Her scarf dropped for a second when she turned around and waved the gun at everybody."

"I see. And is the woman you saw in your restaurant, the one who shot Vincent Rosamund, here in the courtroom today?"

"Yes."

"Would you point her out to us, please?"

He raises his hand and points to the defense table, flapping his fingers slightly. "It was one'a those two."

Parnell and Ericsson are immediately on their feet again, shouting objections. Parnell waves Ericsson quiet and holds the floor. "Move to strike as nonresponsive. Defense demands that the witness be asked to answer the question, 'Is the woman in the courtroom,' and point her out!"

Genet raises her chin slightly and drops the corners of her mouth, as though she were helpless under the circumstances. "It's the prosecution's witness," she says. "He can get the answer any way he likes."

"Let the record reflect," I say to the court reporter, pointing to the defense table, "that the witness indicated the defendants, Diane Pierman and Lisa Pierman."

The reporter nods as she enters my comments. I let Parnell and Ericsson fume helplessly for a few more seconds. I have no more questions for Mavidian—indeed, all I can do now is ruin things if I ask any more—and I make my way back to my seat as slowly as I can without appearing obvious, sit down, look through my papers as though contemplating more questions, and then tell Genet, "I have nothing further."

Genet barely gets, "Your witness, Mr. Par—" out of her mouth before Parnell is on his feet, pointing at Lisa and addressing Mavidian. "Is my client the woman you saw?"

"Objection!" I get to my feet. "Lisa Pierman has not been charged with murder, so this is an inappropriate question. We're not maintaining that she is the shooter."

"Sidebar, your honor," Parnell demands, and the four of us troop up to the bench together. Genet folds her hands and looks at Parnell.

"Who's kidding whom, your honor?" he begins in a loud whisper so the jury can't hear, then waves a hand at me. "The prosecutor knows he is free to file additional charges against my client later, and I want it on the record that this witness failed to identify her!"

"That's totally irrelevant for this trial," I argue. "His client hasn't been charged with the shooting so what's he doing, obtaining testimony for some fictional future proceeding? That's misusing a voluntary witness!"

"It *is* relevant! Our entire defense is based on an inability to positively identify the shooter. If I can demonstrate that the witness is so confused that he can't even say for certain whether somebody else, somebody who isn't even charged with the shooting, pulled the trigger, then it supports my case!"

I shake my head and smile. Parnell is getting confused over his own strategy of trying to split these two cases apart. "Your case doesn't need supporting, remember? Nobody said your client committed murder."

Everything else aside, Parnell has now openly admitted what his strategy is. It will be difficult to change his mind later, even impossible, if Genet bases any rulings on that strategy. But right now, once again, Janine Ericsson surprises us.

"Fine," she says, glaring at me. "In that case, I'll argue against the objection." She turns back to the judge. "The witness's answer to Mr. Parnell's question will strengthen *my* case for Diane Pierman, so the question should be allowed."

She's right, and I can't argue against it, so Genet overrules my objection and sends us back to our places.

"I'll repeat the question," Parnell says to Mavidian. "Is my client, Lisa Pierman, the woman you saw in the restaurant on February nineteenth?"

Mavidian shrugs. "I don't know."

I expect Parnell to ask Mavidian if he can tell the twins apart, but he doesn't and I realize it's a good move. This way, they can later say simply that the witness failed to identify the defendant and there need be nothing said about a twin mix-up.

Parnell has no further questions, and Ericsson rises, pointing to Diane. "Was it my client you saw?"

Mavidian looks at Diane, hard, as though trying at this late date to discern some subtle differences, but it is futile. "I'm not sure, but I think it was one of those two."

"Your honor," Ericsson says to Genet testily, "would you kindly direct the witness to answer the question as asked?"

Genet looks at the reporter. "Please read back the question."

The reporter reaches back into the Plexiglas catch tray behind her recording machine and pulls up several sheets of the fan-folded paper that hold the encrypted text only she can read. She searches for the proper spot. "Ericsson: Was it my client you saw?" She looks at the judge, who nods, then drops the paper back into the tray.

"Mr. Mavidian?" Ericsson prompts him icily. "Was this the woman you saw or wasn't it?"

He looks angry and embarrassed but has no choice other than to be honest. "I don't know."

"Uh-huh. Well, then—" Ericsson takes a deep breath, like she's getting ready to do something daring and hasn't quite made up her mind; then she does. "Are you willing to swear to a moral certainty, without any doubt in your mind whatsoever, that the woman you saw was one of these two sisters?" She is trying to strengthen their case for lack of identity well beyond that of a twin mix-up, by implying that it might not have been either of them. Our witnesses' lack of certainty gave them the opening, but it's still an extraordinary risk, one she obviously hasn't discussed with Parnell, who is blanching visibly.

Mavidian looks at Diane, then Lisa, then back again before dropping his head to look at the floor. "I'm pretty sure."

"I ask you again: are you *dead* sure!" It's more of a directive than a question.

He shakes his head. "No."

Ericsson lifts her chin in triumph. "Thank you. No further questions."

She gambled and won. On redirect I get up again and say, "You are reasonably certain that it was one of these two women?"

Parnell pops up yet again. "Objection!"

"Grounds?" Genet is admirably calm and unflustered through all of this.

Parnell's eyes dart back and forth. "Withdrawn," he mumbles.

"Witness will answer the question."

"I can't be one hundred percent positive," Mavidian says, "but I believe it was one of those two."

I release Mavidian and call Dr. Judeco Vasili, an orthopedic surgeon who was dining at Tawqinah. His testimony is much along the lines of Mavidian's: he saw the woman's face when the scarf fell away; he is fairly sure that it was one of the twins; he doesn't know which one; if pressed, he couldn't positively swear it was one of them; there was nothing he saw that would eliminate them as a possibility. The matter of whom he was dining with doesn't come up.

I call Peter Jaffe, a priest at St. Catherine's. It goes much the same, as it does with David Brenner, a real estate attorney from Irvine; Tracie Bonaface, a copy machine saleswoman for the local Ricoh branch; Linda Tobias, a graphic artist; and Christopher Elman, a city gas-line inspector. These last two were celebrating Elman's recent promotion and were nervous on the stand, said celebration not having included invitations to either of their respective spouses. The witnesses profess varying levels of certainty with respect to how good a look they got at the shooter and whether it was one of the Piermans. The matter of Parnell and Ericsson making objections and me arguing them becomes almost a ritual.

After Elman is dismissed, Genet calls us all to a sidebar. I'm surprised it took her this long. "Milano," she says to me when we are all gathered before the bench, "are any of your witnesses going to make an absolute, dead positive ID on the shooter?"

I turn to indicate Diane and Lisa. "You know that's not possible, your honor."

She shakes her head, her eyes half closed. "That's not what I mean. Will any of them swear to a certainty that it was at least one of the twins?"

I'm forced to admit that's not likely.

"Then it seems you don't have enough to establish guilt beyond a reasonable doubt, certainly not in a murder case."

"That's probably true," I agree, "but that's not the core of my case here. I have a lot more beyond these witnesses." I realize the jury might be able to hear me so I lower my voice and move closer to the bench. "What's important right now is that not one eyewitness is willing to state the negative, that it couldn't have been one of the twins. The *plausibility* of identity, not the *certainty,* is my objective at this stage."

Genet nods thoughtfully then addresses herself to Parnell. "Are you willing to stipulate that the shooter looked like the twins, so we can move on?" No attorney likes to refuse a judge's suggestion to expedite matters, but Parnell is clearly uncomfortable with this particular idea. Genet sees it in his face and adds, "I'm just interested in saving some time here."

"I'm not interested in saving time," Parnell fires back, "I'm interested in saving my client."

He's instantly sorry for his impromptu wisecrack, but I understand his point. They are pinning their entire case on the extraordinary technicality of nobody being able to identify the shooter, and he wants to preserve the defense team's ability to exploit the identity confusion to its maximum effect, which is bolstered by the fact that none of my witnesses can say for certain that it was even one of the twins, much less which one.

Nevertheless, it's in his best interest to try to be accommodating to the judge. "If I were to stipulate to such a similarity," he asks Genet, "how would you phrase it to the jury?"

"I'll tell them we all agree that the shooter looked like one of the twins," she answers.

"No problem here," I agree amiably, but Parnell is shaking his head.

"Forget it." He leans forward. "I'll agree to the stipulation if you tell the jury that not a single witness can positively identify either of the defendants."

Now I'm shaking my head. Neither side is willing to budge. We go back to our places and spend the rest of the morning and part of the afternoon calling more witnesses. I cannot make an absolute case that it was at least one of the twins, but I get close. Parnell and Ericsson ask the same questions and make the same objections, just to get them on the record for appeal later. The jury is starting to get annoyed and bored, thinking the point well made. I try to make it look like I'm doing the right thing and it's those other guys who keep making trivial distinctions, that if they would only back off we could move on. I'm not very successful in this regard: we all look like pedantic idiots.

Finally, about midafternoon, we run out of restaurant witnesses. I try to give the jury the impression I think we've beaten this up enough, that I'm going to do everyone a big favor by dropping this line of inquiry and moving on. I put on a witness from outside the restaurant to bring out that it was Lisa's car that fit the description of the one gotten into by a woman dressed like the shooter several blocks from Tawqinah. This comes off as a bit flaky, as I intended, and Parnell leaps right on it in cross-examination.

"I've gotta ask you something," he says to the witness, a city bus driver named James Apodacia, who was on his break when he saw the woman. "You're sitting in the middle of Santa Monica, people all over the place ... how come you just happened to notice this one woman not doing anything out of the ordinary, just getting into a green Lexus and driving away?"

" 'Cuz she was parked in a handicapped zone, that's why," Apodacia snaps back.

"In a handicapped zone?" Parnell echoes.

The bus driver nods. "With the lights flashing. Like she was only gonna be gone for a second."

"Objection," Ericsson says without hesitation, not standing up. "Calls for speculation."

"Sustained. Remark is stricken."

Stricken, hell. How do you strike it from the jurors' minds? The woman who got into that car hadn't been shopping in the mall for two hours; she had jumped out of the car, shot Vincent Rosamund as planned, and then gotten back in and driven off, all in a matter of a few minutes. And James Apodacia, whose brother is a paraplegic, truly hates people who park illegally in handicapped spaces.

There's no putting a good face on this one, and Parnell doesn't even try, just moves on. "Did you get a good look at her face?"

"Nah, was kinda dark. But like I said, she was wearin'—"

"That's fine, sir. No further questions." Apodacia already testified under my direct that the woman was wearing jeans and a Stars sweatshirt.

I put on Sergeant Jeffrey Renfrew of the Santa Monica Police Department. He testifies that both sisters were calmly sitting at Lisa's house when the police showed up.

"Calmly?" I ask.

"Yeah. Like they were waiting for us."

Parnell and Ericsson are both on their feet shouting objections based on the speculative nature of Renfrew's answer, and I withdraw the question without waiting for a ruling.

I have done a good job of laying the groundwork for a conspiracy case against Lisa: it was her car and her house. But the defense has also done a good job, deftly engineering their case through well-timed objections and careful cross-examination, without calling any witnesses of their own. Under other circumstances, I'd be admiring their work, but right now I'm starting to get stirred, challenged. I can feel the old familiar fires getting nicely stoked, which only adds to my ambivalence and confusion. I wonder how successful I'll be in suppressing the ethical conundrum that plagues me so I can concentrate on doing my job.

My job. It's not like shoveling coal or toting up the accounts receivable, not an automatic, rote execution of clear procedures laid down over years by efficiency engineers. If it were, trials could be heard by computers instead of juries, and when the judge ordered that a remark be stricken, it would happen literally, the offending words electronically erased from the cyber-jury's memory boards. No tricks allowed: you program the machine with the written law, feed the evidence in, sprinkle it all over with the judge's rulings and emerge with a perfectly considered and technically correct verdict. Determining which witnesses are credible and which are not could be a bit of a problem, and tempering justice with mercy is right out as well, but what the hell: that's the price you'd have to pay to get it done right.

We break at four o'clock. All I want is to get out of here, go home and have a cigar, so Marsha and I both bypass the office and head out the front door of the county building, running smack into the still-assembled demonstration.

Ernestine Denier's well-honed radar homes in on us immediately, and she is standing in front of me before I even reach the bottom of the four small steps just outside the door. She appears to be gloating.

"Would seem Regis and Kathie Lee in there are making a pretty good case for the defense," she smirks.

"You mean Parnell and Ericsson?" I ask. I don't bother to try to figure out how she got wind of the trial goings-on so fast. She wasn't in court.

"Yeah. They making your life tough . . . I hope?"

I'm in no mood to banter with Ernestine. "What they're doing is playing with technicalities," I tell her. "A killer may go free because of it."

She seems untroubled and waves it off. "Sometimes those technicalities work on the side of the just."

"Who knows when they're working on the side of the just?" Marsha asks her.

An enigmatic smile. "You can always tell."

"That's what Joe McCarthy thought," I say. "Hitler, too, for that matter. That's why we have the law, see? So your friends don't get to make those decisions."

I should have known better than to get into it with her. If I really didn't want to talk, I should have just walked away.

"That's also why we have technicalities, Sal," she says, suddenly serious. "So *your* friends can't subvert the law, and use it to harass the citizenry for your own political ends."

"Yeah, well it was just such a technicality that got Vincent Rosamund's case thrown out in the first place, so what do you think of that, tell me!" Haven't we already had this conversation? Why am I doing this?

She closes her eyes and shakes her head with exaggerated frustration. "Like I said, you're a small thinker, Milano." With that, she walks away, and I'm too tired to bother to point out to her that she lost this one. She wouldn't believe me anyhow.

Nestor Parnell is standing beside my car in the parking lot. Ericsson is nowhere to be seen, so I wave Marsha off to the side and walk over to him alone.

"How you doing?" he asks.

"Not too bad. Yourself?"

"The same. Lemme ask you, though, just out of curiosity: how come you haven't requested that the jury be sequestered, away from all these protesters"—he waves a hand at Ernestine and her troops—"editorials, TV, all that stuff?"

He makes it sound like two mutually respectful colleagues having a genteel discussion, but I know he's goading me into motioning for a sequester. He'd love that, me standing in front of the judge, making the request in open court and bearing the full brunt of the jury's fury as they're locked away from home, friends and family for the duration of the trial.

"No need for that," I tell him. "The protesters are demanding a finding of justifiable homicide, but since you and Ericsson aren't making that claim, all this clamor and noise is off-base and irrelevant."

I try to convey by my tone that we are supremely confident of the outcome of this trial and could care less about the little nuances that might be valuable if our case were weaker. He acts skeptical but I also detect that he is slightly rattled: what could we possibly have that makes us so sure of ourselves? I walk away and rejoin Marsha.

"What was that all about?" she asks as we turn away from where Parnell is still standing.

I wave my hand dismissively. "More bullshit."

She turns her head to glance at Parnell, who is looking at us as though some betraying body language might clue him in to what we're talking about. "Let's go get a drink," she says as her head comes back around.

"Don't want to. I'm tired."

"Me, too, but we have a problem, and I'm buying."

"You're buying?"

"Yeah, and you're approving the expense when I turn it in."

We drive in separate cars to DC-3, a restaurant adjoining the Museum of Flying right off the runway at the local airfield. Originally called Clover Field, Santa Monica Airport was the place where the DC-3, the breakthrough Douglas plane that proved airlines could make money carrying passengers rather than cargo, was built and flown, and it's now the busiest single-strip airfield in the country. Neighborhood residents complain bitterly about the noise, but the airport was here before they were.

Marsha flies single-engine planes in what little spare

time she has and is well-known in local aviation circles. We get an outdoor table overlooking the runway but it takes us a while to get there, owing to all the table-hopping Marsha is obligated to do with fellow pilots. She loves this place and could easily spend the whole day watching the endless parade of Cessnas, Pipers, antique biplanes, corporate jets and a wide assortment of home-built and vintage aircraft taking off and landing less than two hundred feet away. Today, she doesn't even look in that direction.

"The problem ..." she begins when her vodka and orange juice arrives.

"I know," I say, when I'm settled with my own grapefruit juice. "Our eyewitness ID's sucked." I pull an Arturo Fuentes cigar out of my pocket and hold it up, waving it so Nicholas, the maître d', can see it. He takes a quick glance around, ascertaining that there's nobody around us at this early hour. He may also be aware that there is a light breeze blowing from the west. He nods and shows me thumbs-up, and I half-salute my thanks.

Marsha barely notices and doesn't even make any snide comments. "In a nutshell," she says in response to my last comment.

We knew going in that the identification of the shooter by the restaurant patrons was a weak point, but under Parnell's battering cross-examination it looked worse than we had envisioned. We had hoped to demonstrate that the physical descriptions closely matched the twins, knowing it wouldn't be enough to convict but would at least enable the rest of our case. Now Marsha voices the corollary to that theory.

"I could write the closings for both those lawyers right now," she says, stirring her drink idly. "They'll keep them completely separate, like there were two different trials ..."

". . . and they'll get up and say that nobody could identify their individual clients."

They won't admit that at least one of them killed Rosamund, but even if they did, the jury has no right to convict Diane for murder if they don't know for certain it was she. And without a murder conviction, there is no logical way for them to arrive at the conclusion that Lisa was guilty of conspiracy. How could they convict for conspiracy but not for the crime allegedly conspired to? It would be like convicting one person for accepting a bribe another person was acquitted of giving: certainly possible under our legal system, but totally illogical.

Marsha looks glum, and I tell her to relax. I'm not being deceitful in this regard; I can feel the fires getting still hotter, and I am truly confident about this case. "Parnell, the reporters, all of them, they all think we're dying in there. But we haven't brought out the big guns yet." I'm trying to take a lesson from the Gustave Terhovian school of judicial demeanor and decorum: let 'em all think whatever they want; all I care about is the end result, and I'm pretty sure I can win this trial.

Marsha turns to watch a Cessna Citation jet as it spools up its engines at the east end of the runway. We can picture the pilot's feet coming up off the toe brakes, allowing the plane to lurch forward and accelerate dramatically as the powerful engines whine their way up to full speed. Just when the sleek machine is directly abreast of us, the nose comes up and a second later the wheels leave the ground, the engine noise a full-throated scream now as the plane rockets for the sky.

"You think Marty's gonna come through for us?" Marsha says as the sound recedes and the plane dwindles against the horizon and the setting sun.

It's a rhetorical question, just some out-loud musing, because there's no way to know, but I'm glad to share in it. "Might need a small miracle, but I think he will."

"Why?" She takes a sip of her drink, the first one since we got here.

"Because we're right, that's why," I answer between puffs as I light the cigar.

That's really the thing of it, there. We're right. Therefore, there has to be evidence to support our case. I'm not entirely sure where we're heading—a damned interesting situation when a trial has already begun, but that's what happens when the defense doesn't waive its speedy trial rights—and I've started to get a feeling, a most familiar and delicious sensation, the one that tells me that a part of my brain I'm not very familiar with is churning away on the problem. When it's good and ready, it'll let me know. The challenge is to let it simmer while I concentrate on the trial.

I look at Marsha's mahogany face as the dying sun hits it, and I flash back to Diane's face the night we had drinks on the pier. A faint wave of nausea ripples downward from my throat to my intestines.

It'll come to me. I just know it.

18

"Prosecution calls Gilbert Bascomb."

I watch Nestor Parnell's face carefully as Marsha rises to summon the witness to the stand. I noticed a hesitation in his step as we came into court this morning and he spotted Bascomb seated in the third row. Bascomb was on our witness list, of course, but I never explained why, and I'm certain Parnell never really expected us to call him: it would be stupid, and even though we're temporary enemies, Parnell doesn't think I'm stupid. Which is why he's worried.

"Please state your name and occupation for the record," Marsha says.

"Gil"—he clears his throat—"Gilbert Bascomb, owner and manager of the Santa Monica Gun Club."

"Mr. Bascomb, were you on duty in the club on Saturday, February eighteenth?"

"I was." Bascomb is no survivalist lunatic who runs around in military fatigues but a serious aficionado and collector of both antique and modern small arms. He runs a clean club, strictly by the book, and people with stolen or illegal weapons know to steer clear of his place: Bascomb calls in the police if he suspects unlawful activity. A lot of law enforcement people, Marty McConagle included, frequent the club because they can use private weapons not permitted in the police ranges.

"On that occasion, did you have any unusual patrons in the club?"

It's an overly broad question, an invitation to an objection, but Parnell remains silent.

"Sure did."

"Would you describe them?"

"Two women. Twins."

"And are they in the courtroom today?"

"Yes."

"Would you point them out, please?" He does. "Let the record reflect that Mr. Bascomb has identified the defendants. Sir, were the defendants firing weapons at the club?"

"Yes. Well, one weapon."

"And what was that weapon?"

"A forty-five-caliber automatic pistol."

"Objection," Ericsson says, rising, acting as though she had been patient up until now but can't contain her exasperation any longer. "Of what possible relevance is this witness to the prosecution's case?"

I had been sweating as Marsha slowly dragged out Bascomb's questioning, hoping, as we planned, to draw an objection, like a basketball player draws a foul on the way to an easy layup. Once again Janine Ericsson jumped in to save the day.

I think I'm starting to understand Ericsson. She's very good in prepared situations—her opening to the jury was powerful, her cross-examination of the restaurant witnesses was very capable—but she's a whole lot less adept at thinking on her feet, and she's also impulsive. She had every opportunity to consult with Parnell, who's sitting right there with her at the defense table, but she went for the drama and leaped right up to heighten the appearance of spontaneity. For a support player on the team, she doesn't know the rules very well, and Marsha is going to make her pay for it now. Doubly so, for having made her wait this long.

"Your honor, Ms. Ericsson's client is charged with premeditated murder. All we're trying to do here is demonstrate that Diane and Lisa Pierman were practicing for the killing." Marsha mentions both sisters because it is entirely possible that they didn't make the decision on who was to be the shooter until the next day. "This gun club manager has never seen these two in there before the day in question, and all of a sudden, days after Vincent Rosamund was acquitted and the day before he was murdered, Diane and Lisa Pierman show up in a gun club to pour forty-five-caliber slugs into targets!"

Parnell looks like he wants to strangle Ericsson with his bare hands, but he has no choice but to play the cards he's been dealt. "I object to that, your honor," he says, rising to stand next to his colleague. "There's been no testimony that they were never in the club before."

"Do you wish to make a proper objection, Mr. Parnell?" Drama or not, Genet isn't about to let the rules slide.

"Assuming facts not in evidence," Parnell replies.

"If I may be allowed to continue," Marsha says frostily, looking at Parnell, "I'll get them in evidence."

"Both objections are overruled," Genet says, without having to think about it. "You may continue, Ms. Jones."

"Thank you. Mr. Bascomb, had you ever seen Diane or Lisa Pierman in your club before February eighteenth?"

"No, they've never been in there before."

"How can you be certain?"

He originally wanted to answer along the lines of *Who are you kidding?* but we urged him to something more formal.

"They don't have a signature or questionnaire on file."

"What questionnaire?"

"Everybody who uses the club has to fill out a detailed form, about safety and club rules, and then sign it. We keep it on file." He points to the defense table. "They came in and went through the whole procedure for the first time on the eighteenth."

Thus have we turned what could have been a serious liability into an asset. I've no doubt Parnell will flay Ericsson to ribbons after court today, but for now, as soon as Marsha is finished, he will have to try to repair the damage.

"Just one last question," Marsha is saying. "Did the Piermans rent a gun from you or did they bring their own?"

"They brought their own."

"And that was a forty-five automatic?"

"It was."

"Thank you. No more questions."

Marsha turns away from the lectern and resumes her seat. Parnell has been scribbling notes furiously during the last few minutes. Once, Ericsson tried to interject a thought, pointing to something he had written, and he angrily brushed her hand away.

"Your witness, Mr. Parnell."

He stands, looking at the pages in his hands as he makes his way to the lectern. "Mr. Bascomb," he says, but he's just buying time to review what he's written.

Finally, after an uncomfortably long pause, he begins again. "Mr. Bascomb, how long were Diane and Lisa Pierman in the club?"

Bascomb looks up at the ceiling, then back down. "I'd say, oh, about an hour, hour and a half."

"How much shooting did they do?"

"Well, they bought a lot of ammo, about two hundred rounds, I think. Fresh stuff, too, not reloads."

"I see. Did they carry any out with them when they left?"

"They're not supposed to but, you know, anybody can pocket a bunch of bullets and just leave. There's no way to tell."

Parnell frowns theatrically. "Did they break any other rules?"

"No."

"Then what leads you to believe they might have broken that one?"

I rise to object. "Facts not in evidence, your honor: he never said he thought they took any bullets." The objection is sustained, but Parnell has made his small point. He knows we're unlikely to produce any other evidence as to where they might have purchased ammunition on short notice. I could care less: so far, I can't even show where they got the gun. I don't even *have* the damned gun.

Parnell isn't finished. "Do you know which one of the two sisters fired the most rounds?"

Marsha flashes me a look. Is Parnell falling for our feint, that we're somehow going to try to claim that the one with the most gunshot residue was the shooter? Only one way to find out.

"I object." I get to my feet slowly so I can phrase this

right. "Of what possible relevance is who did the most shooting?"

Parnell whips his head around and looks at me as though I just landed from the planet Neptune. I can sense his panic and it gives me a physical rush. Up until this moment, he has been thinking that our case will be based on some claim that Diane had more GSR on her clothing than Lisa and therefore fired the gun more recently—i.e., into Vincent Rosamund—a claim he could easily beat. But now I've questioned the relevance of what would appear to him to be the key question in such a claim, and he knows now that he was dead wrong in his assumption.

But it is too surprising and too sudden for him to be able to regroup, so he has no choice but to voice it out loud. "Your honor, the prosecution stated in its opening statement that they intend to use 'sensitive forensics' to identify the murderer. Obviously they mean the preponderance of gunshot residue on one of the defendants, and therefore I am merely trying to establish—"

"Excuse me!" I interrupt, then wait for a second until I have both Parnell's and Ericsson's full attention. "Your honor, I have no such intention, and I'd sure be appreciative if defense counsel would let me prosecute my own case!"

Genet looks to Parnell, and there is a visible sheen of sweat on his upper lip as he struggles to assimilate this abrupt paradigm shift. He does so admirably. "I'd still like the question answered. Whatever the prosecution does intend to do, if forensic evidence is to be introduced we have the right to have all the information available."

Marsha is tugging at my sleeve, and I bend down so she can whisper in my ear. She has an idea, and I straighten up to address the judge. "Your honor, let me suggest that we both reserve the right to recall Mr. Bascomb at a later time." It is a master stroke on Marsha's part: she knows that Bascomb has some information that is critical to our case, and we were planning to reserve the right to recall him anyway. This way, we make it look like a concession on our part, like we're doing the defense a big favor so we can all move on.

"I'd like the question answered anyway," Parnell says.

Genet thinks this over for a few seconds, tapping the

side of her chin. "I'll allow the question, and you may have the right to recall this witness later." That right applies to both sides equally.

Parnell turns back to the witness. "Mr. Bascomb, to repeat: do you know for sure if my client fired more or fewer rounds than her sister?"

"Which one's yours, again?"

This draws some chuckles from the jury and audience, and Parnell smiles, too, to show he's still got a sense of humor. He steps to the defense table and puts his hand on Lisa's shoulder. "Lisa Pierman."

Bascomb shakes his head. "No way to tell. They were dressed differently, but I don't know which one was which." I wonder why he didn't say that in the first place, rather than ask Parnell which one was his client. Smartass witnesses I don't need.

"Well," Parnell says, starting to regain his composure, "didn't they each sign separate forms?"

Bascomb shifts forward slightly on his seat, holding out one hand with the palm up. "Sure, but what am I supposed to do, memorize who was wearing what? Besides . . ." He settles back and folds his hands together, one elbow up over the back of the chair. ". . . they didn't use their own names."

Parnell's jaw drops almost to his chest, as does mine. I can feel Marsha stiffen in the seat beside me, but she does a much better job of hiding her shock than I do, and I quickly close my mouth and try to pretend nothing happened. It's not easy, not when some guardian angel just flew over and dropped a king-size Christmas present into our lap.

Parnell is staring stupefied at Bascomb, who blinks several times wondering about the stir he has just caused. For once, Parnell's theatrics are truly spontaneous as he says, "I'm sorry: what did you just say?"

Bascomb sniffles and looks around, his elbow coming off the chair back so he can straighten up and try to look respectable. "They didn't use their own names. On the forms, I mean."

Parnell turns slowly to me, his look baldly accusing, like we were trying to hide this piece of information. On the other hand, his clients have been exposed in a deception, so he decides, wisely, to let the witness go and not ask for sanctions against us. I'm loving it, but I'm going to have a word with Marty about why I'm hearing this for the first time. And I don't want the jury thinking we were trying to pull a fast one.

"Redirect, Ms. Jones?"

Genet is looking at us with suspicion, and I whisper a quick instruction to Marsha: "Get *us* off the hook first!" She nods in understanding as she stands up.

"Mr. Bascomb." I can see the flustered witness almost wither under the weight of Marsha's menacing and accusatory tone. "Did you at any time ever inform the district attorney or any investigator that Diane and Lisa Pierman didn't use their own names on those forms?"

Bascomb shakes his head.

"Please speak up," Marsha says.

"No."

"And why is that?"

He shrugs. "Lotta people don't use their real names. Didn't seem like a big deal—at the time, I mean."

"Thank you. Now think carefully: are you absolutely certain, without a shadow of a doubt in your mind, that these two defendants"—she points to Diane and Lisa without turning to look at them—"are the same two women you saw in your club on February eighteenth?"

He takes a moment to study them, but it is a perfunctory look so Marsha will think he's concentrating. "Absolutely."

"You're dead sure?"

"Jeez, gimme a break. I'da remembered even one of 'em but two like that?" He frowns and shakes his head. "Gimme a break."

Marsha nods, then turns away and looks at the jury, spreading her hands in sarcastic imitation of Parnell: *See? We didn't try to pull a fast one.*

It looks like Parnell won this round anyway, and not because of this inconsequential flub on our part. The reporters are smarter than that, and I can see from the way they're looking at me that they think I've made a big mistake.

What they're thinking is that we've made it possible for Parnell to explain away the gunshot residue on the sweatshirt. We handed it to him on a silver platter by putting on the gun club manager without Parnell having to call him up himself. We might be able to claim that the Piermans were practicing for the murder, but that would not be enough to convince a jury beyond a reasonable doubt that one or the other is guilty of the actual murder.

I sure as hell hope we know what we're doing. It all hinges on Marty.

19

Marty finally called this afternoon. I haven't seen him in a couple of days, and I was starting to get worried. I gave him some grief about not uncovering the false names on the gun club questionnaires, and he was appropriately chagrined so I dropped it.

"Heard things didn't go so hot in court today," he said.

I didn't bother to ask him where he heard it. "Like what?"

"Seems Nestor shat all over our GSR evidence."

"Couldn't have scripted it better myself. What else?"

"Your 'sensitive forensics' piece of bullshit. How'd that go?"

"Beautiful!" I couldn't keep the glee out of my voice, and Marty laughed over the phone.

"I love it!" he said, then sobered quickly. "You think Parnell's figured out I went to see the manager?"

Marty spent half a day with Gilbert Bascomb at the Santa Monica Gun Club the day after the shooting. That was unrelated to the deposition Bascomb gave later in the week, the one Parnell read. Marty's conversation with Bascomb was never written down.

"Never even came close," I told him, and the tension in his voice dissipated immediately.

"Let's you, me and Marsha do dinner tonight," he said.

"Y'know, you're getting a lot of meals out of the county lately. You at least got any news?"

"I got news."

"Okay, where?"

"Where else?"

Giovanni's in Playa del Rey is possibly my favorite restaurant on the planet earth. The single-story structure occupies all of what has to be the smallest block in the state, a triangular blot of land three blocks from the ocean and situated directly on the continuation of the Pacific Coast Highway. WELCOME, BUT DON'T EXPECT TOO MUCH, says a little sign at the entrance, an open doorway with a curtain of beaded strings serving as a door.

Giovanni himself is a Neapolitan who fought with the Allies in World War II and determinedly avoided learning much English during his forty-odd years in the United States. He greets us expansively; we're to his dinner business what we are to Kumito-san's lunchtime. It's about the only opportunity I get in LA to practice my Italian.

"Milano, comé sta, eh?"

"Tutti bene, e lei?"

He shrugs and rocks a hand in the air. *"Si tira avanti,"* roughly translated as *life has its burdens but moves on.*

Marsha and Marty have to duck as they walk in; the ceiling, and I mean literally every square inch of it, is festooned with an explosive profusion of ribbons, Chianti bottles, strung corks, streamers, balloons, model airplanes, college pennants, Christmas lights and whatever else Giovanni or his customers come up with. Once something goes up, it never comes down. The same is true of the walls, which sport a variety of decorative Italian cooking plates, the kind with recipes baked right into the ceramic, celebrity photos with personal inscriptions, pictures of the Italian countryside and hundreds of business cards. How this place passes its fire inspection is a complete mystery.

"You looka like you no eat," Giovanni says to Marty as he slaps his stomach, which hangs noticeably over his belt but not enough to warrant Giovanni's approval. He takes anything less than a beer belly as a personal affront, his own physiognomy a testament to his love of his own cooking.

"That's why we're here," Marty tells him.

"I hate this place," Marsha says.

"Whyzzat?"

" 'Cuz then I gotta stop eating for three days afterwards."

"That'sa why you so goddamn' skinny." Marsha is not skinny.

Giovanni waves us over to our traditional booth, just on the other side of a giant fish tank that keeps us partially hidden from the front of the restaurant. We're hardly seated, Marsha and I opposite Marty, before one of the busboys Giovanni periodically shanghais from the home country sets plates down in front of us, a simple green salad dressed with oil, vinegar and some aromatic spices, a few slices of pepperoni and a soft bread filled with a mild cheese. There is also a plate of *bruschetta,* crusty bread topped with chopped tomatoes and olive oil. Marty holds up a fist toward Giovanni, his thumb and little finger sticking out, and wiggles the thumb at his mouth.

"Whadda you want?" Giovanni calls out across the full length of the restaurant. "Chianti?"

Marty looks at Marsha and me and we both nod. *"Ragazzo!"* Giovanni screams sternly in no particular direction. *"Una bottiglia d'Chianti, sùbito!"*

One of the busboys smiles, shaking his head, and scurries into the back, appearing a few seconds later with a bottle and three glasses. He sets the glasses down, threads an enormous corkscrew into the bottle, and pops the cork with a downward stroke of the levers. He pours full glasses for all of us. I once asked Giovanni why he doesn't show us the label before he opens the bottle and then let someone taste it first. "You no like, you no pay," he answered simply: what could be fairer?

When the wine is poured and we all have a first sip, I ask Marty what his news is and where the hell has he been.

He sets the glass down, looks around and then leans forward, elbows on the table. "I been up in Bakersfield, snooping around."

"Bakersfield?" Marsha says. "What, about Rosamund?"

Marty nods. He's still bothered by all the loose ends,

unwilling to let them go. "Remember those 'unspecified' charges on his rap sheet?" Of course we do: neither of us had ever seen such a thing before. "They were for two prior rapes."

Marty quiets down and pulls back just as Giovanni shows up at our table. "You wanna eat?"

We order after some intense debate with Giovanni. Marty goes for the veal *osso bucco,* a large dish that includes a veal shank surrounded by a generous portion of *spezzatino,* smaller bits of veal marinated in a red sauce. Marsha, who likes to eat light in public, orders the *scampi vesuvio,* jumbo shrimps sautéed in a hot, garlicky broth, and I take my favorite, *braciòla,* listed on the menu as "best in the west." This is the only restaurant I know of that serves it, a thin slice of beef covered with prosciutto, cheese and boiled eggs then rolled up into what looks like an Italian burrito and cooked in tomato sauce. My grandmother used to make it; it was my father's favorite.

Giovanni breaks out into a rousing chorus of *"Ritorno a Sorrento"* as he walks away and I'm tempted to join in, but I'm too anxious to hear what Marty has to say. "Two prior rapes?"

He nods and leans forward again. "It took a little unorthodox persuasion. . . ."

He raises his eyebrows at me questioningly, but I hold up both hands. "I don't want to know!"

"No, you don't. But it seems one of the women was paid off to drop the charges, and she may have been intimidated." He means this in a legal sense, like someone forced her.

"How do you figure?" Marsha asks.

"I tracked her down," Marty says, taking a sip of wine. "To Eureka. Two days it took me, and about five hundred miles of driving. I knock, tell her who I am, and a shotgun comes out the door."

"You told her you were a cop and she pulled a gun on you?" I ask, incredulous. It tells me how scared she was.

"Yep. She says, don't you know I'm a dead woman if I talk to you? Only not so polite. I took the hint and split."

"What about the other one?"

"Disappeared. All the charges dropped."

"Sure," Marsha says. "No witness, no charges."

"Uh-uh," Marty replies, looking down and shaking his head. "Charges were dismissed first, and *then* she disappeared." He looks up. "Without a trace." He means, if even he couldn't find her, it probably wasn't a simple train ride out of town.

It seems to me all too contrived to have been pulled off that cleanly. "So why were the charges dismissed? How did the record get cleaned up?"

"I don't know. But remember that code, 'CA,' the one on the rap sheet? A guy I know up there says that may be a data entry operator's shorthand for 'charges absent.' Like she didn't find anything on the form and didn't want her supervisor to think she forgot to enter it, so she puts in 'CA' to fill the space."

"Charges absent," I muse out loud. "Doesn't explain *why* they were absent, though."

"Sounds a lot like an ACD," Marsha ventures. An adjournment in contemplation of dismissal, common practice for letting some offenders, usually young first-timers, get away without a black mark on their records if they stay out of trouble afterward. "But that's unheard of in a rape case." She echoes my exact thought.

"Can you do any more digging?" I ask Marty.

"I can try. But it does explain how Rosamund was savvy enough to cover his tracks and beat a rape charge, although I gotta tell you . . ."

"What?"

"Doing two women at once was really dumb. In front of anybody but a fucked-up judge like Arigga, he woulda been convicted." Another attempt to make me feel better. I let it pass, but it brings back memories and sets my teeth to grating.

"Everybody says he was a hothead," Marsha reminds us. "Said he would've gotten himself killed eventually."

We all laugh uneasily at the irony of Marsha's comment, and then the food shows up. Each of the entrees includes a side order of pasta, and there's a basket of fresh rolls, so almost the entire surface of the small table is filled. Giovanni pulls a chair up beside the booth and sits on it backward, facing us, his arms up on the back of the chair, to watch us eat. Marty breaks off a piece of bread and starts to put it in his mouth.

"Ey, why you no put inna sauce?" Giovanni admonishes him, miming with his hand over Marty's plate. Marty pauses for a second, then pops the bread into his mouth, still dry. *"Contadino!"* Giovanni mutters, shaking his head: *Peasant!*

We eat and talk with Giovanni for a while until he's called away by some crisis in the kitchen, then Marty asks me what kind of sentences we're going to go for if we get a conviction. I tell him it's premature, that it's dangerous to get too overconfident.

He rocks his head back and forth, gesturing with a piece of bread that's now dripping with sauce. "Yeah, yeah, yeah: so when we gonna drop the big bomb?"

"Well," I tell him, "if you would be so kind as to honor us with the graciousness of your presence in court, maybe tomorrow."

He stops eating long enough to look up at me. "Really?"

"Really."

"Hot damn!" He stuffs the bread into his mouth and turns to attack the side order of *mostacelli*. "Hot damn!"

We're talking like lawyers again, not even a mention this entire evening that the defendants used to be our friends. That's okay. I can't allow us to be distracted by that right now, nor let my colleagues see how much more I am affected by it than they seem to be.

When the main courses are finished, we linger over cappuccinos—also "best in the west"—and cannoli for nearly two more hours, rehearsing Marty until his eyes start to roll up into his head. I get a check from Giovanni and we walk out without paying: he doesn't take credit cards and I don't carry checks or much cash, so I'll mail it to him in the morning, as usual, along with a generous tip for the *ragazzi*.

"You ready?" I ask Marty as we step out into the cool night air, a slight smell of salt water wafting in on a westerly breeze from the shore.

He takes a toothpick out of his mouth and lets out a

long, resonant belch, smiling in self-satisfaction as it dies away. Marsha groans and screws up her face in disgust.

"I'm ready."

20

As we walk through the courthouse plaza, the protesters are a happy lot. Like other observers of the courtroom proceedings thus far, they believe we haven't got a prayer of sustaining any convictions, that our case is beginning to unravel. Ernestine Denier grins at me but doesn't approach, her idea of rubbing it in, like it doesn't even require conversation to make the point.

But I don't care about the protesters; it's Parnell I want to keep off guard. I try to look as pensive as I can, to boost his confidence. The better he feels now, the worse he's going to feel later. Interesting how he was my friend and supporter barely a few weeks ago, and now we're mortal enemies, yet we're both still the same people. It must be the same kind of contempt prizefighters try to muster up for each other, not just to work up the necessary motivation but to make sure they don't feel sorry for the guy they're about to beat to a bloody pulp.

My studied air of desired isolation notwithstanding, *LA Times* reporter Eleanor Torjan sees me and peels off in my direction, ready to accost me with her usual attacking style. It doesn't put me off the way it used to: I know she just uses those techniques to quickly ferret out the substance, to preclude her interview subjects from pontificating without really saying anything. But I don't want to see her now, and I must have somehow communicated that to Marsha—maybe I unconsciously let out a growl—because she puts a restraining hand on my arm and leans in close while keeping an eye on Eleanor, who looks like an intensely focused rhino as she barrels through the crowd toward us.

"Keep it in your pants, Flash," Marsha admonishes me as she steps away, leaving me alone with Eleanor. I notice that Nestor Parnell is within earshot. If he has any lingering suspicions that my feelings for Diane Pierman are ameliorating my enthusiasm for this case—I can't believe that Diane hasn't clued him in to what went on, or what I think went on, between us—I want to quash them as firmly as I can.

"Milano!" Eleanor is calling. "Hey, Sal, y'got a minute?"

I try to drum up a smile. "Sure, Torjan. What can I do for you?"

She's slightly out of breath but her writing pad is at the ready. She jerks a thumb over her shoulder toward the chanting demonstrators. One sign reads: MEN — YOU'RE NOT SAFE UNTIL WOMEN ARE SAFE! Another shows a crude line drawing of a penis and says: TOOL OF OPPRESSION! I let out an involuntary laugh at that one.

"Don't you feel that what these women did might have been justifiable?" Eleanor asks me.

"It's certainly possible," I answer. She wasn't expecting that and it throws her off.

"Then why are you prosecuting?"

I shrug, like it was obvious. "First of all, it's only a possibility. Second, that's not up to me to decide. I'm a prosecutor, not a judge." I shouldn't do this but I can't help it. "That's the great thing about the law, see? We don't just ask people what they think ought to happen and then act on it, we have a system to decide these things."

"Okay, fine." She hates when I lecture her. "Then what do you think, Milano?"

"What difference does it make?"

"What the hell do you mean, what difference does it make?" she says angrily. "You're the goddamned prosecutor!"

Why do I do this? I can't possibly win. My sarcasm is being heard by all of one person, but if Eleanor decides to be tough on me when she writes her story, she can make me look like an idiot to millions. "I repeat, what difference does it make?"

She hasn't a clue as to what I'm talking about, but it's clear I'm going to be a pain in the ass, so she walks off in a huff. Marsha rejoins me, shaking her head. "Do you have to work at shooting yourself in the foot?" she asks. "Or is this, like, something that just comes natural to brainless white boys?"

"I was serious," I tell her. "It doesn't make any difference what I think. My job is to press the case if there's a case to be pressed, and let the court sort it out."

"It makes a difference and you know it," she spits back. "If you believe it's a lousy case, you have the discretion to let it go. You do it ten times a day, so it makes a big damned difference what you think!"

"Yeah, but I can't tell a reporter that."

"True, but you don't have to make her feel like a schmuck, either."

Marsha has that estimable ability to poke holes in my balloon without half trying. I remind her that Torjan, who should know better, was asking questions based on a justifiable homicide defense even though the defense attorneys have already announced in open court that they're not using that defense. Hasn't she been listening to the same trial as I have?

Marsha stops in her tracks and whirls to face me, real anger flashing in her eyes. "The fuck is wrong with you, Sal!" she hisses through clenched teeth. "You think she gives a rat's ass about your opinion of her?"

Marsha's rage takes me by surprise, and I glance around uncomfortably to see if anyone else is noticing her tantrum. "Christ, Jones; what got into you all of a sudden?"

Her lower jaw is trembling. She pounds a fist on my chest. "I don't want you to lose your job, you dumb wop!" She leaves her hand on my suit jacket for a second, then steps back, straightens up and adjusts the shoulder strap of her attaché. "Shit, what would I do if you left?"

"Marsha," I say, making my voice high and squeaky. "Don't tell me you got a thing for me after all this time."

"Yeah, I got a thing for you," she says, regaining control

over her voice. She holds up a clenched fist. "I got this, you don't wise up."

"You want me to go make nice to Eleanor?"

I scout around until I see the miffed reporter sniffing out a more amenable target. "Yo, Eleanor!"

She turns, sees that it's me and starts to tighten up her face. I wave her off to the side.

"Listen, I'm sorry," I tell her, meaning it. "I'm under a lot of pressure and I took it out on you."

She can't believe she's hearing this from me. "I think I like you better as an asshole, Milano."

I smile broadly. "It's sure a lot easier. Look, you got first shot at me after today, okay?"

"What's today? Is something gonna happen in court?"

I rock my head back and forth, trying to look enigmatic. "Just pay attention. It gets too complicated, I'll explain it after. Deal?"

She seems to consider it. "Okay, deal. But if I see you chatting up that slut from AP before I get my shot, you get the bimbo bomb." She's referring to one of those stories where a woman suddenly feels it her civic duty to come forth and disclose that her illegitimate child is the progeny of some public official, or that they were engaged in a twenty-year tryst right under everybody's nose.

"It'd certainly enhance my reputation around the office," I tell her, "but don't worry."

Eleanor smiles, tells me to have a nice day in court, and lets me go.

Thank you, Marsha.

I still have a pleasant buzz as court is called to order. Not only did being nice to Eleanor put me in a good mood, I'm jazzed about what could be the last day of this trial, or at least the last substantive day. It's a chore for me to look worried for Parnell and Ericsson.

Judge Harriet Genet gavels the room to silence. She knows that people in the audience—reporters, friends of the defendants, some people from Parnell's firm, Janine Ericsson's parents and the usual group of retired senior citizens who have discovered that criminal trials are the cheapest theater in town—are anxious to compare notes since last they met, but she runs a tight ship and wastes no time settling everybody down and getting us to our next witness. I'll be handling this one myself.

"The prosecution calls Deborah Gonzalez."

She's a beautiful young woman of Mediterranean extraction, with black hair cut down to her shoulders, smooth olive skin and doelike eyes. Her gait as she walks to the stand is graceful and unhurried; she's been here before, many times, testifying in her capacity as a senior criminalist in the Physical Evidence Section of the LA County Sheriff's Department Criminalistics Laboratory, also known as the Scientific Services Bureau. Parnell stays relaxed as I establish her credentials. He knows what's coming, or thinks he does, and isn't worried. There are no challenges from him or Ericsson, since Gonzalez's credentials are impeccable and beyond reproach, and although I could probably get them to stipulate to her expertise, I want the jury to hear her long list of bona fides.

When those are out of the way, I start in on the heart of the matter.

"Ms. Gonzalez, did you have occasion to examine any of the defendants' clothing for evidence of gunshot residue?"

"Yes."

"Which articles of clothing?"

Gonzalez's voice is calm and confident, her thoughts clearly articulated, and yet they seem unrehearsed, as though she were hearing these questions for the first time. She's the best witness you could ask for, as long as the facts are on your side. "I was asked to examine a sweatshirt, an L.A. Stars sweatshirt. It fit the description given by an eyewitness at the scene of the sweatshirt worn by—"

"Objection!" Parnell sounds personally offended as he rises. "Ms. Gonzalez didn't take the alleged eyewitness's statement, and there is no evidence she even spoke to the witness!"

"What is the grounds of your objection?" Genet asks, ever the stickler. In this case, though, I'm surprised, because the grounds of the objection seem so obvious.

"Hearsay," Parnell says politely, nevertheless.

"Mr. Milano?"

The grounds may be obvious, but they are dead wrong.

"Your honor, experts from the crime lab do not examine evidence in a vacuum but in the context of the scenario described by the investigating officers." Detective Dan Pappas is in the audience, and I point to him. "The officers hand the expert the evidence—say, a piece of clothing—and give her as much detail of the circumstances as possible, so she knows what to look for. This scenario is part and parcel of the expert's opinion and is a firm cornerstone of the case law on the subject. In this instance, the investigating officer is already on record as having taken a statement and identified the sweatshirt and pointed it out to Ms. Gonzalez." I look at Pappas and he nods back in acknowledgment. "However, even if this were not the case, for the purpose of smoothing the way for later expert testimony might I remind Mr. Parnell that a witness qualified by the court as an expert is free to rely on any evidence he or she deems relevant to the case, regardless of the source of that evidence, including hearsay."

Genet is nodding before I finish. "Objection is overruled, and thanks very much for the lecture, Mr. Milano. In the future, would you mind limiting your argument to the issue at hand rather than anticipating future objections?"

I smile sheepishly and with good humor, accepting her mild rebuke like a sport. "Sorry, your honor. Got carried away there." I don't bother to look back at Parnell to see if he is back down in his seat. "Ms. Gonzalez, you were saying that you were asked to examine a sweatshirt. . . ."

"Yes, identified as the one—excuse me, similar to the one—seen by witnesses to the shooting."

"Where was the sweatshirt?"

"Hanging in a closet in the home of Lisa Pierman."

"And what did you do at that point?"

"I took several samples from the fabric, mostly from the lowest part of the sleeves closest to where the hand openings are." She points to that spot on her own blouse.

"And then?"

"I took them back to the county crime lab and ran a series of tests for gunshot residue, or GSR, as we refer to it."

"And what did you find?"

"There were heavy concentrations of several elements,

including barium, antimony and lead, with some traces of copper."

"And from this, what do you conclude?"

"There is no doubt that there was GSR on the sweatshirt."

I look at the jury to make sure this is sinking in. I also look at Parnell, who is yawning dramatically and looking at his watch. Ericsson looks confused, like I'm making an awfully big deal about gunshot residue that no longer seems very important. She happens to be right. "No doubt. Couldn't have come by accident?"

Gonzalez shakes her head. "Not that combination of elements." She turns to the jury to explain. "Barium and antimony are relatively rare. To have them both show up by accident, and to do so in combination with lead, is impossible. It was definitely from the discharge of a firearm."

"No question in your mind at all."

"None."

I like that in an expert witness, no equivocation, no searching for the remotest philosophical exceptions so you can look smart and thoughtful. Just the basic, straightforward premises and conclusions. "Thank you. No more questions."

Genet jerks her head slightly as she moves her attention from Gonzalez, clearly intrigued by both her testimony and her compelling delivery. "Your cross, Mr. Parnell?"

Parnell sniffles and rises slowly, buttoning his jacket, feigning boredom. He smiles at the witness. "Ms. Gonzalez, can you tell us what kind of tests are typically run to determine the presence of gunshot residue?"

"Certainly." Gonzalez shifts slightly in her seat and seems to perk up, the first show, however slight, of any arousal with respect to these proceedings.

Parnell sees it and holds up a hand. "In lay terms, please—science was my worst subject." This gets a giggle out of the jurors and a wide smile from Gonzalez.

"There are two basic kinds of tests. The most common is bulk analysis, the other uses an electron microscope. Which one are you interested in?"

Parnell shrugs and turns up a palm. "Which one did you do?"

"Both."

"Ah. Let's start with the first one you mentioned."

"Bulk analysis." She leans forward, warming up now, a scientist given license to talk about her craft. "Well, we supply sampling kits to officers in the field. They spray a suspect's hands with a five percent solution of nitric acid, then swab it off with a Q-Tip. That will pick up any residue that was on the hand. Then we analyze it."

"Analyze it how?"

Enough. I won't allow him to monopolize my carefully planned day. "Your honor," I say as I rise, "is all of this necessary?"

Parnell looks offended again. "Might I remind the deputy district attorney that the jury has the right to know what the expert relied on in coming to a conclusion? I don't believe the idea is to get some scientist to stand up and say, believe me just because I said so."

Genet agrees with him. "Very well, Mr. Parnell, but can we at least forgo the entire history of physical chemistry in this dissertation?"

"That's up to Ms. Gonzalez."

"I'll try to keep it simple." Gonzalez doesn't want to lose this opportunity and tries to appear cooperative. "The analysis takes place in an atomic absorption spectrophotometer. We extract a few drops of the nitric acid into a little cup, then take a tiny bit and heat it up to a very high temperature in a small graphite chamber. The heat vaporizes the solution and a little puff comes out; then we shine a beam of light of known frequency through it. Like, if we're looking for antimony, we use a lamp made of antimony. A detector captures the beam of light and we see if any of it was absorbed at certain wavelengths. If it was, we know antimony was present."

"You know that for sure?"

"Yes."

"What if there was antimony in the last batch you tested, from another case. Couldn't some be left?"

She shakes her head. "No. We use a nitric acid rinse between samples to keep everything clean."

"Yes, but how can you be sure it's really clean?"

"Simple." She turns to the jury. "At the end of the sample tests, we have some dilute nitric acid that was not used for a sample. There's one in every field kit. We run that through and if it doesn't come up clean, we throw out the whole test."

Where can Parnell be going with this? He knows all this already, and he's just making our case look better.

Parnell seems untroubled by this progressively more solid confirmation of the criminalist's methodologies. "I see. So you use this to find everything that was in the sample."

"Sort of. We do a separate test for each element we're looking for. That's because we have to use a different lamp for each element."

"Is it possible that these elements can appear on somebody's hands just by accident?"

Is he going to be all day with these elementary questions, especially ones I've already covered? "Objection. Asked and answered."

He looks at me. "Just trying to clarify the point so there can be no mistakes."

"I'll allow it," Genet says.

"We have sample absorption charts," Gonzalez continues, "for swabs taken from people who have fired no weapons. We know what innocent hands look like."

"Okay." Parnell nods. "I think I understand. Is it very sensitive?"

"Oh yes, incredibly sensitive."

"Fascinating." He shakes his head with the absolute wonder of it. "What's the other test?"

"That's a little more complicated."

"You're kidding! I barely followed the first one!" Another laugh from the masses. Is he really trying to call her credibility into question?

"The other one works best with clothing, because the sampling is simpler. The field officer takes an aluminum disk with Vistanex on it and—"

"Vistanex? What's that?"

"Sorry. It's polyisobutylene."

"Like that's supposed to explain it to me?" he cries in mock consternation, evoking more laughter. He's really getting Gonzalez to warm up to him; he has her talking a lot, which always scares me. I might have to start objecting more just to warn her.

"It's an adhesive. Any loose particles on the clothing will stick to it. We get back in the lab and dissolve it in bromoform, which is very dense and causes unwanted particles to float to the surface."

Parnell frowns. "What do you mean by 'unwanted' particles?"

"Stuff we're not interested in."

His frown deepens. "How do you know you're not interested if you don't even know what they are yet? Don't you want to know everything about the sample?"

Gonzalez is untroubled. "Of course not. We're looking for gunshot residue. All we care about are a few elements."

"But if there was something exculpatory present, something that might get the defendant off the hook, wouldn't you want to know that?"

Now it's Gonzalez's turn to look offended. "Mr. Parnell, in the lab, we don't care if the defendant is innocent or guilty or if he even exists. All we're trying to do is determine the presence or absence of GSR, and that's it."

He uncreases his brow and looks apologetic. "Of course. I see. Please go on."

"So we take the bottom part of the bromoform mixture and run it through a micropore filter that strains out all but the very finest particles. Then we do a couple of other things to prepare the sample and put it under a scanning electron microscope."

"Ah! Then you look at them and you know what they are!"

"Not exactly. There are two viewing screens. One shows an image of the surface of the sample. We look for spherical particles, because that tells us they were molten at one time, which is what happens to metals in a bullet when it's fired."

"Aren't there other particles that are round?" He's like a straight man on some goddamned television science show for kindergarteners.

"Sure. That's why we have the second screen. When the electron beam hits the sample, certain things happen inside the atoms that send back X rays. By looking at the X rays, we can tell exactly what elements are present. As in the other test, if we find the right combinations, it was GSR. Gunshot residue."

"Amazing! That was a very clear description, very scientific and most impressive." He sounds sincere, and Gonzalez looks well pleased. "And these tests, especially the one with the electron microscope, you said these tests are very sensitive?

"Extremely."

What's he trying to do, hang his own clients? "Wow," he says, shaking his head. "Wow! So, did any of your tests tell you which of the two defendants wore the sweatshirt when the GSR was deposited on it?" He turns and begins walking back to the defense table.

Gonzalez blinks. "No."

Parnell stops his walk, looking at the audience, surprise on his face. "Why not?"

"We have no way to tell that."

"No way?" Frowning again. "None? Not with all the fancy electron wachamacallits, spectro-whatevers? You can't tell?"

"No."

He shrugs, like he's willing to forget it. "Okay, no problem. But you can at least tell if one of them was wearing the sweatshirt, right?"

"No."

"No?" Again a shrug. "Okay, can you tell how long ago the GSR was deposited on the sweatshirt?"

"No."

"Can you tell what kind of gun was fired?"

"No."

"Can you tell what kind of bullets, what caliber, how many?"

"No."

His voice has lapsed into a rhythmic cadence, a responsive chant with Gonzalez, as he hammers home the limitations of the GSR test. "Can you even tell us if the GSR taken from the sweatshirt is consistent with the slug taken from the victim's body?"

"No."

"As a matter of fact, you can't even say that whoever wore the sweatshirt even fired a gun at all, can you?"

"No."

"And why is that?"

"The GSR may not have come from that person firing a gun. It could have rubbed off from another piece of clothing, or come from just handling a gun somebody else had fired—"

"Whoa, hold it, wait a minute!" He turns slowly away from the audience to look at Gonzalez, pausing for a meaningful look at the jury. "Another piece of clothing? It could have rubbed off from something else?"

"Yes."

"Did you examine any other articles of clothing in the closet?"

"No."

"Well, why not?"

"I wasn't asked to."

"I see." Parnell marches to the lectern and grips both sides as he raises his chin. "So let me make sure I understood all of this. Let's say the person wearing the sweatshirt had been at a public gun range—"

"Objection!" I've got to puncture this swelling balloon fast. "Stating facts not in evidence!"

"What are you talking about?" Parnell says. "You've already established they were in a gun club."

"Yes, but not that they were wearing that sweatshirt."

"Well, it's just a hypothetical anyway, your honor."

"Objection overruled."

Parnell inclines his head at Genet, an aristocratic gesture of thanks. "As I was saying: let's say the person wearing the sweatshirt had been at a public gun club doing some target shooting two days before the victim in this case was killed. Your examination couldn't tell that apart from the single firing that killed the victim two days later, is that correct?"

"Yes, that's correct." Gonzalez is back in android mode now, flat, factual answers with no trace of emotion. If Parnell is making her squirm, she doesn't show it. She's been through it before.

"And if they weren't wearing that sweatshirt at the gun range but another piece of clothing, it's entirely possible that residue from that piece of clothing could easily rub off onto the sweatshirt if the two pieces of clothing were hanging together in the closet, right? Or if whoever was wearing it even brushed past someone who had recently fired a gun?"

He's incredible: he's making it sound like he just stumbled onto this extraordinary revelation by accident, just in the last few minutes, and is uncovering information we had hoped to keep deliberately hidden.

"That is correct."

"In fact, if they were hanging together and touching, it's a virtual certainty that some would rub off, correct?"

"Nothing is certain."

"Let's not play games." He's trying to intimidate her now, get her to confess following what he has portrayed as her unpardonable attempt at deceiving the jury. "It's damned probable you're going to pick up GSR, isn't it? Especially with all these super-sensitive tests you just told us about."

"Not necessarily. There are circumstances under which we might not pick it up."

Every witness, without exception, has the potential to incline his or her testimony to one side or the other, consciously or otherwise. The reasons are numerous and include bias, pride, prejudice, stubbornness, hostility, fear and contempt for authority. Like anyone else, many crime lab technicians can be influenced to shade judgment calls in favor of whatever side they're on, but on purely factual matters they won't say anything they cannot truly swear to under oath. They're fanatical about their integrity and rightly so: without it, they are useless, just another of the thousands of expert witness whores who sell their services to the highest bidder and are only too pleased to slant their testimony to any end you care to buy. This is Gonzalez's opportunity to stand up to Parnell, to regain some face following his relentless pummeling of her testimony and my reliance on it.

"So, if I pulled out a gun right here in court and fired a round into the ceiling and you took a sample from my hands or clothes and found GSR, you can't even say it came from that shot, can you." Not a question but a statement for her to confirm.

"No."

"Fine. So the bottom line, and correct me if I'm wrong here, Ms. Gonzalez, the bottom line is that you don't have the slightest idea how that GSR got there at all, or when, or how much there was, or what kind of bullet or weapon was fired, or whether the person wearing the sweatshirt even fired a weapon that day or any other day, isn't that correct?"

"Yes."

"Thank you. Let's get out of Lisa Pierman's house and into her sister's. Did you test any of the clothes hanging in Diane Pierman's closet?"

"Yes."

"Really. Who asked you to do that?"

"You did." More laughter. Parnell elicited it at his own expense because he knows this jury and judge like Gonzalez and might resent his treatment of her. Everybody in the courtroom is convinced he's eating my lunch.

"And what did you find?"

"There was gunshot residue present."

"How about that! Do you know how the shooter fired the weapon?"

"What do you mean?"

"I mean, what kind of stance did she take?"

"I was told it was a two-handed stance."

"Arms extended way out in front?"

"So the eyewitnesses said."

"Like this?" Parnell stretches out his own arms and clasps his hands together, as if around a gun.

"I believe so."

"Was it a baggy sweatshirt?"

"What?"

"Were the sleeves very full and long?"

"Not particularly."

"So in this kind of a stance, the wrist is apt to be exposed."

"Depending on the kind of gloves she wore."

"What did the witness say about the gloves?"

"Small, elegant, like opera gloves."

"Small gloves, snug sweatshirt." Parnell thinks about it for a second. He's probably thought about it for weeks. "Seems to me some wrist should have been exposed."

"Can't say for sure."

"Tell me, Ms. Gonzalez: did you do any skin examinations?"

"Yes."

"On both defendants?"

"Yes."

"What did you find?"

"Nothing."

He cocks an ear toward her. "Sorry, what was that? Did you say nothing?"

"Yes."

"Nothing at all? Not even a trace?"

"No."

"Which test did you do?"

"The scanning electron microscope."

"Even more sensitive than the atomic absorption spectrophotometer, right?" He pronounces it perfectly this time.

"Yes."

"And you found what?"

"Nothing. However—"

"Tell me," he cuts her off, "do you know who won the Super Bowl this year?"

"Objection!" Parnell's sudden non sequitur shakes me out of a half-trance and finally gives me an opportunity to interrupt his flow. "How irrelevant can you get?"

"A little leeway, your honor?" Parnell asks Genet.

"Where're you going with this, counselor?"

"I don't have to go anywhere, your honor, if the people will stipulate that the Los Angeles Stars were the first expansion team of any major sport in history to make it to the championships in their very first year and that over fifty-six thousand Stars sweatshirts were sold in a six-week period beginning in late December and the fact that one that was owned by Diane Pierman and was hanging in her sister's closet doesn't mean it was the same one worn by whoever killed Vincent Rosamund!"

"I'm not stipulating anything, your honor, but I'll change my objection from irrelevance to no grounds for expertise, unless defense counsel qualifies Ms. Gonzalez as either a linebacker or the president of a sporting goods company!"

"Question is withdrawn," Parnell says without hesitation. He didn't really need Gonzalez to answer it; he was just looking for an opportunity to make his speech, which I've given him. "That will be all, Ms. Gonzalez."

"Hold it a second!" I yell, still standing. "Your honor, people demand that defense counsel's speech on the retail market in Los Angeles be stricken."

"Grounds?"

"Stating facts not in evidence."

"Granted. Remarks are stricken. Jury is instructed to ignore them. Mr. Milano, redirect?"

"Yes." There is little doubt in my mind that everybody in this room thinks Parnell just smoked our case into ashes. In fact, everything that has just gone on was of minor consequence, but I'm not ready to reveal that yet. However, there are some points to clarify and one major concept to put across. "You say you found no residue on the skin, right?" I ask Gonzalez.

"That is correct."

"Is that unusual?"

"Not at all."

"And why is that?"

Gonzalez sighs, shakes her head, then addresses herself to the jury. "Everybody thinks a gunshot residue test is magical, that we can tell days later if somebody fired a weapon, but that's true only in the movies. The fact is, you can fire a powerful semiautomatic pistol all day long, and if you come home and wash your hands thoroughly, all the residue is completely gone. With just normal activity, about ninety percent is gone in the first hour, and after two hours, only about one percent is left. We won't even bother to run the test if the samples are taken more than six hours after the shooting." She works one hand over the other in demonstration. "Wash your hands and it's gone instantly."

"So you're telling us a shooter can get rid of essentially all the residue, leaving no trace."

"A savvy criminal can completely defeat the GSR test with little effort."

I look at Diane. "Would that apply to a savvy criminal defense attorney as well?" If Parnell can make accusatory speeches, so can I.

Parnell and Ericsson jump to their feet at the same time and shout, "Objection!" simultaneously. It's almost comical.

"Withdrawn. No more questions for this witness."

Parnell may have done it unofficially, but he has managed to point out to the jury that half the people in town have been running around with Stars sweatshirts all season. He has also trashed the impact of Gonzalez's testimony and is about as smug as I've ever seen him. So much so, in fact, that he doesn't seem to even wonder why I would bother with Gonzalez's testimony when we all know that both sisters were firing guns at the range, which accounts for the gunshot residue.

I never tried to get Gonzalez to say anything about the relative amounts, or if she could tell if one fired more recently, which I already knew she can't. In truth, Gonzalez's testimony wasn't critical, but it was important in establishing that there was GSR on the sweatshirt because, despite all the oblique references, the existence of residue had not yet been made for the official record. I needed it to be on the record in case Parnell tried to throw any doubt on the gun club manager's ID of the sisters. Now he thinks he has effectively destroyed my 'sensitive forensics' angle, and I'm guessing that his confidence is up at a dangerously high level.

I try to look as devastated as I can. Even Genet is waiting for a few seconds, giving me time to regain my composure before we go on.

She asks me to call my next witness, and I rise to summon DA's investigator Martin McConagle to the stand. I'm so juiced for this I can hardly keep my voice steady, so wired that I push all thoughts of what this is going to do to Diane out of my head. If she were my own mother I couldn't stop myself now anyway: in real life, lawyers don't get many Perry Mason moments. I glance at Eleanor Torjan and lift my chin slightly. She looks at Marty as he makes his way up the aisle, and then back at me, a questioning look in her eyes. I turn back toward the front without answering. I have her attention and I'm close to delivering on my promise.

Marty is sworn in and states his name and occupation, that he is an investigator in my office. Parnell is listening carefully: he thinks this is the part where I show how

Diane and Lisa were found together in Lisa's house following the shooting, that I'm simply establishing the arrest sequence. What Parnell doesn't know is that Marty wasn't even there that night.

"Mr. McConagle, when did you first learn of the shooting?"

"About two hours after it happened. Detective Pappas called me at home."

"Why did he do that?"

"I was involved in the case against Vincent Rosamund. He had been accused of raping the defendants."

Parnell is on his feet. "Your honor, this is an outrage! Move for an immediate mistrial!"

"Grounds, Mr. Parnell?"

"Sidebar!"

The four of us troop up to the bench. Parnell is already speaking before we get fully there.

"Your honor, who the hell is the prosecutor kidding? We had a long conversation about this in your chambers and agreed not to mention the rapes!"

Genet looks at me, and I'm prepared for this. "I have no intention of mentioning the rapes in the context of anything to do with the case against the defendants. But the first trial is a matter of public record, and my witness did not testify that any rapes occurred, only that someone was accused of them. And it happens to be why Detective Pappas called Mr. McConagle and I have the right to bring that out."

"When you cut through all the malarkey," Parnell says to Genet, "the prosecutor is violating the spirit of what we discussed."

I shake my head. "When you instructed the jury, your honor, you told them we'd all be foolish not to acknowledge that those events were alleged to have occurred. If you read back what just went on, you'll find that my question and the witness's answer don't step one inch beyond what you said to the jury."

This is a tough one for the judge. Parnell and I both made valid points. "Are you planning to go any further with anything to do with the rapes?" she asks me.

"Absolutely not. All I wanted to do was show why

McConagle stuck his nose into this one." Genet is on the fence and I need to push her over the edge. I look at the defense table then back at her. "For pity's sake, judge: those women were our friends. Mr. Parnell knows that; we even met in his office once before the Rosamund trial." I turn to Parnell. "You want me to bring *that* out as Marty's reason?"

Of course he doesn't. If the jury gets wind of the fact that I was friends with Diane and Lisa and am now willing to prosecute them, they'll get the impression that they must be guilty, otherwise we wouldn't be pursuing this case so avidly. It's in Parnell's interest to show a more neutral motivation for Marty's involvement.

"If the prosecutor agrees to leave it where it is and not pursue it further, I'll withdraw the motion," he says.

"Agreed."

Genet accepts our bargain and waves us all back.

I pick up where I left off. "After you learned of the shooting, what did you do?"

"I got as many details as I could; then I came and got you." He leaves out that he got me off a golf course in Palm Springs.

"That was on Monday morning? February twentieth?"

"Yessir."

"And what did you do at the end of the day?"

"I went to the Santa Monica Gun Club."

"Why was that?"

"To practice. They set aside certain reserved hours for law enforcement people. I hadn't been in a couple of weeks, so I went."

"Who was on duty that evening?"

"Gil Bascomb, the owner."

"And did you have occasion to speak with Mr. Bascomb?"

"Sure. I always chat him up for a couple minutes when I'm there."

"And what, if anything, did you learn from this conversation?"

"That Diane and Lisa Pierman had been in there two days before."

This is, of course, old news. Bascomb testified to all of

this already. Parnell looks puzzled, but he's hanging on every word.

"Didn't you already know that?"

"Had no idea. Gil had already told Detective Pappas, or one of his people, but I didn't know."

Janine Ericsson says, "Objection," without standing. "Hearsay."

It's a perfunctory objection. Maybe she's bored or just wants to disturb my concentration. I withdraw the question—it's not important anyway—and continue. "Isn't it a bit of a coincidence, that they would have been in the same club as you, only two days before?"

He shakes his head. "Not really. It's the only place to shoot guns on the entire west side, unless you're a cop and can use the police range. You want to shoot, you go to Gil's."

"What else did you discuss with Mr. Bascomb?"

"I asked him what the girls—I mean, the defendants—I asked him what they were shooting."

"And what did he reply?"

"He said it was a forty-five automatic."

"And that was consistent with the statement he made to the detectives earlier in the day?"

Parnell objects this time. "He just got finished saying he didn't know Bascomb had already talked to the detectives."

"No, he didn't," I say. "Ms. Ericsson objected and I withdrew the question, so his answer was stricken. And besides"—I address myself to Genet—"if Mr. Parnell wants to try to catch my witness in inconsistencies, might I suggest he wait until his cross-examination to do it?"

Genet nods. "That was not a proper objection, Mr. Parnell, as I would have pointed out had you given me a chance, Mr. Milano. Now can we proceed?"

I smile and apologize, ever the good sport, but Parnell is too preoccupied to be appropriately humble and gracious. He's still trying to figure out what I'm up to. I let it go and shift to another tack.

"Officer, what else did you discuss with Mr. Bascomb?"

"I asked him what happens to the shell casings on the range."

"The shell casings . . . ?"

"Yeah. I mean, yes. Spent cartridges from all the bullets that are fired. They wind up on the floor and you sweep them up every few minutes and put them in a little metal basket provided in each station. I asked Gil what happens to them."

"I see. And what did he say?"

"He told me all about how they're gathered and reloaded. He said—"

Parnell objects again, but not before Marty gets his answer started. "This is hearsay. Move to strike." He's worried now. I can tell exactly what he's thinking: I already had the owner-manager on the stand; why didn't I ask *him* what he does, instead of getting it from Marty? He's going to catch on soon, and I want him silenced while I'm questioning Marty.

"Your honor," I say, "Mr. McConagle is a sworn peace officer who took a sworn statement, and he's only describing the statement. However"—I look at Parnell— "if defense counsel insists, I can put Mr. Bascomb back on the stand."

"That won't be necessary," Genet says. "If there was an official statement. Mr. McConagle?"

"Sure was, your honor." He points to the defense table. "I believe they have a copy."

I'm sure Parnell never read it. There was no reason to since, from his perspective, the manager's testimony could only work to the defense's advantage, as it seemed to when Bascomb was on the stand.

"I'm going to overrule your objection, Mr. Parnell," Genet says. "You have the right to put Mr. Bascomb back on the stand if you want to, so I'll let this line of questioning continue."

"Thank you. Mr. McConagle, you were starting to tell us how the shell casings are gathered and reused . . . ?"

"Yes. You can use the casings to make new bullets, so the empty shells at each station are sorted and bagged."

"Why are they sorted by station?"

"Well, they can only be reused if they're in good condition." Marty turns toward the jury to explain. "See, if someone's firing a dirty weapon or one that's out of alignment, it can ruin the casings. Or let's say they were using poor quality ammunition to start with, well, none of the casings from that station are going to be usable. By bagging each station separately, you can look at a few casings and decide to discard the whole bag without having to look at every last shell."

"I understand." I turn to the jury to make sure they do, too. I see some nodding heads and no signs of confusion, so I go on. "Now, Mr. Bascomb said that the defendants bought about two hundred rounds from him. 'Fresh stuff, not reloads,' I believe were his exact words. That means . . . ?"

"It means—"

"Objection," Parnell says. "Are we now asking one witness to tell us what another witness meant?"

"It's just jargon, your honor," I argue. "I'll be glad to qualify Officer McConagle as an expert in firearms if Mr. Parnell insists."

"That won't be necessary," Genet says. "Hell, even *I* know what a 'reload' is." She waits for the expected laughter and then overrules Parnell's objection.

I wave Marty on. "It means that they bought factory fresh ammo, not rounds that were reloaded from spent cartridges." He turns to the jury. "Brand-new bullets."

"So they were bagged separately . . ." I prompt him.

"Right. And their gun was in good condition— according to Mr. Bascomb's statement—so the shell casings were almost pristine and good for reloading. They were set aside, rather than thrown out, along with several other good batches from that day."

I pause for a second while all that sinks in. Parnell is on the edge of his seat, probably waiting for some sort of bomb to drop. "Nothing further," I say.

Parnell sits up straight. Genet invites him to cross-examine. He looks at Ericsson, then at me, then at Genet. "No questions, your honor." Of course not: he hasn't the slightest notion of where this is heading so what's he going to cross-examine about? The best he can do right now is try not to look worried.

I sneak a peek at Diane. In some twisted way, I'm still seeking her approval, and even if it results in her conviction, something inside me wants her to admire me for it. She's doing a pretty good job of keeping her face impassive, but I sense the worry beneath. She knows I'm good at what I do, that the seeming pointlessness of this line of inquiry has to have some kind of purpose. Again I force my mind away from her, tell myself I'm doing the right thing. Maybe this is what soldiers in the Civil War tried to do before they shot at their own cousins.

Marty steps down and walks through the swinging doors back into the audience. He looks at Marsha and me so he doesn't have to look at Diane or Lisa. Parnell is nervously drumming his fingers on the table, fretting about whether Marty's testimony was some kind of diversion or if there was really a point that my next witness might reveal.

If you want to shoot a duck, my father's friend the tailor used to say, advice Parnell could use right now, *aim where it's going, not where it's been.* "Prosecution calls Robert Eagleson."

Parnell knows who this is from the witness list we provided, and he stands up, looking exasperated. "Your honor, *another* expert from the crime lab? C'mon, we already heard from one; why belabor the point? We're willing to stipulate that there was gunshot residue on the sweatshirt so we can just move on, for heaven's sake!" Ericsson is nodding in agreement.

"Give me a proper objection, Mr. Parnell!" Genet says sternly.

"This testimony is cumulative under Evidence Code section three-fifty-two as it shall consume an undue amount of time."

Genet looks at me, some agreement with Parnell evident on her face. "Your honor," I tell her, "Mr. Eagleson is not an expert on GSR; he is a firearms and toolmarks examiner."

Parnell whirls to face me. "You don't even have the damned gun!" he shouts as he pounds the table dramatically. This time I think his frustration is real. "How the hell can you be talking about toolmarks!"

Genet frowns at this outburst, holds out her hand, palm down, and pumps it at Parnell, telling him to keep himself calm. When he has gotten some kind of control over himself and drops back onto his seat, she looks at me, her eyebrows raised. "He's got a point there, Mr. Milano. You want to tell me what this is all about before I allow this witness?"

I didn't want to do this so early, not without laying the necessary foundation, but Marsha's look tells me I have no choice if I want Eagleson on the stand. "Your honor." I turn so the jury and the whole court can hear me. "If I am allowed to continue uninterrupted, the prosecution will prove beyond doubt that the gun that killed Vincent Rosamund is the same one used by Diane and Lisa Pierman in the Santa Monica Gun Club the day before the murder."

There is an explosion of voices and gasps from the audience, Parnell's voice rising above them all as he gets back on his feet to shout at me again. "You don't have the goddamned gun!" he's screaming, and I think I detect a tinge of incipient hysteria in his voice. For two days now I let him think he's gotten the upper hand, that my case is in trouble, and now I've taken that complacency and in a few seconds turned it into panic.

Genet is banging her gavel, trying to quiet the hubbub, and is getting angry. I stand, mute, my hands clasped in front of me, well-behaved while everyone else is violating her courtroom protocol. Finally she stands, places one hand on the bench top and leans forward, then pounds the gavel once more, hard, on the surface of the bench rather than the circular pad. The booming sound, amplified by the hollow woodwork of the bench top, rings across the room and everyone stops talking. She points the gavel at Drew Stengel.

"Bailiff, any more disturbances, you clear the room, got me?"

Stengel nods, and Genet sits down after one more glance around the room. Her gaze comes to rest on me. "You may continue, Mr. Milano, but this better be good." She waves the witness to the stand.

It will be. "Thank you, your honor."

Robert Eagleson is in his late fifties, just under six feet tall, trim and fit. He looks ex-military but has spent his entire adult career with the LA County Sheriff's Department. Retired now, he is a contract consultant with the Scientific Services Bureau. He wears his gray hair in a crewcut, nicely complementing his (undoubtedly short-sleeved) white shirt, brown suit and nondescript tie. He makes his way to the stand like he's done it a thousand times before, which he has.

In my qualification of Eagleson as an expert, I bring out that he is president of the ISFTE, the International Society of Firearms and Toolmarks Examiners, an elite organization with only six hundred highly qualified members. The sole purposes of this organization are to train members and newcomers, because there is no other way to acquire these extraordinarily specialized skills, and to ensure that members adhere to an incredibly strict set of ethical and procedural standards. Without these, their profession would be completely useless.

Eagleson is somewhat of a celebrity in his profession. Among other things, he's the man who discovered two Colt .45's with identical factory serial numbers, a source of much embarrassment to the manufacturer and a key piece of evidence in a tricky case. A photograph of the two guns lying side by side hangs in a glass display case in the lobby of the crime lab. It's the first thing they like to show visitors to the lab, as I discovered when I went there myself to see Eagleson.

"Mr. Eagleson," I ask him, "can you tell us, please, what a toolmark is?"

"Certainly." A veteran, he turns to the jury to explain it to them, since they're the only people who count. "Whenever a weapon is fired, there are little marks on the slug and the shell. Some of these come from minute scratches inside the barrel as the slug travels down its length. You might get a nick from the firing pin as it hits the back of the bullet to set it off. When the cartridge is ejected, if that's the type of gun you have, it can get scratched as it leaves the chamber, or it can get roughed up as it rotates in a revolver. All of those little nicks and scratches are called toolmarks."

"Thank you. And why are those significant?"

"No two weapons will leave the same exact marks. Even guns that seem perfectly identical will always have some differences, and these will show up when you look at the bullets under a microscope."

"So what does this mean to us? Or, let's say, to people in law enforcement?"

"It means that we can tell you whether a particular bullet was fired from a particular gun."

"I see." I look at the jury to make sure they're following all of this. They're paying rapt attention. "How do you do that?"

"We put the rounds or casings under a microscope, a special one that shows us two bullets side by side. Let's say we get a gun from the police, and a round recovered from a victim. We'll fire a test round from the gun and put it under the 'scope to see what kind of marks it left. Then we'll put the recovered round next to it and compare the two. If the marks match up"—he turns up his hands—"the recovered bullet came out of that gun."

"I understand. Thank you for that explanation." I glance at Parnell out of the corner of my eye. His jaw is so tense it looks like a blood vessel might come popping out the side of his face, and he's gripping both arms of the chair so that his knuckles are white. I know with a certainty what he's thinking: *you don't have the fucking gun, what's this all about!*

"Mr. Eagleson, did you have occasion recently to speak with Mr. Martin McConagle of my office?"

"Yes, I did."

"And would you tell us what that was all about?"

"Sure." He clears his throat, crosses one leg over the other and turns to the jury again, completely relaxed and in his element. "Officer McConagle came to me with a bag of shell casings that he said were recovered from a gun club in Santa Monica. He also gave me the casing found at the scene of a murder."

"And what did he ask you to do?"

"He asked me to determine if any of the casings in the bag came out of the same gun that was used to kill the victim."

I can hear the loud exhalation of held breath from not only Parnell but half the jury and a good number of people in the audience. Even Genet, until now an impassive observer, is leaning forward as though this will help her catch every one of Eagleson's words. She even forgets to warn the audience to silence again.

"And did you do that?" I ask.

"Well," he chuckles, uncrossing his legs, "it wasn't easy, I can tell you that! Usually, we get four or five rounds at the most, and he hands me a bag must've had four, five *hundred* in it."

"But you tried . . ."

"Oh, yeah. Me and two of my specialists worked for three solid days."

"Did you go through the whole bag?"

He shakes his head. "Didn't have to. When we got twenty for-sure matches, McConagle said we could stop."

"Twenty matches," I repeat for the jury's benefit. "And what does that tell you?"

He shrugs, like it was obvious. It is, but I want him to say it. "At least twenty of the shells in that bag came out of the same gun that killed Vincent Rosamund."

"Are you sure of that?"

"Dead sure."

"No doubt in your mind whatsoever?"

"None."

"And your colleagues?"

"The same."

Parnell is shaking, but he rises to his feet and does his job. "I object to that last statement, you honor! That's hearsay!"

"If I may be allowed to continue," I say calmly, and Genet nods her head. "Mr. Eagleson, did you rely on the opinions of your colleagues, in part, in formulating your conclusions in this case?"

"Yes, I did."

"Objection is overruled," Genet says.

Parnell looks like he has been skewered. His eyes are darting frantically from side to side, as though looking for a way out of this awful situation. Without ever seeing the gun, we have produced damning evidence that the pistol the twins were firing at the gun range is the same weapon that killed Vincent Rosamund.

Parnell was banking on our inability to do that; it was one half of his entire defense, the other half being the identification problem, which he still has going for him, but now that's *all* he has.

I take a long look at the jury, examining each face,

most of which are still fixated on Eagleson. They got it, all right, and I don't need to drive it home. "No further questions. Thank you, Mr. Eagleson." He shrugs: *no big deal.*

"Your witness, Mr. Parnell."

"A minute, your honor . . . ?" Ericsson says.

Genet nods as Parnell takes a sip of ice water and consults with Ericsson, the first time he has done so in open court since the trial began. She's speaking and he's nodding, then he leans away, scribbles a few notes, and stands up to walk to the lectern, trying to look like he's back in control.

"Mr. Eagleson, is it possible that matching toolmarks could be a coincidence?"

Eagleson shakes his head. "Nope."

"Not even a remote possibility?"

If it were, Eagleson told me during prep, *it'd be the first time in history.* Now he simply says, "No sir."

"Well, you once found two handguns with identical serial numbers, and that was a hell of a coincidence, wasn't it?"

Eagleson smiles and waves it away. "Nah, that's just a machine stamping numbers. The machine sticks for a second, it puts the same number on two guns. Probably happens all the time; this was just the first we could prove." The smile leaves his face. "Toolmarks are different. There's not a chance of finding two the same."

He's an old hand at this. When faced with the standard "Isn't it even remotely possible . . ." question, he just says no, because he believes it to be so.

But Parnell won't quit. "But it's not very scientific, is it? I mean, you don't have some kind of standard for how many scratches have to match up, or which ones you can ignore, before you reach a conclusion, isn't that right?"

It's a compound question and I could object, but I decide to just let Eagleson handle it. Which he does.

"Isn't what right?"

"What I just said," Parnell replies.

"You just said several different things. You said it wasn't very scientific. That's incorrect; it's extremely scientific, it's just not easy to codify into a hard standard.

That's why we have a multiyear apprenticeship program for people coming into the trade. Just because it requires judgment doesn't mean it's unscientific. Just damned difficult."

Parnell must really be rattled, because he should know better than to take on a guy like Eagleson on his own turf. He gets off it quickly. "How can you be sure it was Diane or Lisa Pierman who fired the weapon that produced those casings?"

"I have absolutely no idea who fired the weapon."

Parnell looks surprised and sees a glimmer of hope. He goes into his I'm-so-shocked routine. "What was that again? You don't know who fired the weapon?"

"Of course not."

"Then how can you testify that one of these defendants fired it?"

Now Eagleson goes into his own act. "Who said anything about who fired it? All I'm telling you is that the shells given to me by Officer McConagle came out of the same gun that killed Vincent Rosamund. That's all I know and that's all I'm testifying to."

"So you're telling me that somebody else at the gun club could have fired the murder weapon?"

"Listen, for all I know, Santa Claus could have fired it. How should I know? I examine toolmarks."

It's time for me to step in. Parnell's getting hurt, but he's doing a good job of hiding that from the jury, and I need to put a stop to it. "Your honor, I object to this entire line of questioning as calling for speculation. Defense counsel is grilling the witness on things he never testified to. All Mr. Eagleson said is that the gun that killed Rosamund is the same one that was used at the gun club. Mr. Parnell is trying to put words in his mouth and then ask him questions as though Mr. Eagleson said them!"

Genet is nodding in agreement as I finish. I'm surprised she let me talk that long. "Objection is sustained. Mr. Parnell, if you have any questions for the witness that relate either to his expertise or his previous testimony, please continue. If not, let's move on."

"I have nothing further," he says, trying to look triumphant.

It comes off badly. No jury in the world is going to

believe that the twins were coincidentally shooting a .45 automatic in the same station of the same club within a few hours of somebody else who then used it to kill Rosamund. Diane and Lisa are linked to the gun without any doubt whatsoever. One of the sisters is the shooter, and all that's left is the issue of which one.

So far it's been a pretty good day. Genet invites me to redirect, but I decline, thanking Eagleson and excusing him, catching Eleanor Torjan's eye as he walks through the swinging door toward the back of the audience. The reporter is smiling and shaking her head, whether out of admiration for me or just because she's got a great story and an exclusive follow-up with me I can't tell. She's scribbling notes furiously.

Genet asks if I have any more witnesses. Diane is holding Lisa's hand under the table but otherwise just staring straight ahead. Parnell is pale and sweating, fingering his notes so that the edges are curling upward. In light of what just happened, he has to be reconsidering whether they're going to put on a defense or even change their case strategy altogether. He is aware, as am I, that the courtroom press section is packed with reporters, many from out of town. This has indeed become a national story, largely owing to Ernestine Denier, and I know that the Piermans' embarrassment is acute. The last thing they need is to have trapdoors spring open beneath them in full view of the world.

"Mr. Milano?"

Parnell is sure I'm going to rest our case on the strength of that last exchange, but I can't. I haven't yet made the case against Diane as opposed to Lisa. I almost feel sorry for him, sitting there thinking that the worst is over, that all the cards have been dealt, that his only remaining task is to drive home the identification issue and salvage his clients. I wouldn't even find any pleasure in watching his face as I address Genet, so I turn fully away as I rise. I feel as though my entire career has merely been preparation for this moment.

"People call Lisa Pierman to the stand."

For a split second there's not a sound in the courtroom. It feels as though time itself has stopped, people waiting in disbelief for others to confirm that they heard me correctly. Parnell's mouth is agape, as is Ericsson's, and now Diane has shifted her gaze to me, her eyes flashing naked hostility. Lisa is whispering frantically in her ear, but Diane ignores her sister.

Finally, Parnell speaks, slowly, drawing out every word and injecting each one with as much cynicism and contempt as he can drum up on short notice. "You—can—not—be—*serious*!"

It takes Judge Genet herself a second, but she comes around as well. "Mr. Parnell, do you have a proper objection to make?"

He looks at her like she's gone senile for even having to ask the question. Where do you start to explain to somebody that two plus two make four? "Last time I looked," he says in a condescending tone, "we had a Fifth Amendment to the Constitution that forbids forcing anyone to give testimony that might incriminate themselves."

I politely allow him to finish and then wait for Genet's hand signal for me to respond. "Lisa Pierman has no fear of self-incrimination," I say, "because we have offered her complete immunity from all charges against her if she testifies." I turn to Parnell, explaining it to him as I would to a first-year law student. "As soon as she takes the stand, and assuming she answers all my questions truthfully, the case against her is dropped and she's free to go." I turn back to Genet and hold out both my hands: *was that clear enough?*

She shrugs—*sounds good to me*—and looks to Parnell, who is standing up, speechless. Ericsson jumps in and requests a sidebar, and as Genet motions us all to the bench, excited yammering breaks out in the audience and she has to gavel everybody to silence again.

This is why Marty and I were desperately hoping not to get an answer from Lisa on the immunity offer we made to her in Parnell's office. We wanted it on the record, but we also wanted it unresolved. Here, in the heat of battle, far along in the trial, there will be no time for the defense to rethink its strategy, no opportunity to make pretrial motions to fend off this attack. And we cannot be faulted: we made an offer, they declined to deal with it at the time it was made . . . so here they are.

In the time it takes to get to Genet, Parnell has found his tongue. "This is outrageous and highly improper!" he hisses, barely able to control his fury.

Genet holds up a hand for him to stop. "Can we keep this off the record?" she asks. I don't know why she wants to do this but we all agree, and she waves away the reporter. Parnell starts to speak again but she interrupts him, leaning toward us so nobody else can hear. She folds her hands in front of her so we all know this is important and she doesn't want to be interrupted.

"There are very serious charges in this matter and I want to give the defense every opportunity, but I have to confess . . ." She looks directly at Parnell, and if Ericsson is annoyed at this, she doesn't show it outwardly. ". . . I'm badly troubled by this case. The theories underlying standard procedure seem to be weighing too heavily in favor of exonerating two people who undoubtedly conspired to commit a murder." Now I know why she wanted this off the record: she's sharing some private thoughts that indicate bias in the case, although there is absolutely nothing in her rulings thus far that would show they have affected her conduct as judge.

"On a larger front," she continues, "there would seem to be no way to convict identical twins for any crime in which no positive, distinguishing ID is made, even if such confusion was engendered intentionally by the perpetrators. And I don't believe the framers of our laws contemplated such an abuse. Now, one unconscionable result has already been reached in this matter, and I'm referring to the dismissal of charges against the alleged rapist." She's as much as telling us that Judge Arigga screwed that case up. "And there has also been an unforgivable aftermath, namely the murder of that rapist, and I'm telling you in no uncertain terms that I'm not about to preside over yet a third if I can help it."

This degree of candor from a judge in midtrial is not unprecedented in my experience, but it isn't usual, either. I know for a certainty Genet won't do anything out of line from a technical point of view even if it means a third, terrible injustice: what she's doing is just telling us that, with her discretion, where the edges are unclear, she is going to err on the side of justice rather than legal purity.

And she's telling Parnell that this is going to help me more than it is him.

"Mr. Parnell," she continues, "I'm inclined to call Lisa Pierman to the stand unless you can mount a sound legal argument against my doing so. I also know that I can get overturned on appeal. On the other hand, I may not. So there's risk both ways, and what I want to know is, what do we all want to do about it?"

Genet has cleared away all the bullshit with one master stroke, away from the jury and spectators and the record, enabling us to get to the heart of the matter absent the usual posturing.

Parnell says to me, "Does the offer of immunity extend to the charge of murder?"

We're replaying the scrimmage in his office; only then, he misunderstood the game. Now he understands it only too well. Or thinks he does: we're not quite through yet.

"Your client hasn't been charged with murder," I tell him.

Parnell whips his head around to Genet. "I thought we were through playing games, your honor! Murder is very much a factor in this case, and my client's Fifth Amendment rights protect her against self-incrimination for charges which may not have been brought yet but which might be in the future. Therefore, she cannot be compelled to testify."

I rock my head back and forth a few times, like I'm mulling this over. "Are you telling us that Lisa needs protection from a murder charge?"

"Whether she actually *committed* murder is irrelevant to whether you might decide later to *charge* her with it!" he tells me angrily, and correctly.

There is a murmur back in the audience again, and Genet buys herself a few moments to think by calling for silence. "He has a point," she says to me. "His client doesn't even have to tell us why she won't testify if there's a chance you might lodge additional charges against her in connection with this matter."

Parnell thinks he has me now. "Unless you grant Lisa Pierman immunity from a charge of murder, we have nothing left to discuss and she won't testify."

Genet is nodding her concurrence, and when I don't

respond, Parnell slaps his hand on the bench and turns to leave.

"Agreed," I say to Genet.

Parnell freezes in his tracks, his back to us.

"Agreed, what?" Ericsson asks me.

"Agreed that Lisa Pierman has immunity from any and all charges that could possibly be filed in connection with this case."

Marsha, who hasn't said anything at all yet, is staring at me, stunned, as is Ericsson. Parnell turns to try to read my face, and I can read his easily: all he has to do now is put Lisa on the stand and let her confess to murder, whether she did it or not, and she is free forever. Further, we'd have to drop the murder charge against Diane because there is now an on-the-record confession from someone else, namely her sister. *Why the hell would I possibly agree to this!*

Genet sits back and lifts her hands, then waves us back to our respective tables. Parnell is walking slowly, trying hard to figure this out, and I walk even more slowly, giving him time to do so. By the time he reaches his seat, I can tell from the slump in his shoulders and the way he rubs his forehead with one hand, leaning against the table with the other, that it just sank in.

If Lisa lies on the stand, or refuses to answer my questions, the immunity is automatically withdrawn. If she confesses to the murder, there is little I can do about it, but Parnell knows that I will grill Lisa intensely, for days on end if I have to. And I'm free to ask her just about anything I want. I will make an absolutely airtight case against Diane, if not for murder, then for conspiracy, obstruction of justice, criminal solicitation and a host of other things that will add up to a sure conviction. I could put her away for life.

To avoid that and to protect Diane, Lisa would have to lie her way through a million details, and the odds are overwhelming that I will catch her in a tidal wave of inconsistencies. Whether Diane is really the murderer or not, I will nail her for sure and probably get Lisa for perjury as well, afterward, which would nullify her immunity.

Either way, if they take this deal, Diane is sunk as soon as Lisa hits the stand. And even if Diane decides to go ahead and take the fall, Lisa won't go along with it: she'll lie and I'll catch it. So the sweet-sounding immunity is purely illusory, and Lisa may not have the sophistication to instantly grasp all of this, but I know Diane and Parnell will. I know they both already have.

"Ericsson doesn't look so good," Marsha whispers to me. Indeed, the defense attorney's face appears to have taken on a slightly greenish cast.

"Every Cinderella has her midnight," I tell Marsha. I don't know what's making Ericsson feel worse: that she suspects her case is lost, or that she's being left out of the heated conversation that's going on between Diane, who is supposed to be her client, and Parnell, who is supposed to be her co-counsel.

Lisa also feels excluded, and she is growing more agitated and confused with each passing moment. Finally, because there's little else for them to do, Lisa and Ericsson begin talking to each other, but I can tell from their gestures that they're each asking questions to which the other has no answers. Then Ericsson gets aggressive and sticks her head between Diane and Parnell, insisting on being included. Parnell looks annoyed and then Genet breaks the whole thing up.

"Mr. Parnell, Ms. Ericsson: do you wish a ruling on your motion to prevent the prosecution from calling Lisa Pierman to the stand?"

Parnell waves Diane and Ericsson to silence. "Your honor, defense requests a short break to confer with our clients."

"How much time do you need?"

Ericsson jumps in to preempt whatever Parnell was going to ask for. "We'd like to reconvene in the morning."

"Mr. Milano?"

"No objection, your honor. Sidebar?"

Genet waves us back up to the bench. "I think nobody should talk to the press," I tell her.

Parnell is nodding his head vigorously. "Agreed. You want to issue a gag?"

"Not necessary," Genet says, "but one word from any of you and I'll hold you all in contempt. Understood?"

She polls us individually and we all acknowledge the warning.

"I'll be available throughout the day," she says as she begins gathering the books and papers on her desk. She knows what's going on and that we are likely to need her before the day is through.

"Where?" I ask.

"In my chambers, or within a few minutes of there." She waves Drew Stengel over. "Any of these four call today," she tells the bailiff, "find me. Got it?"

She orders us back to our places without waiting for Stengel's reply, then stands up to address the room.

"This court is adjourned until ten tomorrow morning. I've ordered all of the attorneys in this matter not to discuss the case with the press." Genet is taking all the heat for the decision, so that none of the reporters will be mad at any of us attorneys for cutting them out of the loop. I'm off the hook with Eleanor Torjan. Genet bangs her gavel, and the courtroom is a sudden swarm of activity as people jump excitedly to their feet, the reporters the most frenzied as they hurry to get to the bank of phones down the hall. Two or three of the more seasoned veterans linger for a second to make sure we're taking the judge's supposed gag order seriously, and when they see none of us is talking to any of their competitors, they leave as well. They don't have to rush to the phones; they all have hand-held cellulars.

I can see Marty standing off to the side, and when he catches my eye, he flashes me an inquiring look. I nod very slightly, hoping nobody else notices; he makes a fist and pumps it once, chest high. Stengel and his assistants are clearing the room, and as I begin stuffing papers into my attaché, I notice out of the corner of my eye one of the massed bodies pushing against the swell, which is unusual because she just made it past Stengel. Nobody makes it past Stengel so I turn fully and see that it's Diane, her eyes fixed on me, heading in my direction.

Marsha notices, too, and taps my arm before she can see that I'm very much aware of what's going on. Parnell reaches past Stengel to grab at Diane's arm but she shakes him off—angrily, it seems—and then Lisa, almost in tears, says, "What are you doing!" but Diane whirls on her and tells her to go home, immediately. Lisa backs off, hurt and confused, and now she really is crying. I pull my face away because the sight of Lisa's naked distress is more than I can take: the depth of her anguish hits me very hard, and I realize the degree to which I've been suppressing any thoughts of her and her sister's suffering.

I've little time to wallow in it. A second later Diane is standing in front of me. "I want to see you. In your office, now, just the two of us."

I look up at her and then over her shoulder to see if Genet is still in the room. Then I turn to where I last saw Parnell, when he was reaching for Diane. He's still there, looking from her to me with a look of deep consternation and indecision about what he ought to do in the face of Diane's obvious determination.

"This is highly improper, Diane." If she catches the faint irony, that this is the same excuse I gave her for not ever asking her out, she doesn't show it. There is nothing in her expression to indicate that there is anything that could distract her from whatever she has in mind. Her intense focus is disconcerting, and I'm not sure I'm strong enough to refuse her. "Does your attorney know about this?" I incline my head back toward Parnell, who is not technically her attorney but really is.

"That's not important," she says, never taking her eyes off mine. Her voice is tight, determined. "I'm the defendant; the attorney serves at my discretion. I want a meeting with the prosecuting attorney. Now will you do it?"

I find myself nodding. I have no basis to turn her down. "I don't want us to be seen leaving together. Can Parnell bring you?"

She shakes her head. "I'll meet you there."

"Twenty minutes."

"Is that necessary? Why not now?"

"Twenty minutes. But you have to at least let Ericsson know."

"I'll tell her."

For some reason I don't trust her, and I want this by the book. So long as Ericsson is the attorney of record, I can't meet with Diane without her knowing about it, even if she's not invited, and Parnell as counsel for a co-defendant also has the right to know. I wave Marsha over and tell her to let the two defense attorneys know that I'm going to meet with Diane in my office.

Diane ignores this and walks swiftly toward the rear doors. Marsha frowns at me. I shrug and tilt my head to one side: *who knows?*

But I do know.

The room completely cleared, Marsha forgets about my odd exchange with Diane when Marty joins us. He wraps his arms around me in a smothering bear hug and lifts me about two feet off the floor, turning my face instantly red.

"Yer a flippin' genius, me boy-o!" he says expansively, then sets me back on the floor.

"Jesus!" I gasp hoarsely, trying to get my breath back. "Wait until it's over before you kill me: you want a mistrial on account of dead prosecutor?"

Marty looks at Marsha then back at me. We are both trying to smile back at him but it comes out strained and false, and his own grin starts to fade. He folds his big arms across his equally big chest, looking down at the floor. "Ah, shit . . ." he says sadly.

It's different in the heat of battle, be it a war or a trial. Soldiers are conditioned to do things like think about glory and medals and honor and yelling *banzai!* as they slaughter somebody else's soldiers, and attorneys are likewise conditioned to think of the courtroom as a giant Nintendo game where they can rack up convictions or acquittals for their personal scorecards, being more brilliant than their adversaries, more clever than their colleagues, more devastating on cross-examinations and more brutal in impeaching witnesses.

Then it gets quiet, and there are bodies strewn all over the place, and weeping mothers, orphaned children and your own conscience, a nagging and intrusive presence always there to spoil all your fun. We've won, or nearly so, and in the excitement of executing our heroic battle plan, we've lost sight of what such a victory means.

"So let's just say it, okay?" Marty says, looking up. "We're putting two essentially innocent women in jail, is that it?"

No, it isn't. "They're *not* innocent," I respond, trying to sound convincing. "What they did is wrong, and they're guilty."

"Wouldn't you have done the same?" Marsha asks me.

"No, I wouldn't have."

"Maybe you don't understand rape," she says.

"Maybe I understand it better than you think I do."

She doesn't respond, only looks at me. "Would I kill the guy?" I ask myself out loud. "No. Would I harass and hound him? Probably."

"Okay, but do they deserve to have their lives completely ruined," Marsha says, "this whole thing having started without any of it being their fault?"

"Hey, Jones," Marty says, unfolding his arms and letting them drop to his sides. "This is a helluva time to be asking that!"

"No," I tell him, putting a hand on his arm. "It's a fair question." I sit on the table and look at Marsha. "It's true, Diane and Lisa are not habitual offenders; they pose no danger to society. They're decent women who were thrown into a hell not of their own making. But here's the thing—"

"Yo, Milano!" It's Stengel, coming through the rear doors. "You camping out or what?"

Marty turns to him and holds up his hand. "A couple minutes, Stengel, whaddya say?"

"No problem." Stengel walks past us and out the bailiff's door near the front of the room.

"Okay, what's the thing?" Marsha says.

"Diane was the shooter—" I begin.

"How do you know that?" Marty asks.

"I just know, okay? The whole thing was her idea; she thought it was the only way to save Lisa's sanity. She felt she had no choice."

Marsha mulls it over. "So?"

"So what if she was wrong?" I let that register before I continue. "What if Lisa could have been helped with the right professional care, given enough time, and then we managed to put Rosamund away on something else?"

"Maybe," Marsha says. "But what Diane did wasn't a selfish act; she had an altruistic motive. She knew what she was doing when she took her chance, and doesn't deserve to have her life destroyed."

"Oh yeah? What if she was *really* wrong? Maybe Lisa wasn't so bad off. Maybe it was really Diane who was all fucked up and she pinned it all on Lisa to excuse her own private revenge. Because just between you and me, Lisa didn't look so damned crazy to me. She was upset as hell, sure, but maybe we're not giving her enough credit."

"But how do you know that?" Marsha asks.

"I don't!" I nearly yell. "That's the whole goddamned point! *Nobody* knows, and that's why we have the law!"

Marsha thinks about it and then takes a deep breath, letting it out slowly. "I still don't believe she deserves to have her whole life wrecked. And now we're in a position to do just that."

"That's not certain," I tell her. "We've still got weaknesses in our case; we're not certain of winning."

They both see right through that. We've crafted an enormously powerful case, and we've done it without the murder weapon and without a positive ID. It'll likely get written up in the monthly journal that goes to every prosecutor in the state.

As we head back to our offices through the back halls to escape the press, Marty tries to cheer me up. He drapes an arm over my shoulder. "Wonder what Mr. Elected District Attorney Gerard Beckman is going to be feeling when he hears about this one!"

More points on the scoreboard. Whoopee for me.

21

I'm in my office with Diane, I behind my desk and she facing me in one of the visitor's chairs. The large scarf and sunglasses she wore to try to hide her face from the reporters are in her lap. Her hair is still slightly matted against her head where the silk fabric pressed in on it, but she hasn't made a move to fluff it out or even to smooth down the wrinkles in her skirt where it rides up against her thigh. She has just told me in a firm, controlled voice that she fired the gun that killed Vincent Rosamund, and also tried to tell me why.

I had no real idea of the anguish Diane and Lisa have been going through, starting with the Rosamund dismissal. Diane feared desperately for her sister, who was taking it worse than she, and felt that the only reason she herself was holding it together was for Lisa's sake. But she could also feel her own personal universe decaying under the weight of the shame and rage, and it was she who concocted the scheme to kill the cause of it all. She knew Lisa could never do the deed herself, and even doubted her own ability, but the more they talked about it the easier it seemed. That's the amazing thing about the human animal: it can get used to damned near anything if given enough time and exposure.

"Are you telling me this on the record?" I ask her.

"No. Not yet."

"Can you prove it?"

She says that witnesses at the scene could probably

corroborate a wealth of small details that didn't seem important before: did she walk around certain tables on her way to Rosamund, how long did she wait before pulling the trigger, was the light at the corner green or red when she pulled out of the handicapped spot.

Maybe. But there is really no need. My initial hunch that Diane did it is confirmed, and I have a voluntary confession from her. I ask her what she wants in exchange for signing a written version, and her answer is what I would have expected.

"I want a sentencing deal for me, and Lisa goes free. That last part's not negotiable."

Diane knows she can't let Lisa get on the stand: she'd incriminate the both of them. Diane would rather spend the rest of her life in prison than see Lisa do one day. I have to see how far I can push this.

"I can't do that, Diane. Lisa willingly participated in a murder conspiracy."

"You still have to prove that, and even if you do, you risk losing on appeal. The offer is take it or leave it."

I think about it, wondering if I have any leverage left, knowing that I'll take the deal if I don't. I really have no choice. There's a knock on the door, and Marion comes in without waiting for an answer.

"Nestor Parnell is on the line," she tells me before I can speak. "He says it's urgent."

"Tell him I'll call back."

She shakes her head. "He's insisting. No way I'm going to get him off the line."

I'm annoyed but pick up the phone and punch the lit button. "What is it, Nestor?"

I listen as he speaks. Then I put a hand over the mouthpiece and look up at Marion. "Would you take Ms. Pierman out into your office, please? Just for a second."

Diane looks at me and frowns but then gets up and goes out with Marion, who closes the door behind them.

"Give me that again," I say into the phone.

"Lisa just confessed to me that she pulled the trigger herself. She can prove it because she knows where the gun is and Diane doesn't. I'm telling you all this at Lisa's insistence, against my counsel, and it's off the record for now."

I tell him that Diane just confessed to me. I think he knew that already.

"Sal," he says, "we gotta end this."

"I agree," I tell him.

22

Santana Jamison cackles gleefully as I miss an eight-foot putt. "USA!" he calls as the ball sails past the hole, coming to rest about four feet on the other side of it. That's his favorite expression on the golf course; it's ethnic shorthand for 'You still away!' meaning your putt was so bad you're still farthest from the hole and it's your turn again.

"Christ, Sandy, give the boy a break, will ya'?" I suppose being nearly fifty years my senior gives Melvin Silver the right to refer to me as "the boy."

"You go ahead and putt, your honor," I tell Jamison. "I need to refocus here."

"What you need is lessons, son." Jamison takes his time lining up and neatly drops the two-footer in for a par, his jet black face beaming with pleasure as he looks at me to rub it in.

We're playing at Penmar, a city-owned, nine-hole course barely five minutes from my office. The average age of the players here is higher than my typical eighteen-hole score. I love playing with these guys, and I wonder if the mere passage of so many years is enough to give one a uniquely wise perspective on life. Despite a wild profusion of geriatric infirmities, they're out here all the time, trying to squeeze a few more drops out of life and enjoy their waning years. Whenever I'm convinced my own life is going down the shitter, I come out here for a few hours and regain some perspective. There is more quiet courage and tenacity continuously on display here than in any other setting I can think of.

I've learned over time not to ask questions when a regular group shows up minus a member: the answers are often too painful, not for them to say but for me to hear. It depresses me terribly to see these great old guys dropping out because they've gone into the hospital for the last time or couldn't make it out of bed or just passed away quietly in the night.

I fish Jamison's ball out of the hole for him. He's a retired superior court judge and he suffers from Parkinson's, as well as the peculiarly virulent self-centeredness that seems to inflict old men. I also tee up his ball for him at every hole, and if he hits a bad shot, it's of course my fault. When he hits it well, he'll rag on about exactly how he did it, urging me to watch him and do the same.

Melvin Silver used to be a deputy DA in the downtown office. He has macular degeneration, and there is nothing but a giant black circle in the center of his vision. He has to look about two feet behind the ball until he finds it in his peripheral vision and hit it that way. Needless to say, both Jamison and Silver trounce me with embarrassing regularity. I don't feel guilty taking the afternoon off because I've been giving them both the background on the case as we play. They'd rather lose a leg than violate a confidence so I'm safe doing that. I need to talk this over with people I trust, people not connected with what's going on.

"What do you think, Sandy?" I ask the judge as we walk to the next hole.

"You already know the answer, fool," he says to me. A Stanford-educated attorney, he likes affecting black lingo now that he's off the bench, thinks it goes well with his black golf cap with a big silver X embroidered on the front. "You just lookin' for some other fool t'tell you it's okay." He pokes the end of his putter into my shoulder, throwing me off stride for a second.

"Do what's right," Silver says as he comes up behind us, trying to wrestle his club back into the bag he's pulling on a handcart as he walks. "What, you need guys to tell you that?"

"What's right, Mel? Is that according to the ends or to the means?"

"Whatever you can live with afterwards, for the rest of your life."

Jamison nods in assent, and I look from one to the other. "That's not very helpful," I tell them, with perhaps a trace of petulance, as we reach the tee box.

Mel shrugs, the scorecard in one hand, a pencil in the other. "Whaddya want, I should give you the answer? Whadja get?"

"A six."

"A six," Jamison spits in disgust.

"What if it were you?" I ask.

"But it's not me." Mel slips the scorecard back in the plastic holder on his cart handle and starts to pull out a club. "It's you."

I can't hide my exasperation. "Yes, Mel, I *know* it's me. I understand that; I don't need you to tell me that: what I'm asking, what would *you* do!"

He stops, then leans forward to poke a finger in my chest. He's even shorter than I. "No, boychik, you really *don't* understand. What I would do is completely irrelevant. I would do what *I* could live with. You have to do what *you* could live with."

"But I don't *know* what I could live with!" I'm almost whining now. "What if I make a mistake? That's why I'm looking for guidance here. . . ."

"Listen," Mel starts to say. "Suppose—"

"Hey, will you guys get a move on!" we hear from somewhere behind us.

Jamison turns to look, and yells back, "Yo, Jimmy: watch yer damned blood pressure!"

"Never mind my blood pressure; time you guys hit the ball I could be *dead*!"

Mel laughs and shakes his head. "In his case," he says to me in a low voice, "he could be right. Now look: suppose you want to get into the sack with some nice girlie, hah? You say to me, Mel, what would you do?"

"Be a damned fool, he asked *you* that question," Jamison mumbles as he heads for the tee box. He hands me a ball and I tee it up for him, making sure the height is

perfect and the label is facing just the way he likes it
before I step back to let him hit.

"What would you do, you ask me," Mel continues,
pausing for a second while Jamison swings. It's one of
those old man shots that galls me, no great distance but
dead straight, right in the middle of the fairway.

Mel goes on before Jamison can gloat about the shot. "I
say, Sally, what I would do, I would say to her, hey, you
play the violin? She says no, and I say, great . . . let's
shtup! When I was your age, you know what, for me that
used to work about half the time. For you?" He sizes me
up, looking from my head to my shoes and back again.
"Not a prayer." He walks to the tee box and bends to set
up his ball, then straightens up and looks at me. "You see
what I'm saying here?"

It goes on much like this for the remaining four holes,
and when we're finished and I'm forking over the fifty
cents I lost to Silver and the buck to Jamison, I say, "You
know what, Mel, you're a real pain in the ass."

"*Truth* is a pain in the ass, Sal," he says to me. "Not the
guy that tells it to you."

"You make it Saturday?" Jamison asks him.

"Yeah, but call me first, make sure I'm still alive."

The judge and I walk over to the snack bar. "You think
she'd go for it?" I ask him.

I'm referring to Judge Harriet Genet, and Jamison
shrugs, then seems to nod his head slightly, but I can't tell
for sure. "Was me," he says, thoughtfully, like he was
deciding on the spot, "I might."

It's one of the most elegant rooms I've ever been in outside of a museum. The ceiling is at least thirty feet high
and puts me in mind of an imperial ballroom or a great
European railway station. Wooden beams, intricately
carved and painted gold, divide it into about a hundred
panels, each painted in complementing mosaic designs of
muted colors. Paintings of heroic proportions hang on the
walls; there are hunting scenes, woodland motifs with
waterfalls and streams, a British castle and two portraits,
each of which seems to depict either a turn-of-the-century
corporate executive or an accountant, I can't tell which.
The walls themselves are done up in rich cherrywood

wainscoting and green baize panels, giving the whole room the atmosphere of a private billiard parlor, but in place of a table there are two leather couches, four wing chairs, several footstools and a number of antique end tables with ornately shaded lamps. There are two enormous windows on the west wall, each the size of double balcony doors, and the deep yellow light pouring in from the late afternoon sun burnishes the whole room with a soft golden glow. Dust motes hanging in the sunbeams add to the impression of quiet dignity.

The California Club in downtown Los Angeles houses a good percentage of the city's old-money power elite. I see several members I recognize pass the open doors to this private room, ranging from the pampered sons and grandsons of ancient industry tycoons to some of the tycoons themselves, teetering past on legs weak either from age or early-in-the-day imbibing, or both. I myself am not a member: not many Salvatores or Milanos on the register, or Goldbergs or Washingtons, for that matter. One month of dues would break me anyway. No, this is Parnell's club, and I'm just an invited guest on somebody else's turf.

It's just the two of us in this room. We don't want to complicate things, and we both know without having to mention it explicitly that Janine Ericsson isn't needed because her inclusion on the defense team was just a tactic to begin with. We have agreed to meet, completely off the record, with the permission of both Piermans. The judge knows we're here and didn't ask a lot of questions. Parnell and I know that, whatever we come up with, Genet won't approve it unless we address her concerns as well as our own.

Our ostensible objective is to put the bullshit aside and try to make the right thing happen, not to parry, weave and try to figure out where the other guy stands before getting down to cases. Naturally, the final decision as to a deal or continuation of the trial is up to the two women. Parnell offers me a drink or a piece of cake, and I ask only for some hot tea. I find that, in times of stress, slamming some burning liquid down my throat keeps me alert. Besides, taking a drink while negotiating with Parnell is like leaving a chamber empty in a gunfight.

Parnell is drinking grapefruit juice. "I'm comfortable with my argument against putting Lisa on the stand," he says, "despite the offer of immunity. These two cases are so tightly related . . ." He lets his voice trail off, waving a hand in the air, like the rest is obvious.

It isn't. "You're the one who's done everything humanly possible to separate the cases in the first place, Nestor. You going to tell me you hired Ericsson because of her long experience defending murder cases?"

His entire case rests on that separation, but I leave it at that. I don't point out that if his case was so strong he wouldn't be here talking to me. We both know it, we both know the other knows it, everybody who comes to a settlement discussion knows it, and rule one is, you don't mention it. If I were so confident in my own case, I wouldn't be here either. Neither wants to call the other's bluff and walk out. It's too risky either way so we play this like gentlemen.

Parnell doesn't nod or otherwise acknowledge my comment. "If Genet forces Lisa to the box, she'll stand on her Fifth Amendment rights anyway and not say a thing."

"Genet will hold her in contempt, indefinitely."

"And I'll fight like hell to get her out, and in the meantime, Genet will eventually have to release Diane for lack of evidence. Lisa is prepared to do that for her sister," he tells me without guile. "After all, she was willing to take the whole rap anyway."

There is a certain temptation here: I could threaten to keep Lisa in jail forever, undoubtedly forcing Diane to a public, formal confession to take all the blame and get her sister released.

But then Lisa would confess publicly, too, and we'd be right back at the beginning. I'd be faced with the problem of trying to exonerate one sister in order to get a murder conviction against the other, which would effectively put me in the role of defense attorney.

However, if we don't go back to court with some kind of plea agreement, I still have one trick left, and it will doom both sisters. I'm sure of it. It will secure a conviction and might set a new precedent, might even make me famous, and I decide to blow it completely by describing it to Parnell now, in detail. If he really wants to fight me, he'll know in advance what I plan to do. My divulging it to him is not an expression of good faith but an inducement to bargain.

"If we don't work something out here," I tell him, "I'm going to go back and amend the charges."

"A little late to be adding charges," he says skeptically. "Kind of gonna turn the clock back on the whole trial, I should think." He's telling me that we'd have to start all over and that usually hurts the prosecution more than the defense.

I shake my head. "I didn't say add, I said amend. As a matter of fact, I'd be withdrawing charges." Which means the trial continues without interruption. I have his attention now. "I'm going to withdraw the murder charge against Diane."

He's waiting for me to tell him I'll then lodge it against Lisa. He's praying for it. It would make me look a total idiot, switching gears like that in the middle of a trial.

"I'll leave both sisters equally charged with conspiracy, obstruction of justice and criminal solicitation," I tell him instead. "I'll then move to combine both cases into a single trial, with both sisters acting as a single defendant, a common unit, two people acting in concert even though they might have had separate jobs to do."

I tell him that I think the law will accommodate the inescapable logic that says that it doesn't matter for these amended charges who pulled the trigger, that they are equally culpable. "I believe I can prove beyond a reasonable doubt that Diane and Lisa conspired to kill Rosamund, one of them had to have done the shooting, and they both acted to cover it up."

I have to hand it to Parnell; he's keeping his features impassive, just rubbing a cheek with one finger as he listens. "What about the confessions?" he asks me when I reach a pause.

"Neither will hold up," I answer. "The details Diane claims to know from the scene can't be definitively proven, and just because Lisa was tasked with disposing of the gun doesn't mean she was the killer. But think about this." I take a sip of tea, now grown cold. "They both offered to confess, and I can use that to demonstrate that there was a conspiracy."

"Those were both off the record," Parnell reminds me, even though we both know that concept doesn't apply here, but there is no need to get into it with him.

"True. But they'd both put them on the record if they each thought it would get the other off."

"They won't stick."

"They won't have to, not if the murder charge is gone, remember? All I care about is the conspiracy. The evidence is so compelling that no jury in the world is going to believe that one of them didn't do it, nor will they believe she acted alone. And if I don't care which one was the shooter, I'll convict them both."

He knows I'm right and elects not to belabor the point. "Would you truly be satisfied without a murder conviction?"

I wouldn't give a damn if they both went free. I'd trust either one of them to baby-sit for my kids, if I had any. They're not criminal personalities, social misfits, or threats to society. They're the worst of all victims, innocents who believed, however arguably, that their lives lay in ruins and who were left without a means of restitution. My problem is a larger one than just these two people: if they get off, it will send a message throughout the judicial system that there is a case to be made for private revenge, where revenge is rightly the province of the state.

"Do you look at criminal justice as revenge?" Parnell asks me wryly.

"The return of a little righteous anger to the process might be helpful," I tell him. "I'm frankly sick to death of guys like you screaming for a chance for rehabilitation of clients with rap sheets running to fifteen pages."

"Sounds like a helluva campaign speech, Sal." His hinting that my zeal is politically rather than philosophically motivated brings me up short, but he moves past it smoothly. "What kind of a message do you think Rosamund's dismissal sent throughout the system?"

"That dismissal was a crime in itself. You know; you were there."

"You think it was right that one flick of a judge's gavel exonerates an evil pig like Vincent Rosamund?"

"Are you kidding here or what, Nestor? Off the record,

just you and me, are you seriously making the case for justifiable homicide?"

He looks at me for a moment, then takes a deep breath and rubs his eyes. "No, of course not." It's an honorable answer. He takes his hands away from his face and drops them in his lap. He suddenly looks very tired, and his fatigue mirrors my own. "What do you want, Sal?"

"Who pulled the trigger, Nestor?"

"I don't know."

I believe him. I don't bother to point out to him that he hasn't denied that one of them did. We're off the record and neither one of us is stupid.

"What do you want?" he asks me again. It's time to get down to business.

"They need to do time," I tell him. "At least ten years each."

This doesn't seem to surprise him. "What are you prepared to offer if they identify the shooter?"

"I don't care who the shooter was." *This* surprises him. "It's of no consequence. Hell, it was probably a coin toss anyway. Besides, under California law, it's irrelevant." An aider, abettor or conspirator is just as guilty as the triggerman. The only reason we cared about the shooter's identity during trial was because we thought it would be impossible to get a conviction without showing who pulled the trigger. But that's not an issue anymore, not with the new strategy of convicting them both on lesser charges. I wonder to myself if the real truth is that I just don't want it confirmed to be Diane, as I think it was: I find the tiny doubt comforting, like a firing squad rifleman who hopes that it was his weapon that held the traditional blank cartridge. "What I want is to make sure this case doesn't become the model for a perfect crime and to make sure a felony doesn't go unpunished. And that's what I think Genet wants." It has nothing to do with Vincent Rosamund. As far as I'm concerned, he got what he deserved. I don't mention this to Parnell. There is? no need.

"Would you settle for five years?" he asks. We both know that would put them out in three. I'm trying hard to suppress the image of these two beautiful, fiercely independent daughters of hopeful political refugees locked away for three years, because if I give vent to it I'm afraid I might do something I'll regret forever.

"I'll accept five years," I tell Parnell.

"How do we handle it?"

"They both plead *nolo* to conspiracy and obstruction of justice." *Nolo contendere*—literally, *no contest*—means that they're willing to accept the consequences of a guilty plea but without admitting anything. "The deal would be final. The offer of immunity to Lisa is hereby withdrawn."

"If the time is minimum security," he says, "we have a deal."

"You haven't conferred with your clients yet."

"It won't be a problem."

"You absolutely sure?"

"I guarantee it."

I nod thoughtfully and wait a few seconds. "I don't want the deal," I finally tell him.

Parnell's eyebrows rise up in shock, and the beginning of a snarl appears on his face. I hold up my hands and tell him to stay calm. "I just wanted to see how far you'd go, so I know what I'm dealing with. I have an idea I'd like you to listen to."

He's still glaring at me but he's listening. "Look," I press him, "I just told you how I could nail them both by dropping the murder charge"—he answers with a barely perceptible nod—"and you're sitting there thinking I could have done that days ago, and I didn't. You and I both know that. But I didn't, and you don't have any idea why." He nods again. "So why don't you just listen to me for a few more minutes, okay?"

I just did away with all the gentlemanly pretense since we now agree that I could convict both his clients in an eye blink. He admitted it by agreeing to a plea bargain. I did it to make sure I have the upper hand, not because I want to continue the trial. But I have to admit to myself, it feels pretty good.

I wait until he sits back and takes another sip of his juice, and then I lay it all out for him, slowly and methodically. He has no trouble following any of it.

"You think Genet'll buy it?" he asks me when I finish.

"I think so."

"How can you set it up so I don't get blindsided?"

"There's still one more element left," I assure him, "and it might be a long shot, but here's the point: no matter what happens, it'll never be worse than the five years each you were willing to give, so you have no reason not to trust me."

Now he understands why I behaved like a rug merchant, seeming to go back on a plea-and-sentencing deal in midstride. He thinks about it, then holds out his hand, and I shake it.

"Can I order up some cigars and brandy?" he asks. "To seal the deal?"

For the first time in years I don't cherish the thought of a good cigar, which in this place would likely be a Havana. Something tells me I wouldn't enjoy it.

"Can I just sit here for a while?"

"Certainly." He stands up and buttons his jacket. "I'll phone Genet and set up a meeting for tomorrow morning."

I nod my agreement, and he leaves. I motion to a passing steward for a phone and try to reach Marsha and Marty, but I can't get either of them.

23

Harriet Genet bangs the gavel and court is called to order. Marsha is looking at me strangely; I never did get a chance to brief her, and it's just as well, because I don't need that kind of scrutiny right now. It isn't every day that a man gets to compromise a handful of his most dearly held beliefs, knowing he is going to spend the rest of his life doubting himself. And for someone like me, who enjoys mouthing off about what's right and wrong, it's a double damnation.

Parnell is standing up, addressing the judge. "Your honor, in light of the amended complaint filed by the prosecution, defense hereby waives its right to a trial by jury and requests that the court hear and decide the case pending before it."

"Co-counsel agree?" Genet asks Ericsson.

Ericsson throws me an angry look. She didn't like Parnell working out a deal without her involvement, and I don't blame her: for someone who started out as window dressing, she acquitted herself well. "Agreed," she says eventually.

"People?"

"People are agreeable," I say without standing. I told Eleanor Torjan this was going to be happening minutes before court began. I said that Genet was honorable and decent and knows the law. She'll decide the case herself, and it will have the weight of a jury verdict behind it.

Genet turns to the jury, folds her arms and gives them

all her attention as she speaks. "Ladies and gentlemen, at times, and for good and valid reasons, certain things occur outside of the presence of the jurors which make it impractical or inappropriate to proceed with a jury trial. Unfortunately, I am forbidden to mention any of those reasons at this time, but trust me that most all of such circumstances are for good and just cause and in the interests of justice. This is one of those cases." She straightens up and picks up her pen, tapping it on the writing pad in front of her. "You are all dismissed, with the thanks of the court."

Most of them look stunned and confused as the bailiff leads them out of the box and out of the room. "Somebody want to motion for a mistrial?" Genet asks.

Parnell, who is still standing, says, "Defense so moves, your honor."

"Granted. Retrial is scheduled for tomorrow morning."

I stand up and make a motion to readmit all of the evidence and testimony from the first trial into the new trial. It will effectively pick up right where this one left off. Parnell and Ericsson agree.

"So ordered," Genet says. "Court is adjourned."

The reporters are all over us the instant we're out the door. Parnell and I give similar statements to the press, that both sides agreed that the issues here are too complex to be left to a lay jury, and so we're going to let the judge be the jury. Eleanor is long gone: I gave her all this before court and she's already off filing it. I think she and I are square now.

That's all the reporters can squeeze out of me, now and for the rest of the day. As he promised, Parnell also stays mum except for the comments we agreed upon in advance.

The next morning we're back for the start of the new trial. Genet bids me to call my next witness. I rise and say, "People rest, your honor."

"Mr. Parnell?"

"Defense rests, your honor."

"Ms. Ericsson?"

She says the same, albeit with a trace of reluctance. Genet stands and gathers up some loose papers, a notebook and two law books. "Court is recessed while I contemplate my verdict." She picks up the gavel, awkwardly balancing everything else in her other arm, and bangs the little pad twice, then turns and walks out the door behind the bench.

As soon as she's gone, the room bursts into excited chattering, people out of their seats and trying to get to us in the front. Bailiff Stengel and two of his people hold them back. Diane and Lisa sit still, looking straight ahead and trying to ignore the crowd. "Hey, it's still a courtroom!" I hear Stengel yell angrily at some particularly aggressive people in the first row.

Less than ten minutes later, Genet comes back through the door and resumes her seat. When everyone is settled down, she says, "Defendants please rise." Diane and Lisa get shakily to their feet.

"Court finds both defendants guilty as charged," Genet says, and she's slamming her gavel down to silence the room almost before she's finished. Another second later and Parnell is on his feet moving for an OR release pending preparation of an appeal. It is a ridiculous request.

"Defendants are released on their own recognizance pending appeal," Genet agrees.

Marsha looks at me with so many conflicting emotions crossing her face I can't begin to sort them out. Marty is walking briskly up the side aisle, elbowing his way past the crowd, flashing his badge. Reporters are shouting questions at me: How did I get a conviction without a deal? How'd I know the judge would rule my way? I try to answer with the standard, meaningless demurrals, but they're insistent: they didn't sit through this whole trial just to be shrugged off when the good stuff came.

"You gonna run for DA?" one shouts above the others, who quiet down for a moment so they can hear my answer. I turn without answering, just as Marty makes it to our table.

"That's it?" he asks. "It's over?"

Marsha nods. "Not with a bang," she says, still frowning at me, "but a whimper."

Not quite, I think to myself.

24

I'm driving out of town, alone in the car, with nothing to divert me from my thoughts. There has been a great public outcry, that justice was not done, that the twins did not deserve a conviction, that the defense rolled over too easily, etc. I may not be popular, but I am clean, having stood behind the courage of my convictions. I have been stoic amid the barrage from the likes of Ernestine Denier and come off well in the press. A half dozen of the politicos who abandoned me following the Rosamund fiasco have crawled back into my life urging me to run, promising me support and money. DA Gerard Beckman has been unavailable for comment since the trial ended. It's time for me to indulge my ambition.

I turned off Highway 99 a little while ago and am now heading northeast toward Breckenridge Mountain. The dusty road runs along the Kern River for a few miles before gaining altitude. It's hot out and the shimmering waters of the slowly moving river look cool and inviting. I haven't seen another car for several minutes.

The café is less seedy than I'd imagined, housed in a two-story detached building of boxlike construction with no architectural pretensions. People assume that drug tycoons always wallow in opulent luxury but this is not so. The smarter ones keep their business venues purpose-fully nondescript: the idea is to make money, not flaunt it, at least not to the general public. In this business, where ego is a bigger killer than federal authorities or rival out-fits, you keep your toys at home, preferably in another country.

I walk in as casually as I can, fighting my fear. I don't know what the man I'm supposed to meet looks like. I look around, head for the bar, and order a tequila on ice. There are no menus available although there is a liquor license on display. The establishment is legitimate, but I know that the food served to ordinary citizens is unpalat-able, the bar service despicable. This discourages them from patronizing the place, which is the whole idea. It's not meant to be a money-making venture. Nevertheless, being a roadside establishment, it's always going to have customers, even if they are always new ones and few ever return.

There are four other men at the bar. One sits in a long raincoat despite the heat, nursing a beer. He is so out of it he doesn't even look at me. Another seems a bit more alert, but his ignorance of me has more to do with derision than disinterest. He wears a black leather motorcycle jacket and studded boots. The other two look like businessmen, maybe in sales, who are on their way somewhere and need a few pops to get their engines moving.

The men I can see at the tables on the other side of the bar and in my peripheral vision look like they'd rather not be noticed. The thugs are obvious; three of them, at three separate tables, eyeing me warily and shifting their shoul-ders to let me know they are armed.

The bartender serves me without a word and refuses my money. He points to somewhere behind me and I turn to look. There is a well-dressed man sitting alone in a booth, mid-to-late thirties, lighter in complexion than I would have imagined. He is wearing sunglasses despite the dim lighting. There is nothing on the table before him but a pack of Gauloises cigarettes and a lighter, large and heavy and gold, probably a Dunhill. He is smoking a cigarette, doing his best to look bored, staring straight ahead as though unmindful of me. A fourth thug is at the next table, sitting alone. I turn back to the bartender, who nods at me; I pick up the tequila and head for the table.

* * *

"Sly?"

His name is Sylvester Pontanegro, but I am told that if you call him by his full first name, you are likely to receive the same reaction as calling Benjamin Siegel "Bugsy."

He looks up slowly and gives me a crooked grin that is supposed to appear street-confident and snappy. "Mr. District Attorney," he slurs out lazily. "A pleasure." He holds out a hand, the fingers limp. It is like shaking hands with a dead fish but the message is clear: he has no need to engage in such immature and unproductive displays of manliness as a firm shake. Pontanegro's power is deeply entrenched and untouchable. This is what I am supposed to think. He points to the opposite side of the table and motions me to sit. An unspoken command. Another display of power.

"I appreciate your taking the time to see me," I say politely, and he waves it off magnanimously, as though he is the one inconvenienced despite my two hours on the road to get here. All four of his goons have their eyes on me now. It's important that I play his game, make him look good in front of his men. A district attorney traveling all this way to see him, coming to his bar, being deferential: if there is a gap in this display, he may feel the need to fill it in some unpleasant way and I don't need that. I'll do what it takes to get what I came for.

"I see you have a drink," he says softly, making me strain to hear him. "Something else, perhaps? Have you had lunch?"

"No, nothing else, thanks. I don't have much time."

Pontanegro nods knowingly. "Of course. You have to get back to the office. I understand." He understands that I'm a working stiff, further underscoring the gulf between our stations. He stays silent, not bidding me to speak, making me make the first move.

"Our mutual friend—" I begin, pausing for a second to see if there is a question. There isn't. "Our friend tells me we might be of some benefit to each other." He purses his lips but still says nothing. "That we might be able to do a few things for each other."

Pontanegro takes a long drag of the powerful cigarette—

is he telling me he is contemptuous even of death?—
and says, "Such as?" through a thick stream of grayish
smoke.

"I need a few things, you need a few things . . ." I make
some back and forth motions with my hands. I'd kill for a
good cigar right now.

Pontanegro fixes me with what is supposed to be a
steely gaze. "What could you possibly want from me?"

I lick my lips and look up to see the goon at the table
behind Pontanegro, and then I lean forward and lower my
voice. "What I want, Sly, is to be district attorney of LA
County. Not a deputy. I want to be the man."

He raises one eyebrow, the first overt sign that he is
even remotely interested in what I have to say. "That's an
elected position. You want me to rig an election?"

It's a loaded question. There is no way he can do that.
Maybe his boss can, but he can't. If I tell him that, the
poke at his vanity will elicit an unproductive reaction.
"No, I don't want you to do that. It's too risky, too
obvious. Besides, I don't want that big a debt."

He smiles and nods his head in appreciation of my
savvy, and of my growing credibility in his eyes. He sees
that I'm cautious, not blundering, and not so stupid or
grasping that I'm willing to hand him my life. There is an
alternative, a narrower bargain, and now he's intrigued.
"Something less," he cues me to continue.

"Something less. A few things here and there, over
time. Tell you the truth, I'm not sure it can be done." I
state it in the passive grammatical voice, careful not to
say I don't think *he* is capable.

His eyes narrow at the clear challenge. "What?"

"I'm a good attorney," I tell him. "Damned good, in
fact. I win most of them—"

"But you also get to choose which cases you handle,
right?" he interrupts me for the first time. I show some
surprise, not only at his understanding of the workings of
our office, but that he knows I'm the head deputy who
assigns the cases. This seems to please him, as though it
hints of some great, dark personal intelligence organization which he controls. The truth is that habitual criminals
know the justice system like the chronically ill know
hospitals.

"That's true, but it isn't like I get to toss anything that looks hard. My boss would have my ass if the citizens didn't lynch me first." He likes my use of the word "citizens." It's the same one used in his outfit to refer to the great unwashed that constitute his customer base, ordinary people above whom he feels himself several atmospheric layers. I hope this makes him think that I might be a kindred spirit in my contempt for the masses.

"Okay, so you're a good lawyer." He lifts his eyebrows and turns up a palm: *so what?*

"So I deserve to be the goddamned DA. My boss is a fucking idiot, a political hack, barely knows which end is up in a trial." I get a little heated up now, more animated and angry. "A week doesn't go by I don't cover for him a dozen times. Like yesterday, he says—"

Pontanegro has held up a hand, and I skid to a halt. He waits, testing my respect, takes another hit off the Gauloises. "I don't give a shit why, Milano. That's your business. I asked you, what do you want." A mild rebuke.

I nod, accepting the reprimand with deferential humility. "Once in a while we get a case, a big one. Very public. Career makers, we call them. Usually, they're close calls, can go either way. The easy ones, nobody says you did a good job, but win a big one, stuff starts to happen. You see what I mean?"

"Of course." It's the same in his own business.

"So, like I said, they can go either way. Sometimes, it's just a question of getting the judge on your side, throw the rulings your way. Smart judge can manipulate things; you wouldn't believe it."

"Yes, I would," he says meaningfully. *If you can't find a lawyer who knows the law, find one who knows the judge.*

"Now"—I hunch closer—"what I hear, you can make things happen. . . ."

"Things . . ." It's a prompt, not an agreement or a question.

I'm in for good now. Cards on the table. "You can get to judges, right? Certain judges. Who knows, maybe even juries." I hold up my hands quickly. "I don't want to know, okay? All I'm saying, you're in a position, you could do me some good now and again. Not often. Only when I smell something going bad."

He hesitates for a painfully long time. "And?"

"And, enough of them go my way, I pick 'em right, maybe for Gerard Beckman they don't go so right . . . and I'm the new DA."

Pontanegro waves the cigarette impatiently. "I told you, I don't give a shit what you do with it. What I'm asking, what's my end? So far your piece of the bargain is all I'm hearing."

"You're telling me you can do what I want done, just like that?"

"I'm telling you nothing. We're just talking."

"Okay. Okay." I nervously run a hand through my hair, hitch my shoulders and lean forward again. Pontanegro pulls away from me slightly, as though reluctant to breathe the same air as I do. "Sometimes you need something, too, am I right? You don't have it all sewn up, people everywhere. Sometimes, maybe you need it to look real good, so nobody gets suspicious." We both know that an enormous amount of Pontanegro's street work happens within my jurisdiction. It is my belief, based on Marty McConagle's investigation, that my people have prosecuted at least twenty-seven members of his organization and won a goodly number.

"Like what?" The cigarette is motionless in his hand, the burning tip only millimeters away from the filterless end in his fingers. I'm getting to him.

"Like a plea bargain you may not have been able to get otherwise. Like a junior space cadet deputy DA getting lost in technicalities your hotshot defense attorneys can jump all over. Halfhearted bail requests. Cases thrown out for lack of evidence." It's specific enough that he knows I'm serious and I can do it. But I also need to stay credible and not go overboard. "Not every time. Not even often, only every once in a while, when you need it badly, and only if I think it's safe. That's gonna be my call, without argument." This last is pure nonsense, a bravado show. Once he has me, I'm his.

For the first time, he nods and shows some real interest. "I could maybe use some of that."

Sure. Like Popeye could maybe use a little spinach. How many of his buddies have a head deputy DA in their pocket? "Yeah, well, I told you what I can do. And we both know I can do it because we already know what I do for a living. Now: how do I know what you can do?"

"Because I tell you I can. That's good enough." He feels the heat from the cigarette and drops it quickly into the ashtray, hoping I didn't see him start to get burned, to lose his poise. I'm becoming sensitive to where the outside of the envelope is.

"Bullshit." I lean back and let him think about that one. No way is he going to strong-arm me now. I'm the most valuable possibility to plunk itself down in front of him in a long while. The temptation is too great for him to blow this by a macho show of force. "I gotta know what you can do or I'm out of here." I wave a hand indicating the various pieces of beef scattered throughout the room. "And don't tell me your monkeys are gonna fuck with a district attorney if I decide to leave." The monkey at the table behind Pontanegro clearly doesn't like this.

Pontanegro waits, apparently getting a grip on his temper until he's sure his voice will be steady, and he smiles, spreading his hands expansively. "Whaddya gettin' so hot for? Jesus Christ, relax a little." He makes a hand signal to the bartender, pointing to my drink. "You drove all the way up here, what, to get me angry, to insult me? Is that why we're here?"

This reference to an insult is something he must have picked up from one too many mob movies. I'm supposed to think that's the worst thing in the world I can do to him, insult him, and that he would rather kill me on the spot than let it go. Now I'm supposed to help him save face so we can continue, which is all right, the both of us having set our boundaries. "No. No insult intended. Just a little nervous, okay, being here like this. With you, I mean." That's part of the trouble with these nouveau wiseguys, these drug-pushing street rats who got too rich too quick and didn't learn the right way to behave from their elders. Everything they know they learned from the movies.

"It's finished." He reaches out his hand, granting me

absolution with another mackerel handshake, and I take it. The bartender arrives with a fresh tequila for me and an espresso for Pontanegro. Another Sicilian affectation, as if we were in a social club on Mulberry Street in lower Manhattan rather than a dusty roadside bar in Bakersfield. "You want to know, what can I do for you, am I right?"

"Right." I take a long hit from my glass. It's two o'clock in the afternoon. I can't remember the last time I had a drink during a working day. Maybe never.

Pontanegro stares at me intently, evaluating the risks, savoring the upside. He takes a sip of his inky espresso. "You mind taking a little trip into the back room with Bornejo here?" He jerks a thumb at the table behind him, and I look to see the beginnings of an unpleasant smile on the thug's face.

"No problem," I answer, and rise voluntarily.

Bornejo leads the way through a door to the left of two others labeled DUDES and DAMES. It's a small supply room, reeking of stale beer from old broken kegs and bottles. Bornejo twirls his forefinger in the air and I turn around, raising my arms up above my head. He taps me on the shoulder without otherwise patting me down, and when I turn back to face him, he says, "Gimme your clothes."

I hesitate, but there's no turning back, and quickly strip down to my briefs. "Everything?" I ask.

"Everything." He watches me carefully, professionally, waiting until I'm buck naked, my clothes on a shelf at his side. Then he says, "Now you can turn around."

It is supremely humiliating, maybe for him as well as me, but he doesn't show it. He is methodical in his examination of every orifice and crevice, but also noninvasive. There is, it seems, a limit even to Pontanegro's paranoia. For some ridiculous reason I wish I weighed fifteen pounds less.

The clothes are next, not a square inch left unexamined. Perhaps as some small revenge for my monkey remark, he returns each item to the shelf rather than let me put it back on. He also sees fit to take the two Macanudo cigars out of my jacket pocket, remove them from the metal tubes and break them in half, crumbling the tobacco onto the floor, which is cold and sticky against my bare feet. There is no malice in this action—it's a common place to hide a listening device. All in all, we're in there about ten minutes. Any earlier trace of bravado on my part is gone in the face of my total vulnerability. Soon, he finishes tapping my left shoe and twisting the heel, throws it at my feet, and opens the door, wide, so I am partially visible from the near side of the bar. "Get dressed," he says, closing the door behind him.

I put everything back on hurriedly. There's no mirror, so I put my tie in my pocket before walking out, chin high, trying to recapture some self-respect, like I know this is standard operating procedure and am cool with it. There's a fresh drink at my place, and I try not to reach for it as I sit down.

"Sorry about that," Pontanegro says solicitously. "A necessary precaution."

"No problem."

"What do you want to know?"

Now I reach for a drink and take a relaxed sip. "Who's in your pocket? What can I count on?"

Pontanegro waits for a moment and then waves Bornejo away. "Hey," I call out, and he turns to me. "No hard feelings, okay?"

Bornejo looks at Pontanegro, who dips his head slightly, then looks back at me and touches two fingers to his temple before heading for the bar. Pontanegro and I are alone.

"Arigga you already know about. That's why you're here, right?" He waits for an answering nod from me. "Tough, though, not a volunteer."

"What do you mean, not a volunteer?" I know exactly what he means.

"We tried to buy him, but he's got some kind of plum up his ass, this integrity bullshit. What, he didn't tell you anything?"

"Not much. We're not exactly buddies."

"I bet," he snickers, reaching for his pack of cigarettes. "So how come he sets you up with me?"

"The hell should I know?" I think for a second. "Maybe he figures, he does you this favor, you'll get off his back."

He laughs loudly, causing several heads to turn. "Stupid bastard! Doesn't he know what you want? That I'm gonna need him to give it to you?"

"Didn't see any need to tell him."

Pontanegro is smiling, shaking his head. "A complicated world, no?"

I nod, like it was a profound observation, the wisdom that comes with power. "I had a feeling that Vincent Rosamund had more going for him than a good lawyer."

"You bet your ass. He had me. The kid was as good as dead and he walked." He puts the cigarette to his lips and speaks around it. "Dumb asshole's dead anyway."

"But if Arigga wasn't paid . . . ?" I leave the question in the air.

Pontanegro, forgoing the expensive lighter, strikes a match and touches it to the tip of the Gauloises, sucking the flame into the tobacco. He flicks the match out with a fingernail. "There's ways."

"What ways?"

"The fuck difference does it make?"

"It makes a lot of difference. I know these guys better than you. I work with them every day. I gotta know what can be done and what the risks are."

Pontanegro sees the truth in this. "Arigga's got a daughter. Beautiful thing, an only child. Maybe he don't think his own life is worth shit, but his kid?" He purses his lips and shrugs a shoulder. "We snatch the little poon and give her a ride to Daddy's house. We don't hurt her, just let him know we can. Bornejo over there, he takes out his wang in the car and waves it at her, she's hysterical— *boom:* the judge is mine. Hadda go one step better than a photo."

I try to keep my voice calm, but it isn't easy. Maybe that's okay: in Pontanegro's eyes *I'm* a citizen and not expected to absorb this kind of thing easily. He seems to get off on my discomfort. "What photo?" I ask.

"The other time, with Rosamund. We took a picture of the daughter, messed it up a little and showed it to him. Told him next time it wouldn't be just a picture."

"What are you talking about, Rosamund."

He looks at me with a frown. "When Arigga was here in Kern County?" I shake my head. "The first time the little prick was picked up for rape," he says. "Arigga was the judge. That's how we became such good friends." He takes another hit off the cigarette. "Imagine that *culo* thinking he could move away and get rid of me. Pissed me off. I was almost glad when Vinny did it again, so I could show the great judge who he was fucking with."

I'm having trouble speaking. "Was that the first time? I mean, since he moved?"

"Nah. Was a small matter a while back. One of my people handled it, but it was a close one so Arigga didn't raise much of a fuss. Somebody ratted out a newcomer . . ."

"Friehling," I say, half to myself.

"What?"

"Peter Friehling. That was the case Arigga threw out for you, wasn't it?"

"Yeah! How'd you know that?" It was the case I prosecuted that Diane Pierman defended. The memory of my shock and her embarrassment when Arigga dismissed it come flooding back to me.

"It was one of mine."

Pontanegro lets that sink in and then laughs loudly again, genuinely this time, reaching across the table to slap my arm. "Holy shit, you imagine that? I like this, you know? You seen me at work! It's like, uh, like a reference, right? A sample of the goods!" He laughs again, getting more and more relaxed in my presence.

I shake my head ruefully, the painful reminiscence evident on my face.

"Hey, don't take it so hard," he says expansively. "Now you're on the right side. My side. Soon, you're fartin' in silk."

I take another long slug of the tequila and smile weakly, showing him that he's winning me over. Another thought has occurred to me: "Anybody else into Arigga? Besides you?"

He tilts his head slightly. "Maybe a couple guys. Not important."

It all makes sense. Arigga's "periods of irrationality" Parnell told me about, the ones that always worked in favor of the accused. Pontanegro may have played hardball with him, but I now suspect that it was because he already knew Arigga was dirty. Makes me feel less guilty about destroying the good judge's career.

"Who else?" I say.

Now he's anxious to brag. "Ravensburg."

That figures. Stanwell Ravensburg was an awful judge to begin with, the spoiled son of the biggest land speculator in Ventura County, elevated to the bench in a series of backroom deals involving his endorsement of a county supervisor and his father's investments in at least three failed S & Ls that I know of. "A volunteer?"

Pontanegro nods. "Too good. Sonofabitch's got no sense of proportion. Greedy type, gonna get us all in trouble some day."

I ask him about a few other judges, starting with Harriet Genet. I know with a deep conviction that she's clean, and Pontanegro doesn't disappoint me.

"The fucking Virgin Mary," he says. "Forget about it. Best we can do, get Arigga to switch some cases to somebody else, like Ravensburg. That's gonna come outta your end, though."

I ask him what he means.

"Means you gotta pay him off. Or at least come up with the dough and we'll get it to him."

"No way."

"Whaddya mean, no way? You want me to pay your bills on top of everything?"

"That's it. Or else there's no deal."

Pontanegro is enjoying this. Me, too. *I* like it because we're on the same side now, just getting down to details. He's starting to trust me. *He* likes it because his need to prove himself to me is behind us now, and we're just feeling out the possibilities. He's also just scored big in the negotiation because if he makes payoffs out of his own pocket, it only increases the depth of my indebtedness. He thinks I don't realize this yet, that he'll spring it on me later when it's too late to turn back. As if that mattered. Once we do a first deal, I'm sunk anyway. We silently agree to drop it for the time being.

"What about Tsielonek?" I ask about a judge I have long suspected.

Pontanegro shakes his head. "He's one of Sappo Pestovic's. Locked up tighter than a safe." This unnerves me but I try to hide it. Pestovic is a shadowy figure in organized crime, rumored to be Ukrainian, but that outfit has traditionally operated out of New York. I don't let on that I'm out of the loop on this one. I decide to press my luck.

"How'd you get to Terhovian?"

"Who?"

"Gus Terhovian, the guy that defended Rosamund."

A funny expression crosses his face. "What's that got to do with anything? You want juice with other lawyers, too?"

"I'm just asking." I don't like the look on his face at all. "Why'd you go so far for Rosamund anyway? He wasn't a heavy player."

He keeps looking at me. "Vinny was a lowlife scumbag," he says, finally, and I breathe a sigh of relief that he has forgotten my question about Terhovian, although I still want to know.

Yesterday I confronted Arigga, and he told me the story of what Pontanegro had done to his daughter. He was terrified, and his hands shook uncontrollably as he spoke. He told me that when Vincent Rosamund was arrested, Pontanegro came to him and told him to assign himself the case. Arigga told him he couldn't possibly get away with anything this blatant. So Pontanegro asked him who the best defense attorney in town was, and Arigga told him Gustave Terhovian, who eventually latched on to Rosamund's savvy in leaving no physical evidence and engineered a dismissal that was highly questionable but not so absurd as to warrant a full-scale investigation. Arigga didn't know how they got to Terhovian in the first place, got him to take the case and agree to a risky fix, and now I might never know, because Terhovian took an overdose of sleeping pills and died two days after Genet found the Piermans guilty. I told Arigga that if he didn't cooperate with me, give me the people who threatened him, I would put him away forever and go after his daughter, too, for conspiracy to obstruct justice and failure to report a crime. He said he was too afraid that he would be killed. I told him that this was certainly a possibility but that I was just as worthy of his fear. If I could put those people away he might be safe, but if he didn't talk to me, then for damned certain I was going after him and I would take him down. Which is how I got the meeting with Pontanegro.

Figuring out that Arigga's decision in the Rosamund case was rigged wasn't hard, not once I gave full rein to the possibility and started fitting the pieces into place. It's why he maneuvered to get himself appointed as the trial judge in the first place. Terhovian didn't make any motions in municipal court because he was waiting to get to superior, where he knew Arigga would be sitting, and he didn't have any jury selection consultants because you don't need good jurors when the outcome is a foregone conclusion. It also explains why he was so uninterested during jury selection: he knew the jury wouldn't be deciding the case; Arigga would.

Part of the tip-off came from the little *ex parte* conversation Arigga and Terhovian were having when I first walked into chambers. Arigga said they were "shooting the shit" after not having seen each other for months, but I checked the court records: Terhovian had argued a parole case in front of Arigga not two weeks before. It also explains why they were both so agreeable to my request to keep a low media profile for the Rosamund case, like they were doing me a big favor, when all they were doing was helping themselves to hide the fix. Terhovian then decided to switch gears and advance that cause by making his inflammatory statements to the press. It was to protect Arigga, planting the notion that a dismissal of all charges was the only rational outcome for the lamentably ill-considered prosecution of his client, Vincent Rosamund. It was supposed to make Arigga seem compassionate rather than crooked when he refused to allow us to file an emergency appeal and threw the case out instead.

Making the connection to Pontanegro was easy. Marty eventually tracked down the source of Rosamund's bond collateral, which was a mansion in Palm Springs, owned for the record by a low-level employee of an import-export business being run by a retired attorney who really occupied the house. Principal shareholder in the business: Sylvester Pontanegro. I threw the name at Arigga, told him I knew Pontanegro was behind the fix, and asked him if I should call the police to come and arrest him, as well as his daughter, or would he just like to talk to me and set up this meeting. To help him make up his mind, I showed him a copy of Rosamund's rap sheet, the one that Marty had turned up in Kern County, the one with missing charges. I pointed to the "CA" code next to the entries and asked him if they stood for Constantin Arigga, the judge who dismissed the charges.

Pontanegro is still talking about Vincent Rosamund. "Had a temper, I'm tellin' you, he could take your fuckin' head off with a penknife. But slowlike, you know? Step by step. It wasn't like he got mad and lit out after you. He got quiet, intense . . ." He gropes for a description. "He got evil. Yeah, that's it. Forgot about business, just about hurting somebody. Not that I'm saying that's bad necessarily. But you should only do it for business." He pauses to stir his espresso. "Like if you need to make a point." He looks hard at me as he says this. The beginning of the tutorial phase of our relationship.

"Sounds more like a liability than an asset."

"Yeah, but." He stops stirring. "Vinny would do anything to get ahead in the organization, and I mean anything. Pulled off jobs, man, I'm tellin' you—" He held up a hand and shook it back and forth. "Nobody else with that kind of *cojones*. And he was smart. Junkie-smart. Could think fast and make shit up on the spot. Long as you could control him, he could get things done. I knew someday I was gonna lose him." He puts down the little silver spoon. "Too bad it hadda happen so soon. But while he was alive, I had to go balls to the wall to protect him. My people knew he took chances for us. Woulda looked bad, I leave him hangin' out to dry." He fixes me with what he supposes is a stare fraught with meaning. "I take care of my people. Period."

My curiosity is getting the better of me. "Then how come you were ready to let those women get away with killing him? The twins?"

He shrugs. "He's dead. That's the end of it. What do I need, revenge on a pair of broads?" He lifts the little cup to his lips and stops it there. "I save revenge for the competition. For business. Besides, I bet the little poons'll have lots of fun in jail."

"Prison," I say.

"Huh?" The little cup stops an inch from his mouth.

"Prison. They're not going to jail; they're going to prison."

He looks at me like I'm crazy. "What the fuck ever. Time they get out they'll be a couple of useless dykes anyway." He sips at the hot liquid.

"You really are one stupid, sorry sonofabitch, *Sylvester,*" I say easily, leaning back in my chair.

"What was that?" Pontanegro moves the cup from his mouth. "What did you say?" It is beyond his comprehension that I could have said what he thought he heard.

"What part of *stupid, sorry sonofabitch* didn't you understand?" I answer, carefully enunciating each word.

He is frozen. There are no moves in his repertoire to deal with this situation. It is utterly alien to him, like asking your first-grade teacher if she wants to step into the coat closet and do the nasty. He can't take his eyes off me. Finally he manages to croak, "The fuck are you talking about?"

"I'm talking about your career being over, Sylvester. About spending the rest of your putrid life in prison, or jail, if you prefer."

He's not quite sure what's going on, but some thawing brain cells take over, and he swings around to signal to Bornejo, who jumps up from his barstool only to bump his cheekbone into a nine-millimeter Glock being held by the leather-clad biker type. A goon from the next table leaps up with remarkable speed for a man his size, pulling a Colt revolver from inside his jacket as he rises. Just as he swings the weapon around toward me, the man in the raincoat whirls suddenly and plants the side of his fist into the goon's solar plexus, eliciting a strained *whoof*ing sound. The gun flies out of his hand and arcs in the air toward me. I duck to avoid it, but as I drop below the table and twist to the side, I see Pontanegro reaching out across the table with both hands, right toward where I had been sitting.

The gun clatters to a stop a few feet away from the table. I kick off from the side of the booth as I fall, propelling myself toward the weapon. I slap my hand down to retrieve it, and my fingers wrap neatly around the handle and trigger. I can sense a shadow looming my way and realize it's Pontanegro coming out of his seat. I pick up the gun and swing it around, bringing my left hand around and cupping it under the right, pointing it toward the shadow. I'm flat on my back now and the shadow stops moving, Pontanegro's face a scant two feet from the barrel of the revolver. I've never seen such naked hatred and rage in a man's eyes before.

I hear a loud rattling sound and somewhere in my peripheral vision I see the man in the raincoat pump a sawed-off shotgun, doing it loudly to emphasize its immediacy as well as his expertise. The two salesmen are holding semiautomatic handguns, both aimed at the remaining thugs, and six uniformed officers from the Bakersfield police department are coming into the doorway. They halt as they see me pointing the gun at Pontanegro.

This man of power is stopped dead in his tracks. All his influence, money and backup personnel are as worthless as sand in this bit of frozen time. The twenty ounces of metal I'm holding in my hand just became his entire world, the key to his mortality sitting at the base of a four-inch barrel. In the totality of his universe there is now only one question, one decision branch that counts: is this guy—meaning me—going to pull the trigger and kill him or isn't he?

That my hands are shaking badly and my breath is coming in rapid, throaty rasps only makes it worse for him. I think he suspects that I've never held a gun in my hands before and this gross inexperience scares him. My finger is on the trigger—how much more pressure would it take to fire it? I honestly don't know. I don't even know if I'm supposed to pull the hammer back first, or click off a safety device. . . .

I stare back at him and feel my breathing begin to slow down and grow steady. One squeeze of my finger and Sylvester Pontanegro is dead. Just like that. He knows it and he's motionless, scared. He has no options but to stay still until I allow him to do otherwise. I feel a tremendous sense of power pouring in from the gun, through my arm, filling me up with strength and confidence. It's a tangible, physical thing, like sex only much better, much stronger. Everybody in this entire room is waiting on me, waiting to see what I'm going to do. I've never been in such total and complete control. . . .

"Mr. Milano . . . ?" A voice from near the bar. It's asking me what I plan to do. I don't ever want to let go of this gun as long as I live. "Sal?"

Some of the uniforms at the door begin to stir. The goon on the floor, the one who used to own this gun, groans and tries to roll over onto his back. I blink, then tilt the revolver so the barrel is pointing upward slightly, aimed somewhere over Pontanegro's head. He leans back, never taking his eyes off my hand, then drops back fully against the side of the table as a hand reaches in from behind me and wraps itself slowly and gently around the gun. Reluctantly, I let my fingers loosen up and then it's gone.

Pontanegro pulls himself back up to his chair. He forces a smile and tries to make himself relax. No one has touched him yet. He jerks a thumb back over his shoulder toward the bar. "You can't be serious with this shit, Milano."

He has recovered much faster than I. I make it back to my own chair with as much dignity as I can muster. Without the Colt I'm the same person I was before, a mortal, and it feels like an empty shell. I don't speak until I'm sure I have control of my voice. "Does it look serious?"

"It looks like bullshit." He puts his hands on the table palms up, a barely perceptible note of panic in his voice. He knows I'm not suicidal, that I must have thought this through. I can practically hear the tape recorder in his head spin its reels as he replays our conversation to try to figure out what he has said to me that might be incriminating. "It's entrapment, and you know it, so what is this crap?"

"Entrapment?"

"All that bullshit about you wanting to be DA, how

we're gonna help each other, all the stuff you want me to do? You asked first, I didn't offer. You solicited me. Like askin' a hooker does she wanna do you before she asks you. Entrapment, just like that." He looks around the café. Nobody is moving. The uniforms are in position, waiting for instructions. "So why don't you get your fag-ass cops outta my place, go bother somebody else?"

I shake my head and reach into my jacket pocket for the cigars that I have momentarily forgotten lie in pieces on the supply-room floor. The leather-clad biker sees my disappointment and puts a hand inside his own jacket, pulling out an Upmann No. 2 and tossing it to me. I try to catch it lightly so it doesn't break. "Thanks," I say, with no further acknowledgment. I don't want Pontanegro to know who Marty McConagle is. Even from where he's going he might have the juice to reach out and hurt Marty, the man whose tenacious investigation led me to this café in the first place. "I don't give a rat's ass about our little deal, Sylvester." I relish the look on his face whenever I mention his full first name. I pat my pockets down looking for a cigar clipper, then give up and bite the end off.

"So then you got shit." His growing impatience with my deliberately annoying cigar dance is in his voice.

"No, what I got is you confessing to fixing judges, kidnapping, obstruction of justice, solicitation of felonious acts"—I wave a hand in the air—"couple other things I haven't thought of yet. Can I borrow this?" I reach for his Dunhill lighter without waiting for a response. "Oh, yeah, and Bornejo over there for kidnapping and sexual assault." I flip up the top on the lighter and flick the knurled cylinder on the side a few times. "For what he did to Arigga's daughter," I say around the cigar.

He laughs, or tries to, but it sounds forced and theatrical. "You fuckin' kidding me or what? You got no evidence!"

I look up at him as though surprised. "No evidence? Sure I got evidence. You just told me the whole thing. Jesus, this lighter is a piece of shit." It probably cost over a thousand dollars. I finally manage to get a flame out of it. No wonder he used a match for his own cigarette.

Pontanegro is worried now. This is more ridiculous

than it should be. "Milano. You outta your mind? It's your word against mine."

I pause in mid-light and look at him, puzzlement and concern on my face. "You mean you'd lie in court? Commit perjury?" Like it was the most horrible thing I could think of. I hear the *biker* and the two salesmen stifle giggles.

Pontanegro looks around to see if anybody else is clued in to this absurdity he's hearing. All he gets are blank faces. And I'm getting tired of toying with him. I make a hand motion to a man in a plain suit standing by the doorway. He walks up to the table and hands me a dictating machine. I hope he has picked out a good spot on the tape. Pontanegro can't take his eyes off the device as I push the slide switch into the play position.

"We snatch the little poon and give her a ride to Daddy's house." It is his voice, tinny and shot through with static because it's a copy of the master still safely out in the surveillance van. But it is unmistakable and besides, I made the recording myself, with a court order, so I can testify to it. "We don't hurt her, just let him know we can. She gets a good look at Bornejo over there, he takes out his wang in the car and waves it at her, she's hysterical—*boom:* the judge is mine." I lip-synch the word "boom" as it emerges from the little machine.

Pontanegro's eyes are frantic now, the pupils darting back and forth without seeing. Then he notices me again and leans across the table, putting his hands out toward me. Marty McConagle starts to step forward, but I hold up a hand.

"Bornejo searched you!" Pontanegro is practically screaming, tugging at my lapels and punching at my pockets. "There's no fucking wire, goddammit!"

"Easy there, Sylvester." I grab his forearms and shove him backward. He is thin, wiry, but also overcome with anxiety, and I can feel it in the tautness of his arms as he falls back heavily. "You gotta keep up with the technology." Which I am not about to share with him. My thick watch contains a thin film battery and a miniature transmitter about the size of a nickel. The strap serves as an antenna, the winding stem a highly directional microphone: very effective as long as I keep my hand on the table facing whatever it is I wish to record. The battery has remarkably high output but, as a result, only lasts about fifteen minutes. I can turn it on and off by pressing the watch face into my leg or any available surface.

Pontanegro is dead in the water. Now it's about saving face in front of his men and looking good for the bosses. "You got nothing on Bornejo. He never touched the girl."

"Doesn't have to." I take a long drag on the cigar and blow the smoke toward the ceiling. "How'd you put it, 'waving his wang at her,' or something like that? Sexual assault. Like a flasher, kind of."

"What about the other guys?"

"Concealed weapons." I wave my cigar around the room; the business types, the man in the raincoat, and Marty hold up handguns they have removed from Pontanegro's toughs.

"They got permits," Pontanegro says, like I'm supposed to release them immediately upon hearing this.

"Yeah? Let's see 'em." There are very few permits for concealed weapons issued in southern California. Even the new police chief in LA had to wait months to get one. I waggle a finger toward the door and the police and federal undercover operatives dressed in business clothes start moving everybody out. Three uniforms are on Pontanegro, pulling him to a standing position and cuffing him. He struggles briefly and the uniforms start to tighten up, but it seems to me he is trying to get to me. "Hang on a minute, guys," I say, and they reluctantly let him go and step back. He leans down to me and speaks in a whisper.

"Why the big show, Milano? You got any idea what I coulda done for you?" I don't answer right away, and he finds this encouraging as though there is maybe still some room here, some chance. "So what is it?"

"I'll tell you what it is, Sylvester." I doubt he's worth the breath but I cannot help it. "There is nothing in this whole world, nothing that I hate worse than a crooked judge. Not murderers, not pushers, not corrupt politicians, not the mob, not anything." Not even people like Pontanegro himself.

Soon after my grandmother died, quite comfortably in that beautiful room at Columbia Presbyterian arranged by

"Mikey" Prestigiacomo, men began coming into my father's bakery without buying anything. They would nod at my father without smiling, or touch a finger to their nose or hat brim, and head for one of the unused back rooms that we had hoped someday to fill with display cases for custom wedding cakes and other specialty items. Sometimes they stayed in there even after closing time, and young boys barely older than I, some of whom I recognized as dropout street punks from the neighborhood, would run in and out carrying small paper bags. The timing of this mysterious enterprise coincided with the genesis of a progressively debilitating depression in my father, though I didn't know to call it that at the time. Despite the surprising, post-embargo reappearance of real Havana cigars in our house, his anxiety and general apprehension increased as the quiet men came more and more often, and his irritability with his family became a gulf between us that was never filled in. One night, out of absolutely nowhere, as my mother told me later, he suddenly cried out, "*Basta!* Enough!" and crushed a newly lit cigar in the ashtray, the tobacco leaves splaying out from between his fingers like bristles on an old broom. He put on his worn leather jacket and left the house without a word of explanation. Three days later a pipe bomb leveled the bakery and took my father with it. I was in my second year of law school.

Pontanegro looks around uncomfortably: he's thinking, is this guy really giving me a morality lecture?

"Whatever else is going on out on the streets or in corporate offices or crack houses, the people are entitled to believe that when they get to court, they're going to see justice done. It might take some time, it might not always go the right way, there are some funny rules you have to live with . . . on the whole, it works."

I tilt my chair back to get a better look at him and to make sure I can be heard beyond our table. "The judges are the gatekeepers. They enforce the rules. If the judges can't be trusted, then the rest of us are left as animals, biting and tearing at each other until somebody wins or loses for all the wrong reasons. Without a clean legal system ordinary people have no chance against the likes of you. And make no mistake about it, *Sylvester*"—I let the chair drop loudly back to the floor—"you are scum."

Pontanegro is taken slightly aback but recovers quickly. He doesn't like being lectured in front of his men, and he doesn't like me having the upper hand. He smiles broadly. "What was he supposed to do, somebody snatches his kid . . ."

"He was supposed to have some faith in the system he represents!" I nearly shout, this time mostly for the benefit of the young cops in the room. "He's supposed to do what he would demand of anybody who comes before him in court!"

Pontanegro is unimpressed. "That ain't always so easy."

Arigga's own response to the same high and mighty lecture had been somewhat less sanguine than Pontanegro's. "What the hell do you know about it, Milano!" he had shouted at me. "You have nobody! Your old man's dead, your mother's in an institution, you got no wife, no kids, nobody who gives a shit if you live or die, so don't you fucking tell me what I was supposed to do!" His words still sting my ears. But I hit him back, hard, for making a stirring opening speech to a jury when he knew in advance he was going to dismiss the case.

"Nope," Pontanegro is saying. "Not so easy."

"I'm doing it," I blurt out without thinking.

"Yeah." He smiles benignly and leans toward me, whispering in my ear. "And you're a dead man."

"That so?"

"Yeah, that's so. And that goes for that fat fuck Arigga, too." He pulls back again. "You got any idea, any fucking idea at all, how big we are? What we can do? What do you think you're dealing with here, some high school purse-snatch gang?" Without glancing at the officers behind him, he steps around the table toward me, and I hold my ground.

"I know," I tell him. "You got judges, you got cops, you can do it all, that what you're gonna tell me?"

He smiles. "You don't understand shit, Mr. Deputy DA." He's no longer concerned about being recorded. "What we got is the people. While you're running around trying to protect the citizens from me, those same sorry bastards are running around you trying to *find* me. Who do you think it is spends billions on the shit I sell? Men from Mars?" He pulls back, grinning now. "You ain't protecting the people, ass-wipe. The people are on my side." He shakes his head. "All you're doin' is raisin' prices."

With a final swagger, he turns back to the police-men and says, "Let's go already," and leads the way to the door.

After he's gone, Marty walks up and sits down opposite me, pulling another cigar out of his pocket. "You two have a nice little chat?"

I find it hard to crack wise back at Marty. I have the sickening feeling my life just changed forever, and for the first time I'm glad I'm single. "Yeah. Decided we're gonna wear powder blue to the prom."

Marty nods and chews lightly on the cigar without lighting it. "How soon you gonna swear out a warrant on Ravensburg?"

"Today. This afternoon."

Marty nods again. "He's right, you know."

"Who?" I know who.

"Pontanegro."

"About what?"

"About you being a dead man."

I don't like this coming from Marty, whom I trust more than any other human I know. "That supposed to be comforting?"

"Nuh-uh."

"So what do I do?"

He thinks for a minute, then pulls out a disposable lighter and flicks it. "Stay visible." He puts it to the tip of the cigar and starts puffing in the flame, little balls of smoke blowing out the sides of his mouth, until he has an even red glow at the end and lets the lighter go out.

"What's that supposed to mean?"

He leans back in the chair. "You're already committed to putting Pontanegro out of action, as well as a couple judges. Too late to do anything about that." He puts up a hand quickly. "Not that you'd change your mind."

"So?"

He takes another hit from the cigar. "So. You need to make a big deal out of it, like one of those big cocaine hauls the feds make? Where they go on television and try to convince everybody they made a real serious dent in the traffic?" He grunts with heartfelt derision.

"I don't get it."

"When you're visible, these guys will be reluctant to take you out. They don't need that kind of publicity."

"But they're going to get plenty of it by the time I'm through."

"No, they won't." Marty puts the cigar down in the ashtray and leans forward. "They're going to circle the wagons, distance themselves from Pontanegro, from the judges. They're going to cut them all loose. The only connections will be the ones you make, and I don't think you can make many of them, except by conjecture."

"You're telling me, get famous and that's how I'm gonna protect myself?"

He plants the cigar in his mouth and turns his palms up. "That's it. Whole thing blows over, Mr. Milano wiped out corruption in Santa Monica, the law-abiding citizenry goes back to snorting cocaine they got from elves, drinking booze and telling their kids to stay off drugs. . . ."

"Everything goes back to normal."

"Right. And you run for district attorney."

This last remark brings me up short. Run for DA? Pontanegro will have helped me after all. And everybody will think I'm busting judges for my own personal aggrandizement and advancement, and I get to be DA over the dead bodies of Vincent Rosamund and Gus Terhovian and the ruined lives of Diane and Lisa Pierman. Then I spend the rest of my career pandering to every political voice in Los Angeles who might possibly have an influence over the next election, to the Ernestine Deniers of the world tossing mindless platitudes around like so many bouquets, polarizing everybody to unnecessary extremes to the point where compromise and practical results are impossible. Worrying about the press I'll get if I undercharge a child molester or overcharge a panhandler or fail to indict some other miscreant whose criminal liability is judged heinous by the fads of today but would have been merely mischievous in a previous generation, or the other way around. Dispensing justice according to the whims and caprices of the same voting public who might have pardoned the Pierman twins and castrated Vincent Rosamund, then gone back to the office to harass their secretaries and then home to blow a little dope to get the evening started.

Arigga had laughed at me after one of my more idealistic comments during our confrontation. He taunted me about the extraordinary degree to which people in law enforcement are bought, if not with irresistible amounts of drug money, then with threats. He asked me if I remember a certain case of an alleged murderer the year before and how he got a mistrial after a hung jury. Of course I did, and he said all the defendant's two brothers had to do was get to one juror and scare the shit out of her and that was the end of the case, because jurors don't have to defend their decisions, no matter how ridiculous. And law enforcement has become so compromised and unreliable that people no longer have faith in the system's ability to protect them from such threats. I listened as Arigga went on and on, and his total surrender to what he perceived as powerful forces invading the system was depressing beyond words.

"There aren't any winners, are there, Marty?"

He is looking at me curiously, smoking his cigar. He made a remark to me once, in a bar on Ocean Avenue when I was feeling particularly morose at the lack of impact I was having after losing a tough case. He said that the best that most ordinary people could do to make the world better was not to go after the whole planet at once but to make sure they did as much as they could in their own little corner of it. Do right by the people working for you, take special care with your friends, casual or otherwise, and if you're a prosecutor, put away as many bad guys as you possibly can.

"Sure there are," Marty says, rising stiffly from the chair. The strain of this day is showing on him. "Just different ones day to day, and sometimes they're hard to spot."

We step outside into the brilliant sunlight, squinting as the last of the squad cars and unmarked vehicles pull out of the dusty lot and head down the mountain road. I look up and hope that my father is looking down, pleased at me for racking up another notch in my hopeless and pitiably endless quest to avenge his death.

EPILOGUE

It's not a bad starter house for a budding young attorney, tucked away in a cul-de-sac near Brentwood. Unlike the purchase of my own fiasco of a condo at the height of the real estate market, this place was a shrewd investment at the bottom, bought from a newly unemployed aerospace engineer who had built it himself some twenty years ago. It was a gift to Diane in the form of an extended loan when she passed the California bar, financed equally by Lisa and their parents. Lisa had made her money early and saw no reason why she shouldn't share some of it with her mirror-image sister, who would undoubtedly make hers later. When they all drove up and took off the scarf they had used to cover Diane's eyes, the house was wrapped in an enormous pink ribbon tied in a bow over the roof. It was the last time Jack and Anne Pierman had visited California before their daughters' trial. I hadn't even known they were in the courtroom.

I'm starting to get conspicuous sitting in the driveway without opening the door to my car, so I shake my head hard a couple of times and get out. Flower beds line the front walls on either side of the door, new tulips, daffodils, and rhododendrons spraying a wild profusion of colors into the warm spring air. A pair of work gloves, a small pail and a three-pronged gardening tool sit at the border where the flower beds meet the grass. I falter at the sight of the beautiful plants, neatly tended by Diane's own hand. The front door has an antique brass knocker.

Two fresh flowers poke out of a hole at the top. There are no sounds in the quiet neighborhood other than a few birds chirping and flitting about in the nearby bushes.

Diane is wearing old jeans, a sweatshirt, worn running shoes, and a plain gray scarf to protect her hair. Her pupils are slightly dilated from dark adaptation, and she squints as she opens the door. The sun shining behind me illuminates her face so that her skin seems to radiate its own light, and she steps aside to let me in. "Good news?" she asks.

I nod in answer. "Good for you, not so good for a couple of other guys."

She offers me a drink but I decline, looking at my watch and telling her I can't stay long. I don't really have anywhere else I need to be, but I'm setting things up so I can leave quickly whenever I want to. What I really want is to never leave, but who ever gets what they really want?

I take a straight-back chair at the small dining table, and Diane sits opposite me on a couch done in muted plaids. Light streams in through the half-open blinds behind her, striping the walls and floor. Tiny dust motes play in the bands of light.

"Vincent Rosamund's trial was fixed," I tell her as calmly as I can. I don't want any histrionics—what I have to tell her is too important to risk getting lost in a lot of noise—so I try to keep myself on an even keel and transmit some of that to her.

I can see a small shiver run across her shoulders, but other than that she only stares at me intently, then asks, "By whom?"

"Sylvester Pontanegro." She draws back and inhales audibly on hearing his name; she remembers it from the Friehling case, didn't expect to ever hear it again, and can't make the connection. "Rosamund worked for him," I continue, "and he got to Arigga and Terhovian both and rigged the whole thing." I let that settle in. Pieces start to fly together in Diane's mind. I can see her eyes dart back and forth as some form begins to emerge from all the disparate data she's trying to process.

"Terhovian made it look good," she says after a while.

"That was his job. If Arigga just threw the case out, it'd be too obvious. Terhovian found some technical hooks and made it possible for it to look almost legitimate. Not quite, because we had a clean case, but enough so that there was maybe some doubt as to Arigga's judgment but not much to claim it was fixed."

Diane tries to take a slow, deep breath to help get her bearings, and I can hear a shudder as she inhales. I can only guess what's going through her mind. She and Lisa were dealt a terrible injustice, and that would make her angry, but maybe it will also lessen any pangs of remorse she might have about killing Rosamund. It will also shake her idealistic faith in the legal system.

"Did Pontanegro also fix the Friehling thing?"

I nod. "And he also got Rosamund off on two prior rape charges in Kern County. Arigga was the judge in both those cases, too."

She puts her hands up to her mouth, fingers steepled as though in prayer, and tears begin to fill her eyes. "How do you know all this?" Her voice is choking and strained. She's looking past me.

"I met with Pontanegro this morning."

She jerks her head back to look at me. "Met with him?"

"In Bakersfield. I just drove back. I pretended to solicit his help in exchange for some favors and taped the conversation. He gave up Arigga, and Ravensburg and Tsielonek, too."

The details don't seem to interest her. I thought she'd be horrified at learning this about two more judges, but it didn't even register. "You did that?" she asks. "For me?"

No, I did it for me. "For a lot of things. It needed doing."

She doesn't believe that. I can see it in her moistened eyes. She's looking at me like I was a hero, her Prince Charming on a great white horse. She's not naive, she knows the terrible risk I took walking into the lion's den wearing a wire. "What happens now?" she asks. Back to business. She knows better than to embarrass me with fawning admiration after I shrugged off her gratitude, no matter how moved she might be by what she thinks I've done for her.

I clear my throat and take my eyes off her smooth oval face and pale neck, focusing instead on a framed photo of a couple and their two small children, the little clan surrounded by bags and trunks. There is Cyrillic writing visible on some of the larger boxes, stenciled letters spelling out "KIROV." It's a snapshot of the Pirosman-ishvili family at the Moscow central station just before they boarded a train for Vienna, a trip from which they would never return to the Soviet Union. The two little children are Diane and Lisa Pierman.

"It'll all be public tomorrow morning. By the after-noon, there'll be a great hue and cry in the media." The papers will report that the people are outraged, so by the next day they will be. "Nestor Parnell will go to Judge Genet and request that she reexamine your convictions in light of this devastating new information, this outrageous miscarriage of justice. The prosecution won't object."

She is looking at me wide-eyed, her mouth slightly agape. She blinks as I finish speaking. "What do you think's going to happen?"

"No way to tell. Maybe Genet will intercede on your behalf with the appeals court, see if something can be worked out."

She leans forward on the couch. "You think maybe we won't go to jail?" The childlike hopefulness in her voice is testing my resolve.

What will happen is that Parnell will argue against a drawn-out, stressful and unpopular appeals process, offering to have the twins both plead guilty to reduced charges, Lisa to involuntary manslaughter and Diane to misdemeanor conspiracy. Genet will accept the new pleas and change their sentences to long probation and several thousand hours of community service, thus bypassing the appeals court. Diane, having pleaded guilty only to a mis-demeanor, will be allowed to retain her law license but as part of the deal must switch over to civil law, abandoning the criminal side forever. This was at my insistence: one who takes the law into her own hands has no business being in this business.

I don't tell Diane any of this, that it was all planned in advance, a three-way deal among Parnell, Genet and me made prior to our waiving the jury and putting the case in Genet's hands. The whole arrangement was contingent on my proving that the Rosamund trial was a sham. Had I not been able to do this, Parnell would have dragged out the appeals process forever, with Genet's unspoken complicity, and ultimately accepted a plea bargain with a short sentence, perhaps smaller than the five years they were willing to take originally. That's why I got Parnell to agree to the five years before I laid out the deal: I needed to establish the outer boundary in advance, so we could seal the arrangement without knowing whether I could finger Arigga.

I rock my head back and forth as I pretend to ponder Diane's question. "My guess, you won't be doing any jail time, but you won't get off without a record, either."

She looks at me a moment longer, then drops back to lean against the back of the couch. She turns her head so one of the beams of light hits her face full on, closing her eyes and enjoying the feeling of the warming rays.

I'm a real star now, or will be when the papers come out tomorrow. Despite my zeal in prosecuting the twins, I went after Arigga anyway, undercutting my own prosecution because it was the right thing to do, a demonstration that I'm a fair and righteous public servant. I'm going to run for DA, bolstered by all of this extraordinary exposure, having gotten a drug kingpin and three dirty judges busted and justice served in the case of two innocent victims of high-level judicial corruption. I still believe that the twins shouldn't have done what they did, and will go on saying that to the press and anybody else who will listen. But none of this would have happened if the fix wasn't in, so their light punishment, while perhaps a disappointment to me as defender of the public well-being, need not be of further concern. I have thus offset the original fix with one of my own. Whether they now balance or instead have doubled the volume of injustice, I'll worry about at another time.

Marsha did her best to try to introduce a sour note into my triumph, during a conversation last night while we were planning the Bakersfield meeting. Didn't I feel bad about hanging Arigga, knowing the enormous pressure Pontanegro had put him under? I explain that I don't feel bad, because Arigga is a jurist, and ultimately the power and reliability of the system rest in his lap, and he violated that explicit trust.

Marsha thought about that for a minute and then said, "Congratulations."

"Thanks," I responded modestly.

"—for one of the most cynical perversions of the system ever perpetrated by a responsible official."

My smile hung idiotically on my face. "What do you mean?"

She shrugged like it was obvious, or should have been. "You got a pair of murderers walking around free. Essentially off the hook."

"Not exactly," I countered. "They have convictions on their records. It'll hang on them forever. That's enough punishment."

"According to whom?"

"According to you. To me. To Marty and all of us." I look at her as though she hadn't been a part of this from the first day. "Christ Almighty, Marsha, what's the big surprise here all of a sudden?"

"I want to know who the hell exactly are you and me and all of us! Who are we to say who goes free, who goes to prison, who gets prosecuted and who doesn't?"

"But we make decisions like that all the time. You pointed that out to me yourself just a few days ago!"

"We make tactical judgments based on the strength of the case, not who our friends are. The *system* makes the decisions. Prosecutors fight for convictions, defense attorneys fight for acquittals, everybody puts on their best show and the system sorts it out. When one side bends and doesn't do its job, the whole house comes crashing down. Am I telling you something new?"

"Far as I'm concerned, it came crashing down the day Rosamund walked."

"So you figured, what the hell, might as well pull down a few more walls, put everything right."

I wasn't nuts about the analogy, but okay, she basically had it right. "So what's so wrong with that?"

I knew exactly what's wrong with it, but I listened anyway as Marsha spelled it out. "What's wrong is that you forgot about the law, Sal. You remember the law, don't you?"

"Sometimes justice is above law." A terrorist slogan. What the hell was I talking about?

"Maybe. But *people* are never above it. What if these had been the proverbial waitresses or dishwashers? Or poor black kids? What if they had been gang members? You wouldn't have done any of this because you wouldn't have believed they deserved the break. You wouldn't even have known the whole story, would you, or bothered to find out."

"But this is a damned if I do, damned if I don't, Marsha. You'd condemn me either way, no matter what I did!"

She shook her head from side to side several times, wide swinging motions. "No sir! You engineered the most brilliant prosecution I've ever seen, and I cheered you on all the way. We may have commiserated about how painful it was, but I never told you to ease up. If you hadn't pressed for a harsh sentence, that would've been okay, too. Nothing wrong with tempering justice with a little mercy. But what you did was not only illegal, it violated your public mandate."

She paused for a breath but wasn't quite finished. She could tell from my face that it wasn't sinking in, or thought she could; in truth, I was being crushed under the weight of it. "You're so convinced they didn't deserve to go to jail, Sal," she continued, "but here's the thing: they murdered a human being in cold blood."

"A human being who escaped punishment."

Marsha leaned back and crossed her arms. "Yeah, but what do you figure his punishment should have been? What do you think would have been a reasonable winter plea? He left them mentally traumatized but physically unharmed. Sure, he was a lowlife scumbag and I don't stay up nights feeling bad for him, but did he deserve to die for what he did? And even if he did, did these women have the right to mete out that punishment, without due process?"

"But due process was denied them! What the hell do you think this Bakersfield thing tomorrow is all about? I'll prove it then!"

"Okay." She mulled that over. "Okay, but suppose there *had* been due process. Suppose the fix *wasn't* in. He still might have been let go, he could've gotten a year in the joint or a suspended sentence, or, Jesus, Sal, maybe he really didn't do it and that might've come out in court. You're arguing bullshit!"

I started to get angry. I don't know why. We have discussions like that all the time and I never take them personally. "So tell me, queen of all that's just and legal: what would you have done?"

She fixed me with a steady glare. "You really want to know?"

"I really want to know!" I nearly shouted.

She looked away; I could tell she wasn't prepared for that question, maybe hadn't thought of it before. It's a little too easy to criticize when somebody else is faced with the hard choices.

Finally she turned back to me. "I'll tell you what I would have done: probably the same thing as you, but I hope I wouldn't feel so goddamned smug about it."

We were friends again. You've got to love a woman with that kind of self-possession. "But I didn't do it for me; I did it for them," I said.

"I don't buy it." She was calmer now. "Ultimately everything we do is for ourselves. Maybe it was because you wanted to be DA, maybe you wanted to win the girl in the end, maybe it's compensation because everybody thinks you fucked up the Rosamund trial—which we both now know you didn't—and you want your manhood back. Or maybe it was because you really cared about them and wanted to see real justice done, the right thing. What the hell ever, the point is you did it for yourself, because it's what you wanted, because it would make you feel good. That's what you did. And I can't help but feel a little soiled having been a part of it all."

I tried to wave it off. "We plea bargain all the time."

"Sure, out in the open where everybody can see it. But not a backdoor deal that we hide because it would make people mad."

Now she had gone too far, not thinking straight. "That's a crock: we make backdoor deals all day long and you know it."

"But when was the last time we got a fake conviction and then gave away the courthouse on the sentence?"

I didn't need to hear all of this the night before the

meeting with Pontanegro. "What people?" I asked her. "Who'd get mad?"

"Huh?"

"You said we hid it because people would get mad. Who?"

"People in the neighborhood where I grew up, where you grew up. People doing hard time because they got no break. Maybe Vincent Rosamund's mother or his brother. What're you gonna do if one of them caps Diane or Lisa in a restaurant some night because the white bitch that murdered their son or brother walked on the rap after the deputy DA put his own fix in? What then, Sal?"

Why was I even arguing with her? She was only succeeding in voicing out loud my deepest misgivings and fears about what I had done. I just didn't like hearing it.

Diane's voice snaps me back into the present. We had both been lost in our private reveries, and I can't tell how much time has passed since either of us spoke.

"Don't you even want to know who pulled the trigger?"

I shake my head. "I know it was you."

She doesn't blink. "How?"

"Lisa doesn't have that kind of strength. Sorry, bad choice of words. She doesn't have the stomach."

"And I do?"

"Obviously. You're the one who kept telling me you had to save Lisa, to preserve her sanity and let her get on with her life. Personally, I think you underestimated her strength."

"So you think I was really talking about myself, right? Projecting my own fears onto Lisa?"

It had occurred to me, and may be partially true, but it's beside the point for this conversation. "I'm not smart enough about things like that to know. I do know that Lisa may not have had a lot of legal sophistication, which confused her when all us legal beagles were using obscure jargon, but she had more inner resolve than any of us gave her credit for." I saw it in her eyes when Diane was on the stand and Lisa was listening. "All I'm saying, if you were really out to save her, it wouldn't make a lot of sense for you to stick a gun in her hand and send her off to commit murder, to let her take such an enormous risk of being exposed or captured." I hold up a hand. "Don't bother to corroborate it. I know it was you."

"Then why didn't you pursue it in court?"

"Because it was too soft, from a legal point of view. No way to prove it beyond a reasonable doubt."

She stays quiet. She doesn't believe that was the real reason. "Tell me," I go on, "why did you—and I mean the both of you, now—why did you really do it? What was going through your minds? Did you really think you were going to get away with it? That there was no chance of at least one of you doing some hard time?"

"Getting away with it was a secondary consideration," she tells me. "It was the only way to put Lisa back together again, and it didn't matter if she did time or not: better to be in prison for a while as a whole person than free as a zombie."

There's a distant look in her eyes and again I wonder, is she talking about herself or Lisa? Is she leaning on Lisa's craziness as a substitute for her own? Maybe Diane *needed* Lisa to be crazy, and she used her sister as a crutch to save her own soul. "Jesus!" I hear myself blurting out, under the strain of wishing this would all go away. "You only got raped, not killed or crippled; was it worth committing murder?"

"Yes!" she spits at me defiantly.

"Did it work?"

No answer.

"How's your sister now, Diane?"

I can tell from her face that her master plan failed even worse than my prosecution of Vincent Rosamund.

We get past it. There's nothing more either of us can say on the subject. I look into the kitchen. "Is that coffee on the burner?" I ask.

Her eyes are dry again, and she goes into the kitchen to get me a cup of coffee, hands it to me and sits down on the other side of the dining table. I take a long sip. "Excellent. Grind your own, do you?"

"Yeah. So tell me"—she sits back and folds her hands in her lap. "How do you feel about being involved with a cold-blooded murderer?"

I take another sip and set the cup down. "We're not involved."

"No, of course not, I understand. You've got an election coming up; who needs that kind of political baggage, right? What I mean is, after that. What's a decent interval a girl's gonna have to wait?" She's smiling now.

I keep telling myself I did it all for the love of the law and an orderly system, but as I listened to Pontanegro in the bar I found myself slipping into a fantasy about really going in league with him. What could I have done if the rest of the bar patrons were not law enforcement officers, if people in the surveillance van hadn't been listening to my every word? I've been kidding myself all along. It's not my love of the law, but my love of power: if I had freed Diane I might have had her forever, but by prosecuting her, I've reentered myself in the DA election. But I didn't really have a choice, did I? Not really. This is what I keep telling myself. Marsha said everything we do we do for ourselves. Even Mother Teresa does what she does because it makes her feel good, because she wants to go to heaven.

But then there's the question of how far I pushed that prosecution, how I engineered its outcome. The way I figure it, coming up in my life I've got several thousand nights during which I somehow have to fall asleep, despite whatever it is I've done to disrupt that process, and several thousand shaves during which I have to look at myself in the mirror. In everything there must be balance, some cosmic reckoning that requires equal distributions of recompense for all the injustice.

I fought a three-sided war among my heart, my principles and my ambition. The first two definitely lost, but it's not yet clear to me that even the third was victorious. Even if I win the election it won't be clear. Early on, it was easy to view these competing motivations as distinct, even mutually exclusive, but over time the edges of the definitions began to blur and run together, like the colored cubes of wax in those candles we made in the sixties when we thought there was an artist within each of us. There wasn't. Bitter disappointment was the only result for many who bought the party line, that we all had the capability to be Michelangelos if we could only unlock the creative beast that surely dwelt within all of us. It wasn't true. Me, I thought I could be a hell of a lawyer. You learn the rules, memorize the cases, work your ass off and, hey: you're Oliver Wendell Holmes.

It was the rest I was unprepared for. How those "cases" would make me feel. How sometimes I wouldn't feel anything for them at all, except as they provided the means to rack up debits and credits in the balance sheet of my life. Not to stretch the metaphor, but right now all I'm feeling is impending bankruptcy, an emotional insolvency that no infusion of career successes is going to salvage.

I told you this wasn't going to have a happy ending.

"We're never going to be involved, Diane," I tell her as gently as I can. "Not ever."

There is no use explaining to her why. Call it my penance, if you will, my punishment for having participated in the subversion of everything I hold dear, for setting her free after she took a man's life. I'm probably going to be the new DA, and that is my reward, and I'm giving up Diane, and that is my punishment. Every time I looked into her eyes I would be reminded that I took advantage of my position and my authority, power not available to the everyday street miscreant who commits a crime for reasons every bit as understandable as Diane's and Lisa's. Besides, do I really want to spend the rest of my life with someone who is going to spend the rest of *her* life trying to come to grips with what she has done, and who already shows signs of failing miserably in the attempt?

And there is another thing I have come to consider: there was a lot of evidence that the sisters colluded after the killing to confuse their identities, but what happened before? If I sit down and try to walk through it all in detail, I wind up unable to shake the feeling that Diane shot Vincent Rosamund without ever telling Lisa she was going to do it, and then enlisted her assistance in trying to get away with it. That's why the police found them both at Lisa's house: Diane drove there after the shooting and that's the first Lisa heard about it. And how could a twin refuse to help her sister beat the rap? If that was really the case, Lisa was doubly victimized and Diane is doubly damned, having surrounded Lisa with a dark cloud for the rest of her days. Even though they will never see a minute in jail, Lisa is now not only a rape victim but a conspirator in a murder plot. To my grave I never want to know if Diane really did this to her without her permission, under the guise of "saving" her.

Either way, Marsha was right: what Diane did was wrong. We could have maybe gotten to Rosamund another way: first expose Arigga, brand Rosamund as a habitual criminal and rapist in the eyes of the public, hounded him into another mistake, put heavy surveillance on his drug-running activities and busted him all over again, even prosecuted him on federal civil rights charges. That tactic's been used before to circumvent the double jeopardy problem. Who knows what we might have been able to do, we self-righteous tenders of the flame of justice?

But executions by private citizens without due process? Never.

Not when I'm the new DA.

Acknowledgments
(alphabetically)

Gail Abarbanel, LCSW, founder and director of Santa Monica Hospital's Rape Treatment Center—unflinching and dedicated, one of those who truly makes more than a symbolic difference in this world

Deborah Anderson, Cristina Gonzalez and James G. Bailey, criminalists in the Physical Evidence Section of the LA County Sheriff's Department Criminalistics Laboratory (a.k.a. Scientific Services Bureau)—their descriptions and demonstrations of laboratory methods were both fascinating and sobering

Mike Duarte, deputy district attorney, Santa Monica, California—for his gracious, patient and tireless efforts to educate me in the workings of both his office and criminal law as practiced in real life

Nick Ellison—friend and savior; no more need be said

Bob Hawkins, retired LA County deputy sheriff, now an independent contractor to the Firearm Analysis Unit of the LA Police Department and president of the Association of Firearm and Toolmark Examiners—a giant in a narrow specialty, who took the time to make sure I got it right

Santa Monica Jail Manager Jackie Jones—generous in spirit and with her time; I highly recommend her facility if you're ever arrested

Scott Klippel, criminal defense attorney, Austin, Texas— for sharing with me his insights into the arcane minutiae of legal maneuvering

LA County Deputy Sheriffs Dave Sprengel and Kim Braden—my on-site education in courtroom and lockup procedures was greatly expedited by their explanations of what I was seeing and hearing

Robert J. Tobias, attorney-at-law, Santa Monica—immensely knowledgeable, he took an extraordinary amount of time straightening me out on countless points of law

Also—Sara Bixler, Marti Blumenthal, David M. Brenner, Jan Christie, Louise Collazo, Dr. Herman Falsetti, Dr. Bernard T. Ferrari, Irwin Goverman, Christina Harcar, Joe Pittman, Errol Southers, Jim Stein and Liz Ziemska

Author's Note

I've mentioned several attorneys who assisted not only with interpreting the gnarled intricacies of the law but also with ensuring accuracy regarding proper procedure in Los Angeles County courts. In many cases, I've deliberately taken liberties for purposes of pace and clarity. These are minor variations of little consequence, but more important, they are there despite their identification as such by the experts who reviewed the manuscript and who share no responsibility for their inclusion. Observations and opinions regarding the judicial system are also strictly those of the author.

The county court branch in Santa Monica was chosen as the venue for the novel purely by dint of proximity and prior familiarity, not because it is a hotbed of judicial impropriety. To the contrary, that branch has the reputation of being one of the finest in the county, if not the entire state, and its judges, several of whom I am familiar with, are widely admired for their integrity and skill.

The quote by Ilosha Pirosmanishvili in Chapter 4 was originally by Winston Churchill. The golf advice in Chapter 11 is attributable to Sam Snead.

Finally, the detailed critiques of various drafts of the manuscript by my wife, Cherie, added immeasurably to the finished work. During the writing of this book, she also found time to win her age division in the Hawaiian Ironman and half a dozen other long-distance triathlons, becoming the top-ranked triathlete in the country among females 50–54. The discipline and perseverance she displayed in reaching those heights were major inspirations in my own work, which is typically as undisciplined as one could possibly imagine.